Once a reporter for Independent Television News, Gerald Seymour is the author of eighteen best-selling novels, including *Harry's Game*, *The Glory Boys* and, most recently, *A Line in the Sand*. He lives in the West Country. One of his novels, *The Waiting Time*, has recently been adapted for Carlton Television.

Also by Gerald Seymour

HARRY'S GAME
THE GLORY BOYS
KINGFISHER
RED FOX
THE CONTRACT
ARCHANGEL
IN HONOUR BOUND
FIELD OF BLOOD
A SONG IN THE MORNING
AT CLOSE QUARTERS
HOME RUN
CONDITION BLACK
THE JOURNEYMAN TAILOR
THE FIGHTING MAN
THE HEART OF DANGER
KILLING GROUND
THE WAITING TIME
A LINE IN THE SAND

and published by Corgi Books

HOLDING THE ZERO

Gerald Seymour

CORGI BOOKS

HOLDING THE ZERO
A CORGI BOOK: 0 552 14666 8

Originally published in Great Britain by Bantam Press,
a division of Transworld Publishers

PRINTING HISTORY
Bantam Press edition published 2000
Corgi edition published 2001

1 3 5 7 9 10 8 6 4 2

Set in 10/12pt Palatino by
Phoenix Typesetting, Ilkley, West Yorkshire.

Corgi Books are published by Transworld Publishers,
61–63 Uxbridge Road, London W5 5SA,
a division of The Random House Group Ltd,
in Australia by Random House Australia (Pty) Ltd,
20 Alfred Street, Milsons Point, Sydney, NSW 2061, Australia,
in New Zealand by Random House New Zealand Ltd,
18 Poland Road, Glenfield, Auckland 10, New Zealand
and in South Africa by Random House (Pty) Ltd,
Endulini, 5a Jubilee Road, Parktown 2193, South Africa.

Printed and bound in Great Britain by
Mackays of Chatham plc, Chatham, Kent.

For Jacqui and Susie

Prologue

What he feared most was fire.

He was wedged into a shallow space between the slight angle of the tin roofing and the beams to which the rough planks of the room's ceilings were nailed.

The darkness around him was total.

If the hut were set ablaze, if the flames licked up and the smoke surged, he would be flushed out, roasted or suffocated to death.

Where they had put him, he thought, was the most precious and secret place in the village, where an honoured and respected guest would be hidden from danger. He lay on their cache of rifles, angular and hard under his body, and was pressed against the sharp shapes of the ammunition boxes. Because he was the guest, he – alone – had been thrust up with their hands, as his feet scrabbled for a grip on their shoulders into the hidden cavity. He had been granted their hospitality and therefore his life was more important than their own.

He could hear the voices around the hut, some raised and abusive and some that wheedled and pleaded.

It had been late in the communal meal he had shared with the village men when the jeeps had come up the barren stone track towards the village, their lights shafting ahead and on to the mountain scrub flanking the track. As the guest he had been sitting cross-legged at the right side of his friend, sipping the juice that was poured for him, dipping his fingers into the iron pot to search for scraps of meat, scooping the palm of his hand into the rice bowl, and then the jeeps had arrived. Moments after they had heard the engines, as they had seen the lights, he had been plucked up and dragged like a rag doll away from the rug on which he'd sat, and the clutch of men around him had stampeded him into the hut, had opened the trapdoor and pushed him into the small cavity. The trap had been closed and he had heard scraping fingers smear mud and charcoal over the outlines of the opening. The darkness had been around him and he had lain so still, barely daring to draw breath. He had listened and he had prayed that the hut would not be fired.

He heard the abuse of the soldiers, the pleading of the village men, the screams of the women, and the single shots. He did not know the language of the soldiers, or of the village men, but he understood the sounds of the women's screams and the message the shots sent.

The soldiers would have come from the garrison town of Amādīyah to the west or from the camp at Rawāndiz to the south. The information would have been given, for reward, that he was in the village. He would be a prize capture. He would be portrayed as a spy, not as a harmless, innocent guest of the mountain people. He understood, lying on his stomach on their old firearms and against their ammunition boxes, that the soldiers shouted at and abused the village men to make them reveal his hiding place. The men would be pleading that they did not know, had not seen a foreigner, a spy, and they were beaten, taken from the main corralled cowering group, while the women screamed for their lives as they were shot.

There was the smell of fire and the crackle of it from other huts in the close-set village that perched above a patchwork of fields and below the steep orchards. A few huts, chosen at random, were burned but it was a still, cool night and the flames did not spread from those to the adjacent ones.

The soldiers were in the hut, moving below him. He heard them rummage in the bedding and there was the crack of plates breaking as a cupboard was emptied. He stifled his breath. As a spy he might be hanged or shot, he might be tortured, and his protestations of a simple friendship would be ignored. When the soldiers left the hut in which he hid, the sound of the chaos they brought continued. Any of the village men who were condemned, or their women, might have saved themselves by denouncing him and showing the soldiers the camouflaged trap-door. He was in their hands, they held his life.

He lay in the roof space all through the night, and he was not betrayed.

The jeeps drove away down the track and headed back to the garrison at Amādīyah or the camp at Rawāndiz. He was in debt, he owed his life to the silence of the people of the village.

The trapdoor was opened.

The light of the dawn flushed onto his stiff, shivering body.

He was helped down. He walked out into the low early-morning sunlight.

9

They had already started to dig the graves in the burial ground beside the grazing meadow that was closest to the village. He saw the sweat beading on the faces and chests of the men who swung pickaxes to break the concrete-hard ground, while others shovelled away the rocky earth. The women cradled the heads of the dead and keened their sorrow. He stepped around the ejected cartridge cases and the pools of drying dark blood that had been spilled so that he, their guest, should live.

The burden of obligation crushed him.

He said to his friend, 'Tell them that I will always remember the value that they have given my life and the depth of their sacrifice, that the shedding of their blood for me is something that I will never forget to my last, dying day. Tell them that I will, and I do not know how or when, repay the debt of blood and life.'

His friend translated, but the repetition of his words in their own tongue seemed not to be heard by the people in their grief. Then, his friend said quietly to him, 'It is time to go, esteemed Basil, time to leave.'

'I meant what I said.'

'Of course, esteemed Basil, of course – but you did not say how or when.'

He was put into an old, rusted truck and driven away from the village, where some of the huts smouldered, away from the deepening grave pits. They would have thought his words were empty and his promises worth nothing. They drove towards Nimrud where he had left his car in the care of the archaeologists before taking the journey into the mountains in his friend's truck. He would be back at the base beside the Euphrates river by nightfall, in the officers' mess in time to celebrate the

10

third anniversary of his Queen's accession to the throne that night, and the talk around him would be of Prime Minister Churchill's health, and rising taxation at home, and the worsening security situation in Kenya, and the new Bob Hope film. He would say nothing to his fellow officers of where he had been, and of the debt that he owed.

Many times, as they went down the track, he looked back at the smoke spirals and the diminishing figures of the men who swung the pickaxes, and he thought of the blood that was dry on the earth and the bright sheen of the cartridge cases.

He had pledged his word.

Chapter One

Their home was a single-roomed building for the family to live, eat and sleep in.

Augustus Henderson Peake sat cross-legged on the floor of stamped-down earth within the circle of women around the fire.

The stones of the walls, some roughly shaped and some rounded by the torrent in the gorge below the house, were held in place by mud substituting as cement or mortar. In places there were gaps through which the wind off the mountains came in stiletto stabs. There were no windows and the door of crude-cut wood planks was closed on the night, but the wind shook it, and the penetrating blasts whipped at the smoke from the fire inside the circle. It scurried up towards the room's rafters of tree branches with peeling bark. Nailed above them was a sheet of flapping white plastic, and through the plastic's ripped tears he could see the dried-out underside of the turfs that were laid over the roof. There was a hole in the centre of the roof through which the smoke escaped.

Against one wall was an old mattress covered by scattered sacking and blankets, and he thought it was where the parents of the children would sleep. The children's beds were at the wall facing the closed door, more sacking and blankets but no mattress; there were four children pressed close to each other for warmth and each of them, in turn, hacked deep coughs from their chests and throats. The light in the room, by which the women worked, was from a single stinking oil lamp that threw cavorting shadows of the women's heads and shoulders against the upper walls and into the ceiling where the smoke gathered before finding the release of the hole.

There were no hand-woven tapestries on the walls, nor any photographs, but on the wall in front of him, hanging from a hook where it was at an easy height to be snatched down, was an assault rifle with a magazine fitted.

Behind him, against the door, the men watched in silence and waited for the women's work to be done.

Gnarled fingers with broken nails and dirt-grimed wrinkles fought with needles to gather in pieces of the garment. It had once been a suit of overalls that a mechanic would have worn; it was drab olive green. Two women were busy sewing the heavy canvas strip that had been cut from an old tarpaulin to the front. Another pulled for possession of the knees and elbows, to sew smaller canvas squares onto them. Another stitched a veil of soft, sand-coloured netting to the front of the hood, which had already been fastened to the collar. Three more women clawed at the back, shoulders, body, legs and arms, wherever he pointed, and sewed to them short-looped straps of hessian fabric. The garment was wrenched from hand to hand, over the smouldering fire of wet wood, past and around the

13

hurricane oil lamp. Each time a strap was in place and the cotton snapped, the eyes would look to him and he would point again to a place where the surface was not broken, the hessian strap would be torn for the necessary length and the needles would dive and flash in the light. They talked softly among themselves. It was a language of which he knew nothing, but when they caught his glance the older women cackled, gaptoothed, in amusement, and the younger ones, who were little more than girls, dropped their heads and giggled.

The fire gave little heat, only smoke; the lamp gave a small light and many shadows. The smoke was in his eyes, watering them, and the smell of the oil from the lamp was in his nose and his mouth.

The shape of the overalls was changing. The clear lines of the body, arms and legs were gradually distorted by the mess of hessian straps; the sharpness of the outline was broken in a hundred places. The needles darted, disappeared, then rose again. Each time the garment was pulled by a new hand the smoke billowed under it and fanned into their faces and his. It was good work, and he could not have accomplished it himself. When they were finished he thanked them. There was laughter all around the room as he stood and held the garment against his body.

A man stepped forward and tugged at his arm, as if to tell him that his time had run out.

Gus untied the laces of the old hiking-boots he had brought with him, then kicked them off. He pulled on the loose overalls over his denims, shirt and sweater. He wriggled and shook into the garment, pulled up the zip from crotch to throat. A woman broke the circle around

14

the fire, went to the mattress bed, took a small broken shard of mirror from a plastic bag of her treasures, and handed it to him. He stood to his full height, his head close to the plastic-sheeted ceiling, and the smoke curled around him. He looked into the mirror to study the front, then held it out to the side at arm's length and tilted his head so that he could see part of his own back. He pulled up the cowled hood and dropped the veil over his face. There was more laughter.

He told them that, in his own country, this was called a 'gillie' suit, and he said it was the best he had ever seen and that, pray his God and theirs, he would be invisible to the enemy of them all – and they seemed not to understand a word he said. And he thanked them. With his hands and his eyes, he thanked them, and there was a murmur of appreciation. The oldest woman pushed herself up arthritically from her place by the fire and touched his arm, a gentle, sweeping brush as if now he was understood.

After he had laced his boots, the oldest woman took the mirror from him and held it where he could best look into it. He lifted the veil then bent to take the small tubes of camouflage cream from his rucksack. He smeared lines of ochre, black and green on to his hands and throat, his nose, cheeks and chin.

The door opened behind him. The wind howled into the room, guttered the fire, spread the smoke and flickered the lamp. The children cowered under their tent of sacks and blankets.

'It is time, Mr Peake? You are ready?'

'Yes, Haquim, I am ready.'

Kneeling beside the rucksack, he put the tubes of cream back into a side pouch and gazed down at the rifle around which the hessian bandage was already wound. The lens of the telescopic sight flickered in the lamplight. Abruptly, he zipped shut the camouflaged, padded carrying case that held the rifle. He turned for the door.

They would be finished now. The night would have fallen heavy on Stickledown Range, his colleagues of the Historic Breech-loading and Small-arms Association would be gone. They would have had their last beer, worried over their scoring charts, packed their cars, locked up their caravans, and would be on the crowded roads going their separate ways to their homes. He doubted that they would have missed him . . . The owls would be out now over the quietness of the range, hunting for the rabbits that would have emerged once the boom of the old rifles was silenced. He breathed hard then rocked slowly on his feet before slipping the strap of the carrying case over one shoulder and the loop of the rucksack over the other. His shadow leaped from the assault rifle on the wall towards the children shivering on their bed. He wondered if any of those in their cars at the end of their day's target shooting knew the true force of fear. But it had been his choice to come, his decision . . . Without a backward glance he went out through the door.

The men were around him. The wind gripped at the hessian straps and caught the billows of his gillie suit. He thought of the Lee Enfield No. 4 Mark 1 (T) in its secure cabinet at home, and the collection of silver teaspoons, awarded for competition marksmanship, in the sideboard drawer. He walked towards the lights of the vehicles.

Close about him was the darkness, the smell of

16

fighting men and the scent of struggle ... It had been his own decision, his own choice.

It is a place that is an afterthought of history.

The Tarus and Zagros mountains are the kernel of this region and its people. The natural limits, recognized only by the inhabitants of a harsh, wind-stripped land, are the plains below the mountains to the south and east, the upwaters of the great Tigris river to the west, and the Black Sea shores to the north. The modern frontiers, created artificially by long-dead diplomats in faraway chancelleries, have divided up the territory with a confluence of boundaries scarring that kernel. The present-day nation states of Syria, Turkey, Iran and Iraq now have uncertain stewardship of the towering mountains, the razor-edged ridges running between them and the cliff-faced valleys below, and jealously guard their sovereign rights with aircraft, artillery pieces, armoured vehicles, infantrymen and the shadowy agents of the secret police.

The people of this arbitrarily carved land are the Kurds. They have an old history, a culture unique to themselves, a language that is their own, and no country. Only when they are useful in gaining greater political advantage to outsiders is their dream of nationhood supported, or when their pathetic lot in defeat pricks foreigners' consciences. Most days of the week, most weeks of the year, most years of a decade, most decades of a century, their dream and their struggle are ignored by blind eyes and deaf ears. They are not Arabs, not Persians, not Turks; they do not fit conveniently.

A war progresses fitfully in that part of the Kurdish heartland that is nominally within the territorial boundaries of the Republic of Iraq. It is like a restless man's sleep, sometimes aroused and flailing intensely, sometimes dormant. The enemy of today, as he has been for twenty years, is the President in his palace in Baghdad, Saddam Hussein. Since the Gulf War, the modern army of Saddam has been kept out of the Kurdish territory by the threat of aerial action from American and British warplanes based at the Turkish NATO base at Incerlik. The army waits for the opportunity. It is a poised cobra watching for a prey's moment of weakness.

Some Kurds say that the life, always waiting for the cobra's strike, is not worth living, that it would be better to sidle up to the reptile and lie under its protection. Other Kurds say that the comforting words from Washington and London are hollow, spoken from toothless mouths. And a few Kurds say that the present time offers the last best hope of a military thrust to recapture their old capital city of Kirkūk.

By the frail light of a small torch, a child was buried beside the road going south to Kirkūk, her legs taken off by a V69 Italian-made anti-personnel mine laid by Iraqi army sappers.

The girl's legs had been severed at the knees when her running footfall triggered the tripwire. She had been gambolling ahead of her father towards a meadow of yellowed grass where the family's four goats grazed. He had known there were mines close to the small collection of homes that made a village, but it was the first day of April, it was eleven days after the sparse celebration of the Kurdish New Year, *Newruz*, and the winter fodder for the goats was exhausted. They must find their own food if they were to fill their udders and give the family the milk of life. Had there been a hospital close by, had there been a four-wheel-drive vehicle in the village to take the child to it, then a life might have been saved. As it was, the child had died of trauma and blood loss.

Her father and brothers paused by the pit they had dug beside the road under the shelter of battered, storm-tossed, leafless mulberry trees. The father slid down into the hole on his backside, and the eldest of the brothers took the small wrapped bundle from the mother and passed it to him. The tears ran on the father's cheeks, dribbled with the rain on his face, and all the time the mother cried the dirge that was familiar to all women, all mothers, in northern Iraq.

'Saddam! Saddam! Why do you sow mines in our fields?

'Why do you hang our sons, why do you bulldoze our villages?

'Why do you bury us alive? . . . We beg you, America!

'We beg you, United Nations! We beg you, God!

'Help us and save us . . .

'For our lives are destroyed, and we have become beggars.'

The small convoy of vehicles passed her as she sat swaying her shoulders and crying her song. Her hands were folded tightly against the emptiness of her chest, where she had held her dead, desecrated child. The vehicles were travelling slowly along the rutted track on dulled sidelights. The torch that lit the burial of her child, with a weakened, failing battery, threw a wide cone of grey light into the first dun-painted, mud-scarred truck that passed her. She did not recognize the man who drove, or the men squashed into two rows of seats behind him, but she recognized the young woman sitting beside the driver. The mother had never before seen the young woman, but she recognized her from the rumour slipping through the villages. It had been brought, as surely as the leaves of autumn eddied from the orchards, by nomads. She saw the young woman's face, the combat fatigues on her upper body, the rifle against her shoulder, and the chest harness to which the grenades were hooked. All the mothers in her village had heard the whispered rumour of the young woman who had come from the north, many days' walk away, where the mountains were highest.

She shouted at the limit of her voice: 'Punish them. Punish them for what they have done to me.'

More vehicles passed.

Her child's father and brothers were pushing the clods of wet soil and the stones back into the pit. Then the father stood and held up the torch so that the brothers might better see stones to heap on top of the shallow grave to protect it against wild dogs and foxes. There should have been a man of God there, but they lived too far from any mosque to receive that comfort. There should have been neighbours and friends and cousins, but they were too close to the positions of the Iraqi murderers and the front line of their bunkers for any but the close family to venture into the darkness. The boys gasped under the weight of the stones.

The light of their father's torch caught the last vehicle in the convoy. It had a closed cab and an open back in which were huddled men in fighting clothes who clutched weapons to their bodies. The men saw the

20

mother, they saw the father and the brothers, they saw the stones that marked the grave, and all but one raised their fists, clenched, in a gesture of sympathy.

One man, squatting in the back of the last vehicle, was different. He gazed at the mother but his hands remained firmly on the straps of a many-coloured container, green and black, white and deadened yellow, and his rucksack. The beam of the torch caught the smeared lines on his face. He was different because he was not of their people. The mother saw the strange garment that the man wore, bulky, covered with the little strips of hessian net in the colours of the hills and earth, foliage and stones among which she lived. She thought he came from far away.

'Kill them,' she shouted into the night. 'Kill them as vengeance for taking my child.'

And the line of lights drifted into the distance. She knew nothing of history and nothing of politics, but she knew everything of suffering, and she knew what the rumour had told her of the young woman who had come from the distant north.

When his bed was cold, long after his woman had left it, the shepherd crawled from under the blankets.

He heard the sound of the generator throbbing, and he smelt the rich coffee that she had already placed in the pot for heating. The fire was lit but its warmth had not yet spread through the room. With the coffee was the scent of bread baking. She worked hard to look after him, but he deserved a good woman because he had brought her the electricity generator and fuel for the fire, ground coffee and sugar and food and money to spend in the bazaar in Kirkūk away beyond the checkpoints and road blocks. He gave her the money to buy carpets for the floors, and bedclothes and drapes for the walls, which were dry under a roof of new corrugated iron.

He waved to her and she scurried from the stove to the window and pulled back the drape. He saw the slow-moving clouds against the light gold sky of the dawn. He knew the colour of gold, the best gold, because sometimes he could buy it at the bazaar in Kirkūk. It had been a bad night, but the storm buffeting his home had moved on. The shepherd usually slept well. He was a contented man. He had a fine house, a fine flock of sheep, he had a generator for electricity, he had food, he had an old biscuit tin filled with dinar notes issued by the Central Bank that he kept against the wall under his bed, and a smaller box beside it held four chains of eighteen-carat gold . . . and he had their equipment.

By taking their equipment, the shepherd had sold himself.

He pulled on his loose-fitting trousers, knotted the string at the waist, then drew over his head that week's shirt and a thick woollen sweater, gently unravelling where the thorns had plucked at it, then a heavy coat. He sat on the bed and slid into his still-wet shoes. He wound a turban loosely around his head. From a hook beside the door he took the Kalashnikov and the binoculars that had come with the equipment. She gave him his first coffee of the day in a chipped cup. He grunted, drank it, belched, and returned the cup to her. He lifted an old television set from the floor – wires snaked from it across the room and climbed the walls before disappearing into the ceiling – pressed down the button and waited for the picture to form. It showed, in black and white, a steep-sided valley, and at the bottom of it were the gouged lines of a vehicle track. It was the same each day, and each night, deserted. But he checked it many times each day. The shepherd was conscientious because he valued the things given him when he had sold himself.

He went out into the dawn light. He cut along the side of his home, shielding his eyes from the low slant of the sunlight, and hurried to the small building of concrete blocks that protruded from the end of the one-room house. He rapped three times on the wood door, the signal, heard the footfall within, then the grate of a bolt being withdrawn. The door was opened. As he did every day at the end of the night watch, his son embraced him, kissed both his cheeks.

The shepherd stepped inside. There were no windows in the room. The generator chattered in the corner. In the dim light the dials of the military radio glowed brightly. The television on the table beside the radio showed the same picture of the valley floor. His son shrugged, as if to say, as always, nothing had moved on the track below in the night, then ran for the door. His son always went first to the pit at the back to shit and piss, then to his mother for his last meal of the day; his son would sleep during the daylight hours then resume watch as night fell.

It was a few minutes before the time when the shepherd was scheduled to make his morning call on the radio. There would be another call as dusk fell but there was, of course, a frequency he could use in an emergency. He threw the switch that killed the television picture, and the second switch that governed the alternative camera capable of thermal imaging, and the last switch that controlled the sound sensors at the floor of the valley. He did not know the age of the equipment or its origins, but he had been taught how to operate it by men of the Estikhabarat in the headquarters of the Military Command at Kirkūk. Everything he owned – the gold, the money in the biscuit tin, the stove, the fresh coffee, the oven for baking bread, his flock – was his because he had agreed to work the equipment they had given him.

He went outside and padlocked the door behind him.

On the south side of the valley, above a sheer cliff face, was a plateau of good grazing grass covering an area of a little more than eleven hectares. Though he did not have the education to measure it, the shepherd was some 150 metres above the valley floor along which the rough track ran. To the left and right of the plateau were higher, impassable cliff faces. Three kilometres down the track, past two sharp bends in the valley's narrow passage, was the nearest Iraqi checkpoint. The cliff below the plateau was climbable, with great care, by a sure-footed man, if he followed the trails used by the shepherd's animals. The shepherd was a tripwire, an early-warning system for the troops at the checkpoint.

He was not aware that the summit of the valley on the far side was exactly 725 metres from the front door of his house, but he knew it was a distance far greater than a Kalashnikov rifle was capable of firing. He believed himself impregnable, safe from his own people, and he had the big radio to back him, if men tried to climb the sheep trails to the plateau.

He stood by the door of his home, drinking the air. He watched an eagle making slow circuits above the summit of the far valley wall. He had strong, clear vision. The far side of the valley was as it had been, exactly, the day before and the day before that. He raked his eyes across the landscape of yellow grass tufts, grey stone, brown, exposed earth and the sharp greens of the bilberry leaves. If anything had changed, if man or animal were on the summit across the void, the shepherd would have seen it. His stomach rumbled, called on him to return inside, take his first food of the day and more coffee. But he stayed the extra moments and gazed at the simple peace around him. Later, while his son slept, he would lead the sheep towards the west of the plateau, but always he would have his rifle with him and his binoculars, always he would be able to see the track along the valley floor and he would be a few seconds' hard running from the room of concrete blocks and the live radio. He had lost sight of the eagle. He blinked as the sun was in his eyes . . . and then the blackness came. He heard nothing.

The shepherd felt as though he had been hit by a great iron hammer full in the centre of his chest. He slid, against his will, down onto the short, sheep-cropped grass in front of the door.

His life had passed within a second. He had no knowledge of a .338 bullet fired at a range of 725 metres and fracturing his spinal column between the second and third thoracic vertebrae. He could not know that his wife and his son would cower under the table of their home and be too terrorized to open the door, run to the radio and send the coded signal summoning immediate help. Nor would he know that, as the dawn spread light on the paths made by his sheep over the precipice face of the cliff, men would scramble up the heights, break his radio, smash his television, cut the cables to the cameras, drink his coffee, find his biscuit tin and the smaller box holding four gold chains, and he could not know what the men did to his wife and son – the *jahsh*, the little donkeys, the traitor Kurds who sided with Saddam. And he would not know that amongst the men was a young woman, sweating and panting from the exertion of the climb, who summoned the spittle in her mouth and spat down onto his still-open eyes.

The first hour of the day shift was the busiest for the technicians in Kirkūk working at the radios of the Estikhabarat al-Askariyya. Early in the morning the new shift handled the volume of check calls and radio signals sent to the Military Intelligence Service. At the end of the day, the new night shift would be deluged by a similar number of calls. There were transmissions that were classified as important, and there were the regular checks that had low priority because nothing of worth was ever reported on them. In a cubicle compartment, four yawning, scratching, smoking technicians listlessly ticked off radio calls received, and wallowed in boredom.

The role tasked to the regional office of the Estikhabarat in Kirkūk was to provide military intelligence on armed Kurdish factions north of the army's defence line, and to infiltrate the factions so that a *peshmerga* commander could not shit, could not screw his wife, without it being known and reported on down the line to national headquarters in the Aladhamia area of Baghdad. Low priority, bumping the bottom of the barrel, was given to Call-sign 17, Sector 8.

Call-signs 1 to 16 had reported in, nothing of significance. Call-signs 18 to 23 had been received on clear transmission. Only Call-sign 17 in Sector 8 was not ticked off. The technician who should have received the call alerted his supervisor when the transmission was forty-eight minutes late.

'Probably poking sheep,' the supervisor said, and walked away. 'He'll come through in the evening.'

But the technician, a conscript who would follow military service with an electronics course in higher education in Basra, was not satisfied until he had personally checked the file for Call-sign 17. Call-sign 17 was issued with a Russian-made R-107 radio. It had a four-to-six-kilometre range, which meant it relied on a booster antenna in the mountains. The radio, in the opinion of the conscript technician, was poor and the antenna, during the night, would have been battered by the storm that had raged over the high ground north of Kirkūk. He made a note to refer it to the technician taking over from him at the end of the day. Of course, the sheep poker was low priority or he would have been given more sophisticated equipment than the R-107 radio.

At dawn that day, a little crack had been opened in the many-layered lines of defence separating the Kurdish enclave from their spiritual capital of Kirkūk, and it was not seen by the technician, or by his supervisor.

They had all played a part in moving the letter. Written in a spidery hand by Hoyshar, the father of Jamal, father-in-law of Faima and grandfather of Meda, it had begun its journey six weeks earlier, while the snow was still falling in the northern mountains and valleys. Now in his eighty-fifth year, a remarkable age for a man who had lived the greater part of his life in a village community where the houses clung to the steep slopes, near Birkim, of the mountains of Kurdish Iraq, it had been a great effort for Hoyshar to write to an old friend whom he valued as a brother.

There was no postal service out of the region, and Hoyshar had no access to a facsimile machine or to a satellite telephone. The letter had moved by hand, growing grubbier, accumulating the fingerprints of people Hoyshar did not know. The young woman, Meda, had started her march out of the northern fortress uplands in the week that the letter was written. All of those who had moved it woke that morning unaware of the small fissure opened in the outer extremity of the Iraqi army's defence line.

The letter had been given by the old man to Sarah, an Australian working in northern Iraq for a London-backed children's charity. She had been in the mountains investigating reports of a diphtheria epidemic, and the letter had been pressed into her hand . . . That morning, an hour after a single bullet had sung across the emptiness of a steep-sided valley, she nursed an aching hangover from the farewell party for her regional director . . . She had passed on the letter.

Joe had taken it from the aid-worker. He was Scots born, a one-time soldier in the Royal Engineers, and was in northern Iraq to clear minefields. She had pleaded, explained, and he had stuffed it into his shoulder-bag and gone back to the ground around a village well where he taught local men, by example and practice, how to kneel and probe for the anti-personnel mines . . . That morning, with his bodyguards, interpreter and three Kurdish recruits, he was staking out the pegs round a field of V69s and POMZ 2Ms and Type 72As that had been laid in an orchard of pomegranate trees . . . Three days later he had handed on the crumpled envelope.

Lev had taken the letter, been told its history. Everybody knew the overweight and balding Russian. He was equally loved and loathed: loved because he could smooth paths and provide comforts, loathed because of his corrupt amorality . . . That morning, he spat orders to his houseboy, who carried to the boot of the Mercedes two crates of bourbon, a video-cassette recorder and an Apple Mac computer . . . He had slid the envelope down into the hip pocket of his trousers, where it wedged against a gross roll of American dollar bills, and delivered it at the end of the week.

Isaac had been given the letter and had, of course, steamed open the envelope. If it had not interested him, it would have gone into the plastic bag of shredded waste-paper beside the table where the banks of monitoring equipment were stacked. He was an Israeli, an employee of the Mossad, in charge of the most God-forsaken post offered to any agent sent from Tel Aviv. His equipment, his dishes, his antenna, in the high, empty country south of the Arbīl to Rawāndiz road, could eavesdrop on every communication between army headquarters in Baghdad and Fifth Army head-quarters in Kirkūk, and the signals of the Estikhabarat, and he could monitor the SIGINT and ELINT operations of the Project 858. As a result of the strange alliances of northern Iraq he was protected in his eyrie by a platoon of Turkish paratroops. That morning, he had listened to Call-signs 1–16 and 18–23, in Sector 8, broadcasting news of nothing to Kirkūk, and he had noted that

Call-sign 17 had failed to make scheduled contact. Then he had begun to listen to a radio conversation between armoured corps commanders in the Mosul area . . . A Turkish air force Blackhawk helicopter, with no navigation lights, came in at night once a week to the small LZ, shaking the roof of his building and tugging at the tents of the paratroops. The helicopter had taken the letter, resealed.

The letter handled by the aid-worker, the de-miner, the entrepreneur and the intelligence agent had been delivered four weeks after it had left the mountain village to a vicarage in southern England, and none of its couriers yet knew of the consequences of their actions.

Sometimes their voices were raised, at others they bickered quietly. Gus Peake did not know the cause of the dispute. He sat on his haunches with his back against the wall of the shed, with the map and plan they had drawn across his knees. They were within earshot but out of his sight, around the edge of the shed, and beyond the thorn corral where the goats were. Nor did he know why the advantage from his single shot was not exploited. He had seen with his binoculars how the men had swarmed on the cliff face and run to the building in front of which the body lay. He had seen the main door of the house beaten down, and he had heard the screams, the smashing of the equipment from inside. And she had come back down the cliff, descended nimbly, as easily as a deer, and later she had reached where he waited. He did not understand why they had not, immediately, pushed forward. He tried to shut from his mind the argument raging near to him.

Gus worked on the plan of the bunkers they had given him and married them to the old map. He used a compass to measure distance, because he had been told he should never rely completely on the technology of his binoculars. From the map, he tried to locate a vantage-point amongst the whorls of the contours that he could approach using dead ground. He accepted that luck had been with him that morning, that a clean kill at 785 yards without a sighting shot was more than fortunate. He had little conceit, and less arrogance. He believed in himself and his ability, but he was seldom less than realistic. He had been lucky, more than fortunate. He tried to find a point on the map that he could reach in darkness, that would offer him cover and protection and give him a range of not more than 650 yards.

Their voices were angry again. He pictured them, toe to toe, eyeball to eyeball. Some of the men had been left on the plateau, some had come down, and they sat in the shade of trees where the vehicles were hidden around a small fire. Their faces were impassive, as if they heard and saw nothing of the argument.

He did not know if the map was accurate, or whether the plan that had been given to him of the bunkers was loosely drawn or to an exact scale. Then he heard the silence. The lines on the map seemed to bounce in front of his eyes. She was walking away, crossing open ground, skirting the clump of trees where the men sat and the vehicles were hidden. He saw her sink down and her head fall into her hands. Suddenly the smell of the goats seemed revolting. He folded away the map, dumped the plan into the rucksack's pouch, threw his calculator and the compass in with it. He kicked at a stone and watched it career towards the track.

31

'You have a problem?'

Haquim limped the last few strides from the corner of the shed to where Gus sat and used the butt of his rifle as a prop while he clumsily lowered himself down.

'Only that I don't know what's happening. I don't know why we are here. I don't know what everyone is arguing about. I don't know why she's not speaking to me . . .'

'Why do we not go forward, Mr Peake? Because we wait for more men. I try to tell her and she abuses me. Why do we wait for more men? Because there are very few who will follow me, and many who follow only the orders of their *agha*. Yes, because of her, because simple people believe in her, illiterate people, people who have old rifles to keep bears and dogs away from their live-stock, she can raise an army that would be butchered by machine-guns, artillery and tanks. We need trained men who are familiar with the tactics of battle, who will receive and carry out orders, who know how to use weapons. The men we need, the *peshmerga*, which in your language means "those who face death", are con-trolled by the two *agha* of the Kurdish people. They have promised a few men, only a few. They want to fight a war, yes, but only if they believe they will win that war. So, the supply of men will be like a drip feed. Each time we advance, a few more men will be sent. I cannot change it. I have to wait for more men . . . She does not understand . . . I tell you, Mr Peake, sometimes I can be angry with her.'

'I was called, I came, and now I am ignored.'

'Also, I tell you that without her we would not have started to march, we would not have had the dream. Without her there would be nothing. Being ignored is a small price to pay . . . I am experienced in war. She has no experience, but at every step she will question me. But without her nothing is possible, and I believe you know it.'

'Thank you.'

'We move at last light . . . You want to hurry to war, Mr Peake. You will be there soon enough . In a week or two weeks, tell me then if you still want to hurry . . .'

Carried on the wind, he heard, faintly, the sound of the furious revving of a vehicle far down the track, around a gentle sloping escarpment that rose to the valley's cliff wall, beyond his sight. Haquim had stiffened, lifted his head to hear better, then pushed himself up with his rifle. He said coldly, 'When you meet a target that can shoot back, Mr Peake, then you will have found a war.'

The first fires of the day pushed up a pall of hanging smoke that merged with the fumes of cars' exhausts, which hung as a thickening carpet across his view of Baghdad awakening.

He had stayed too long, should have been gone before the sun was up. It was suicidal for him to have remained there until daylight broke over the city.

He had stayed too long because, for the fifth night, the target had not appeared. The frustration bit into him. He should have been gone an hour earlier, at least, while the shadows still hugged the streets. Although the sun's early warmth was on the flat roof beside the water tank, Major Karim Aziz shivered. Throughout the last hour he had known that the chance of the target coming diminished with each passing minute, and yet he had stayed.

His legs were cramped and stiff, all feeling gone. His

eyes watered from the long hours of gazing into the aperture of the sight's lens. His shoulders ached from holding the rifle butt at his shoulder for so long. He realized that for the last fifteen minutes, as the smoke and fumes had formed a cloudy haze, he had barely been able to see the driveway, the steps and the door on which his telescopic sight was locked.

He took a last look through the sight, cursed, then began to pack his gear quickly. He wrapped the sight in a loose towel, snapped the butt-release button and reduced the weapon's length so that it would fit easily into the anonymous sports bag, then his binoculars, then his bottle of water, and his box for salad and bread, then the larger bottle, tightly corked, to hold urine passed during the night. He rolled up the thin rubber mat on which he had lain motionless for eleven hours and dropped it inside, zipped the bag and stood up. As he had calculated it from the city's maps, it was a distance of 545 metres from the leading edge of the building's water tank to the front door, across which, up which, through which, he had now waited five full nights for the target to come.

He checked around him. His life and the lives of those he loved depended on the care with which he checked the concrete of the roof beside the water tower for scraps of paper and drops of urine or water.

Below him were the sounds of radios, shouting children and banging doors. He pulled the hood of his army windcheater up over his head so that his features were masked, and hurried towards the service door to the roof of the block. Behind him was the view across the apartment blocks between Rashid Street and al-Jamoun Street, past Wahtba Square, across lower blocks between

34

al-Jamoun Street and Kifah Street, and into a gap on the far side of Kifah Street that offered a small window view of the few yards of driveway to the villa.

He took the rough concrete service steps three at a time, clattered down them. He had spent a week searching out his vantage-point, trudging into building after building, gaining access by his military uniform, giving a false name on a forged identity card, claiming he was looking for accommodation for himself and his family. He had made a great circle around the villa to which he had been assured the target would come, and found only the one rooftop, of a seven-storey building, which was between 400 and 700 metres from the villa and offered a view over the surrounding wall of the short way the target must walk between his bomb-proof car and the front door.

Maybe the bastard's penis did not itch enough: when it itched, when it needed stroking, sucking, then the bastard would come. He passed two smoking, gossiping maids on the service stairs. They saw him, looked for a moment at his army coat, then flattened against the wall and averted their gaze. They would have assumed that he, too, had an itching penis, and they would not dare to speak of an army officer's assignation for fear of a beating from the Military Security Service . . . It was all about the President's itch, and the visits to the villa of his current mistress.

Major Karim Aziz let himself out of the side fire exit of the building, and joined the pavement throng heading for the Shuhada Bridge that crossed the Tigris.

He walked quickly, imagining that every eye was on him, believing that every eye was in the head of an agent of the regime. The weight of the sports bag banged against his thigh. At every step, he expected a hand to grab him, a body to block him, and the bag to be snatched and opened. He crossed the bridge over the wide, slow-flowing mud brown of the river, swollen from the thaw of the snow in the mountains far to the north. The tiredness bred the fantasies of danger.

He reached Haifa Street, crossed it near to the central railway station, and came to his home.

Major Karim Aziz's home was a modest two-storey house, with a muddy front garden where the roses that Leila tended would bloom in a month's time, where Wafiq and Hani played football, where her parents would sit in the summer months. They were all in the kitchen. The boys were gathering their books together for school. His wife was shuffling through papers she would need in her day's work at the hospital. Her father was listening to the radio's news bulletin, and her mother was clearing the table. His own place was laid, a piece of melon, a slice of bread, a square of cheese. They all looked away from him and he gave no explanation as to why he had, for the fifth time, been away from his home for the night. It was impossible for him to give any.

He kissed the boys sharply, touched the arm of his wife and nodded to her parents. They would have seen the tiredness in his eyes, and they would have looked down and wondered what he carried in his sports bag.

It was too late for him to sleep.

He showered, shaved. By the time he had changed into a clean uniform and come back into the kitchen, the boys had left for school and Leila had gone to the hospital where she nursed children. Her father stared at the radio while her mother rinsed the plates at the sink;

they wouldn't have understood even if he had been able to tell them. He thought it was better that he had not come home earlier. The previous time, he had slipped into his home, a thief in the night, and snuggled against her back and known that she only pretended to sleep, and he had heard the tossing in their beds of his sons, the cough of her father, then the fear of the consequences he might inflict on them had ravaged in his mind.

Aziz took the family car, the old Nissan Micra, to his workplace at the Baghdad Military College.

37

Chapter Two

After the engine of the distant vehicle had stopped, he saw them come round the escarpment's bend. There were two men with rifles, the escort, and a man and a woman who were unarmed and European. When they'd passed a small clump of winter-dead trees, the woman pointed to the smoke of the fire near to the track and ahead of them, and their pace quickened. They would have seen the spiral of the smoke, then the vehicles parked in the trees close to the shed.

They had started to run. The unarmed man, the European, ran badly as if he had wrenched his back, but the woman turned, grabbed his arm without ceremony and heaved him forward to keep up with her. He stumbled and seemed to cry out, but she just tugged harder at him.

Gathering strength to climb the other side of the valley and witness the result of his shot, Gus sat in the sunshine against the wall of the shed. The sweat ran in faint driblets against his skin under the weight of his gillie suit. The woman saw Meda sitting alone in the pasture grass, released her burden, let him slip then fall, and waved to her. He heard the broad ring of her fierce Australian accent.

'Christ, am I glad to see you. We are in shit, Meda . . . You might just be a goddam angel . . . I'm trying to get my regional director to the border. Too much Irish last night – Christ, do we have hang-overs. The driver, the arsehole, took the wrong turn – alcohol poisoning's his bloody problem. Obstinate bastard won't admit he's cocked it. We're in the back end of bloody nowhere and aren't the Iraqis just round the corner? Christ . . . We tried to turn but the bloody Cruiser's stuck over a goddam rock. Do you believe it? We don't have a bloody rope on board it or on the back-up. Do you have a rope? And maybe some bodies to help? If I don't get him to the border, it screws everything, all the schedules, the exit visa, the flights, every bloody thing . . .'

She was laughing, and Meda with her.

'I mean, Meda, that arsehole was taking us into the Iraqi army checkpoint. Christ, they'd have thought it was bloody Christmas.'

She was mud-smeared, her hair a flash of blond in the wind. Meda was leading her towards the shed and shouting to her men under the trees. And because she pointed to the shed, and the men ran ahead of her towards where he sat, the European man hobbled faster towards him.

He didn't know what he should do. He sat rooted to the ground, his back hard against the wall. A stampede was closing on him. He heard Haquim's whispered voice, but didn't respond. And then he saw the way the European man gazed at him with bright, staring eyes. He had been wearing the gillie suit for so many hours that it no longer seemed special.

Haquim's fist closed on his shoulder. 'Get in, Mr Peake, get out of sight.'

He was wrenched up, pitched inside the windowless shed, and crawled towards the far corner, into the darkness where his rucksack and the rifle he had cleaned earlier were. Perhaps he should have been sleeping, perhaps he did not realize the necessity of taking any opportunity to sleep. He had been too captivated by the tranquil beauty of the valley, and the eagle's soaring flight, and too angered that Meda ignored him. Now, exhausted, he did not know why he was hurled into the back of the shed.

The doorway was crowded, a torchbeam roved over the floor of stamped dirt and goat droppings. Before they found the length of rope among the ammunition boxes and the stacked heap of armour-piercing grenades, the beam of the torch discovered him. He couldn't see the face of the European man who was framed in the doorway with fierce sunlight behind him. The beam lit him and the rifle propped against the wall close to him.

'*Mr Peake?* Is that English, American?'

Without thinking, he muttered, 'English.'

'A long way from home. Where is home?'

Still without thinking: 'Guildford.'

Haquim spat at him, 'Don't give them your face. Shut up. Don't say anything.'

He was startled by the venom of the order, flinched instinctively, turned his head so that the torchbeam fell on his neck, then moved to the rifle and lingered on the camouflage strips of hessian material wound round the barrel and the telescopic sight. Then it jumped away because the coil of rope had been found. As fast as it had filled, the shed emptied. He sat in the darkness. His mind cleared. He did not need to be told that he had made a mistake, but he knew that when the aid-worker's vehicle had been pulled back on to the track and had driven away, Haquim would return and batter him with criticism.

When he had climbed down from the cab of the lorry that had brought him from Guildford in south-east England to Diyarbakir in south-east Turkey ten days before, he would have said that he could cope with isolation. He would have said just as firmly nine nights ago, when he had been taken along a smugglers' route over the mountains, the border and into northern Iraq, that loneliness did not affect him. He sat in the darkness with his head drooping – he had wanted to talk to somebody, anybody, in English and about home, about what was safe. He clenched his fists and ground his fingernails into the palms of his hands so that the pain would wipe out the guilt of making a small mistake . . . and then he closed his eyes.

It was about visualization. It was about each crawling movement towards the firing position, each moment of preparation, and each controlled breath when he aimed at the forward bunker that was on the plan drawn for him, and each contour of the map over which the .338 bullet would fly.

But it was hard for him to erase the memory of the mistake.

The regional director, Benedict, waited until they were back on the open road.

'Did you see that man?'

'What man?'

'Called Peake. Said he was English, from Guildford.'

'Didn't see him.'

'He was a professional soldier.'

'I see what's good for me to see – and I get on with my job.'

'He had a sniper's rifle in there.'

'It's not my business.'

'It's my damn business. Don't bloody laugh at me, I worry about you more than any other of Protect the Children's field-workers. That's honest, more than the guys in Afghanistan or Somalia. Yes, you're protected by goons, but we all know that's just show. The Iraqis could take you any day they want.'

'You're a bag of bloody fun today, Benedict. It's best you forget it.'

'No way. If the British military is deploying expert snipers in northern Iraq, that jeopardizes the safety of British-employed aid-workers.'

'Leave it.'

'I'm raising the roof when I get back.'

She turned away, shut her eyes. Her head throbbed. It was a good place to be drunk, pity was it didn't happen often enough. She heard his breath hissing through gritted teeth. She knew he would raise the bloody roof, and she knew the Iraqis could kidnap her at any time they chose.

'And who was that woman?'

She didn't open her eyes. 'You don't need to know, so don't ask.'

They crowded around Gus.

Haquim said they had all seen Russian-made sniper

rifles, but never a weapon as large as the one he carried.

The hands groped towards it, but he did not let any of them touch it for fear that they might jolt the mounting of the telescopic sight.

Four days before, he had zeroed the sight. He had gone off alone on to a flat, sheltered meadow of grass and spring flowers. He had paced out a distance of 100 yards and left a cardboard box there with a bull blacked in with ink. He had paced out a further 100 yards, and left another cardboard box, and a final one at 300 yards. He had gone back to his firing position, turned the clicks on the distance turret of the sight to the elevation for 100 yards, fired, examined the target with his binoculars, found the shot low, had made adjustments to the mounting, fired again, checked with his binoculars where the shot had clipped the top edge of the four-inch bull, had made more adjustments, fired and been satisfied. Then he had moved to the 200-yard target, and then to the 300-yard target. Only when he was completely satisfied with the accuracy of his shooting had he packed away the rifle. Then, an hour later, he had met Meda. No talk, no gratitude, no curiosity as to how he had made the great journey, nothing about family, no recall of the past. She had handed him on to Haquim, and had not spoken to him since.

Gus let them look at the rifle, but he would not let them touch, feel or hold it.

He counted forty-two of them. There were forty-one men and a boy. He was slim, had stick-like wrists and a thin throat. On the smooth complexion of his cheeks and upper lip there was a haze of fluff, as if he was trying to grow a man's beard. Most of the men were middle-aged, some shaven and some bearded, some in fatigues and

43

some in their own tribal clothes. There was one who pressed closer than the others – turbaned, an old torn check shirt under a grey-blue anorak with a face masked by stubble and dangerous flitting eyes. They were bad, hostile eyes, and they raked him. His mouth had narrow lips, between which the tongue was turned and rolled in the mouth to gather the spittle. It was directed down between his boots. There was the single croaked word, spoken with contempt: 'American.'

Gus stared back into the man's face, shook his head and said, 'English.' He saw the eyes and mouth relax, then the man turned his back on him.

He thought them proud men, but with the common features of cruel eyes and brutal mouths. His grandfather would have described them, in the language of long ago, as 'villains'. They carried assault rifles and grenade launchers; one had a light machine-gun and was wrapped with belts of ammunition. Then, in a moment, he was no longer the centre of attention because they had seen her, Meda.

They were around her. She spoke softly, with the glow in her eyes. They hung on her words. The one who'd spat, his mouth gaped open as if the foul old bastard had found the light of God and was mesmerized. Gus thought they danced for her.

Haquim, at his shoulder, said, 'I can tell them about the tactics of frontal attack, and about clearing trenches with grenades, and about enfilading fire, and they tolerate me. She tells them of destiny and freedom, and they will follow wherever she leads. I fear where she will lead us, Mr Peake.'

'When are we leaving?'

Haquim said dully, 'We go when she says we go.'

'I counted forty-two new men – is that enough?'

'Forty-one men and a boy, Mr Peake. Forty-one fighters and a boy to wash and cook for them. And there were eighteen of us, and you, and her. You go to war, Mr Peake, with fifty-nine men, a boy and her . . . It is what we have, it has to be enough. I told you it would be a drip feed. Today, *agha* Bekir has sent us forty-one men and a boy from the slum camps of Sulaymānīyah. In Arbīl, *agha* Ibrahim will watch to see if we are successful. If we are he will not wish to lose status and he will send a hundred men, who will also be the scum from the slums. I told you how it would be.'

Her hands moved, outstretched, as she spoke. They seemed capable of carrying the weight of the world. He watched the power with which she held them, then ducked inside the shed.

When he came out, the rucksack and the carrying case hooked over his shoulders, Meda was leading and they were following up the narrow paths on the cliff face that generations of sheep had made. He heard their singing, in quiet, throaty voices. Haquim was ahead of him, labouring over the rocks. He climbed slowly and carefully, never looking back or down. Around him, he heard the songs of men going to war.

Sarah stood by the two Landcruisers, the bodyguards crowded around her. The customs men on the Syrian side of the river were waving urgently for him to hurry, and the man in the ferry-boat was shouting for him. Her regional director kissed her awkwardly on the cheek. She didn't know whether she believed what he'd said, that he worried more about her than any of his other field people. When he was back in his London home, with his wife or partner or boyfriend, would he be worrying about her? The visits were little light lines in the darkness of her everyday life, but they unsettled her. It would take a week to reassemble her existence, fall back into the routine of the isolation and exposure to suffering that were commonplace.

'Keep safe, Sarah.'

'Give my love to the office,' she said flatly.

'I'm going to do what I said I'd do.'

'What's that?'

'British snipers hazarding your safety . . . raise hell.'

Under the glare of the afternoon sun he scrambled down the track towards the ferry. She waved desultorily. She watched him climb aboard and the ferry carried him across the Tigris, towards Syrian territory, towards safety. Tomorrow she would be back in the high villages and her concern would be for children who had no school, no clinic and no hope. What could one sniper do, however fucking expert, however big his fucking rifle, to give the children hope, a clinic and a school? The ferry reached the far side of the river, and he ran to the car that would drive him to the airstrip for the feeder flight to Damascus.

She shouted after him, 'I hope your back's better in the morning. Don't tell them in the office that you did it getting the Cruiser back on the road. Tell them you were escaping from a battalion of the Republican Guard . . .'

Gus had made the climb up the far side of the valley his bullet had crossed.

Only once before had he stood, silent, and looked down on the dead. Then, more than nine years before, he had steeled himself, erect, tall, and adopted a concerned expression. Hands had plucked at the sleeves of his coat and led him between the clusters of wrapped shapes. He had tried, then, to close his ears to the persistence of the sobbing of the living. Men had wept and women had cried out in their anguish and the tears had rolled down children's cheeks. He could remember, then, that he had worried how they would bury so many bodies because there was little earth between the rock outcrops and that was frozen under the sporadic patches of snow. He could remember the endless crawling line of people coming down a track on a far slope towards the swaying rope bridge with their bundles, bags, cases and more dead. Sometimes, that was clear in his mind, the cloths that wrapped the corpses had been unwound so that he could see the faces of the dead, as if it was important to those who lived that he should share with them the agony of their loss. They had died from hunger, thirst, cold, exhaustion, from wounds into which gangrene gas had spread infection, and from the cruelty of eccentric accidents. She had been with him as he had toured the panorama of the dead, always behind him and never speaking, never interrupting her father and grandfather, never weeping, never crying out. Her gaze had been impassive as her father had drawn back blankets and sacking to show the crushed faces of her sister and brother killed by a pallet of grain bags parachuted down from an American mercy flight. He had witnessed her strength.

Before they had left, then, the mountain slope of tents and plastic sheeting, the shivering living and the cold dead, he had said the unthinking words that he had mouthed several times before and since. At the doors of English crematoria and at the gates of cemeteries, he had

47

taken the hands of mothers, widows and daughters, and murmured, 'If there's anything I can ever do to help, absolutely anything, then make contact, and I'll do my best...' It had been the decent thing to say. Empty words spoken before he had turned his back and hurried for the border, the car, the hotel and a damn great drink, all long ago, and the chance to put the dead from his mind.

Again, he saw the dead.

Again, the plucking hands pulled him forward.

The flies were on the face. They flew, buzzed, settled around the gaping mouth and the wide stare of the eyes and over the stubble set in the opaque skin. He saw a fly go into the man's mouth while another rested on his eyeball.

Gus was brought closer.

He wanted to shrug their hands off him but he did not, could not. There was a pool of blood on the chest and more blood, which had earlier seeped from the hole in the corpse's back. That, too, was a focus of the flies' feeding frenzy. The coat and shirt that the living body would have dragged on in the dawn cold a few minutes before its owner's death were pulled back to reveal the matted chest hair and the neatly drilled hole into which a pencil or a biro, of less than .338 diameter, would have fitted comfortably. He remembered the moment at which he had fired, as the target had seemed to arch his back and his head had tilted to face the heavens and his god, to drink the freshness of the air. A man clawed a hand around his shoulder and cackled, squeezing his flesh as if to offer congratulations at the accuracy of the shot. He thought he belonged. A bullet of .338 calibre moving at supersonic velocity, killing, had won him the respect of the men crowded close to him.

With a babble of voices around him he was taken into the home of the carcass, through the door that had been hammered down. The table was toppled over, the food trodden into the floor: there was a woman's body and a young man's, and the flies were worse. They rose in swarms from the bloodied wounds at the corpses' throats. He understood why the woman and the young man had been killed: they should not be able to carry away news of the attack over the plateau to the military position. He knew why they had been knifed: if they had been killed by gunfire the crash of the shots might have carried in the stillness of the early-morning air across the roll of the hills to the bunkers.

Gus thought of Stickledown. It would be quiet there after the previous day's shooting, the targets would be lowered and the flags down. Would any of those who had fired the old weapons the afternoon before, his friends and his fellow enthusiasts, the other lunatics, comprehend what he had done, what had brought him to this place?

Perhaps the men around him had seen him rock on the balls of his feet, perhaps they had seen the pallor spread over his face . . . They took him out and around the building, through the crazily hanging door and into the annexe block. He was shown the smashed screen of the television, the cut cables and the radio. Grimed fingers jabbed at the typed sheets of paper that he presumed carried the codewords, frequencies and schedules of transmission.

Outside, with the sunlight on his face, he too drank at the air, gulped at its purity.

They ate from an iron pot that the boy had heated over the last embers in the stove inside. With his fingers he

49

snatched saffron-flavoured rice, and palmed up the juicy swill of tomato and onion. Twice he found small scraps of meat, goat or mutton.

She had not eaten with them.

As the light sank they moved off.

She was ahead.

In the middle of the straggling column of men was the boy, burdened by the bags of food and the emptied iron pot. He skipped between the men, talking all the time, and stayed with each one until their patience was exhausted and he was cuffed away to dance on, light-footedly, to his next victim.

Gus trudged alongside Haquim at the end of the column, and realized the *mustashar*, the commander, was finding the going hard over rock and scrub, over shallow gorges and up rock inclines. He saw the pain in Haquim's grizzled, heavy-boned face and the sharp biting at his lower lip to stifle it. When Haquim stumbled and he put out his hand to offer help, it was pushed away. He wished he had slept more in the day, when the chance had been given. They would march in the evening, then he and Haquim would go forward in the night. The sun was dazzlingly fierce and starting the slide below a rim of granite rock. Twice, now, Haquim had stopped and steadied himself, breathing hard, then sighed and gone on. At the head of the column, he saw Meda drop down into a gully, near to the last ridge. He stayed with Haquim. He did not know whether he should insist on carrying part of the load balanced in a backpack on Haquim's spine. The column ahead waited for them in the gully.

Gus hadn't seen the boy turn when he materialized from among the rocks and wind-bent scrub close to them. All the time that he had been walking alongside Haquim, peering into the sun's fall, sometimes blinded by it, he had not seen the boy's charge back towards them. The boy said nothing, came to Haquim, stripped off the backpack, heaved it up alongside his rifle, the food bags and the cooking pot, and there was no protest. Then, again, with the sun in his face as it cringed below the ridge, he lost sight of the boy between the greying rocks and the darkening trees.

Haquim challenged him. 'You think I am not able?'

'I think nothing.'

'I am able.'

'If you say it then I believe you.'

'You, you are the worry.'

'Why am I the worry?'

'I doubt your strength. I may have a broken knee but I have strength. When I look down at a body, at a man I have killed, my stomach does not turn, I am not a girl. Let me tell you, Mr Peake, what you saw was as nothing to what the Iraqis would do to any of us, and to you. Do you know that?'

'Yes, I know that.'

'Today, for you, it is simple. Tomorrow, perhaps, it is easy. After tomorrow nothing is simple, nothing is easy. After tomorrow you will not look at me as if I am an aged cripple worthy of your sympathy, you will look at yourself.'

The first shadows of darkness cloaked them as they moved towards the second target.

He had showered, cold water to keep himself awake, eaten with the family, and gone out into the evening darkness.

51

Major Karim Aziz had yearned, again, to give some sign to his wife as to why he went out with his heavy waterproof tunic on and with the sports bag in his hand. There was nothing he could have told her. He could have lied about 'Special Operations' or manufactured an excuse involving 'continuing night exercises', but she always knew when he was lying. She'd done her best with the cooking for the family meal, and her mother would have spent hours on her slow old feet going round the open market stalls for the vegetables they could afford and a little meat. He had risen from the table, circled it and kissed in turn her parents, his boys and his wife. Then he had dressed for the night and left them.

The colder night air had cleared the smoke and smog. His view of the edge of the driveway, the steps and the villa's main door was crystal sharp through the sight.

As a trusted professional soldier, with twenty-six years of proven combat experience behind him, Major Karim Aziz had access to any equipment he cared to demand. It would be bought abroad and smuggled by lorry from Turkey or Jordan into Iraq. But his needs were simple. He told the officers and senior NCOs he taught at the Baghdad Military College that in the area of infantry operations the art of sniping was as old and as unchanged as any. They should beware of state-of-the-art technology. He would say that if a child learned only to count with the aid of a pocket calculator, then went into a mathematics examination without it, he would fail – but the child who had learned to add, subtract and divide in his mind would pass that examination. He had learned the measuring of distance as a primitive skill, and had never asked for range-finding binoculars.

The distance from rifle barrel to target was critical, but he was satisfied he had made an accurate measurement. With correct adjustment to the elevation of the sights, the bullet would be two metres above the point he aimed at before dropping for the kill. Too great an estimation of distance, the bullet flew high and the target lived; too low, the bullet dropped too far and the target suffered a non-fatal wound . . . but he was satisfied with his appraisal of the distance. It was the freshening wind gusting around the edge of the roof's water tank that bred the anxiety.

In daylight, he could have watched the flutter of the washing hung out on the roofs of the blocks of apartments fronting on to Rashid Street, al-Jahoun Street and Kifah Street. Through his binoculars, he would have seen the mirage of dust and insects, carried by the wind, and there would have been the drift of smoke and smog. At night, peering through the black curtain of darkness towards the illuminated window of the driveway, the steps and the front door, there was no accurate way he could tell the strength of the wind beyond the blow around the forward edge of the water tank. At that range, his bullet would be in the air for one and a quarter seconds; one surge of wind gusting for two or three hundred metres between buildings would bend the bullet's flight a few, several, centimetres and make the difference between killing and missing. But, with his experience, he did not require a calculator to make the adjustment to his PSO-1 sight. His intuition told him to compensate for a 75-degree wind direction at a strength of ten kilometres per hour, and his adjustment to the windage turret meant that his actual aim, if the target came, would be some eleven centimetres to the left.

If he was wrong, the bullet would miss, and if the bullet missed, a black hell would fall on the conspirators and on their families. What Major Karim Aziz feared most was that he would shoot and fail.

But he believed in himself, in his ability, in the certainty of his intuition. If he had not, he would not have been chosen.

An hour after he had taken up his position, he had seen car headlights sweep in a half-circle on the driveway 545 metres from him. The radio linked to his earpiece had remained silent. He had stiffened – in case the radio malfunctioned – aimed, and rested his finger on the trigger. He had watched the woman go up the steps and through the villa's door. She'd been flanked by men, but she was tall and they were a step behind her. He had seen, through the sight's lens, the auburn richness of her hair, and the proud swing of her shoulders. She was carrying boutique bags . . . The target had not been with her, and his finger had slid away from the trigger. A shop, importing Italian or French clothes, would have been opened especially for her in the evening. The dresses she carried in the bags would have cost, each, more than he earned as an army major in a full twelve months. Not that she would have paid, not that the bastard's most recent mistress would have been asked to delve in her wallet or purse for banknotes.

If she had new clothes to show off, then perhaps the bastard would come.

Aziz lay on his stomach on the mat, and the stiffness crept through his limbs.

The villa in the side road behind Kifah Street was closed off behind road blocks. The pedestrian public of Baghdad were denied access to that side road and to others in the city where high dignitaries lived or kept their women. From the end of the side road, when he had reconnoitred, Major Karim Aziz had seen a wall, a patrolling pair of sentries and a solid gate. There was no chance of inserting a culvert bomb in the streets at either end of the side road, and less chance of putting a marksman closer.

He had once met the target, in Basra, in the third year of the war with Iran. He had stood in a line and waited for an hour, had been frisk-searched for weapons by agents of the Amn al-Khass. He had shaken the limp wet hand and had gazed for a moment into the cold power of the face, then watched the armour-plated car drive away. Aziz thought of himself as a patriot, but there would be many who would denounce him as a traitor.

The radio stayed open. In his ear was the constant murmur of static. If the target came, there would be three tone bleeps in his ear. The man with the radio was above a butcher's shop on Kifah Street, opposite the side road.

The night wore on, and the streets below him gradually emptied. All the time his skin nestled against the cheek-pad on the butt of his rifle. It was because of his experience and his skill that he could concentrate totally on the small, brightly lit area enclosed by the telescopic sight.

The concentration dulled the enormity of the risk he took with his life and his family's lives.

'All I can tell you is that there are no British military personnel – I repeat *no* – stationed in northern Iraq.'

'Are you calling me a liar?'

As soon as he'd reached a payphone at Damascus

International, the regional director had called the embassy and demanded of the duty officer that someone with the rank of first secretary should be at the airport within an hour.

'It's best you listen carefully – there are no British military personnel deployed in northern Iraq, period.'

'I saw him with my own eyes. Seven hours and ten minutes ago, I saw a sniper in camouflage gear with a sniper rifle. His name is Peake and he told me he comes from Guildford, Surrey . . . My people live on the edge there. They fulfil a humanitarian role in circumstances of difficulty and enormous personal risk. I have a responsibility for my people who are beyond the reach of help, most especially when a British marksman – I assume he's Special Forces – is roaming loose on their territory. If I don't have your immediate guarantee of action then, on my arrival in London, I'll be phoning every tabloid newspaper.'

'That won't be necessary. I hope you have a good flight.'

They lay beside each other, waiting for the dawn, among the rocks.

Haquim said that he did not know whether the position, the network of bunkers and trenches, would have thermal-imaging equipment.

It would be two more hours before they would see, for the first time, the scattered shapes of the bunkers, the radio antenna and the unit's pennant. There was a single pinprick of light for them to watch, as if one lamp burned in a low cement-hardened bunker and was visible through a firing-port. There were high stars in shapes – he recognized some of the formations – but there was no moon. Ahead of him was the single lamp's light with an endless seam of blackness around it. Somewhere, close to the light, was the officer that Haquim had told him he would target. He thought the man would be young, still in the first flush of youth, and he would be sleeping, and in his mind would be the image of a girl or his mother, or his home. He never thought, lying still and stiff, feeling the damp creep through the rubber mat, through the reinforced canvas knee and elbow pads of the overalls with the hessian straps, that the target would toss on a camp bed in the horror of a nightmare of fear.

When he closed his eyes to rest them, when Haquim did not grunt and break the quiet, hallucinations played in his mind of a line of men who had gone before him, the ghosts of his trade.

He made fantasy pictures of them to go with the remembered words he had read.

He lay with the Indian fighter, Tim Murphy, who had sniped the British general Fraser in the Hudson river valley. Beside him was Major Wade of the 2nd Battalion 95th Rifles, the marksman who had held the wall of the La Haye Sainte farm barns at Waterloo. Close to him was Jim the Nailer on the makeshift parapets around the Residency at Lucknow . . . and there was Hesketh-Prichard, his favourite, the big-game hunter turned sniper, who had said Germans in their trenches should be treated merely as 'dangerous soft-skinned game' . . . and there was Billy Sing, the Australian who had shot 150 Turks at Gallipoli. There was the marine at Saipan in the Pacific, who had destroyed a Japanese machine-gun nest at 1,200 yards with his vintage Springfield rifle, and the soldier at Hue in Vietnam who was seen to gain a kill at a measured 1,400 yards. They were all around him, close and near to him. The heritage was passed down to him, hand to hand, rifle to rifle, target to target. Would any of them, in the darkness before dawn, in the cold of a slow wait, have cared whether the chosen target slept easily or shook in the hold of a nightmare?

'I'm Carol Manning. This is Captain Willet.'

'What time is it?'

'If it matters, it's eight minutes to five. Don't get any persecuted ideas that I enjoy being out of bed at this time of night. It makes it legally easier if you invite us in.'

'Who are you?'

'I'm Security Service, he's some sort of soldier. Are you inviting us in?'

'If I don't . . .'

'Then my foot stays in the door while we ring for the police to come with a search warrant. I wouldn't advise that – things get broken then.'

'Why are you here?'

'Because the electoral roll tells us this is the home of Augustus Henderson Peake.'

'This is Gus's place, yes.'

'You're inviting us in? Thank you, that's being sensible.'

She stood aside to let them pass. Willet had done dawn raids in the old Belfast days. The woman's confusion, failure to demand credentials and proper explanations, did not surprise him.

'Are you Peake's wife?'

'Not exactly.'

'What are you then? Tenant, lodger, common-law, partner?'

'Girlfriend, I suppose you'd call it, maybe just friend. My name's Meg. If it matters, I'm divorced, I have no children, I'm a junior-school teacher.'

'It's not important. Where is he? Where's Peake?'

'I don't know. I haven't the faintest idea.'

At last, the way it always was, a little spark had come to the woman's eyes. Ken Willet, captain, detached from his regiment to duty at the Ministry of Defence, heard Ms Manning swear quietly. The woman's nightdress hung like a heavy, bulky shroud over her body.

'Maybe I should make a cup of tea,' Willet said.

'No, we will.'

It was an instruction. Ms Manning turned and gave him the eye. He understood. The kitchen for the women, and for him the search through the living room and the bedrooms. Willet had never worked alongside the Security Service before. His telephone had gone an hour and thirty-five minutes earlier. It was about a sniper, he'd been told by the night desk, and he knew a little about sniping – though not as much as he'd have wished – and he'd be picked up. Throwing on his clothes, he'd heard a horn hoot down in the street. He'd expected a smelly old blighter in a dirty raincoat, his image of a counter-intelligence officer, and she'd reached over, held open the door for him, then accelerated away before he'd settled, before he'd belted up. She'd grumbled all the way down about the assignment, the time, the condition of the car, her rates of pay, the weather . . . but she drove well and fast.

He started to search. He heard the whistle of the kettle and the clatter of mugs. Carol Manning was expert at her work, and the talk had already begun. He heard the murmur of the woman's voice.

'Everything in Gus's life is about shooting at targets with that old rifle. I'm not complaining, but I come after shooting, way after . . . I suppose we need each other. We go to the cinema, we watch television, we eat together. Sometimes I stay over, sometimes I don't – never on a Friday because that's the night before shooting, never on a Saturday because that's cleaning the rifle after shooting. I'm just around, whether he notices, whether he doesn't. It suits me and it suits him, but the shooting's what matters.'

The silver spoons were thrown carelessly at the back of a drawer, and he didn't think they'd been polished since the day they were handed out as prizes.

'He cut his hair short four years ago, not because I asked him to, but because he hadn't shot well one day and he thought the wind blowing his hair across his face had distracted him. Three years ago, he gave up smoking overnight, not because I wanted him to but he thought it affected his breathing pattern in the moment of aiming and firing. We jog three evenings a week, but that's because a target marksman needs to be at top fitness. Look, up there, there's a diet sheet. He barely eats before he shoots so that his stomach's comfortable. He lives for his shooting. For pure happiness, he should just put up a tent on Stickledown Range, at Bisley, and live there. He's in this club, the Historic Breech-loading and Small-arms Association, and they fire these old rifles. There's a Martini-Henry and a Mauser, a Mosin-Nagant M1891, a Garand, and the secretary shoots a Sharp's breech-loader. I know what they're called because I take a picnic and go with him most times, not that I get any conversation. They're funny people – nothing wrong with them, they're decent – and they're

60

obsessed with these rifles that are a hundred years old. All they talk about when they're shooting is wind-deflection and the humidity that affects the fall of the bullet, ammunition quality, and holding the zero. Do you know? They were quite upset when he didn't turn up for the last club shoot. Jenkins, that's the secretary, rang me – rather aggressively, I thought – to find out where Gus was, why he hadn't been there. Was he ill? Why hadn't he phoned? There's been complaints from the group that they'd shot poorly because Gus wasn't there. They shoot at eight hundred yards, right up to a thousand, and Gus wasn't there, no explanation, and they couldn't perform – and that was Gus's fault. He's the best one amongst them, you see, far and away the best, and they need him. I wouldn't call them friends, but they lean on each other. They're all a little sad, really, to an outsider – not that they'd think so.'

In the back of another drawer, not hidden away, was a packet of photographs that showed posed groups of men who held old rifles and stood or knelt as a celebration of comradeship. They were not sorted, not in order, as if they were unimportant and seldom looked at.

'He's very ordinary – that's not a criticism – no interest in making an impression. I met the people he works with at last year's Christmas party. I think they were quite surprised to see him turn up with a woman . . . I didn't tell them, and none of them mentioned the shooting, didn't know about it. He hardly shares it with me. We were drifting along, a boat on a canal, and then the letter came – you know about the letter, do you?'

First he discovered the keyring, hanging from a thin

nail on the underside of the bed's wooden leg, then the gun cabinet bolted to the wall at the back of the wardrobe. He recognized the Lee Enfield No. 4, with the telescopic sight, and the box of ammunition of match grade with the Full Metal Jacket of cupro-nickel casing. He locked the cabinet, returned the keyring to its hiding place.

'I'd met him after work, on Newlands Corner. It's good for running there – it's wonderful, because you can go for miles, high up and with the wind on you, and the village lights all below you. You run better in the dark, it's liberating. He was quite chatty on the way home, and I thought I'd stay. We're not much good, either of us, at the sex bit, but some nights it's better than others – why am I telling you this? His post was on the mat. There was a letter from his grandfather, and another letter with it. He just sat in his chair and read the other letter again and again, and never showed it me. I didn't even bother to cook, there was no point, and I went back to my place.'

In an old folder in an unlocked desk, held together with a bulged paper-clip, were the scoring charts. Under the heading 'ALL-IN SCORE DIAGRAM FOR LONG-RANGE TARGET' were the tables for wind-deflection, weather conditions, and the target circles. There were no neat crosses in outer, inner, magpie or bull. All the crosses, on every scoring chart, were in the V-Bull circle, which was sixteen inches in diameter, and the ranges for the charts were eight hundred yards, nine hundred yards and a thousand yards. He felt a sense of respect.

'He packed up, it was like he was closing down his life here. I've never made demands of Gus, certainly I've never pestered him with questions, but I did ask, "What's it about? Where's it from, the letter?" He didn't answer. I know he went to see his grandfather the next day, but that's all I know, and that's nothing . . . He paid off all his bills. He dealt with everything outstanding. He spent more and more time away, before he finally headed off. I'd be here, and sometimes he'd show up late and dump his stuff in the hall, sometimes his brief-case and sometimes his rucksack. Old people do that, don't they, when they're going to go into hospital, deal with everything? We didn't have much of a life by other people's standards but, God, I miss him.'

In the hall, on a line of coat-hangers behind a curtain screen, were old, dry, mud-smeared trousers and a patched all-weather coat that hadn't been cleaned. On a hook was a wide-brimmed, shapeless hat. He noted that there were no boots on the floor below the hangers. Of course, a man would have taken his boots . . . Later he found tax documents in the name of Peake, Augustus Henderson, and electricity, telephone and gas bills, cheque book stubs and bank statements. He noted the last withdrawal and whistled to himself in surprise – eight thousand pounds taken out and the deposit account almost cleared.

'I came round two weeks ago. I thought that if he was here I could cook a meal for him. He was packing. It wasn't a suitcase but the rucksack, and everything he put in was old, should have been thrown away years ago. I never did get round to cooking anything. We made love on the bed beside the rucksack, and I wept all through it – it's none of your business, but it was the best loving we ever did. He seemed to need it. I woke up early, and he'd gone . . . I don't know why because he didn't tell me, and I don't know where he is.'

The music beside the stereo was bland, popular

classics and easy listening. The books on the shelves were all technical shooting volumes. The pictures were anonymous prints of dull, well-worn country views. He thought that target marksmanship with an historic rifle consumed the man's life – but there was nothing to tell Ken Willet, from what he rummaged through and saw, of the soul of the man. But there had to be something more, or he'd be here, not slogging in the missing boots through northern Iraq.

'He's just a nice man, a good man. I can't tell you anything more.'

They left her.

Carol Manning drove the car away, down the road below the cathedral, from a cramped and unremarkable two-bedroomed maisonette.

'Well?'

'What do you want to know?'

'Is he a military wannabe – into all that *Rambo* crap?'

'No. He shoots at targets with an historic weapon, and with great skill. His rifle is fifty-plus years old. He's an enthusiast.'

'A bloody anorak? Like one of those idiots on a platform writing down train numbers?'

Willet said evenly, 'He shoots very straight. He wins prizes for hitting targets at a range of up to a thousand yards.'

'It's one thing to hit targets. What about killing people?'

'I found nothing to indicate that he has the slightest interest in the military situation in—'

'So what the hell's he doing there?'

'She said the letter was passed on by his grandfather. Ask him.'

'Can't today. Health and Safety says we're entitled to a full day off after a night call-out. I've a lieu day tomorrow. Have to be the day after.'

'I thought it was urgent.'

'We do have entitlements. Doesn't the army?'

'Do you mind if I have a cigarette?' Willet was reaching into his jacket pocket for the packet and his lighter.

'It's Service policy that no cigarettes, cigars or pipes are to be used in our vehicles.'

Willet said brightly, 'Aren't we lucky? Where he is, stomping through northern Iraq, passive smoking would seem low down on the problem list.'

It was a cheap point. He should have, but hadn't, apologized. He wanted, rather desperately, to know more of a man who had packed up his life and gone without training and without military background to fight in someone else's war.

'I'd like, Ms Manning, to be with you on this one and follow it through. I'd like to learn about him.'

Her eyes never left the road. She asked brutally, 'How long do you give him?'

'Not long. Sorry, not long at all, but he'd be an idiot not to know that. If he's gone to fight, front line, as a sniper, alongside irregulars, against a trained modern army, then he won't survive. No chance at all.'

Chapter Three

'I have to leave you, Mr Peake,' the voice whispered in his ear.

Gus had not been thinking of Meg, or of the office at Davies & Sons, or of his parents and the old wing commander (retired) who was his grandfather, and he had not been thinking of the Stickledown crew. They were all erased from his mind, as if a new life had replaced them.

He did not care whether Meg had slept that last night in bed at her home or whether she had been in his bed. He did not consider that his parents might have tossed through the last night, and those of the weeks before, in anxiety for his safety, or that they held his grandfather responsible for his going.

'You have what you need, Mr Peake. You know what you will do?'

His view, through the fine netting over his face, stretched away from the rocky outcrop where he lay with Haquim across a slope of yellowed grass in which were set clumps of bright flowers, mauve, white and blue. There was then a ridge where the wind had eroded the soil and exposed more of the grey stone, then a valley gorge from which he could hear the tumble of a stream, then the further slope of the valley, pocked with more outcrops and more flower clusters. The sun was behind him, and intruding against the gentle blue of the sky was a single military pennant. Gus had a moment of doubt.

'What if he doesn't come?'

Gus could see a clean-cut low slit in the forward bunker's facing wall of pale grey concrete, and further back was a similar shape over which the pennant flew. Between the forward bunker and the pennant was a narrow column of smoke, drifting haphazardly, but the pennant gave Gus an indication of the wind strength at what would be the end of the bullet's flight, if he had a target to aim for. When his eye was off the sight, he watched the colours of the flowers and the movement of grass tufts, because the sway of the petals and the waft of the grass stems told him what would be the deflection of the bullet when it left the barrel at 2,970 feet per second, at 2,640 revolutions per second, if he had a target.

'I know the way of officers. Each morning, however junior, if he has responsibility, he will inspect all his positions.'

'What if I don't see him? What if he's going low through the communications trench?'

'He is an officer of the Iraqi army. He will not permit his soldiers to see him cower.'

'The radio?'

'Do you think I have nothing more to do than to place you in position? Of course there is the radio. My problem is the radio, the wire, the mines, and my problem is wondering whether you make a hit. You have one chance. Everything depends on you taking that chance.'

Haquim's hand caught at the back of his hood and held his hair, vice-like, then loosened it. It was not a gesture of friendship, or of support. Gus thought the man had tried to reinforce what he had said. They depended on him and there would be the one chance with the one shot. If Gus missed there would not be a second. The radio would be used to call up reinforcements; the advantage of surprise would be lost.

A different man, one from Augustus Henderson Peake's past, might have crumpled under the burden of that responsibility. But the past was obliterated. A man had told him about positive thinking – can, will, must – the critical importance of mental conditioning, and the corrosive effect of stress. He had no time to wallow in the past. First, at dawn, he had estimated the distance, then confirmed his estimate with the range-finding binoculars, and all the time he had studied the flowers and the grass fronds, the smoke and the pennant for the wind. His mind was as tunnelled as his view through the ten-times magnification of the sight. Alone, spread-eagled among the rocks behind his rifle, his concentration only settling on the clear window through the sight's lens, Gus never saw the goatherd and his flock's slow progress far to the right.

The goatherd understood weapons. Hooked across the width of his back was a Russian-made SKS46 carbine, mass-manufactured half a century before. Its worn barrel was incapable of accurate shooting. If a wild dog was harrying his goats he could drive it off by firing over it, but to hit it he would have to be within fifty paces, and he could have thrown a stone that far. But the rifle was as much a part of him as the knife at his belt or the heavy footwear that carried him between the high grazing lands; it was a segment of his manhood. His friendship of more than twenty years with a shepherd was the most likely source of a new weapon.

His friend had access to influence and to weapons. Over the last few weeks, the goatherd had been worming towards the direct request to his friend that a rifle might be found for him – not a new one, a working replacement for his carbine.

The previous morning, he had heard the single shot. He had been an hour's walk with his flock from his friend's home, with the first warmth of the day's sun on his face, when he had heard the long, rippling echo. He knew from the sound of its carry that the bullet had travelled over a great distance, further than his friend's Kalashnikov was capable of firing. He had left the goats in a small sloping valley and gone on his stomach to a clutch of rocks that gave him a vantage-point above his friend's home.

His eyesight was as keen as his hearing. From the cool of the early morning, through the heat of the day, into the cold of the evening, he had watched the home of his friend, the body of his friend, and the killer. He had seen the rifle that had taken his friend's life, and the sight mounted on it. He had waited in his secret place until the killer, and the murderers with him, had moved off into the dusk.

In the darkness, keeping the goats with him by using the reed whistle to which they responded, he had gone slowly and quietly towards the military bunkers. He felt the anger aroused by a blood vendetta – and if he were fortunate, and brought good information, he might be given a new rifle.

The pennant flew slackly over the bunkers, and he whacked his goats' backs and haunches with a short stick each time they found sparse grass to feed on. He hurried them forward so that he could report what he had seen.

The lieutenant was woken.

He cursed viciously at the conscript, no younger than himself, who had woken him and not brought fresh coffee. He threw on his uniform, dragged on his boots, then yelled at the soldier that the boots were not cleaned, and that a fresh shirt had not been laid out for him.

He bent his head, emerged from the dank shadows of his bunker and strode along the trench connecting it to the command post. Only the lieutenant, because of his rank and education, was permitted to use the radio. He made and received all transmissions. The set bleeped, a red light winked for attention.

He slotted on the headphones and threw the switches. He responded to the call from Kirkūk. There was anxiety. The forward observer, codenamed Call-sign 17, had now missed three transmissions: probably a malfunction, or maybe storm damage to the booster antenna. He was ordered to check the cause of the malfunction, to retrieve the radio if he believed the fault lay there, or to visit the booster antenna on the summit point to the west if that was the likely area of the problem. He would respond, of course, to the order, and immediately. He ended the transmission.

The lieutenant cursed again. To reach the location of Call-sign 17 he must go on foot. There was no track passable to a vehicle between his own position and the Call-sign's location. It was six kilometres across country, and it would be six kilometres back. To cover twelve kilometres over that ground of rock and bog, where he could stumble and bark the skin on his knees on the rock or sink to his thighs in hidden mud, would take the entire day, in the company of the peasants he commanded. He was twenty-one. He was the eldest son of a family of the Tikriti tribe. He had a future ahead of him as bright as that of his father who commanded an artillery regiment in the Basra region and his uncle who led an armoured division of the Republican Guard facing the Kuwaiti frontier. But the future, bright and glittering and perhaps one day offering him a place in the Hijaz Amn al-Khass unit that protected the President, was deferred until a year of military service in the north was completed. He hated the place. It was cold, wet, harsh, and he was marooned in a small complex of damp bunkers with only idiots for company. He hoped that one day, soon, the President, the leader of the Tikriti tribe, would give the order for them to mount up in the armoured personnel carriers and ride further north, right to the borders, and bring the bastard Kurds back under the authority of Baghdad. There was an old corporal, double his age, in the position, the only man with whom he could talk, and each time he told the corporal of his hope that, one day, the President would unleash the columns of armoured personnel carriers to drive north, the corporal gazed at him as if he were a fool and knew nothing. When his duty was over, when he was posted back to Kirkūk, he would see that the corporal suffered for his silent insolence.

He came out of the command post. Four men would go with him to the location of Call-sign 17, leaving four and the corporal behind in the bunkers.

There was coffee now, steaming but failing to improve his temper, and the lieutenant said that he would take his breakfast when he had inspected the position, then start the cross-country trek. And the lazy bastards, with the corporal, would sleep all day without him there to goad them on with their work. The early-morning light was into his face, and sprang little diamonds of brightness from the wire that ringed the areas in front of and flanking the position where the mines were laid.

The corporal led him on the morning inspection. The corporal always scurried forward, like a hurrying rat, along the communications trenches. He had been in Kuwait nine years before, at the time of the Mother of all Victories.

The lieutenant never bent his back. It was not right that an officer of the Tikriti tribe should cower, and he knew of no danger confronting at him as he went along the trench.

He rounded a corner reinforced with sandbags and rocks. A soldier had laid his rifle down in the mud and was urinating onto the side of the trench. With his full strength, the lieutenant punched the man in the back of the head, saw him stagger and crawl away.

He went to the forward bunker of rough concrete, around which were defensive coils of wire where the mines were laid most thickly. He went inside. He thought the soldier on sentry in the bunker had shit there. He could smell it. A candle was guttering low, throwing shadows towards the firing port through which the morning sunshine streamed. It would have burned all night. It was expressly forbidden to have lights inside the bunkers during the darkness hours. He came behind the sentry, peered over his shoulder and out through the gun port. To the extreme right he saw the distant movement of the goatherd and his animals. To the left and ahead there was nothing, just the rock, the green of the grass over the bog areas, and the wind-flattened small bare trees. He steadied himself and kicked the sentry hard. When the sentry fell to the bunker floor, whimpering, he kicked him again, belted the hands that covered the sentry's groin, then squeezed out the candle flame with his fingers.

He knew they loathed him, the corporal included. His father had told him, and his uncle, that his men should be more afraid of him than of any enemy.

He stepped out of the bunker. He swore again, because he now had the sentry's shit on his boot. He was not thinking of home, or of the daughter of his father's cousin, or of his mother, or of the discothèque music that he played on the radio beside his bed, or of a bright and glittering future . . . but of the shit on his boot.

The corporal was going on down the trench, bent, scampering.

The lieutenant died, not gloriously, as he wiped the sentry's shit off his boot, spreadeagled against a sandbag.

The bullet came into the broad width of his back, created an instant hydraulic shockwave through his life organs, yawed in his chest cavity and destroyed the shape of his heart, making a hole the size of a well-juiced orange as it burst out past his tunic buttons. Misshapen, tumbling, it flew past the corporal's head and splattered into the mud wall at the back of the communications trench.

His life lingered a few seconds before he died. His last

73

sensations were those of a burning numbness through his upper body. His last sight was of the corporal turning to stare at him in wide-eyed shock. His last hearing was the hammer of a machine-gun beginning to fire. His last thought was that, without him, the peasants would break and run.

He was the future of the regime, a favoured son, and he died with a sentry's shit on his boot.

The goatherd had heard the single shot, as he had heard it the day before. For a moment he froze in his tracks, and the silence settled, then the machine-gun started up.

He watched the bright lines of tracers arc across the open ground and fall on the roofs and walls of the bunkers.

He whistled sharply and started to run. The persistence of the goatherd's whistling and the clatter of the machine-gun, and the blast of individual rifles firing on automatic, drove his animals in flight after him, as if he were their salvation.

He set off, at the best speed he could muster with the goats, for a long journey across pathless ground. It would take him all morning and most of the afternoon before he reached the next army unit based below the high ground, at the Victory City, where he sold his goats' cheese and their meat.

The guilt hit him, sea waves of remorse broke over Gus.

He had seen the face of the target, the shoulders and the upper chest, before the target had gone down into the forward bunker, and the face had been that of a young man. A smooth-skinned face, with a dark moustache, and unkempt hair, as if he had just risen from his bed. All the time he had waited, while the target was inside the forward bunker, while the sight was locked on the few feet of ground outside the entry to the bunker, he had been unable to discard that face, and he had played pictures with the life of the officer – had seen him standing proud in the doorway of a home, had seen his mother kiss him, his father shake his hand, had seen a girl standing back and shy but with the love-light in her eyes, had seen him walk away from home with the big pack on his back, waving a farewell. He had seen the tears in the eyes of the mother, the father and the girl.

The officer had come out of the bunker and stopped. Gus's aim was on his back. It was as if the target stopped to blink in the sun after the darkness inside the bunker. He had fired. The rifle was fitted with a muzzle brake that reduced the recoil and the jump of the barrel to a minimum. His view through the sight had been constant. He could follow the flight of the bullet. Some called the vortex of the bullet's journey the 'wash', others called it the 'contrail'. Whatever it was, he could see it, a swirl and disturbance that fluttered the air. He had seen the bullet's track all the way across the valley and he had seen it strike. Arms had gone high into the air, and the target had fallen.

Then the chatter of the machine-gun had begun.

He had tried and tried again to clear the face of the officer from his mind . . . The machine-gun that Haquim had sited played a pattern of fire onto the bunker above which the radio antenna. There had been sporadic return fire. He understood why Haquim had left him, alone and with his guilt, to go back and position the machine-gun. With the officer gone, only a very brave man would have risked exposing himself to the battering of the machine-gun shells on the bunker. The *peshmerga* had pushed forward in a straggling line.

He had watched her, then lost her as she descended into the valley, and had seen her running up the far slope towards the ridge, the wire and the pennant. Through the telescopic sight, he could see her urge the men forward with a wild sweep of her arm. He had raked back across the ground, through the line of men with whom the boy ran, then found open ground and had seen Haquim limping behind them. When they were close to the wire and bunching to go through the corridors between the mines, slashing the view of his telescopic sight, he had seen the soldiers in flight from their bunkers. Weapons and helmets were thrown down. They took their wounded with them, but not the corpse of their officer.

She was on the roof of the command bunker snatching down the pennant. It was then that the guilt died, when he, Augustus Henderson Peake, shed the last trace of remorse. She stood on the bunker's flat roof, punching the clean, clear air around her in triumph. He felt a desperate state of exhilaration, and was not shamed by it. Time after time, as the *peshmerga* gathered around and below her, she raised her fist to the skies.

The lines of the sight were on her in her moment of victory. If a marksman as good as himself had had that aim then she was dead. He collected up his equipment, stood and massaged the muscles in his legs to restore the circulation and stretched, arching his back to ease the stiffness.

Slowly, with an uneven, unsteady stride, Gus walked towards the bunkers.

The life of the corporal hung on a slender thread.

If he were believed his flight would be forgiven. If he were not, he would be shot as a deserter.

Across an endless wilderness of rock plains and marshes, up escarpment cliffs, down into gullies with swollen streams, he had led his men to safety. As the sun fell, he had reached the village and the company-sized unit of mechanized infantry.

He sat in the corridor outside the captain's room in the biggest house in the village that was classified by the regime as a Victory City. The cries of his two wounded men echoed down the corridor. He sat on the floor with his hands clasped on his head. If his hands moved the guard kicked him. He recited in his mind, over and over, the story he had told the captain.

'I often said to him that he should always use the cover of the communications trenches. I do not wish to speak ill of a martyred hero but he did not listen. Major Aziz of the Baghdad Military College can confirm that I attended his course two years ago. He taught us about the sniper. It was what he called "crack and thump". You hear the crack beside you, then you hear the thump from the firing position. If the crack and the thump are together then the sniper is close. The major said that you would know how far away the sniper was by the time between the crack and the thump. It was between one and two seconds – so I think that is about seven hundred metres. We all fired but none of us, even with a good Dragunov, could hit the targets at that range. Only he, and he is the best, was accurate. It was a very expert sniper that killed the lieutenant. We are forbidden to use the radio, but it was impossible anyway to reach it because there was heavy machine-gun fire at the approach trench to that bunker. We had wounded, we were about to be overrun. There were many scores of saboteurs attacking us. I have many times served my country in northern Iraq, but I never heard of a "primitive" who could shoot so straight at seven hundred metres with a rifle. It was my duty to report it.'

If they did not believe him he would be kicked again, hit around the head with a rifle butt, taken out of the building, stood against the wall and shot. It was the truth: in all the years he had fought in the north he had never confronted a 'primitive', a tribesman, who could shoot with accuracy at such a distance. He could hear the low voices behind the door as the captain and his two lieutenants discussed what he had told them. He had not mentioned that a woman led the final charge towards the bunkers because that would not have been believed.

The door swung open.

The captain stood over him, took the final breath from a cigarette, then ground it out against the corporal's forehead. He screamed. He heard the rasping voice denounce him as a coward, as a disgrace to his unit. The kicks came fast and hard into his body. He had betrayed the sacred trust of the Iraqi army. The rifle butt crashed down on to the hands that protected his scalp. And then he smelled the stale old stench of the animals.

The goatherd had been brought into the corridor by two soldiers. His arms were held tight.

The corporal believed that his ribs were broken and he felt the blood on his face. He listened to what the goatherd told the captain, and it was a second thread on which his life rested.

'It was a long shot that killed my friend who was a true and loyal servant of the Iraqi army, and the same long shot this morning took the honoured life of the officer. I saw the man who fires the long shots. Yesterday afternoon, before he went to walk in the night towards the place where he shot the officer, he sat outside my friend's house. He has a big rifle, the devil's rifle, bigger than I have and you have. I do not think he is a *peshmerga*. He wore clothes that also I have never seen before. It is only when he moves that you see him. If he does not move then he is like a rock or a pile of earth. I have never seen a man like this devil before.'

The corporal reached forward and took the ankle of the goatherd and held it tight, as if to thank him for the saving of his life.

He crawled to his feet and he was not kicked, not hit. He heard the captain inside his room shouting on the radio.

He whispered to the goatherd, 'You did not tell them about the woman . . .'

'I told them what would be believed.'

It was his birthday, and he had forgotten it.

When he had woken that morning, after three hours' sleep, the children had been round the bed and had shaken him so that he could open the presents they had brought him. His elder son had given him a pen of sterling silver, and he had unwrapped the white shirt offered by his younger son. His wife's present was a narrow gold ring that fitted easily onto the little finger of his right hand. He had kissed each of them, and thanked them hoarsely.

Major Karim Aziz had gone to work in his office at the

Baghdad Military College, and in the afternoon he had locked his door, pulled down the blinds, put his feet on the desk and slept for two and a quarter precious hours. As he slept, the fingers of his left hand clutched the gold ring. Before drifting off, he had thought that it was as though Leila sought to bring him back to her, to wrestle him from the grasp of devils. It had been a good, deep sleep, free of dreams and nightmares.

He had returned home refreshed for the family meal in celebration of his forty-fifth birthday. The children had changed from their school uniforms to their best clothes, his wife wore a fine blouse of Indian silk, her father was in his favourite suit and her mother in the dress she took out of the cupboard only on special occasions. At another time, on another day, he would have criticized his wife for the extravagance of the presents and the cost of the food she served, and there was a bottle of Lebanese wine that had been imported across the Jordanian border. But the wine poured for him stayed in his glass, because he did not dare to cloud his mind. He picked at the rice and cubes of curried beef and ate little, because he didn't dare to fill his stomach with food. What hurt most, they all tried so hard to make it a happy day for him . . . and he could tell them nothing.

He resented what they had spent on him. Only at work, only at the Baghdad Military College, was his life not subject to the sapping frustration caused by the shortages. An American had said that Iraq would be bombed back to the Stone Age of history.

And what else was there to talk about around the table? Any conversation inevitably entailed more discussion of the shortages, whether in the street markets, at school or the children's hospital. He ate little and drank nothing, and the silences around the table grew longer.

The telephone rang. Wafiq ran to answer it, hurrying to escape the quiet of the celebration.

A year after his marriage he had been posted to the Soviet Union for six months to learn infantry tactics. He had written to his wife twice every week while he was away, and babbled conversation to her of what he had seen for days after his return. Two years later he had been in Lebanon's Beka'a Valley teaching those tactics to militiamen, and he had told her everything when he had come home. On leave from the battle fronts of Khorramshahr and Susangerd, he had written home of the war with Iran – careful letters that would not offend the censors – and he had talked to her on leave, walking on the esplanades beside the Tigris river where he would not be heard, of the horror of the street fighting. He had held back nothing of his times in Kirkūk and Mosul and Arbīl in the north. Everything he had seen in Kuwait City, at the start and at the end, when he had fled from the advance of the American tanks on the charnel-house road through the Mutla Pass, he had shared with her, because he loved her. Now, he had nothing to talk of, and he pecked at his food, and her eyes never left the ring she had given him.

The boy came back, said the call was for him.

He pushed aside his plate, scraped back his chair, and went into the hallway. He lifted the telephone and gave his name.

The call was from a duty officer at the al-Rashid camp of the Military Intelligence, the Estikhabarat. He was ordered to attend the al-Rashid camp at nine o'clock the following morning. The call was terminated.

81

He rocked on his feet. It was a familiar pattern, known about by every officer of his rank and experience but never talked of. The Estikhabarat always summoned a suspect to the al-Rashid barracks, but watched his home through the night to see if he fled, and to block him if he did. He knew of such calls, and of the desks cleared the following day by strangers, then occupied by new men, and of the officers who were never seen again after they had travelled to the al-Rashid complex.

Major Karim Aziz breathed hard, and the sweat ran on his stomach and down the small of his back.

Around the table, beyond his sight and reach, his family – everyone he loved – was waiting for his return and wondering why he was so troubled.

He went into the bedroom, took his heavy coat from the hook on the door, and knelt to pull the sports bag out from under the bed. From the small cupboard beside the bed, always locked and closed from the sight of his wife and his sons, he took a Makharov automatic pistol and a single hand grenade. It was possible, with planning, for a general to cross the frontier if he used his authority, or his relatives, or a dignitary, but for a major at the Baghdad Military College, with his family, it would be a journey of exceptional difficulty. He put the hand grenade under his shirt, tightened his belt so that it could not slip down, and reassured himself that his fingers could feel the loop of the pin.

He went back into the dining room. The table had been cleared. Leila was coming out of the kitchen with the cake her mother had made that day. It was iced, decorated, it would be sugary sweet, the cake he liked best. He kissed Wafiq, and the boy stared down at his table place; then he kissed Hani and the tears ran on the child's cheeks; then his wife; then her mother and father.

He could tell them nothing.

All of them, the officers who went under orders to the al-Rashid camp, believed in the faint hope of survival, went with the hesitant innocence of lambs herded to the butcher's knife, deluding themselves that the anxiety was unfounded.

He stood in the kitchen doorway, holding the sports bag, and faced them. Behind him was the hallway, the front door, the concrete pad where the car was parked, the shadows of the poorly lit street. If the anxiety was well founded, the agents of the Estikhabarat would already be in those shadows, watching his house. Sometimes the bodies were brought back, if their families paid a few dinars for the bullets that had been used.

He turned away from them, switched off the kitchen light, then went out through the back door. He slipped past the new building where her parents slept, and scrambled over the wall at the end of the yard.

He would spend one more night beside the water tank on the flat roof. And, if they were waiting for him, if they were there to take him, he would pull the pin from the RG-42 high-explosive fragmentation grenade. Major Karim Aziz knew of no other road he should follow.

He thought it was his duty, in the name of Arab nationalism, socialistic modernism and his country, to go to the roof and pray that all was not known and that the bastard would step into the handkerchief of light on the driveway. He wondered if, without him, they would eat the cake . . . He walked briskly. Alone, without the responsibility of his family, he could again cloak himself with the assurance, confidence, self-esteem that marked him down as a master of the military science of sniping. It was why he had been recruited.

AUGUSTUS HENDERSON *PEAKE*.

Profile of subject compiled by K Willet (capt.), seconded MoD to Security Services.

Role of K Willet (capt.): In liaison with Ms Carol Manning (Security Service), to assess AHP's capability as a marksman, and the effect of his presence in northern Iraq on military/political situation in that region.

AHP is British national, born 25–10–1965. Resident at 14D, Longfellow Drive, Guildford, Surrey.

Background: AHP's presence in northern Iraq witnessed by Benedict Curtis (Regional Director of Protect the Children registered charity) on 14 April. AHP seen wearing combat sniper's camouflage kit, with unidentified sniper rifle. No known past or present links with Ministry of Defence or other government agencies.

1. Conclusions after search of AHP's home (see above). Subject is a competition marksman of the highest quality using a vintage weapon (Lee Enfield No. 4). From his undemonstrative lifestyle, I would

consider him to be of placid temperament
and not subject to personal conceit;
necessary characteristics of a champion
target shooter. I found, however, no signs
of his having made a study of military
sniping – no books, magazines etc. – and
no evidence of any interest in that area.
Also, there were no indications as to the
motivation of AHP in going to northern
Iraq. At first sight, he presents the picture
of an eccentric enigma.

SUMMARY: Without strong motivation,
military background, and a hunter's
mindset, I would rate his chances of
medium-term survival as extremely slim.

(To be continued.)

Willet shut down his computer. Had he sold the man
short? Without motivation, the background, and the
necessary mindset, Gus Peake was as naked as the day
he was born. What a bloody fool . . .

'So serious, so heavy . . .' The twinkle was in her eyes, as
if she mocked him.

Gus had watched her approach. She had moved
quietly and effortlessly over the rocks towards him. He
had lit a small fire that was deep down and sheltered by
the crag stones. He was wrapped in a blanket. A half-
moon was up. She had come amongst her men: some
reached up to touch her hand, some brushed their
fingers against the heavy material of her trousers, and

he'd heard her gentle words of encouragement. Haquim followed her, then the boy.

'Maybe tired.'

She sat close to him. She had no blanket but she did not shiver. 'I do not think so, I think angry.'

'Maybe angry.'

'It is the start of a journey – why angry?'

'In fact, it's the end of a day . . . and I think you're probably the reason for my anger.'

'Me?' She pouted as if he amused her. 'Why?'

'It was just indulgence. You stood on the bunker, you waved your arms around like a kid on a football pitch. Anyone within half a mile could have shot you.'

Haquim hovered behind her, and the boy. She waved them back as a parent would have dismissed children. 'Were you frightened for me? It is because I lead that I have the strength to make men follow me.'

'In the American Civil War, at the Battle of Spotsylvania, the last words spoken by General John Sedgwick were, "What, what, men, dodging? I am ashamed of you. They couldn't hit an elephant at this distance." He didn't say any more, he was dead. Someone shot him.'

'Who else can make the men follow them? Haquim? I do not think so . . . *Agha* Bekir, *agha* Ibrahim. They won't lead. *I* lead. Because I am at the front, not frightened, I will lead all the way to the flame of Baba Gurgur that burns over Kirkūk. The simple people pray to the flame as if it were God, and I will lead them there. Kirkūk is the goal. If we must die, then we must die for Kirkūk. We will sacrifice everything that we have – everything, our lives, our homes, our loved ones – for Kirkūk. It is only I who can take the people there. Do you believe me?'

Her eyes never left him. She was, he thought, neither beautiful nor pretty. There was a strange simplicity about her. He would have been hard put to describe it to a man who had never seen her. Her nose was too prominent, her mouth too wide. She had high, pronounced cheekbones, and a jaw that showed nothing of compromise. To a man who had never met her, he would have talked of her eyes. They were big, open, and at the heart of them were the circles of soft brown. With her eyes, he thought, she could win a man or destroy him. He had seen the way the *peshmerga* clustered around her to win a single short spasm of approval from her eyes, which never wavered, stared into his. Gus looked down and tried to snatch a tone of bitterness.

'I have to believe you, I have no choice – but the "simple people" won't get to see their flame if you are shot, prancing on a bunker.'

'Is that the limit of your anger?'

'You've been ignoring me . . .'

'Oh, a criticism because I have forgotten my social manners. That is a very serious mistake. My grandfather tells me that the Iraqi Arabs in Baghdad used to say that all the British taught them was "to walk on the pavements and iron our trousers", to behave like them and you, Augustus Peake. I apologize for my rudeness. Between my duties of raising and leading an army, I must speak to my newest recruit. Don't sulk. If I spend time with you, favour you, then the *peshmerga* believe I bend my knee to a foreigner. Because of foreigners, where are we? We are hopeless, lost, destitute. We were abandoned by the foreigners in 1975, in 1991, in 1996 – is that enough for you? You saw in 1991 what was our fate when we trusted the word of foreigners – on the mountain, starved, dying, fighting for food thrown down from the sky, for a few hours you saw it. If you believe you are superior, should have special attention – sheets to sleep on, comfort, food to your liking – go home. Turn round, take your rifle, go back, and read of me when I take my people to Kirkūk. Is there any other cause for anger?'

She lectured him gently, tauntingly, but with a soft sweetness at her mouth. It was as if she manipulated him, and dragged the irritation from him.

Gus said, surly, 'You treat Haquim badly. He's a good man.'

'He is old.' She shrugged. 'Has he shown you his wound? The wound took the fire from him. He is a *good* man at arranging for the supplies of food for the men, and the ammunition they will use, and he knows the best place to site a machine-gun. Without the fire the simple people will not follow him. Always he is cautious, always he wants to hold back. He will never take us to Kirkūk. I will. Is there more, Gus?'

He would have said that he loathed arrogance above everything – a man with arrogance could not shoot. Sometimes at work it was necessary for him to deal with arrogant men and afterwards, in the privacy of his car or the quiet of the small office, he despised them. If written down, her words would have reeked of arrogance, and yet . . . Her spoken words, he thought, were the simple truth. They would all, and himself, follow her because she believed with a child's simplicity that she would win. Her confidence was mesmeric. He remembered when he had first met her, nine years before, and had thought her silence sullen, had not understood the strength her god had given her.

'If you reach Kirkūk . . .'

'*When* – and you will be with me.'

'When you reach Kirkūk what will you do then?'

'Return to my village. Tell my grandfather what I have done. And I will be a farmer. We have goats there, and a pig. Kurdistan will be free, my work will be done, and I will collect the fruit from the mulberry bushes and the pomegranate trees. I will be a farmer. May I tell you something?'

'Of course.'

The boy came with a plastic bowl of food for her, but she waved him away. Her hand rested on Gus's shoulder, the gesture of an older man to an inexperienced youth. 'If you had not fired the first shot and killed the officer, if you had not come, we would still have taken their bunkers. A few of the men behind me would have been killed, and some would have been wounded, but we would still have taken the bunkers – and whether you are with us or not, we will march to Kirkūk where the flame burns over the oilfield. Can we forget about your anger now?'

'Yes.' Every criticism he had made had been ignored.

'And will you follow me to Kirkūk?'

'Yes.' Gus laughed and saw her eyes flash.

'Do not be so solemn. How is your grandfather's health?'

Chapter Four

'I suppose I'd better start at the beginning. That would be the orderly way to do it.'

'Yes, start at the beginning,' Ms Carol Manning said.

Ken Willet sat at a table behind her. Among the plates, the empty glass and the cup with dregs of coffee in it, he opened a foolscap notebook. At the top of the page he wrote, 'WING CO BASIL PEAKE'. Immediately underneath the page heading he scrawled 'LETTER', and half-way down the page 'MOTIVATION'. Ms Manning's temper had sounded grim at midnight when she'd rung to tell him that her lieu day was postponed; there was no improvement now.

'It all began at Habbaniyah – I don't suppose, my dear, you've ever heard that name.'

'I haven't, but I'd be grateful if you'd get on with it.'

Willet thought the old man's eyes glittered in covert amusement.

They'd come up the drive to the vicarage, found it locked, shuttered, and a solitary cat had run from their approach. After circling the darkened building, late Georgian or early Victorian, they'd seen the modern bungalow – where a dull light burned – set back amongst trees beyond lawns covered with the winter's leaves. But the daffodils were up, and made a show with beds of crocuses. It was five to eight when she pressed the bell button.

'Habbaniyah is just north of the Euphrates, about forty-five miles west of Baghdad. Of course, there's a vegetation belt alongside the river, but where we were was surrounded by desert dunes, flat, horrible, lifeless. It's 1953, before you were born, my dear, I think. There was an RAF base there. It was ghastly. There was a single runway of rolled dirt reinforced with perforated metal plate. There were only three permanent buildings: administration, sick quarters and a damn great control tower. Everyone, men and officers, right up to the CO, lived in tents. We were "in the blue" – that's colloquial, my dear, in the forces for being posted out to the back end of nowhere. I was one of the nine hundred and ninety-nine penguins – you know what they call the RAF? The *penguins*, only one in a thousand flies . . . Sorry, just joking . . .'

'Best you stick to the point,' she said.

'As you wish. I was a wing commander, in charge of movements. The control tower was mine. We were a little island in hostile territory. The King and his government in Baghdad were marionettes for our ambassador to play with, but increasingly there was resentment from the civilian population and the younger army officers about our presence – so we lived on camp. All the food was flown in. We had a swimming-pool of sorts, a marquee dropped down into a sand scrape, and we had sports pitches – we didn't play the locals, we'd go as far as Nairobi, Aden or Karachi for cricket, hockey and soccer. To get out, if we had a few days' leave, we

91

hitched rides to Cyprus or Beirut – few of the officers and none of the men were permitted to travel inside Iraq.'

He was eighty-four years old, widowed for the last six. Willet thought the straightness of his back remarkable. Wearing worn carpet slippers, flannel pyjamas and a heavy dressing gown, he'd let them in, sat them down, then excused himself with old-world politeness. He'd come back still dressed in the slippers, pyjamas and dressing gown, but shaven and with his fine silver hair carefully combed. He'd checked their identity cards, then eased into a high wing-backed chair. He hadn't challenged them, had seemed in fact to have expected them.

'You passed on a letter to your grandson, Augustus Peake.'

'Patience, my dear, always a virtue . . . We had two squadrons of Vampire fighter-bombers there. It was a troubled little corner of the world, the Soviet border was less than an hour's flying away, and we had the transports coming through. They used to put down on Malta, then reach us, then go on to East Africa or the Red Sea, or keep going east to Singapore, Hong Kong and Korea. Most of the transports were Hastings, 53 Squadron. They came in and went out in the early morning; that's when everyone did their day's work. After that, in the heat – mad dogs and Englishmen stuff – we played sport. In the evening, officers anyway, we dressed for dinner, drank, ate, drank, played cards or took in a film in the open-air cinema, drank, and went to bed. We had to wear our issue greatcoats over our pyjamas, it was so damned cold. An evening a week, I was out on guard duty in support of the RAF regiment, shooting at

92

shadows out of our trenches – the Arabs would steal anything they could creep in and get their hands on. It was damned dull. That wasn't good enough for me. All I saw of the local culture was the traders at the main gate, nomads crossing the desert, and the thieves looking for a gap in our defences at night. What a waste . . . Barbara – that's my wife – wrote to me from the married quarters in Lyneham and pointed out what was just over the horizon. Well, not exactly – about two hundred miles, actually. Antiquities. Do you know anything about antiquities, my dear?'

'No, I don't, but I expect you're going to tell me.'

A myth, handed from grandfather to child, says that the Ark of Noah grounded as the floods fell back on the summit of Mount Cudi in present-day Iraq, 4,490 years before the birth of the Prophet Muhammad. The survivors were the first Kurds.

They were, through history, a warrior people.

Another myth, from ancient Jewish lore, tells that four hundred virgins were taken out of Europe by devil spirits who had been exiled from the court of Solomon, the *djinn*, to the Zagros mountains and their bastard children became the unique and isolated Kurds.

Xenophon wrote of the retreat of 10,000 Greek soldiers towards their homeland after defeat by Cyrus of Persia, and a week-long epic battle through the mountain passes, harried by the ferocious Carduchi tribesmen. The victor over the Crusader king, Richard the Lionheart of England, at Hittin by the Sea of Galilee was Salah al-Din Yusuf, the Kurd known in medieval Europe as Saladin. Kurds fought on both sides in the war of total barbarity, four hundred years ago, between Beg

Ustajlu and Selim the Cruel. As irregular soldiers, toughened by the physical hardship of life in the mountains, they were employed occasionally by the governments of Britain, France and Russia. But the reward never came . . . their own country was never given to them. When their usefulness was past they were as bones thrown from the table.

They were an image of the fallen stones from temples and palaces, scattered, antiquities.

Willet saw her fidget. The page in front of him, under LETTER and MOTIVATION was blank, but he was rather enjoying the story and it didn't seem to matter that he hadn't an idea where it was going.

'There I was, sitting at Habbaniyah, bored out of my mind, and six hours' drive to the north were the ruined cities of Nineveh and Nimrud. I obtained permission, took a car from the motor pool with a driver. We had a couple of tents, some food, service revolvers and a rifle, and off we went – the first time. That evening, humbled by the sense of place and time, I walked in the ruins of Nineveh. I actually saw – some blighter's hacked it out and stolen it now – the alabaster carvings in the ruins of King Sennacherib's palace, in his throne room, and he died 2,680 years ago. The next morning we drove the few miles to Nimrud. There, I stood amongst the fallen stones of the palace where King Ashurnasirpal the Second is said to have entertained 69,500 guests. I mean, your mind just falls apart in such a place. There's an observatory there where they studied the stars in the ninth century BC. We had to get back, and, sod's law, the bloody car wouldn't start. Had the bonnet up but couldn't get a spark of life out of her . . . A local wandered by, quite a different dress and stance to the Arabs down at Habbaniyah, watched us for a bit, then came close. The driver thought he was going to steal something from the car and drew his damn revolver. No, he didn't shoot him. I'm not mechanical but the local had a poke about – cleaned something, put it all back in place, then climbed into the driving seat, started her up, and she was as sweet as new. He wouldn't take any money. He was the first Kurd I ever met. His name was Hoyshar.'

Willet thought they were getting there, in the old man's own time.

'I went back a couple of times with the driver. It was purgatory for the poor fellow. He had no interest whatsoever in me picking around among the stones, giving a hand to the three German archaeologists at Nimrud – that became my favourite. He used to find some shade and sit down with a comic book, and this man, my age, Hoyshar, was always there and he worked on the engine and polished the bodywork so that it gleamed, never would take any money . . . The third time I wanted to go the driver was sick and no-one else was available. I had permission to go on my own. Hoyshar was waiting. It's a damn strange language the Kurds have, extraordinary, but, there are English roots. "Earth" is *erd*, "new" is *new*, a "drop" of water is a *dlop*. We got to be able to speak to each other; it was a bit like a comedy sketch but we understood what the other said. He drove me back to Habbaniyah, drove excellently, and took a bus home to the mountains. It became a routine. Every two weeks I'd drive from the motor pool to just outside the main gate, he'd be there, and he'd drive all the way to Nimrud, and then he'd bring me south again.

'By the fourth or fifth time I went up there – and I was then the only married officer who had ever applied for an extension to his posting at Habbaniyah – I'd stopped going to the kitchens for packed meals. Hoyshar brought all the food we needed. Yoghurt, apricot jam because I was important, bread, goat's cheese, dried meat . . . He was old enough to remember the RAF bombing his village, knocking the tribes into submission before the Second World War, but didn't seem to hold it against me. Always he refused money, so I used to take him books. If you went into his house now you'd probably find a stack of them, stamped "RAF HABBANIYAH: LIBRARY", mostly military history. At night, when it was too dark to work on the site with the Germans, we'd sit outside the tents. I'd learn about his people and he'd learn about mine. The seventh or eighth time, he brought me clothes to change into, those baggy trousers they wear and the loose shirts. I was going a bit native . . . That was it, scratching around for fragments of pottery, scraps of glass and gold from necklaces and earrings in the day, and talking at night . . . Do you know, my dear, that King Tiglath-Pileser the Third, from Nimrud, ruled an empire he had himself conquered that stretched from Azerbaijan to Syria to the Persian Gulf? Think of it, the scale of the civilization – and we were wearing skins and living in caves . . . I used to feel, every time I was there, privileged, and doubly privileged to be with such a man as Hoyshar.'

There was, Willet noted, a slight wetness at the old man's eyes. He blinked as if to clear it.

'At the end, before I went home, I was taken to his village. None of his family, and none of the other Kurds there, had ever seen a European. I slept in his bed, and he and his wife slept on the floor. I was shown the tail fins of a bomb that the RAF had dropped on the village twenty-something years before. If I had not been with Hoyshar the men of the village would have slit my throat, probably after cutting off an appendage . . . He is the grandest man I've ever known, my friend Hoyshar. I'm not a blinkered Arabist, and I hope I never stoop to patronizing the "noble savage".'

The old man paused, screwed his eyes shut, opened them, closed them again, then flickered the lids. His angular jaw jutted. The wetness was gone, the moment of weakness banished. Willet realized that some trauma had been released in the talk of the bare detail of the night in the village. He didn't think the former wing commander would degrade himself with a lie but he thought him capable of parsimony with the truth. He wondered whether he should interrupt and probe, but he was not the trained interrogator. She was. He had already begun to doubt his first instinct by the time composure was regained and the voice continued the story.

'What he wanted was freedom, for himself, his family and for his people. As a mature man, aged thirty-one, he stood in the Circle in the middle of Mahabad, that's across the Iranian border, and saw Qazi Muhammad hanged for the crime of proclaiming the First Republic of Kurdistan. I have good recall, I remember what I've read. A Foreign Office man wrote, in bloody Whitehall, about their freedom: "Their mode of life is primitive. They are illiterate, untutored, resentful of authority and lacking in any sense of discipline. The United Kingdom should not offer encouragement to the sterile idea of Kurdish independence." We used to talk about freedom.

'I went back to Lyneham, then to Germany, then was retired. I wrote two letters a year to him till 1979, and had two letters back, then I went out there again to see him. It was pretty hard to get the visa, but the British Museum was helpful. It had all changed . . . That damned man had taken power. There were soldiers everywhere. I sensed the subjugation of the people. There was a French team digging at Nimrud, and we helped them. It wasn't the same, there was an atmosphere of hate and fear. We continued to exchange letters. I was growing older and visas were exceptionally difficult to come by during the Iraq–Iran war, nigh on impossible, then there was the Gulf War, and the weasel messages sent by the Americans for the Kurds to rise up against the dictator. They did, the promised help never came, they fled.

'I thought of Hoyshar and his family, refugees in the mountains. I found the comfort of my twilight life obscene. My son wouldn't accompany me, said he was too busy with work. My grandson came with me. I heard his mother, my daughter-in-law, tell Gus before we set off, "Watch him, he's a complete lunatic where these wretched Kurds are concerned. Don't let him make a fool of himself." I'd have gone anyway, he didn't have to be with me. We were the original odd couple, me at seventy and him a full fifty years younger. They have a saying, "The Kurds have no friends but the mountains." That's where we found them, in their mountains, in the snow. It was incredible, a little piece of fate, that amongst a hundred thousand people we found them. His son had just buried two of Hoyshar's grandchildren. All they had tried to do was to take what is natural to us, their freedom.'

Willet looked up from the page. He had filled all the space under the heading of MOTIVATION. There was a feeble sunlight on the window behind the old man, but he could see the bright boldness of the flowers on the lawns.

'When did the letter come?' Ms Manning asked briskly.

'A month ago . . . That day on the mountains Gus met my friend and my friend's family, and he met Meda, who was then a teenager. When the letter came last month, it was about freedom for a far-away people. Do you think, my dear, I've deserved a coffee break?'

She made the coffee while Willet carried the plate, cup, glass and the cutlery from the table and washed them up. The captain's eyes were drawn to a curled photograph stuck with adhesive tape to a kitchen unit. On the slope of a hill, a thousand blurred faces behind them, a grizzle-faced man sat on a rock with a girl behind him, her hands on his shoulders. Defiance blazed from her eyes, which were compelling and erotic in their power.

Ms Manning carried the coffee mugs back into the living room.

'Right, so a letter came, and you showed that letter to your grandson . . . '

They crossed high, bare ground. Sometimes, rarely, they had the cover of wind-stripped clumps of trees, but the column mostly hugged the little valleys and ravines created by the rainstorms and snow-melt of centuries. Until they reached a flat ridge, pocked with rock outcrops, they were the lone inhabitants of a wilderness.

Gus plodded at the back, weighed down by the rucksack and the rifle bag. The wind diluted the warmth of the sun, and it was hard for him to maintain the pace of the *peshmerga* because the bulk of the gillie suit impeded him. He was behind Haquim who, even with the disability of his knee, seemed to move more easily over the jagged stones and the small, hidden bogs. Gus felt the sting of a blister on his right heel. Meda was in the leading group, moving fast, never looking behind her to see how he coped.

He had formed in his mind what he wanted to say.

The men and Meda had settled on the ground, amongst the rocks in the lee of the ridge. Some chewed at food, some bickered quietly, some laughed softly as if they were told an old and favourite joke, some cupped the water from a spring's source, some lay prone with their eyes closed. Haquim had reached them and sat on a stone and massaged his knee. Gus was going slower, and the tear in the skin at his right heel was opening. The boy was watching two men as they cleaned the breech of their heavy machine-gun . . . Nobody came back to help him as he struggled forward. He was bathed in self-pity. With his rifle and his skill, he was of critical importance to them. He didn't have to be there . . .

Gus heaved the rucksack off his back and carefully lowered the carrying case to the ground, onto the tufted yellow grass and the weathered rock. He untied the laces of his right boot, pulled off the sock, and examined the reddened welt of the blister. He rummaged in his rucksack for the small first-aid box, and selected a square of Elastoplast to cover the broken skin. He let the freshness of the air bathe his bare foot.

'Put your sock and boot back on.'

He hadn't heard Haquim's approach, was not aware of him until the man's shadow fell on him.

'It needs to breathe.'

'Put them back on.'

'When we're ready to move.'

'You need to do it now.'

'Why?'

'If the Iraqis ambush us, we will not ask them to stop and wait, while one amongst us pulls his sock and his boot back on.'

He felt hurt, as if degraded. 'Yes. Right.'

'And, Mr Peake, you do not question what I tell you.'

'My foot hurts.'

'Do you see others complaining? If it is such a big matter to you that your foot hurts, perhaps you should not have come.'

His head down, Gus heaved on his sock and his boot. Haquim was turning away. Gus said, 'I want somebody to be with me, to help me.'

'To carry your sack? Have all the men not enough to carry already?'

Gus said evenly, 'I want someone with me when I shoot.'

'I will choose someone.'

'No.' Gus's voice rose. 'I do it, it has to be my choice.'

'You give yourself great importance.'

'Because it is important.'

'Later, then, when we stop for the next rest.'

'Thank you.' Gus had finished retying his bootlace.

The column moved forward again. He heaved on his rucksack, lifted the rifle in its bag onto his shoulder, and gingerly put his weight on his right foot.

101

When the line of men passed through a small gully that broke the ridge, a great vista was laid out in front of them. Gus's eyes travelled over the sloping ground, the lower ridges, the distant curls of smoke above a faraway cluster of buildings, and on towards the single flame burning bright in a haze of lighter grey. Twenty miles away, and it was still a beacon, the flame at Kirkūk. He looked down on the ground that was to be the battlefield he would fight over.

Once again, the target had not come in the night.

On a bright, crisp morning, before the heat of the day settled over it, Major Karim Aziz reached the al-Rashid camp.

He showed his identification to the sentries at the gate, his name was checked off a list and he was shown where to park.

He'd known many who had come here on similar bright, crisp mornings in their best uniforms, who had been picked up by camp transport and and who had never been seen again. He had shut out the picture of the disappeared men and their families from his mind.

The transport pulled up beside his car. He had driven out to al-Rashid in a daze of tiredness and now he sleep-walked to the van.

Since the bombing of 1991 the camp had been rebuilt, the rubble removed, the craters filled in. The van took him past the many complexes of the Estikhabarat. There were the buildings occupied by the headquarters personnel of the second-in-command, a staff major general, those that liaised with Regional Headquarters, those that controlled the Administration Section, the Political

Section, the Special Branch and the Security Unit. He saw the batteries of anti-aircraft guns, and the clusters of ground-to-air missiles.

The van stopped outside a squat building. From the set of the windows he could see the thickness of the reinforced-concrete walls, painted in camouflage colours, and on the roof was a farm of aerials and satellite dishes. The armed guard opened the door for him and smiled. He wondered whether the guard always smiled at an officer summoned early in the morning to this building.

When he had reached home again after the night on the flat roof, he had clung to his wife briefly, then she had shrugged him off. It was unspoken, but she blamed him for the fiasco of his birthday celebration. The children had gone to school, her parents had stayed in their lean-to annexe at the back of the house. His wife, without a backward glance at him, had gone for the bus to the hospital. Then, alone in his home, he had checked through every item in the sports bag under the bed to satisfy himself that nothing incriminating could be found there . . . He did not know how he would resist torture . . . What could have damaged them, him, he had buried in the garden.

At the inner guard desk of the building he was asked to enter his name. There was another smile, and a finger jabbed towards his belt. He unhooked the clasp, passed the webbing belt over the desk, and with it the holster holding the Makharov pistol.

He was led down the corridor, then up a flight of stairs, then on to another corridor.

He had to make the effort to kick his legs in front of him. The panic was growing, the urge to turn and run insistent, but there was nowhere to turn and no-one to run to. He heard the boom of his boots on the smooth surface of the corridor's floor.

With each step towards the closed door at the far end he remembered the path he had taken towards joining the conspiracy. In February, two generals and a brigadier had come to a firing range to watch his progress in teaching marksmanship to his students, junior officers and senior NCOs. The course, like so much of the tactics learned in the Iraqi military, was based on old British army manuals. As he did, the students had used the Russian-made Dragunov SVD sniper's rifle. It was not the best rifle available in the international market, but he had a curious and almost emotional attachment to the weapon that had been with him for a year less than two decades. His students had had good shots at 400 metres, but at 500 metres none had hit the inner bulls on the targets, a man-sized cardboard shape, when they should have had an 80 per cent probability of doing so. Perhaps they were made more nervous by the presence of the generals and the brigadier. He had then fired his own Dragunov, but at 700 metres. From behind him the generals and the brigadier had watched his shooting through telescopes. Six rounds, six hits, when the probability of a 'kill' was listed as only 60 per cent, and after each shot he had heard the grunted surprise from behind the telescopes.

He reached the door at the end of the corridor.

His escort knocked with quiet respect.

He heard the gravel voice call for him to enter.

Three weeks after the shoot Major Karim Aziz had received a telephone call from the more senior of the two generals. He was invited to a meeting – not in the general's quarters, not in a villa in the Baghdad suburbs, but in a military car that had cruised for an hour with him, the general and two colonels along the city's roads flanking the Tigris river. He could, he supposed, have said that he had no interest in the proposition put to him in the car. He could also have lied, given them his support, then the next morning gone to the Estikhabarat, in this building, in this camp, and denounced them. They wanted a marksman. He had agreed to be that marksman. The general had said that an armoured brigade in the north would mutiny and drive south, but only after word was received that the bastard, the President, was dead. He had been told of the villa, of the bastard's new woman. The detail had been left to him – but without their esteemed leader's death, the armoured brigade would not move. The general had talked of a domino effect inside the ranks of the regular army once the bastard was killed.

The general had been a big and powerfully built man, but he had stammered like a nervous child as he explained the plan. Aziz had agreed, then, there; only afterwards, when he had been dropped from the car, did he consider that he might have been set-up, stung, and he had been sick in the gutter. He had dismissed that thought because he had witnessed the precautions taken to preserve the secrecy of the meeting and seen the nervousness of the officers in the car.

He had tracked for days around the villa and had found the place from which to shoot. He had met the general again, cruised the same route in the same car, and the general had embraced him.

He went inside. His stomach was slack and his bladder full. He tried to stand proud, to pretend that

105

he was not intimidated, was a patriot surrounded by cowards. He thought of his wife and his children, and of the pain of torture.

A colonel had his back to the door and stared at a wall map, but turned at his approach. 'Ah, Major Aziz. I hope there was nothing important in your schedule that had to be cancelled.'

He looked up at the photograph of the smiling, all-powerful President. He stuttered his answer. 'No, my schedule was clear.'

'You are the marksman, the sniper, that is correct?'

'It is my discipline, yes.'

'You understand the skills of sniping?'

He did not know whether he was a toy for their amusement, whether the colonel played with him. 'Of course.'

'Two men dead, two rounds fired, on consecutive days, each shot at a range of at least seven hundred metres in Fifth Army sector. What does that tell you about the sniper?'

'That he is trained, professional, an expert.' He felt the tension draining from him. He was limp, a rag on a washing-line.

'How do you confront a professional sniper, Major?'

'Not by turning rocks over with artillery or tanks or heavy mortars. You send your own sniper to confront him.'

The colonel said sharply, 'You go tomorrow, Major Aziz, to Kirkūk.'

'The north? The Kurds are not snipers.' He wanted to laugh out loud as the lightness broke into the tightness of his mind. He bubbled, 'They cannot hit targets at a hundred metres.'

'I am from the Tikrit people, Major. Yesterday my cousin's son was shot at seven hundred metres in a defence position near Kirkūk. Perhaps a foreigner is responsible.'

'Whatever the nationality, the best defence against a sniper is always a counter-sniper.'

'Be the counter-sniper, then. Your orders will be waiting for you when you reach the garrison at Kirkūk.'

Aziz saluted, turned smartly and marched out of the room. Outside, with the door closed on him, he could have collapsed in a huddle on the floor and wept his relief. He steadied himself against the arm of his escort, and walked away.

A few moments later, the warm air brushed his face, washed it of fear.

Gus sat on a rock and scanned the ground ahead of him with his binoculars, looking for movement.

It was the best place he could find, had the nearest similarity to the terrain of the Common in Devon. It was a practice but it was still crucial. The arguments were finally over, had finished when Haquim had struck a man and knocked him flat, when the knife had flashed, and Haquim had kicked the knife from the man's hand. Before then, the argument had raged savagely. Meda had chosen not to intervene, but had sat apart with an amused smile on her face. He needed an observer to help him with distance and windage and, most important, to guide him in on the stalk to the targets ahead and to work out the exit routes after each snipe. It could not be Haquim – too slow and too involved in the mess of strategy and tactical problems.

The arguments were because each man in the column,

old and young, believed he was the best at moving unseen across open ground. The bitterness was inspired by pride, when Haquim had selected the dozen men from the hundred in the column – from *agha* Ibrahim's men, or from *agha* Bekir's men. The older men who had fought for the most years, or the younger ones with more agility than experience. The larger group, not chosen, sat behind Gus, and scowled or watched the slope of ground ahead with a sullen resignation.

He had four 'walkers' out, as he had seen it done on the Common. Each time he saw a man, magnified through the binoculars, crawling, Gus shouted to the nearest 'walker' and pointed, and the man was tapped on the head by the 'walker', and eliminated. Each time a man was eliminated there was a growl of jealous approval from behind Gus.

Gus counted those he had spotted and eliminated. Some had taken the obvious route for their stalk, along a meandering river trail, some had headed for the single tree in the centre of the open ground, some had tried to use a broken mess of buildings to the right. The river, the tree and the ruins were all obvious points for a stalk and were therefore poorly chosen . . . He saw the last man: his head and chest were low, but his buttocks were up. The 'walker' went to him, and the last man stood.

He had asked too much of them. He had tried to bring an alien culture of warfare from the Common in south-west England to the foothills of the Zagros mountains. He had asked them to crawl, concealed, across a thousand yards of open ground, and none had reached the finish line he had set. Gus cursed. Was it better to take the best of the failures, or was it better to work alone? He pushed himself up.

'It's my fault, my bloody fault,' Gus said to Haquim.

There was a single shot, the crack of it high above him, then the thump of the following sound. The sounds were almost simultaneous. Behind him there was brief pandemonium. As the moment of silence settled he heard the rasped arming of weapons. A dozen men had gone forward and stalked back towards him, and he had identified that same dozen. He had the binoculars up to his eyes and tracked over the ground, across the grassland, over rocks, between the narrow height of the tree trunks, into and out of the stones of the ruins, and he still could not see the man who had fired. They were the best binoculars he had ever used, and he saw nothing.

Gus said to Haquim, 'Tell him to stand.'

Haquim shouted at the emptiness in front of them. Then the silence fell again. At first Gus felt a sense of excitement, but that was whittled to annoyance because nothing moved. He covered the ground again for the outline of a face, the shape of a shoulder. They said on the Common that the stalk didn't count unless the sniper had a clear view of his target when he fired . . . Some clever bastard in hiding, loosing off into the air.

'Shout again.'

Haquim yelled, and the voice bellowed back off the hillside. From clear ground, ground on which there were no rocks, no trees, no fallen buildings, away from the small river, the boy rose to his feet.

There was a sod of earth with grass growing from it, a turf square, on the boy's head. The boy, grinning like an ape, had reached the finish line. Gus reckoned he'd covered that area of grass five, six times with his binoculars, and still hadn't seen him.

'I'll have the boy.'

'You cannot,' Haquim said.

'Why not?'

'The boy is not a person of consequence.'

'I'll have him because he is the best stalker.'

'He has no connection – no father, no family. It will cause resentment.'

'I'll have him, and when it gets harder – as it will, you tell me, and I believe you – then I will shoot better.'

He thought he was already a harder man, as if stones in a torrent battered against his body and forced the softness from it, than he had been three weeks before on the Common. They needed to make further ground before dusk. He walked in the heart of the column and ignored the blister on his right heel. The boy skipped along beside him and had offered to take his rucksack, but Gus had refused.

They went past the ruins of the village. The roofs, of concrete and tin, were collapsed inside the sunken walls, and Gus knew that each building had been dynamited. The grass grew up between the debris abandoned by a fleeing people, pots, pans, clothes faded by wind, rain and sunshine. The old village had been destroyed so that there was nothing for its people to return to. There were two men dead behind him but, passing the ruins of the village, Gus felt for the first time that he was a part of the quarrel. He was a changed man, and in the failing light he imagined that the flame far ahead burned brighter.

The Israeli, in his eyrie where the winds blew, under the sharp light of the stars and forty miles into northern Iraq from the Turkish border, heard the radio transmission from the al-Rashid camp to the Estikhabarat offices at Fifth Army headquarters in Kirkūk.

The computers in the building low slung on the mountain summit had long ago deciphered the Iraqi military codes. The previous evening Isaac Cohen had listened to a signal reporting the activities of a sniper operating in the area north of the Fifth Army's sector. Now, a counter-sniper, a man with a reputation, was being sent to Kirkūk. The old Mossad man chuckled. He worked with the most modern electronic equipment that the factories at Haifa and in the Negev could produce, and before induction into the Mossad he had served as a captain in a tank unit that boasted the supreme technology in the sensors that sought out the enemy . . . The messages revealed archaic warfare – a man against a man, a rifle against a rifle, two men scrabbling on their bellies to within range of the other. Not slings and stones, not bows and arrows, but rifles that only marginally increased the distance of combat. But as the evening wore on, Cohen's amusement was stilled. How could a sniper be so important that a counter-sniper had been sent against him?

Isaac Cohen was a methodical man. As the night settled around him, he began to track back through messages held in his computers. The calls, made at dawn and dusk over the last forty-eight hours, traced a line into, through and beyond the defence lines of the Fifth Army north of Kirkūk. He saw the trail of an incursion, and the decrypting power of his computers broke into the conversations of a satellite telephone that had spoken with *agha* Bekir in Arbīl and *agha* Ibrahim in Sulaymānīyah, the time and place of a meeting.

He no longer laughed. A small army marched across

the God-forsaken wilderness. The adage of the Mossad was 'The enemy of my enemy is my friend.'

And then he wondered what damage could be wrought to the enemy by one man with a rifle.

The dog whined behind the bedroom door.

Major Karim Aziz, with his family, ate his evening meal, and he talked. He spoke of soccer with his children and their games at school; with his wife he joked about holidays they might take one day in the northern mountains, with tents and picnics; with her parents he laughed about their continuous and never-ending hunt for food at the open markets. He talked and joked and laughed because that night he was not returning to the flat roof, and he felt as though a great weight had been shed from his shoulders. He assumed, perhaps correctly, perhaps not, that a general and two colonels would have heard that Major Karim Aziz of the Baghdad Military College was posted to the north. And he had no route by which to pass them any urgent message. He had survived the visit to the al-Rashid camp, which few did, and he had been treated there as a valued expert. No suspicion had fallen over him; the shadow of arrest, torture and death did not lie on him.

The dog scratched at the bedroom door.

It was a familiar experience for a veteran soldier. He ate with his family around him, and before dawn the next morning he would be gone. He could have listed each of the times that he had eaten a last evening meal with the family – before going to Moscow, or the Beka'a, or to the front lines in the Iranian cities of Khorramshahr and Susangerd where the fighting had been in cellars and sewers, to the north for Operation al-Anfal against the

Kurdish saboteurs, to Kuwait City for the first strike then a return in the last days, to the north again for the push into Arbīl and towards Sulaymānīyah – it was a familiar routine for him. Later, before bed, he would visit the home of his own parents and would tell his father, the pensioned civil servant of the Iraqi Railway Company, and his mother that he was going away and that there was no cause for them to worry. He drank more than was normal for him because the weight was off his shoulders.

In the bedroom, with the dog, was his packed and bulging backpack, and the heavy wooden box in which he always carried the Dragunov rifle when he went to war.

As the light had fallen on the city, Aziz had gone to collect the dog. It had been lodged with his cousin for two months more than two years, since his wife's parents had come to live in his home. It had been blamed for aggravating her father's asthma. It was a brown and white springer spaniel, now nine years old, fast, fit and trained with all the patience he could summon. To go to war without the dog would have been to travel without his eyes and ears.

Around the table, with the warmth of his family close to him, the north was not spoken of. His detestation of the north, of the Kurds, had little to do with politics and everything to do with blood. Her father's younger brother had died there in 1974, a dozen kilometres from where he, the young lieutenant in a mechanized infantry brigade, was serving, and he had seen the body and what had been done to it. His cousin's nephew had been killed there in 1991, a prisoner after the fall of the Military Intelligence headquarters at Arbīl, taken out on the street, shot, and his body dragged round the square from the back of a jeep; that body, too, he had seen when the city was retaken. But, at the table, it was not mentioned.

Later, when he had walked the spaniel to his parents' home, and settled him beside their bed, when his wife was in his arms, the master sniper would tell her that she had no cause for anxiety. That night Major Karim Aziz had not the slightest doubt that he would locate, stalk and kill an enemy. He did not entertain the thought that he might fail, that his place in the bed beside her would remain cold, empty.

He said his name was Omar.

He spoke with a piping American accent, and told his story.

He had no mother, no father, no family, no home. His mother had died on the mountainous slopes of the Turkish border, frozen to death with his sister. His father had died a month earlier, killed in Arbīl by Iraqi soldiers. He did not know where his uncles, aunts and cousins were. His family's homes had been bulldozed in 1991. He said the American servicemen bringing relief supplies to the camps in the mountains had found him and cared for him.

Gus idly imagined soldiers bound together by a common sense of compassion, finding a half-dead child, numbed by cold and hunger, and taking him back to their tents, food and warmth, as they would a stray, pretty cat. They would have fussed over the child, spoiled him, and taught him their language. When they moved back over the border, consciences salved by the good work, they would have dumped him on aid-workers. Gus thought of Omar hanging about the offices of a foreign charity in Arbīl or Sulaymānīyah or Zākhō, running messages, scrounging, with his childhood irreplaceably snatched from him. When most of the aid agencies had fled in the late summer of 1996, the child would have attached himself with limpet-like strength to a fighting *peshmerga* unit, helped to carry food and ammunition forward to the sagging front line, and bring the wounded back.

Gus thought of his own childhood, of its calm and its safety. The orphan would have seen horror, and would be feral and savage as a result.

The boy stank. His pillow was a stone. He lay on the ground, without a blanket to cover him, close to Gus's sleeping-bag, and the rifle with the double magazines taped to each other lay across his stomach. He wore drab American army fatigues, torn and still too large for him, and a pair of yellow trainers that had gone at the toes. He had brought Gus food from the cooking pot and watched him eat until Gus had passed him the bowl. He had gulped down the last of the food and licked the bowl till it shone in the evening sunshine.

The camp was quiet and Gus spoke softly. 'The man we have to remember is Herbert Hesketh-Prichard. There had been others before him, but as far as our army is concerned, he was really the father of sniping. He was a big-game hunter before the first war with Germany – he shot lions and elephants, and he turned those skills to shooting Germans. He went to France, where the war was with the Germans, and took with him big-game rifles and telescopes. At first, none of the generals would listen to him, but he kept emphasizing the importance of a quality sniper on the battlefield. The sniper was more effective in breaking the enemy's morale than an artillery barrage. Kill the officer, kill his spotters, kill his machine-gunners, and your troops feel good, they live. Almost everything we know today is based on what was taught by Hesketh-Prichard to his snipers eighty-five years ago . . .'

The boy, Omar, snored in his sleep.

Chapter Five

The helicopter had come in at first light, flying low like a hawk hunting, hugging the contours of the ground. It came smoothly over a ridge to the north, all the time looking for gullies along which to fly, then hovered. For a moment it was a predator, black and without identification, over a prey. The prey was Meda . . . and she had waved it down.

Four men had immediately jumped clear from the open fuselage hatch. Two carried machine-guns, one had an assault rifle, and one held a grenade launcher; all wore a common uniform of jeans, anoraks, face masks and baseball caps, and they had scattered to secure a perimeter area round the big bird. Gus thought that after the guards the next man out was also American. Under his windcheater, his tie was whipped up from his throat as he bent to run clear of the downdraught of the blades, he had a lavatory brush of cropped grey hair, and carried maps in plastic covering. He'd shaken hands perfunctorily with Meda, then turned back and helped two more men, Kurds, down from the hatch.

The American, the Kurds and Meda had settled down amongst stones, the maps spread out across their legs,

117

and Gus saw a Thermos flask passed between the men. Meda refused to drink from it.

The pilots kept the turbines running. Where he had been told to stay, with the *peshmerga,* the boy and Haquim, Gus was a full three hundred paces from the meeting-point and the helicopter.

Haquim said bitterly, 'I am not important enough to be a part of the negotiation.'

Through his binoculars, Gus watched them. He could recognize the body language of the Kurds – one in a suit and one in laundered but old tribal dress. The American was between them, the conduit. Gus sensed deep-held suspicion. Meda faced them and her arms alternated between gestures of frustration and the softer movements of persuasion. He passed the binoculars to Haquim.

Haquim said, 'In the suit, dressed as the Westerner he wants to be, is *agha* Bekir. He controls the west of the enclave. I trust him as I trust a scorpion. Three weeks after the Iraqi attack of 1991, in which his people were murdered, left destitute to starve in the mountains, *agha* Bekir was shown on Baghdad's television hugging Saddam as if he were a favoured cousin. He looks only for power and money. He would sleep with a snake to gain them.'

'But he has men . . .'

'And *agha* Ibrahim has more men. He is more simple but more cunning, which is why he wears the clothes of his people, and he has more greed. He controls the north and the east, and therefore can take the toll money from the lorries that cross the Turkish frontier to go to Baghdad. He should know Saddam, because Saddam tried on many occasions to kill his father. Once

118

Saddam sent Shi'a clerics from Baghdad to talk peace with *agha* Ibrahim's father, and Saddam told the clerics they must wear a hidden tape-recorder so that he could know what was said. When the meeting had started, one of the government drivers outside threw a switch, with radio control. The tape-recorder was a bomb. At the moment the bomb exploded a servant was leaning across in front of *agha* Ibrahim's father and filling his glass with lemon juice. The servant died, and the cleric with the tape-recorder, and many others. But *agha* Ibrahim's father survived to tell his son of the treachery of Saddam. Did he listen? Three years ago, *agha* Bekir and *agha* Ibrahim fought full-scale war over the division of the money from the smugglers, and when *agha* Ibrahim was losing, being driven back, he called to Saddam for help. He was rescued by Saddam's tanks. It was when I was wounded . . . He has many men, fighting men, because he has the money to pay them. It is the miracle of Meda that has brought them together.'

'I think they both want to fuck her,' the boy said.

Haquim lashed out behind him, but Omar laughed and leaped back as a boxer avoids a tiring opponent's punch.

'What is being decided?' Gus asked quietly.

'They are deciding what they will risk. Meda has to persuade them, again, of her vision.'

Gus had taken back his binoculars and watched her. There was something of virginal innocence about her. She smiled and scowled. Her head would drop as if sulking, then would be lifted and a child's happiness would break across her face. Without her, nothing would happen. She wove a spell over them. It was as if, Gus thought, her very innocence – her enthusiasm, her optimism, her certainty – persuaded them. Omar, the vulgar little wretch, had spoken the truth. She sat facing them with her legs splayed out in the combat trousers, and with the upper buttons of her tunic unfastened so that they could see the skin of her chest. He saw, so clearly, Ibrahim's leering smile and the way Bekir gazed into her eyes. The American wore an older man's frown, as though anxiety – for her – raged in him.

After he shook her hand, he stood and shouted to the guards, who backed towards the helicopter and covered the ground ahead with their weapons. Hands were held and shaken, then all were gone into the belly of the helicopter.

She stood with her hands on her hips against the growing power of the rotors. The blast threw back her hair, and thrust her tunic and trousers against the shape of her body, slender and young, without fear. As the helicopter lifted, she didn't wave to them, as if to affirm her independence.

It came low over them, and Gus saw the face of the American peering down. He held the rifle close to him against the blow of the blades.

And the silence came . . . He felt a sense of great loss. The helicopter had been a lifeline. It had come, he could have walked to it, climbed inside it, could have argued himself a seat and been carried back to his home, his work and his life. The chance had been laid before him, and he had not thought to take it. She was walking back towards them, the big grin of triumph on her face.

The men ran to her, and Haquim hobbled after them. Gus cuffed the boy and said he should go, too, while he sat alone with his thoughts. He could never have turned his back on her: she had trapped him. Everything that was home, work, life, seemed now of minimal relevance. She stood and they sat in front of her. He saw the old and the young faces that had been hardened by cruelty and suffering, that were cold and brutal, and the light in their eyes. She trapped all of them.

The boy returned to where he sat.

'What does she say?'

'She says that later today the *agha* Bekir and the *agha* Ibrahim will each send one hundred of their best fighting men to join us. In the morning we attack the *mujamma'a* in the front of us – that is a new village, what is called a Victory City. She says when we have captured it more men will come and we will fight at the town of Tarjil – we will have more men and we will make a battle at the crossroads of the Baghdad road and the Sulaymānīyah road. After that, when more men have arrived, she will lead us past the flame of Baba Gurgur, and into Kirkūk. We are going to Kirkūk. Do you believe her?'

'I have to,' Gus said.

'They believe her, *agha* Bekir and *agha* Ibrahim, because they want to fuck her. They can fuck any woman they want to, but they want her because they know they cannot have her.'

'You are a disgusting child.'

'Do you want to fuck her, Mr Gus?'

He caught the lobe of the boy's ear, where it peeped from under the matt of tangled dark curls, and twisted it hard so that Omar yelped like a hurt dog.

He started to tell the boy of the role of an observer working in close harmony with a sniper. Everything he knew about life told him that when a blow was struck there inevitably followed a stinging counter-strike.

121

Mapped ahead of him was a timetable of war, locations on a map that would all be fought for and each would be harder. He talked softly, earnestly, of the work of an observer, as if the boy, Omar, were an equal to him, as if his very survival would rest on the skill of the boy when the counter-strike fell.

The door to the ageing Antonov howled open on poorly oiled hinges. He allowed his eyes to grow accustomed to the brightness beating up from the tarmac, and waited for the steps to reach the aircraft.

Other men he knew in the army would have refused to take a flight in the veteran transport, but Major Karim Aziz had been often enough in combat for the fear of death to be replaced by a comforting fatalism. Everything was behind him now.

He shouted his thanks to the pilot. He had been the only passenger on the flight, with his dog. He gazed around him. It was three years since he had last been at Kirkūk Military. Then, some of the attack aircraft's hardened bunkers were still under repair, and wooden scaffolding had surrounded the control tower. But there was nothing to see now of the work of the American bombers; the scaffolding and the workmen were long gone.

A jeep was approaching fast from the tower.

Aziz called the dog to heel and went down the steps struggling with the weight of his backpack and the wooden box. When the jeep pulled up he saw from the gaze of the officer deputed to meet him that his reputation had travelled before him. His cheeks were brush-kissed, an offer made to take the box, which was refused. The box was the basis of his reputation and Aziz allowed no other man to take charge of it.

He followed the officer to the jeep. In any unit he worked with, there had never been any love for the sniper. He would be respected for his skill, but not liked. Soldiers in a front line always felt a vague affinity with the enemy across no man's land; Iraqi soldiers had felt that for Iranian soldiers – and the sniper brought anonymous death to the man in the opposing trench. When a sniper came to a quiet front line, killed, moved on, the hell of artillery fell on those left behind. And the sniper's killing was premeditated and took away the random, haphazard chance of shell shrapnel with which soldiers could live.

The officer was wary. 'You had a good flight, I hope?'

'Good for me, but the dog was sick.'

The officer laughed thinly. 'Not a good companion.'

'Oh, yes, the best.' He lifted his box into the back of the jeep and the dog bounded in after it. They drove away. He had kept the name of the dog, Scout. It had been four months old when he had found it on his third day in Kuwait City. It had had a collar on it, with its name on a tag and an address. Major Karim Aziz had flown in with the first assault troops, by helicopter, to take one of the Emir's palaces, but the fighting had been slack. The third day he had wandered the streets of Kuwait City and marvelled at the ostentation. He had found the cowering, terrorized puppy whimpering as the tanks growled past. While fellow officers successfully looted that wealth, he had gone to the address on the tag and found the wrecked, emptied home of an expatriate British oil engineer. He had taken the dog back to the hotel where he was quartered. When, two weeks later, he had returned to Baghdad, he had felt a sense of shame that he took with him the dog, a video camera and a bracelet from the famous gold *souk*. Others had taken back new Mercedes, and BMWs, and had loaded lorries with 'souvenirs'. They had never used the video camera at home because he had not stolen the cassettes to go with it, and his wife had sold the bracelet for money to buy clothes for the children, but he had kept the dog. Scout was now nine years old, but still had the legs and eyes, nose and ears that made him indispensable to Aziz when he went to war.

From the airport, he was driven through the city.

Kirkūk was home to a million people. The jeep wove through crowded streets, past bustling pavements. The shops were open. He saw nothing that made him sense panic, and yet out in the distant hills to the north, beyond the clear, bright, high flame, an army marched on that city. The jeep's horn cleared a path through the laden lorries, donkey-drawn carts and the kids careering on bicycles and scooters. There was no atmosphere of danger.

He was taken into the headquarters compound of the Fifth Army, driven at speed past smart sentries, and lines of T-72 tanks and ranks of BMP personnel carriers.

With his dog at his heel, Aziz carried his box into the command bunker.

He was introduced to a general. He saluted, shook hands. Behind the general was a brigadier who looked up, through him, and returned to the study of the map spread on the table. He knew the brigadier, recognized him, but could not place where he had seen him. He struggled to find it, before it was swept from his mind.

'So, Baghdad has sent us a sniper.' The general spoke scornfully. 'One man to do with a rifle what an army with tanks and artillery and two divisions of infantry cannot achieve.'

'Against a sniper, the best defence is a superior counter-sniper.'

The sneer formed. 'With a dog and the fleas it carries.'

'With my dog, yes.'

'What do you need to know?'

'I need to know the route the incursion has taken, and the exact position of the blocking force you have deployed.'

The silence hung in the room. The brigadier peered up from the map, then ducked his head and played with a pencil.

'A blocking force has been deployed?'

The general said, without expression, 'Your job, Major, is at a level of local tactics. Do not try to teach me strategy.'

'I need to meet the eyewitnesses who saw the enemy's sniper.'

They both stared at him before telling him when he could interrogate the witnesses. He was escorted out.

In a bare room with a small cupboard and an iron-framed bed, he took a square of goatskin from his backpack and laid it in the corner as a mat for his dog, then filled the dog's bowl with water. From a framed photograph on the wall, the President watched him, smiled down on him.

AUGUSTUS HENDERSON *PEAKE*.

2. (Conclusions after interview with Wing Co.
Basil Peake RAF (Retd.) conducted by self and
Ms Carol Manning – transcript attached.)

MOTIVATION: A central focus point for AHP in making his journey to northern Iraq is the powerful influence of his grandfather. Ms Manning believes BP used his manipulative arguments to persuade AHP to travel and involve himself. Motivation is important for a sniper in a military theatre, but that importance will diminish quickly once AHP is involved in combat, and will ultimately be of little relevance. BP has old, legally held rifles, and from his youth AHP was, therefore, familiar with handling firearms, but BP was unable or unwilling to offer information concerning the necessary MIND-SET of the hunter that is crucial if the step from target marksman to sniper is to be made.

SUMMARY: Without that MINDSET, AHP will fail and if he fails he will be killed. No evidence of a military background. My earlier assessment stands: the chances of medium-term survival remain slim to non-existent.

TEXT of letter sent to BP by Hoyshar – see transcript above.
(NB: The letter is the start, and may be the only indication we find as to what AHP hopes to achieve in northern Iraq. In my opinion, the end is a military impossibility.)

Esteemed brother Basil,
I write to you at a time when I have not received any of your valued letters for two years. This letter will be given to SARAH of the Protect the

Children, and only God will decide if it shall reach you.

It is now, esteemed brother, a moment of crisis in the recent history of our people. The Kurdish people, my people, in the mountains and in the towns and in the villages are filled with despair. We believe no longer in the will of the West to protect us from the Great Murderer. We think that we are forgotten. When we have been forgotten then the Great Murderer will send his tanks and guns and aircraft to destroy us. We understand that very little time is left to us. You will remember my dear granddaughter, my Meda. She now has twenty-five years. For one so young she has the fire of a lion in her breast, and she has power over men. I believe, esteemed friend, that the strength in her is God-given.

For a year she has visited many villages in our region and talked to women, and to men, of a new moment when the Kurdish people shall rise up to take their freedom from the Great Murderer. At first she could only talk. Then, three months ago, she was heard in Rost, near to the Sar i-Piran mountain, by a military commander of proven courage, the *mustashar* Haquim. She entranced him as she had the simple village people. He took her to Arbīl and to Sulaymānīyah, and his influence as a fighting man enabled her to meet with *agha* Ibrahim and *agha* Bekir. They are cunning men, men of deceit. They have fought the Great Murderer and they have kissed his cheeks. They bend when the wind is against them, and they go forward when the wind is behind them. They are corrupt dogs but they have power. Meda met them and talked to them about freedom. She looked in their faces, each in turn, Haquim told me, and she asked them did they want to live as the servant of the Great Murderer and in fear, or as proud men who had led their people to freedom? Did they want to be remembered as cowards or heroes? She is just a young woman, and she demanded their answer. They could not refuse her. She promised them that she would bring them past the flame of Baba Gurgur, and into the square of Kirkūk.

Esteemed friend, she has the power over men and they did not dare to refuse her. It will be a small army at the beginning, but it will grow. Each time she wins, more men will be given to her. She will have Haquim, whom I love like a son, at her side to guide her. She will be in God's care. I cannot say whether this letter will reach you. If it is delivered with success to you, please, esteemed friend, look at your newspapers and your television and discover the day that she reaches Kirkūk.

This is not, of course, the calling-in of a debt, or for you to feel there is an old obligation that you carry, but any assistance you can offer would be a gift of the highest generosity. It is a great journey that she is beginning. She is the last chance of the Kurdish people. With pride, I pray for her.

I am, as always, honoured to call myself your friend, Hoyshar.

Ken Willet had read the letter many times. It reached him, touched him. Each time he'd read it, scanned through the clear copperplate handwriting, he remembered the photograph in the kitchen of the old man sitting and the young woman standing beside him. He had patrolled in Northern Ireland before the ceasefire, he had heard shots fired in anger, but all he knew of combat was what had been taught him on the training grounds of the Welsh mountains. From his posting to the Ministry of Defence, he would move on to an administrative position at a barracks, then probably try his luck in the civilian world. He would never know about combat at first hand.

He felt, and he was not ashamed of it, a very great sadness. The force of the words played in his mind: 'chances of medium-term survival remain slim to nonexistent'.

He'd let Omar lead him forward.

For Gus that was the act of faith, the first step.

'You do it well and you stay with me, you do it poorly and you go back to cooking and carrying. There are no second chances, Omar,' Gus had said, at the start of the stalk. He had tried to sound ruthless and brutal, but it was not in his nature. Omar had grinned back at him, then led.

They had come over a ridge and looked down on what Omar called the *mujamma'a*, what Haquim had called the Victory City, his lip curled in sarcasm, and what Gus thought of as a concentration camp. Far beyond the village was a town, then a crossroads, then the flame and Kirkūk, but all were hidden by the heat-haze of the afternoon. He had seen the original village, which had been flattened by explosives. Now he saw the replacement, sited in the centre of a desolate plateau of rock and bogland. No fields had been made, no strips cultivated. Outside a wire perimeter fence were groups of sheep and goats, pathetically thin, hunting for sustenance. Behind the fence, closed in by it, regimented rows of concrete block-houses were linked only by washing lines. Gus made a plan of the fence, the gate, the watchtowers and the single large building that dominated from the centre the ranks of block-houses. There was no grass to brighten the vista, and no flowers. The gate had been opened to admit a water tanker and a lorry.

Very carefully he drew the plan of the village and he began to understand: it had been built away from a source of water and away from good grazing land, so that the village people were dependent on their guards to provide them with life support. Without it they starved. The boy had good eyes and revelled in the power of the telescope. Twice he had pointed to small sandbagged bunkers that Gus had missed. Everything he saw, and that Omar found for him, Gus marked on his plan. He studied the command post. He saw an officer, a machine-gun placed behind a parapet on the flat roof, and the queue of shuffling villagers form at the main door to receive their small packages of food. It was a place of dreary certainty, and he thought that one day would be the same as another . . . but not tomorrow.

While he made the plan, he whispered to Omar about the work of an observer. He was not good at sharing even the little information he knew. All his knowledge of shooting was based on his taking supreme responsi-

130

bility for his own skills and shortcomings. But tomorrow he could not be alone. He was searching for a vantage-point to the side, where there was sufficient elevation for his eyeline to clear the block-house roofs, from which he could see the entrance door to the command post. Away to his left, several hundred yards from where he and the boy lay, was a barren hillside, without obvious cover. If they were there and the machine-gun found them, they would die. If they did not live, the attack would fail.

'Omar, don't move, don't point, don't move your head fast. The hill to the left . . .'

'Where there is nowhere to hide, Mr Gus?'

'Yes, where there is nowhere to hide. Can you see a place for us?'

'Perhaps.'

'Not perhaps. Yes or no?'

'Of course, Mr Gus.'

'Really, *yes* or *no*. Which?'

'There are better places.'

'It's where we have to be, Omar. Yes or no?'

The boy was learning. He moved the hessian-covered telescope, netting over the lens, so slowly. Then he settled and his eye was locked to it. Every bush on the hillside had been cut down for firewood, every tree felled. The slope was of dull brown, winter-dead earth, as if the snow and the rain had eroded the life from it.

'If we are on the ridge, above the hill . . .'

'Too far for me to shoot.'

There was silence between them. Gus tilted his head to watch every movement around the command post, as if each moment that he saw the villagers and the soldiers, tramping in the mud around the building, was precious. The water tanker and the lorry left. He focused

131

on the machine-gun position. Was the officer more important, or the machine-gun? Omar tugged his arm. 'There is a place.'

'I can't see it. Are you sure?' Gus had his binoculars on it, but saw only the featureless slope of the hillside.

'Yes, Mr Gus . . . '

'Omar – do you love Meda?'

'I love her, Mr Gus – not fuck-love, but *love*.'

'If you haven't got a place, if the machine-gun finds us and Meda is leading the attack, afterwards it will kill her . . . So you have to be sure.'

'Very sure, Mr Gus.'

'Can you get me there in the dark, no light, and can you get me out in the day?'

The boy nodded soberly. 'I think so, Mr Gus.'

'If you can't, Omar, Meda is dead.'

He knew tomorrow would be different from any experience in his life. The thought of it chilled him. He wondered how he would sleep that night, if he would sleep.

'Don't try to please me,' Major Karim Aziz had said, to each of them separately. 'Don't tell me what you think I want to hear. Do not be definite about anything you are not certain of. I want only the truth.'

He had heard what the corporal and the goatherd had said, then he had told the guards that both were to be fed a full hot meal but in different rooms so that neither knew what the other had told him. While they were eating, he had gone away to the intelligence unit and demanded they produce for him large-scale maps and aerial photographs. When he had pored over them, he had gathered up those that would help him and

132

had returned to talk with each of them again.

The corporal's story didn't alter, but the goatherd had seen the man, his man. 'My friend was shot from across the valley, and I do not lie to you, Major. God strike me if I lie to you, but I have never known of a man who could shoot at such a distance . . . But I saw him, Major. He was sitting in the sun's light against the wall of the house of my friend, and the rifle he held was bigger than any rifle I have ever seen. He was dressed in clothes that made him look like the earth and the bushes. He is not a *peshmerga*, Major, because I never saw one of them with such a rifle or who dressed in such a way.'

He took the maps and the photographs back to his room. He fed Scout, and when he settled at the table the dog nestled against his feet. The Dragunov was laid on the table with the maps and photographs. It was, he reflected, the moment for which he had prepared himself through a military career of twenty-six long years. He had killed many men, but in battle the ultimate conflict of sniper against counter-sniper had always eluded him. Everything else he now stripped from his mind. It would be an elemental struggle for supremacy, himself against an expert. Alone in his room, with the dog's snoring to calm him, there was no admission in Aziz's mind that the man confronting him would best him.

It was not for glory, medals, the reward of money, for killing; it was the lure of a primitive struggle between two men for supremacy in the science of fieldcraft and the skill of marksmanship. He thanked his god for the opportunity.

The conflicts began in earnest before the attack. Meda wanted to lead the attack. Haquim insisted she stay with him, in the rear. Meda wanted a frontal assault. Haquim demanded they charge the right flank of the village. Meda wanted their own machine-gun to fire on the watchtowers. Haquim said the concentration of fire should be against the command post. Meda wanted Gus close to her, shooting in support of her dash towards the fences. Haquim told her that the marksman would decide where he placed himself.

The commentary came from Omar. It was painful to Gus. His carefully drawn plan of the village was laid on the ground between them, illuminated by a shaded torch. He thought everything Haquim said made sense, but Meda rejected it, as if governed by a wild obstinacy. When his suggestion was rejected, Haquim doggedly, fruitlessly, pursued it. It was just a damn waste of time, and Gus played no part in the running sore of their disputes – her arrogance against Haquim's experience.

'I know about war,' Haquim said, and Omar whispered it.

'You know about losing at war,' Meda said, and Omar giggled as he translated. 'The men follow me, not you . . .' There was a shout behind her, her name was called. She pushed herself up. 'I will lead. I will be the first to the fence, the first to the command post, and they will follow me.'

She disappeared into the darkness.

Gus and Haquim studied the plan. Gus sensed the anger of Haquim at the humiliation thrown on him by her. But he knew that the *mustashar* would not walk away from her, as he would not. They agreed the position to be taken by Gus and Omar, the angle of the machine-gun's fire, and the direction of the charge.

'And she will lead?' Gus asked heavily.

'What am I supposed to do? Chain her to a rock? Bind her legs? If she goes down, is hit, then everything for us is finished.' Haquim shrugged. 'What can I do?'

'I will watch for her, as best I can,' Gus said.

'As I will, as we all will, as best we can, as much as she will allow us.'

There was a growing murmur of voices behind them. Two pinpricks of light were advancing imperceptibly up the incline of the hill, and both took as a beacon the central guttering fire of their camp. Gus watched. It was because of her that the new men tramped across the black wastes of open ground, and came to them. The lights they carried lit their wild, bearded faces and their weapons glinted. They came as gliding, savage caravans in the night, carrying rifles, mortar tubes and ammunition boxes, the silver shimmer of knife blades at their belts. She walked towards them, and Gus saw the way that those at the front quickened their stride, while those at the rear ran to catch up. She held out her arms and the columns broke as they scattered to gather in front of her. They squatted down and she talked to them. They rippled their approval.

'What does she say?'

Haquim responded grimly, 'She says that, through their courage, the Kurdish people will find freedom. That they are the heirs of Salah al-Din Yusuf. And that mercy is shown to an enemy only by a man who is weak. She says the Kurds will not find their freedom before they have killed every Iraqi soldier in the country that is their own. She says . . .'

Gus walked away, turned his back on her.

He would be, and he knew it, tomorrow, a changed man – for ever changed.

All day the Israeli had listened to the radios as they sucked down the crypted and clear messages from Fifth Army headquarters to the forward echelon positions.

In the shadowlands of intelligence gathering, Isaac Cohen understood the need to recognize a crucial moment of advantage. The moment might be micro-brief. In a struggle lasting years, the moment of advantage might exist only for a few hours. Many times in a veteran's career with the Israeli Defence Force, then with the Mossad, the window of advantage had flickered open, sometimes to be exploited and sometimes ignored with heavy and enduring consequences. As a lieutenant in an armoured unit he had been pushed across the Canal in the Yom Kippur war when intelligence had recognized the advantage to be gained from hitting the hinge between the Egyptian Third and First armies. As an operating field agent of the Mossad, he had sat in on those endless debates as to the right time to eliminate activist leaders of the terrorist Hamas organization on the West Bank. Was the better advantage gained from killing the bomb-makers as soon as they were identified, or letting them run under surveillance in the hope of more names or locations surfacing? Once, it had been decided that a man should stay free, and the moment of advantage had been lost: a 10-kilo TNT bomb had killed 13 and wounded 170 more in a bloodbath at the Jerusalem food market. He was now in his isolated posting because of the failure of his superiors to recognize that a moment of advantage had passed. Everything was about advantage.

He believed now that such a moment existed. It was merely a question of identifying it. It was as though a stiletto had made a short but not fatal stab into the ribcage of an enemy. The knife could be turned – two hundred more men were moving forward, the radio intercepts told him – and then the hole would be larger. As the hole grew, as the stiletto was plunged deeper towards the vulnerable heart, so the risk to the enemy increased. But all that they had done was to send a master sniper from Baghdad. Why had a blocking force not been sent north? Why did the Fifth Army not respond to the threat and cauterize the wound?

He did not understand the reason – but he believed a moment of advantage now existed.

He sent a short message to Tel Aviv. In crisp language, he made a suggestion as to what he should do to exploit the moment.

He was fit for his age, but he still dreaded the prospect of a long night march. When the terse response came on the radio, he was already writing a letter to his wife that would be carried out on the next resupply helicopter. Permission was granted.

'Hi! You okay, Caspar?'

'Not too bad, Rusty.'

Caspar Reinholtz was a slave to punctuality. It was seven minutes to ten o'clock. He approved of the young man, who was early for his night shift. If it had been Bill or Luther, they'd have walked in with a half-minute to spare. He had just transmitted his report and the tiredness pulsed in waves across him. He doubted that he'd wander over to the mess where Bill and Luther would be socializing with the pilots and ground crew. He was not in the mood for USAF small-talk.

'Long day?'

'Long enough.'

'But was it a good day?'

'At best satisfactory.'

Caspar ran his hand through his cropped hair. The day, whatever it had been, had started at five, as the dawn sidled over the runways and bunkers of the Incerlik base where the USAF's F-16 Falcons shared space with Turkish aircraft, and the helicopter had lifted him off with four marines for close protection duty. A small bungalow compound, inside the USAF security perimeter, was the home base for the Agency team responsible for northern Iraq. Drinking beer with flies in the froth was about as satisfactory as running American interests in northern Iraq from over the Turkish border. They had flown to collect the fat cat from Arbīl, then on to pick up the second fat cat from Sulaymānīyah, then had headed up and high into the mountains for the scary flight into bandit country.

'You going to tell me?'

'Don't take it personal – same old problem – but it's a Need to Know.'

'That's not a difficulty, Caspar. You want some coffee?'

'I'd appreciate that.'

Rusty was big, strapping, a young man out of the University of California, Santa Barbara. He had an openness that was rare for Agency recruits, and seemed to take it to heart when information was not shared. He'd learn. Long ago, Caspar had learned all that anyone could teach him, and what he knew best was northern Iraq. It had been taught the hard way. He'd been there, first tour of duty, in 1974 – young, like Rusty, and keen – when the Agency, with Iranian and Israeli help, had armed the Kurds to go kick Baghdad's ass, but the diplomats had signed a treaty, the aid had stopped, and the reprisals of the Iraqi army against the Kurdish hill fighters would have made a less focused man weep and slip to his knees. Caspar had gone home to find new fields.

The second tour, he'd been back across the Turkish border in 1988 when Operation al-Anfal had punished the tribesmen, bombed, gassed and butchered them. Caspar had been posted away. When he'd returned in '91, he had been in time to set up the radio station that had broadcast the calls for the Kurds to rise up in armed open rebellion against Baghdad. They had, but the promised support hadn't come: the runways at Incerlik had stayed silent, and the retribution had been repeated.

Caspar had been called back to Langley. But the place was like a damn malarial microbe in his bloodstream. He had requested and badgered for a last time back there – a fourth tour – and he'd made it to the Agency team in Arbīl a month before the disaster when Saddam's tanks rolled over the ceasefire line and ruthlessly drove the Kurds north. He never spoke – not to colleagues, not to family, of the awfulness of their own escape from Arbīl, and what they'd left behind. He'd been at Incerlik ever since, and had five more months to go before they'd call him home a final time. The coffee had been cooking all through the evening as he'd written, encoded and transmitted his report.

'If you don't mind my asking, will it work?'

'What's that?'

'The plan, will it work?'

'I'm tired – sorry, I don't want to give offence here, Rusty. Look, there is a plan. There's lengths of twine that need binding together to make a rope that'll carry the plan. They're not together yet.'

They called the plan RECOIL. RECOIL, in the mind of the author of its name, Caspar Reinholtz, implied the release of a pressured spring of tempered steel with the force to drive back a seemingly immovable object. He was proud of that name. The pressured spring was rebellion, the immovable object was the regime in Baghdad. As station chief, he alone of the Agency team in Incerlik knew the importance of each of the lengths of twine that must be woven to make the rope.

'Can I ask you something?'

'I'm not promising to answer.'

'Did you see her?'

'Am I going to get some coffee? Yeah, OK, I saw her.'

The strands were a woman . . . an armoured formation . . . an action in Baghdad . . . a movement with momentum, pace and bluff. If one frayed, the load of the plan might not be carried. The woman was to kick-start it but each succeeding part of RECOIL was as integrally important, and it worried the shit out of him. He had never before met a young woman, the same age as his second daughter, who had made an impression of such devastating simplicity and confidence. All through the flight back, with the detours to drop off the fat cats, her face, her sweetness and her goddam arrogance had been locked in his mind. He was old, he had seen everything, he was labelled a cynical bastard by those who worked for him, and he'd wished to God, and been as sober as a baby, that he could have followed where she led. If he'd told his guards or the pilots or any of the young ones here what he thought, all of them would have called him a fucking lunatic.

'What's she like?'

'That's pushy, Rusty . . . Actually, she's remarkable. She —'

'Can she get to Kirkūk?'

It was the strand Rusty knew of. He was in total ignorance of the others.

'The coffee, please. Hey, she's a symbol. She gets men off their butts. She's a part of a big picture, no more and no less. Can she get to Kirkūk? I don't know. RECOIL goes further than Kirkūk. Quit the questions . . . What I will tell you, I saw her point man. You been to Fort Benning?'

'No – you want sugar or sweetener?'

'They do snipers there,' Caspar murmured. 'I saw her sniper. The chopper took a run over him. He was in the real camouflage gear and he'd a hell of a big shooter. She said he was important to her. They're going south into real shit, fucking fighting, against experienced tank units, artillery formations. That's before they get to Kirkūk, and she thinks one guy with a rifle is important. Hey, Rusty, don't ever believe good news comes out of this place. It doesn't, I know . . . Do you want to get me some coffee or do you want to get shipped home?'

He sat in his room and he heard Rusty whistling quietly to himself in the kitchen annexe. She was in his mind . . . and when he lost her he seemed only to see the bleak face of the man under the helicopter's flight path, wrapped in the camouflage smock, holding the rifle.

'Major Herbert Hesketh-Prichard had friends among the British aristocracy – that's the people with money and influence. Once he'd made the decision that the way to take on the German snipers was with snipers of our

141

own, he persuaded those friends to help him . . . Are you asleep?'

'No, Mr Gus. How did the friends help?'

'Lady Graham of Arran loaned him a five-times magnification telescope to take to France, and a fund set up by Lord Roberts bought more telescopes to be used by the observers alongside the snipers. Lord Lovat sent all his gamekeepers – the men who guided Lovat's friends into the mountains of Scotland to shoot deer – to the army because they were the best at stalking on the open slopes of the mountains.'

'As good as me, Mr Gus?'

'Of course not, Omar, no-one is as good as you, and no-one is as conceited as you. So shut up and listen. The best of Lord Lovat's men was a corporal, Donald Cameron, who was described as a "very good glassman". The observers spotted the targets for the snipers and protected them from patrols. When Major Hesketh-Prichard set up his school for snipers at Steenbecque in the Forest of Nieppe, he always trained snipers and observers alongside each other.'

'Not the school any more, Mr Gus. Tell me about the killing.'

'Tomorrow.' Gus lay back and stared at the stars. 'Tomorrow we'll talk about the killing.'

Chapter Six

Gus, after a long time watching the night sky, had finally drifted to the sleep he needed when he was shaken awake. He started up at the touch of Haquim's hand on his shoulder.

He heard the voices and blinked to see better. Omar was crouched protectively beside him and was holding his assault rifle as if Gus were threatened. Haquim kicked at Omar's ankle, drove him back, and pulled Gus to his feet.

A torch shone into Gus's face.

'Is this him? Is this the sniper?' The voice, deep and harsh with the Israeli–American accent, came from a shadowy, stocky man who was bent under a backpack.

Gus coughed out phlegm in his throat and spat it on the ground. 'Who needs to know?'

The shadow's breath clouded the chill air between them. The man came forward from a group, and as the men behind him followed, he waved them away dismissively. He reached Gus, poked his finger into Haquim's chest and pointed into the reaches of the darkness. Maybe he didn't see Omar, who was crouched down close to rocks.

The voice dropped. 'Are you the sniper?'

'Who are you?'

'At dawn you attack the Victory City of Darbantaq, yes?'

'Perhaps.'

'It is not often I step outside my front door. Less often I spend a night walking through these goddam hills. Put another way, it is something remarkable for me to have hiked this sort of distance when I could be tucked up in my cot. Isaac Cohen, who in the wisdom and generosity of the government of Israel is stationed in this fuck-awful place. I'm tired, I've twisted my ankle, I smoke too much, I have carried a load of tricks for you – can we talk?'

Instinctively, Gus reached out his hand and took the Israeli's. 'I'm Gus.'

'I have much to tell you, and I want to be back in my bed before dawn. Are you listening?'

'We have a *mustashar* and a leader. Should they not be listening?'

'Do you know nothing? First lesson here, trust no-body. They'll say what they think you want to hear. Believe nothing you are told, accept nothing you see. They are terminally divided and incapable of unity, just watch. You'll have a crowd with you going forward. If you have to go back you won't be able to run fast enough to keep up. So, in answer to your question, I'm only talking to you.'

'Why did you come?'

'To tell you about Darbantaq. If you're a sniper then you've reconnoitred the village . . .'

'Yes.'

'You saw the BMP personnel carriers?'

144

Gus hesitated. 'No.'

Cohen chuckled. 'Then it was worth my coming. You didn't circle the village. There are three BMPs in earth revetments behind the command post. All will be fitted with a 73mm 2A20 main armament, rate of fire at four rounds a minute. Also they will be mounted with a light machine-gun. Unless you can handle the BMPs you won't get near the place – and one of them will be fitted with thermal imaging . . .'

The Israeli had slung his backpack off his shoulders and gasped at the release from the weight. He rooted in a side pocket, produced a folded wad of papers and gave them to Gus. 'It's all here. I'd have thought a combat veteran would have known about BMPs.'

Gus said quietly, 'It's my first week in combat.'

'That's very funny. Your famous British sense of humour? This is perhaps not so funny – you should read it.'

The hands burrowed into the backpack, the fingers working fast. Gus watched. The olive-green dish was expanded to full size and a stubby antenna pulled out in the centre. Short cables were stretched to their maximum length and plugs slid into sockets in the box. Cohen threw a switch, a red light flashed and the dial's needle jumped, then he killed the power.

Cohen said, 'In the command post is an R-123M AFV radio that'll go back to a booster, then to battalion at Tarjil, then on a relay to the brigade HQ on the Sulaymānīyah–Baghdad crossroads, and ultimately to Fifth Army HQ in Kirkūk. This box will block an R-123M's transmissions, but it'll only work at one hundred and fifty metres. So you have to get to one hundred and fifty metres from their command post at Darbantaq, then you can put them off-air. There'll be no hero in a bunker giving a running commentary on the main assault, got me?'

'Yes.'

'It's what I came to give you.'

'Thank you. What do you call it?'

'It's just a box of tricks. You want a name for it? Try "Josephus". Josephus will do nicely. He died one thousand, nine hundred years ago, and he was a big man in the last Jewish revolt against the Romans. Josephus will work well for you . . . That was a joke, that you're really not a veteran?'

Gus said simply, 'I have never in my life done anything like this before, nor wanted to.'

Cohen reached out and his fingers caught Gus's cheek. He held it tight enough to hurt. 'You picked a bad place to learn. Your opposition knows about you and takes you seriously, which is not healthy news for a beginner . . . I sit on a mountain and I hear everything. They've sent a man from Baghdad for you.'

'Have they?'

'They have sent a master sniper to track you. He is Karim Aziz, a major, and they think he's one of their top guys.'

'Do they?'

'He's coming to track you and to kill you.'

Gus batted the fingers from his cheek. 'I hope you get back safely to where you came from, and I hope your ankle's better soon.'

Cohen said grimly, 'Sniper against sniper. Secure your front, secure your flank, secure your back. I'll listen for you, I'll hear each step he takes and you take, until he finds you or you find him . . . It's like something from

146

the intestines of history. I'll be listening, but I hope, and you'd better hope too, that your god watches for you.'

He heaved the backpack up onto his shoulders.

Gus watched the wavering, diminishing light from the Israeli's torch. When it was gone, he called Haquim forward and repeated everything he had been told about the box, Josephus, and the positioning of the BMP personnel carriers, but he said nothing of a man sent from Baghdad to track and kill him.

The cold was around him. In an hour he would go forward with Omar. He felt a suffocating sense of loneliness.

They sat in the cold dining room, at the table, and Ms Manning kept her outdoor coat on. On his pad, at the top of the blank page, Willet had written and underlined the word MINDSET.

'His grandfather told us nothing of this.'

'Well, he wouldn't, would he?'

After another early start, after another early pick-up by Ms Manning, they'd hammered at the door of the vicarage. Henry Peake had not been dressed, had told them firmly to wait. They'd sat in the car for fifteen minutes before being allowed inside. There were sounds of movement in the kitchen, but they were neither taken there, nor offered tea or coffee.

'I don't know – you tell me.'

'We're not responsible for our parentage and I am certainly not responsible for my father's prejudices.'

Henry Peake was a slimmer man than his father, and already more gaunt. He had little of the certainty that the old man in the bungalow behind the big house had shown. But he talked in response to the prodding

147

questions rattled at him by Ms Manning. 'You'll have to explain.'

He was lighting his third cigarette. He retched a cough, then launched. 'Gus's grandfather, my father, wouldn't have talked to you about his grandson's childhood. He didn't approve, you understand me? I was brought up in a service household. I made a crystal-clear decision, and Fiona was right with me on this, that Gus would not be reared as I had been. We let the child run. He was a free spirit. He wasn't hidebound by the diktat of meaningless traditions. It was only later, when my father needed Gus, that he quite shamelessly involved him in this nonsense about northern Iraq. It's where he is now, isn't it?'

They were in a sheep scrape Omar had found. The ground would have been weakened by years of rain, and then the sheep in the last summer, or the summer before, had used that weakness and with their bodies had insinuated a narrow cavity on the slope of the hill. The depth of the scrape was sufficient shelter from a summer squall for four or five sheep pressed close to each other, but was barely big enough for the boy and Gus. To use it and still be hidden by its lip of earth, the two were huddled close against each other.

In the scrape Gus could not take his usual firing position with his legs splayed out behind him. He used the Hawkins position, lying sideways with his upper body twisted so that he could aim out to the extreme left. It was neither comfortable nor satisfactory, but the rule of a marksman was to accept the conditions as he found them. Each time Omar wriggled, the movement reverberated through Gus's body and disturbed his aim, and each time he kneed hard against the back of the boy's legs and hoped he felt it.

In front of Gus, magnified through the telescopic sight, was the Victory City of Darbantaq. He could see the upper casings and the mounted guns on the BMPs behind their earthen walls, women starting to form a queue at a building close to the command post, the machine-gun crew on the roof of the command post, men fussing around their penned goats and sheep beside their concrete homes, soldiers shivering in the watchtowers, and children playing with a deflated football behind the wire.

Behind him and to his right, waiting on his first shot, were four hundred *peshmerga* men, and Meda. They would be crouched, nervous and fidgeting, holding tight to their weapons, waiting for the signal of his first shot.

The boy was more restless, his movements more frequent. Gus could not fault the way he had been led forward, partly at a crouch, and then at the leopard crawl. The last three hundred yards down the slope had taken them a full hour, scraping the ground in the half-light, because the Israeli had said one of the personnel carriers had thermal imaging, and if they were not flat to the ground they would make a signature. The boy had done well but now shifted more often as he raked a greater arc of ground with the telescope.

'Our approach was good, Omar,' Gus whispered, 'but now we must be patient.'

'Then the chance comes to kill them, Mr Gus.'

'Where did you learn to stalk?'

'Going into Iraqi camps, and going past the guards into the compounds of the charities, to take—'

149

'To *steal*, Omar.' Gus laughed soundlessly, and his eye never left the scope's lens, which covered the entrance to the command post.

'It is necessary to live, Mr Gus. And to live I have to take.'

She had ignored the father's question. 'Didn't his grandfather teach him to shoot?'

'God, no. He was into partridges and pheasants, semi-tame birds being driven towards the guns – he calls it sport, I call it murder.'

'Did you teach him to shoot?'

'Never been in the slightest bit interested. It's all down to Harry Billings, a rogue who lived in the village, dead now, and no tears shed. We'd sent Gus away to school, of course, but he was a loner, didn't mix well, and a bit of an under-achiever. I'd hoped that boarding school would make him more sociable. It didn't. When he was home on holiday we hardly saw him. He virtually lived with Billings, just came home late at night to sleep, and was gone again at first light. His grandfather alternately said Billings should be horsewhipped or locked up, never seemed quite sure of the remedy.'

'What was the nature of Mr Billings' roguishness?'

'Poacher.'

'I beg your pardon?'

A grin creased Willet's face, which she would not have seen. He knew from her monologues in the car that Ms Manning lived in Islington, that her parents were also close by in north London, that she had been to local schools and to university down a bus route. She was an urban person: she would know damn all of a country poacher's life. His pen was poised.

'A low-life ignorant poacher. Game birds, rabbits, the occasional deer. It wasn't all illegal, there's a big area of common ground up to the north of the village where they could shoot, but it was decidedly criminal when they were on the Vatchery estate. They were never caught by the gamekeeper there, though not for want of trying. That man used to sit half the night outside the Billings house waiting for the old devil to creep home with the pheasants or a fallow deer carcass. There was a bond between that uncouth man who'd not an iota of education or ambition and my son – I have to say it, a much closer bond than ever existed between Gus and his mother and me. Billings had a son, younger than Gus, a proper little tearaway, quite unsuitable company . . . Anyway, Billings was finally arrested and given three months inside by the bench. The police stopped him with a van full of pheasants. At the time I thanked God that Gus was away at school. When he was released the whole dreadful family moved away, good riddance, never heard of again. You give freedom to a youngster and hope common sense prevails. Sadly, parents are not always rewarded.'

He had been writing hard, taking a note that was almost verbatim. For Willet, it was as if a small light illuminated the darkness. He looked up. 'What was the ultimate for your son, Mr Peake, when he was with Billings?'

'A clean shot. I was once bawling him out, the way fathers do with teenage sons – he'd come home quite filthy from the fields and ditches, and we'd guests in for drinks. His response, as if he were talking to an idiot, was "You have to be prepared to lie up, Dad, so's you get a clean shot under your own terms. Otherwise all you've done is wound a rabbit, break a pigeon's wing. The worst sound in the world is a rabbit in pain, screaming, when you can't reach it, hurt because you rushed your shot, Dad. It has to be a good kill." I had the impression that the hunting was more important to him than the slaughter, though I doubt that applied to Billings.'

'Is that all there is?' Ms Manning was already bored and lost.

"Fraid so. What else? Gus left school with pretty average grades, and I managed to pull some strings, got him into a haulage firm in Guildford. I did business with them and was owed favours. He's been there ever since. I can only talk about his youth because we hardly see him, these days . . . What do I tell my wife?'

'Your problem, Mr Peake, not mine,' she said, without charity.

'What's he doing there? Is he driving a relief lorry?'

'He's gone to fight, Mr Peake,' she intoned.

'But that's a war zone . . .' The man's mouth gaped.

Gus saw the target. He came slowly towards the command post. His own estimate of the distance was 750 yards, and the binoculars confirmed it at 741. There was a short line of soldiers at attention. A moment before, as Gus had done a fast scan with the binoculars, the crew on the roof with the machine-gun had closed up behind their weapon, and the soldiers in the watchtower ducked below their sandbag parapets. The T-junction of the reticule in his 'scope sight was on the target. He would fire at the next moment that his breath was steadied.

'Watch the shot, Omar. Don't move, not a fraction, just watch the shot.'

Gus breathed deeply, then slowly, so slowly, began to empty his lungs. When they were emptied he would relax, then fire. The smoke curled from the homes of the villagers, there was no new adjustment to make for the slight wind's strength. Above the chest of the target were the gold insignia of rank on the target's shoulders.

'No.'

'What?' Gus hissed.

'No. Don't.'

Gus breathed again, his finger was inside the trigger guard.

'Why not?'

'It is not the officer.'

'He has the rank.'

'No, Mr Gus. The soldiers are laughing at him.'

Gus stared through the 'scope. Behind the target figure, level with the insignia on the target's shoulder, a soldier grinned and Gus saw the flash of his teeth, and another man near to him laughing.

'It is not the officer, it is a pretend. They know about you, trick you. They would not dare to laugh at their officer.'

The breath seeped from Gus's body. He eased his finger off the trigger. He felt flattened by the simplicity of the trap set for him. Without the boy, he would have walked into it, fired into it. At that moment he saw his own importance. The life of a soldier, with a family and with a mother, was to be snuffed out so that his own life could be taken.

'Thank you, Omar.'

'It was easy to see the trick – yes, Mr Gus?'

He kneed the boy savagely. The sun crawled up

153

behind him, over the ridge where the attack force lay and waited on him.

'Correct, Mr Peake. Maybe you should chat it out with your father as to why your son is currently in a war zone. Good day.'

She was on her feet. Willet had filled the page below the heading of MINDSET. He put the pad into his briefcase. There were no handshakes at the door. Momentarily Willet saw a woman's face at the kitchen door, grey, lined and harassed. He wouldn't have known what to say to her that might have been of any comfort. The door slammed shut behind them.

They walked to the car.

'What a bloody fool,' she said.

'Who?'

'Peake, of course.'

'Which Peake?'

'The son, that idiot.'

'Why?'

'For doing what he's done – for going where he's gone.'

Willet felt the anger brimming in his mind. 'The last weekend you had time off, what did you do? Where did you go?'

'Actually, I was in Snowdonia, with a group rebuilding footpaths for the National Trust. We were all volunteers.'

Through gritted teeth, Willet said pleasantly, 'It must have seemed, Ms Manning, important. I suppose rebuilding a footpath is about as important as fighting for the freedom of a subjugated people in a war zone.'

She looked at him curiously. 'Are you all right?'

He sat with his head down, his chin on his chest. 'I'm fine – but what about him?'

'The wind's changed.'

'He is coming.'

Gus hissed venomously, 'You didn't tell me, it's veered.'

Omar persisted shrilly, 'The officer is coming.'

'The wind has moved from south-west-south to west-south-west – you've got to warn me about this sort of thing.'

'Do you want to know about the wind or the officer?'

'Both.'

The panic consumed him.

The wind had come up from gentle to moderate strength. A flag on the Stickledown Range would have eased clear of the pole and lethargically flapped free. Its direction had shifted from No Value to Half Value. On that range he could have waited, settled, then tapped into the calculator on the mat beside him and computed whether to alter the windage turret on the 'scope by a full click, or by half a click, or whether to aim off from the centre of the target's V-Bull. Gus saw the officer. There were no insignia on his shoulder but men straightened to attention as he passed. He was within half a dozen feet of the entrance door to the command post and walking. There was no time to settle or make the necessary calculations. He aimed off, his mind racing for an answer to the equation, to compensate for the fresher wind and for the brisk stride of the officer.

'Watch the shot's fall,' Gus whispered.

But the officer, wide-chested, in fatigues, would

pause at the jamb of the command post's door, and that, too, must go into the equation.

Gus fired. The moment that the recoil hammered into his shoulder, he knew that the breath pattern was wrong, and that he'd squeezed too fast on the trigger. The rifle's compensator attachment at the barrel end kept the 'scope sight steady. He saw the hazed shapes of single waving grass stems and the flattening climb of the smoke columns, and the eddy of the air disturbed by the bullet's track, and then he lost the flight.

The bullet would run for more than one and a half seconds. Its trajectory curve would take it to an apex of a fraction more than four feet above the aim point before the sliding fall. The flight, to Gus, was endless.

The target, the officer, at the door of the command post had turned and was issuing an instruction, jabbing with a finger for emphasis. Then he stood as if frozen.

Omar piped, 'Miss. One metre to the right. Hit the wall. Miss.'

Gus slid the bolt back, eased out the wasted bullet. They were all rooted to the ground. It was what he had been told. Men stood statue still in the seconds after a bullet had been fired and had missed them. But that moment would pass. It would pass before he had the chance to breathe in, breathe out, and use the respiratory pause. He locked the aim. His mind made the adjustment on intuition and instinct. He fired a second shot. A soldier dived to the ground. A second cowered, another fell to his knees, as if the ice of the tableau had melted. The officer's jabbing finger was retracted and he seemed to be twisting his hips to turn for safety.

Gus saw him spin, one arm whipped high in the air. He saw the shock on his target's face and watched him

156

pirouette, fall. The officer was on his back and his legs kicked in the air. No-one came to his aid, and across the open ground came the faint whinnying cry of his scream.

He slid back the bolt, ejected the cartridge case. He tried to steady the post-shoot shake in his hands. He loathed himself for his failure to make a good, clean kill and started to analyse the first total failure and the second partial failure, as he had been instructed. And with the analysis came the calm . . . He had asked too much of the boy, he had not allowed enough for the wind, he had not reckoned on the pace of the officer's walk, and he would think about it some more in the evening.

Gus said evenly, 'The old stalkers in Scotland knew it. They'd have a guest fire at a stag and miss, and the stag always stays exactly still for two or three seconds. Then it runs. But, if it is winged, it runs immediately, until the wound kills it. I was lucky with that second shot.'

The machine-gun had opened up behind him and to his right, the tracer rounds arced across the dead ground, scattering little chasing patterns. The view through the 'scope was a blurred, fluid mess as he searched to find the position on the roof of the command post. And behind him he heard the whooping roar as the line of men began their charge.

A soldier yelled his name, waved frantically for him.

Major Karim Aziz was walking the dog alongside the edge of the high wire fence.

He heard his name and ran towards the soldier. The dog at his heel, he was led to the communications bunker.

The brigadier was already there, the general bursting in a minute after him.

He stood at the central map table and listened. The words that came blurted over the loudspeakers, high on the wall, were interspersed with break-up and howl.

'. . . The captain is hit . . . Yes, Corporal Ahmad wore the captain's coat, but was not shot at . . . Captain Kifaar is hit, is not dead, but they cannot bring a medical orderly to him. There is a general attack. We are waiting for Lieutenant Muhammad to take the place of Captain Kifaar in the command post.'

The Victory City at Quadir Beg broke across the transmission – their water tanker was late. When could they expect it?

The Victory City at Keshdan reported the failure of the single-stage air filtration system of a BMP. Could a qualified engineer accompany the next resupply column with a replacement?

'Get those arseholes off the air,' the general shouted.

'. . . There is heavy shooting from the front . . . There are casualties . . . Lieutenant Muhammad has now reached the command post . . . They are led by a woman. She is with their forward force. The machine-gun fires at her, no hit yet, she is protected . . . The medical orderly has not come to the command post to treat Captain Kifaar. The captain is close to death. Are units advancing to help us? In God's name, send us help.'

Aziz asked quietly, 'Please, is it possible to know the circumstances of Captain Kifaar's wounding? It would be useful for me.'

The question was relayed.

'. . . A very long shot, twice. The second shot hit him. We must have help. They are near to us . . . No-one

158

knows where the shot came from. Is help on its way?'

Over the loudspeaker came the sounds, staccato, of the firing. But Aziz had been given the answer he had expected and seemed not to hear the deep, distorted terror of the men under fire.

Gus had hit a man who ran to the nearest of the personnel carriers. He had missed another who made a snaky crawl to follow him but had put the next shot right through the gunport of the command post. A fuel drum, close to the earth walls for the personnel carriers, had caught fire and the deep red blaze of the incendiary threw a lowering pall of smoke across much of the village, which ebbed towards the fence. Between gusts of wind, gaps appeared in the grey-black wall of the smoke, and he caught fleeting glimpses of the machine-gun crew on the roof.

It was a scene of hell. Against him the boy was shivering with excitement.

She was at the front of the long, straggling line approaching the fence. She had no fear.

Suddenly, as if a man had punched him, came the realization of her vulnerability. He saw her turn and face the line of crouched men behind her, and give an imperious wave that they should follow.

Gus saw the machine-gun traverse towards her, then the smoke drifted and thickened. The tracers poked through the cloud, firing at random, searching for her. Haquim was behind her, running awkwardly over the rough ground and hugging the metal box to his chest. The hellish cauldron was a small pocket of life and death, in which she stood and demanded that the *peshmerga* follow.

'Watch for the fall,' Gus snapped.

The wind was stronger: it tugged at the grass and wafted the smoke. He waited for the chance. She was a hundred yards from the fence. He had gone to eight clicks on the windage turret, but the wall of smoke was solid and he could not see through it. The tracers swarmed around her.

The smoke dissipated without warning.

He was gazing through the 'scope at the machine-gun crew. Three choices: the man who called the aim and was crouched at the back, puffing at a cigarette clamped between his lips; the one who fed the belt and whose helmet strap was undone and hung loosely against his cheek; or the one who pulled the trigger?

'She's hit,' the boy gasped. 'She has fallen.'

Gus fired, once, twice, a third shot. The smoke closed around his view of the target. He heaved back the bolt, squeezed the trigger again, and again, heard the empty scrape of the action and knew that his magazine was empty.

'You have them, Mr Gus.'

He choked. 'Does it matter?'

There was a stillness around him, as if the pace and clamour of the world had stopped. It was the silence of remembrance.

'The witch is down.'

Around Aziz there was a growl of pleasure, and the brigadier slapped his clenched fist into the other palm.

The operations officer lifted the microphone to his mouth and yelled at it, 'Are the BMPs now engaged? Come on, man, what is happening there?'

The voice came back at them, echoed down on them.

'They cannot reach them. There is a marksman. There is very great difficulty . . . Our machine-gun, the main defence, they are all dead, it is the marksman . . . Is help coming? Wait . . .'

Aziz felt a detached distaste for such confusion. It had no part in the warfare he practised. The chaotic noise was alien to him. He was at ease with himself, he had learned what he had wanted to know. He had no sympathy for the beleaguered soldiers: they were only a testing ground for his enemy. He yearned to be alone with his Dragunov and his dog, on a hillside, pitting himself against a worthwhile adversary.

'She's up . . . the witch is up. She's—'

The voice was lost in a sea of static.

For several minutes the technicians tried to regain the link, to break the power of the jamming equipment, but the beating pulse of the garrison was gone.

He had seen the little clutch of men around her, had seen them drag her to her feet. She had stood for a moment, dazed, had then swayed, would have fallen again if they had not held her. She had pushed them away. He had lost her in the wall of smoke, and had reloaded five bullets in the magazine. When he had looked again through the sight, she was close to the perimeter wire, a dark stain on her thigh.

Gus watched. She was driving the men over the wire. They reached up and shredded their hands on the coiled barbs at the top. She was grabbing at those who followed, pitching them forward or helping to lift them. Sometimes her face was screwed tight in pain, and each time she ducked her head so that nobody could see. A man threw his heavy leather coat onto the coils, and others lifted her, pushing her feet so that she straddled the wire. More caught her as she fell on the far side.

His body slackened and he eased his hands from the rifle. The fighting was hand to hand, body to body. Like swarms of ants, the *peshmerga* fanned out to hunt down the last defenders. He saw a soldier emerge from a building holding high a white strip of torn sheet, before crumpling, his blood spattered across on the whiteness. Two more were running, only to be engulfed by the mob. He saw a soldier dragged from a bunker and the flash of knives. One of the BMPs coughed exhaust fumes and drove at speed towards the gate, crashed through it, then swerved into a ditch.

There was nothing more for Gus to fire at. He started to ease himself clear of the hiding place then turned and methodically started to pack away his rifle.

She was on the roof of the command post now, strutting her triumph.

'Come on, Mr Gus. If we do not hurry, the killing will be finished.'

It was always the same in every communications bunker behind the lines when contact was lost with a forward position. The stunned quiet as if, buried tomblike in the bunker, each man considered the last seconds of a garrison's life. Then there was shuffling movement and hushed voices to show that the living lived and the dead were abandoned. The general clapped his hands for attention and barked out a series of orders: the battalion force at Tarjil should be alerted and should go to maximum readiness; brigade at the crossroads of the Sulaymānīyah and Baghdad routes should be warned; a situation report should be prepared for his approval before it was despatched to the Defence Ministry with copies to the al-Rashid command and the Abbasio Palace. Quiet conversation was followed by banter, then noisy laughter.

At the back of the bunker, away from the map table, Major Aziz noted that no order had been given for the advance into the hills of a column of tanks and armoured personnel carriers, either from Fifth Army headquarters or from brigade at the crossroads. The lack of that order at first confused him, but then it slipped back in the heap of his own priorities.

His was a sense of private, covert exhilaration.

He slapped his thigh, a gesture for the dog, slipped from the bunker and climbed the steps to the freshness of the morning air. With no thought for the men of a defeated garrison, he went to his quarters to ready his gear. His time was coming.

When there was no more killing to be done Gus had brought Omar down to the village.

Near to the gate they reached Haquim packing away the cables of the box. Gus nodded abruptly to the *mustashar*, should have congratulated him, and did not, should have been congratulated for his shooting, and was not. He was learning. It was not Stickledown Range: Jenkins wasn't there to slap him on the back. He walked through the gate, close to where a thick leather coat was hanging, ripped, from the top of the wire. He passed a sentry, whose body lay stupidly over a low wall of sandbags.

In the sheep scrape he had been protected from what he now saw.

He walked past the homes built of concrete blocks,

Omar following. Some were on fire, some smouldered, some were pocked with bullet-holes. He saw dazed mothers walking aimlessly, holding their babies. One mother carried a bundle from which only a single tiny foot protruded at a broken angle. Another sat in front of the fractured door of her home and rocked in a chilling grief. In front of her were the corpses of two children.

Away to his right were the fathers and adult sons. Some were already digging the pit; some came to join them with spades hoisted on their shoulders. Near by was a toppled corner watch-tower, half of the body of the fallen sentry covered by it.

There was a trail for Gus to follow through the village: the trail of her voice. It led him along a sporadic line of death, towards the command post. The soldiers' bodies had been robbed of everything of value: pockets had been ripped open, chains torn from their throats, their wallets discarded with the money gone and the photographs of their loved ones stamped into the dirt. She was on the roof, hectoring the men of the *peshmerga*, and he did not have the stomach to tell Omar to translate. He didn't need to. He saw the dried blood on the thigh of her combat trousers. There were many corpses near the command post's door, as if it had been a final rallying-point when the *peshmerga* had come over the perimeter fence.

On the ground in front of his boots, by the entrance to the command post, the face of the officer was barely related to the face he had seen through the 'scope. The vomit rose in Gus's chest. The first of the *peshmerga* to reach him had not finished the officer's life with a clinical head shot, but had slit his throat. Gus went into the command post and skirted through the detritus of broken tables and upturned chairs, stepped over the bodies, passed a man whose dead fingers were locked on the dials of the radio, and climbed the ladder to the roof.

He had his back to her. Behind him was the pride of her voice. With slow steps, he trudged to the corner where the machine-gun was sighted, and looked away over the bare ground towards the hillside, searching it for the sheep scrape. He could not find it. The boy had chosen well.

In the machine-gun nest, one man lay with the cigarette still clamped between his teeth. The others were more messy in death. On each was a narrow entry wound at the front and a larger wound at the back.

Haquim had crept up behind him. 'This is not target shooting, it is war. For you it is an intellectual puzzle of distance and wind, the steadiness of your hand, and the quality of your ammunition. To us it is war. For you it is using your very great skills to combat technical difficulties. To us it is survival . . . No matter, you shot well.'

Haquim had said everything Gus had thought as he stood on the flat roof with her voice dinning in his ears. He turned away. On the far side of the camp, where the personnel carrier had battered a path for its flight, he saw a clutch of bodies, where men had entertained a last, hopeless belief in escape.

'We have to harden you, Mr Peake. If you are not hardened then you will be like them, dead. Do not criticize us for behaving as barbarians would. It is what they do to us, what we have learned from them. The month that you saw Meda in the mountains nine years ago, with a hundred thousand others, starving, cold, without shelter, I held a pass with the men of *agha* Bekir that allowed them time for flight. We retreated rock by rock, stone by stone, to make time, and we could not take our wounded with us. We left them to the mercy of their soldiers. You don't want me to tell you what we found when we came back. It is war.'

'Is she hurt?'

Haquim snapped, 'Of course she is hurt.'

'Has she had treatment?'

'Mr Peake, twenty of our men are dead, but twice that number are wounded and cannot walk as she can. There are many people from the village who are hurt – and there are their dead. She is the inspiration. Can she go to the front of the queue and demand, because of her importance, that her wound is treated? If she had not risen when she was hit the attack would have failed. If the men do not believe she can go forward, the advance is finished. She cannot show weakness. It is the price she must pay.'

Gus climbed down the ladder from the roof, went out through the command-post door and past the body of the officer. He walked briskly around the queue of *peshmerga* and villagers, some standing, some sitting and others just lying in the mud, silent or crying in their pain. He headed away from the grave-pit, and away from the last bodies. Her voice behind him was faint. He squatted down in the dirt, his back to the village, and stared out through the wire at the slope of the hills, and the mountain crests.

From behind him, Omar asked, 'Do you think, Mr Gus, he is there, searching for you?'

*　　*　　*

166

The brigadier asked him where he was going. Major Aziz shrugged, pointed vaguely to the hills beyond the flame. Because he had been sent from Baghdad on the orders of the Estikhabarat, he did not have to explain himself. He walked out of the bunker; it perplexed him that reinforcements had not yet been sent, that the great lines of tanks and personnel carriers still rested in idle lines. It irritated him more that he could not recall where, or when, he had met the brigadier, but his mind was too clogged with details of his task for him to pursue it.

Behind him, in his bare quarters, on the floor underneath the smiling photograph of his President, he left the polished box and the folded rug on which the dog had slept. On the neatly made bed he had laid out all the spare clothes that had filled his backpack when he had flown north, and the pouch with his razor and toothpaste. On the chest beside the bed was the leather frame that held the pictures of his wife and his sons. He put his wedding ring and the birthday ring beside the frame.

He walked to the jeep and the driver started the engine. Aziz sat beside him, the Dragunov across his legs and the dog beside his feet. In the backpack, stripped down to necessities, were spare ammunition, his telescope, a half-loaf of bread, a quarter-kilo of cheese, his half-filled water bottle, dried biscuits for the dog, what he called the Dennison suit, maps and a folder of aerial photographs. He ruffled the fur at the dog's collar, saw the pleasure on its face and felt the beat of its cropped tail against his boots.

The jeep drove away from Kirkūk, and passed through the brigade formation at the crossroads for

Sulaymānīyah and Baghdad, climbing towards the town of Tarjil. It was as if he were coming home.

'You know what? It's my last bloody war zone – thank God.'

Dean thought it was the fourth time that night Mike had made that promise, Gretchen reckoned it was at least the fifth. A week of evenings together in the ground-floor bar of the Hotel Malkoc, and the story that had brought them to Diyarbakir was still beyond reach. The whisper was that the spring thaw would provide an opportunity for Saddam Hussein to advance again into northern Iraq. But they were in Turkey, and the border was closed.

'Only war zone I've found is the goddam bathroom. "As dusk fell tonight, a vista of carnage and destruction was witnessed by your correspondent. Under a flickering light I surveyed, quote, scenes reminiscent of the worst horrors of the French revolution, end quote, in which no prisoners had been taken. After a good stamping session, I counted the corpses on my bathroom floor of forty-three cockroaches, their lives taken in the prime . . ."' Dean was a roving reporter for a Baltimore paper and had covered every substantial conflagration in the region over the last seventeen years.

'That's bollocks.' Mike was slumped in a rattan chair, swatting at flies and passably drunk. His Turkish cameraman was in the old city hunting women. Mike was a veteran reporter for the BBC, and was in the fast decline towards retirement.

'You got a better war zone?' Dean grinned.

'Did you get on air tonight, Mike?' Gretchen was conciliatory. She was forty, going on fifty, and worked for the *Der Spiegel* group out of Frankfurt. She was neither a threat nor an attraction to them. At the start of every assignment that brought them together she told them how she missed home and the company of her friend, Anneliese. She dressed like them: chukka boots, trousers with too many zip pockets, open-necked shirts showing their chests, safari tops with loops for pens.

'No. I am not on the air tonight. I *might* get a showing on breakfast tomorrow, but I'm not holding my breath. What about you, Dean?'

'Thank you for your kind consideration. I was dropped – "pressure of space". Gretchen, how'd they take your feature?'

'Took it, probably already used it – to clean the lavatory. I am "on hold pending a peg".'

Mike and his cameraman had tried to film the Turkish army in the streets of Diyarbakir, and been swamped by plain-clothes security men. Dean had filed on the scandal of the decay of the city's medieval mosques. Gretchen had written six thousand words on child labour in the clothing sweat factories. They had all tried to justify their existence as they waited for the permission that didn't come to cross the border that remained resolutely closed. Northern Iraq was near and unreachable.

'If I was to use the word "introverted", and then the word "self-obsessed", who would I be talking about?' Mike finished his drink and slapped the glass down on the table for the waiter's attention.

'You would, of course, be talking about our esteemed editors.'

'It's my last war zone.'

'Fifth time.'

169

'Wrong, sixth, easy.'

'Last war zone – fuck you two – if I ever get to it, *if* – because my loved and admired editor is short on interest.'

'Seem to have heard that record played somewhere before. "Sorry, Dean, but it's the stock-market that's playing big right now."'

Mike banged his glass down again, louder, harder. '"Sorry, mate, but we really need something that'll hook the viewer, like a celebrity visit – that's if you're unable to give us combat footage. Has to be an angle, Mike." Problem is, I shot my mouth off, told them the tanks were going to roll . . . and I haven't heard that Julia Roberts is arriving with an orang-utan, or Goldie Hawn up an elephant.'

'You guys are joking.'

'Or, Gretchen, we would cry,' Dean said.

She persisted. 'It is serious. Nobody cares back home. The editors tell it as it is. We believe that people at home are interested, and troubled, by the world outside their front door. We are old-fashioned, we are not "new". When I go home, my neighbours are polite and ask where I have been. I tell them I have travelled to Somalia or Iran or Sudan, where people are suffering, and they are embarrassed . . .'

'There is no technology to titillate, no smart-bomb videos, no cyber war. That's why interest is spread thin. Doesn't faze me – my last time, thank God . . .'

'And on he goes.'

'Fuck you both. Then I'm off to grow roses and sail a boat – and I will be, I promise faithfully, an anecdote-free zone. Not that anybody would listen.'

'I don't understand why people don't care. In affluent

societies, with safe lives, there is a duty of caring.'

Mike thought she was always saddest when she was earnest. 'Forget it, Gretchen. Just enjoy the beer, the expenses, and the dazzling brilliance of the company around you.'

Dean said, 'We're all in the same shit, but attacking it separately. I don't usually share.'

Mike was twisting and semaphoring to the waiter. 'When it's sharing your money you've stitched-up pockets.'

'No way I'd share if I had a half-chance of screwing you deadbeats. I'm sharing because I can't, as you can't, get across that border.' His voice had dropped, more from habit than the proximity of the Turkish plain-clothes police at a nearby table with their glasses of orange juice. 'I was talking to one of the Turk lorry drivers who goes across, runs food loads for the UN. I offered him five hundred bucks to take me with him.'

'You tricky bastard.'

'You'd have left us here?'

'Damned right I would. Didn't do me any good. You know what he said, big bastard with no teeth? He asked me how I knew he wouldn't drop me off on a God-awful lonely road where an Iraqi agent could take good care of me and give me a lift all the way to Baghdad. He said he'd get ten thousand dollars as bounty for an American illegal – be the same for a Britisher. Sorry, it'd be less for a German lady. Kind of nixed the negotiation.'

'Is this story going anywhere? If it isn't I'm off to force our bloody order down little Peach-bottom's throat.'

'He said there was a rumour of fighting down south on the ceasefire line.'

171

'There's always that rumour.' Gretchen scratched at her armpit.

'This afternoon he said a Kurdish army was being led south by a woman.'

Mike laughed loud. 'Are you winding me up?'

'A *young* woman, good-looking, with tits and an ass.'

'Jesus, I wish I believed you.'

'Why not a woman?' Gretchen scowled. 'Why should a woman not lead an army? Why cannot men be led by a woman?'

Mike said solemnly, 'Because it's Kurdistan, lovely lady, because this is the Stone Age. Because women are in the home to cook, clean and open their legs on a Saturday night. I'd lead the bulletin, might even get a special out of it.'

Gretchen laughed. 'I'd get the cover and ten pages inside.'

Dean stood. 'After a lifetime of alcohol abuse, Mike, you are a total fucking failure at ordering drinks. You want something in this life, you have to do it yourself.'

'Hey, it's just a wet dream, because the border's closed. What a way to go out from the last war zone. So, no Pulitzers for you.' Mike caught the American's arm and mimicked his accent. '"As dusk fell tonight over a vista of carnage and destruction, your correspondent stood beside the newest general to confront the awesome power of Saddam Hussein. She is a woman of soft beauty, who said her hero was the Duke of Wellington . . ."'

'Wrong . . . Schwartzkopf – no question.'

'I'd love to think it's true – two brandies, one straight Scotch, doubles. Go on, hurry up, you try and get some action here. A woman, leading an army, now that would be some story . . .'

In the quiet of the night, she came to the place by the wire where Gus sat.

'The best tale in Major Herbert Hesketh-Prichard's book is about the cat. There was a German trench that was thought to be disused, but this lieutenant from the Royal Warwickshire Regiment – with his telescope – saw the cat sunning itself.'

'He's asleep, Gus.' There was the tinkle of her quiet laughter. 'I think the cat will have to keep until tomorrow.'

He had known the boy was asleep. He was telling the story for himself, for comfort.

She sat close to him. He put his arm lightly around her shoulder and remembered how he had felt when the boy had told him she was down.

Chapter Seven

'Without your grandfather, his friendship for my grandfather, I would be a peasant.'

'Has your wound been treated?'

'Without his books I would not be able to read. I
would be in a village with children, animals, a small
field and a man – and I would have nothing.'

'Stop talking for a moment and answer me. Has
anyone looked at your wound?'

The night was around them, and the quiet. The scant
moon's light shimmered on the wire of the fence in front
of them. Gus held her shoulder loosely, as if she were a
sister or a loved cousin. At home he had neither. He
smelt the stale sweat of her body and the dankness of her
clothes. No radios played behind them, and he heard no
voices. Gus thought the village was stilled by mourning
and exhaustion.

'I know from the books, Gus, of the workings of the
engine of a Hastings aircraft of Transport Command
and the armaments carried by a Vampire jet bomber. I
do not think that many peasant women have such
knowledge. I know the history of the Peninsula war,
and the campaign of the British in North Africa. I know

174

of the lives of Montgomery and Haig, Kitchener and Wellington, and why William won at Hastings, Henry at Agincourt. I read the books well that your grandfather gave to my grandfather. How could I be a peasant?'

'If you're wounded, it must be looked at and treated.'

'How could I work in the fields, clean children, cook, watch goats and sheep, when I have read the many books given to Hoyshar? I think it was destiny, Gus.'

'It has to be looked at.'

'I felt the weakness when I fell. It was God's mercy that very few of the men saw I was hit. If they know I am hurt, believe I cannot go forward, they will be gone by the morning. It would be the end of the destiny. Do you not understand, Gus? I cannot go for treatment where the wound is seen.'

He asked quietly, a murmur in her ear, 'Will you allow me to look at the wound?'

'But you would not tell? You must not . . .'

There had been a fierceness in her voice when she had spoken of destiny. When she spoke of the wound there was, Gus recognized it, a timid slightness about her. The wound made her young, frightened. He understood. Destiny would carry forward the cold, hard, cruel men of the *peshmerga* – the pain of the wound and her fear would cause them to go. If she could not go forward then he, himself, would turn. He would go back to his grandfather, back to Meg, back to Stickledown Range, back to the offices of Davies and Sons; he sensed the burden she carried.

Gus said, 'I'm sorry, I know very little about medical treatment. I'll do what I can.'

'But you won't tell?'

'I promise.'

He slipped his arm from her shoulder and walked across the dead, darkened ground between the wire and the homes of concrete blocks. He stumbled against the carcass of a dead sheep, sloshed in the mud of a sewer, moved past the low houses where muted lights burned. He went into the command post, where Haquim was crouched over the captured maps. He told Haquim what he wanted, and saw anguish crease the face of the fighter, ageing him.

Haquim stood awkwardly, as if the pain had settled again on his old wound, and was gone. If her injury was serious, if she was living on borrowed time, it was all finished.

Gus sat amongst the dark debris of the command post. All finished, for nothing . . . The minutes slipped by. He would return home and the one thing in his life that had seemed to him to be important would have been dogged by failure. He would carry that failure to his grave. Haquim returned.

Gus carried the saucepan of boiled water, the sealed field dressing, the small wad of cotton wool, the narrow roll of bandage gauze and the torch out into the night.

He set down the torch, knelt beside her, and did what no man had done. His fingers trembled as he reached under her tunic, unbuttoned the waist of her trousers and drew down the zip. She was looking into his face and he saw trust there. He put his arm around her waist, lifted her to drag down her trousers and felt the spasm of pain grip her. He saw the clean skin of her thigh, the caked blood and the livid colour of the bruising. He tore off small pieces of cotton wool, dipped them in the water and began to separate the blood from the bruising.

Three years before, Gus had been the first driver to reach a motor accident – chest injuries from the impact on the steering wheel. He had run a hundred yards to the nearest house and demanded that an ambulance be called. He had gone back to the car, held the woman's hand until the paramedics arrived and had vowed to replace his ignorance with the basic skills. He had driven away with good intentions on his mind, and had never enrolled in an evening first-aid course.

He cleaned away the blood, edged his hand high on her thigh to hold her still when she squirmed in pain, and found the wound. An inch to the left and the bullet would have missed her; an inch to the right and it would have nicked an artery or shattered her femur. He worked faster as the water cooled. The wound was a deep furrow in the flesh of her thigh. It was worst for her when the cotton wool touched the rawness, and then he held her tightest, but she never cried out.

He smeared the last strands of trouser cotton out of the wound. The field dressing was old British Army surplus, would have been sold to the Iraqi military at a knock-down price. When he held her, and hurt her, the warmth of her chest was arched against his face and she bled from her bitten lip. He read the faded instructions on the dressing, then stripped it out and fastened it. He lifted the slight weight of her thigh higher and wrapped the bandage round the dressing.

There was a guttural cough behind him.

Gus pulled her trousers up over her thighs and hips, and buttoned them. She sagged away from him and lay on her back.

He lifted the torch and the beam speared into the darkness. The men sat silently in a wide crescent, their backs to him and to her. No man looked at her, had seen her nakedness.

The softness passed from her eyes. The trust was a memory. She dragged herself up and picked up the torch.

Meda walked freely among them and kept the torch on her face so that they could see that she felt no pain.

He was bound to her. Where she walked, he would follow.

AUGUSTUS HENDERSON *PEAKE*.

3. (Conclusions after interview with Henry Peake (father of AHP) conducted by self and Ms Carol Manning – transcript attached.)

MINDSET: In a solitary childhood, AHP received a grounding in countryside lore and hunting. He would have learned to kill and, more important, would have become familiar with the basic techniques of stalking and tracking. In my opinion it is impossible for a sniper to operate successfully unless he has the hunter's MINDSET. However, my assessment of AHP's chances of medium-term survival (slim to non-existent) in the northern Iraq theatre are unchanged. The MINDSET is good, as far as it goes, but a teenager's ability to shoot rabbits and pigeons does not compensate for lack of MILITARY TRAINING. Also, I have no evidence of AHP possessing the necessary TEMPERAMENT that differentiates a sniper from a target marksman.

Ken Willet read it back to himself in the quiet of his London living room. It would be on the desk of Ms Manning's line manager in a few hours, would be read and then filed into dusty oblivion.

Four years earlier he'd failed a sniper's course at the Infantry Training School at Warminster. It had been the only minor setback to his army career, and at the time it had hurt. Not any more. There were five parts to the final examination and he had passed in two, Camouflage and Concealment along with Observation, and failed in three, Marksmanship, Stalking and Judging Distance. To have won a sniper badge he'd needed passes in all disciplines. From his own teenage years he already had the mindset, he'd also been a good shot against rabbits and pigeons, but had realized in the second of the course's five weeks that his temperament was inadequate. And there was nothing he'd yet found, as the character of Augustus Peake was laid bare, to convince him that this civilian had a temperament to withstand the physical and psychological pressures that would close on him.

Ken Willet had failed the course, along with nine others out of the dozen starters. He'd had a fast beer, and driven away from the Infantry Training School. Forty-eight hours later he had been back with his platoon in Belfast. Easy. If Peake failed, there was no beer and no commiserations, and no drive out. He would be dead in a bloody foreign field.

As he started for bed, Willet thought that the man must be damned arrogant to imagine that, without a sniper's temperament or training, he could waft into a faraway war and make any sort of difference.

They had left Omar and the *mustashar* behind, sulking and resentful. No explanations offered, she had walked out of the village at first light. Only Gus was with her. A dozen men had pressed forward, claiming in a babble that they should go with her, and she had flashed her wide smile, then told them they were not needed.

They had walked for two hours, then crawled forward. She had walked well, but the crawling was tough. They had crossed two ridges and the valley separating them. The further valley, now ahead, was steep-sided and rock-sprayed. She should have been in bed, or at least resting, but he didn't bother to tell her. She'd stumbled once, the wound taking the force of her fall against a stony outcrop, and had let out a shrill cry. When they had pressed forward on their knees, she had twice had her backside in the air to keep her weight off the wound, and each time Gus had belted her buttocks without ceremony.

They were at the rim. Below, there was a track on the valley floor, insufficient for a vehicle, perhaps used by a goatherd or shepherd but not since the last summer. He soaked up the wild quiet of the place, and the small clumps of flowers.

'Watch for me.'

It was an instruction. He was no longer the man who had tended her wound. 'What am I looking for?'

'If there is a threat to me, to take me, then shoot.'

'Yes.'

'Your promise, Gus, if they try to take me, shoot me.'

'I promise.'

'Shoot me – promise it, on your grandfather's life.'

'I will shoot you, Meda. Don't move, stand still, don't break my aim. Don't make it hard for me to get a clean kill.'

Could he shoot her? Circumstances had shifted once more. From killing an enemy to shooting a friend. And each time they changed, he was further involved. She had not told him who might take her, or what was the threat. Could he measure the distance, make the windage adjustment, find her body on the T-junction of the reticule in the 'scope, hold his hands steady and squeeze the trigger?

She slipped away. He crawled off to his left, then began a slow search with his binoculars to find a position where he could lie up. She slithered down the sloped wall of the valley, kicking up dust, carelessly cascading stones in her wake. There was a place that was blanketed by old yellowed grass – well away from a tree stump that was the obvious position of concealment, two dozen paces from a small cluster of rocks that was the second most obvious. He spent several minutes tearing up similar strands of the grass and wove them into the hessian loops of his gillie suit, over his back, his shoulders, onto the hood, and put the last pieces into the hessian bandaging the rifle.

He armed the rifle and depressed the safety. She was on the floor of the valley, sitting on a smoothed rock with a child's innocence. She was picking tiny flowers and he saw her slide them across her nose. The one thing she feared, he thought, was capture. He had been brought with her because she could not show the men, or the *mustashar*, the smallest sign of fear . . . She started up, no longer the child. He watched as she transformed herself once more into the warrior. He could not see who approached her. As he had told her, she did not take a step forward. The sight was on her. She was unbending, magnificent. Gus's finger rested on the trigger guard.

The gloved hands came first into the tunnelled vision of the 'scope, reaching for her, then Gus saw the arms in drab military olive green, then the insignia of rank on the shoulders, and then the pocked sallow face with the black brush of the moustache, the beret.

Gus's finger lay on the cold metal of the trigger. He watched as Meda's cheek was kissed by a senior officer of the Iraqi army. They sat together and a map case was opened between them.

His cook-boy came with two buckets filled with dried earth as Lev Rybinsky unravelled the hosepipe at the side of his bungalow home. The water gushed out, he doused the buckets, hurled the mud at his car and sent the cook-boy for more.

His car was a 500SL Mercedes saloon. With old newspaper Rybinsky smeared the dripping dirt over the panelwork, the lights, the bumpers and the windows. When more mud was brought to him, he threw it against the body of the car. The day before, the cook-boy had spent the whole afternoon cleaning and polishing the Mercedes, but that was before Rybinsky had heard the whispered rumour.

Eight buckets of mud went onto the car before he was satisfied that every trace of polish had been removed. Rybinsky wiped a small part of the windscreen clear, enough for him to see through, shouted for the cook-boy to follow him and went back inside the bungalow. The hall and the living room were filled with packing cases.

There were more in the kitchen, each stamped with the names of aid organizations. He skirted around them, went into the rear yard and unlocked the heavy padlock on the steel door of a concrete shed. His two Alsatians leaped at him from their chain tethers.

From the shed, with the cook-boy's help, he carried out a new, never-fired DShKM 12.7mm heavy machine-gun. The cook-boy took most of the weight, and would return to the shed to bring out the ammunition, while Rybinsky had the light wheels as his second load.

Preparing to set out on a journey, Rybinsky would ordinarily have filled his Mercedes with oil, crates of corned-beef, sacks of pasta or flour, packets of computer chips or cases of whisky. He had them all, but because of the rumour he took only the machine-gun, which had an effective range of 1,500 metres and the ability to penetrate 20mm-thick armoured plate, from the arsenal of military weapons stored in the shed.

He supervised the lifting of the gun and its wheels into the back of the Mercedes where they covered the medicines he always travelled with. Lev Rybinsky was a week from his sixtieth birthday; his wife, his children, would be in their home at Volgograd when the date fell. He checked his jacket pockets – he needed to be clear exactly where the documents were. On the left side he kept the passes and letters of authorization supplied to him by *agha* Bekir, and on the right were the papers given him by *agha* Ibrahim. He tapped his bulging buttock and felt the reassurance of the roll of banknotes, American dollars. As a trader, a provider, a milch-cow, needed by everybody and loved by nobody, the roll of notes gave him access, influence and the ability to trade. The rumour he'd heard offered the possibility of a major commercial opportunity. He left a short letter for his junior partner, Jürgen, in the living room on the stacked crates that held an X-ray scanner for a hospital – donated by an Italian charity – and as an afterthought picked up a carton of Marlboro cigarettes.

If the rumour were true, it would be a long journey. He drove away in his mud-spattered car towards a distant war.

The old Israeli had told him to trust nobody, to believe nothing he was told and to accept nothing that he saw. Gus watched Meda shake the officer's hand as if she were his equal. The maps were folded away and the officer had slipped from the sight.

Gus burned. Her talk was of *destiny*. Because of her, the *peshmerga* had charged a machine-gun. He had watched the dead buried and the wounded taken on bumping litters to the north – and she had met an Iraqi officer. She was climbing the slope of the valley wall, slowly and with effort, and he saw the small stain on her thigh where the wound wept. The tears of anger in his eyes misted his view of her. He thought of betrayal, as he slithered away from his firing position and crawled to the far side of the ridge to intercept her.

Meda came over the rim and looked into his face.

There was the haughty whip in her voice, 'What is your problem, Gus?'

'Not my problem,' he blurted, 'the problem of the men, the problem of Haquim, the problem of the villagers. Maybe only the dead don't have a problem.'

She flared. 'Because I meet an Iraqi?'

'Because you go secretly to meet an Iraqi.'

Her hands caught at the hessian loops at his

184

shoulders. 'Do I have to tell you, like a child has to be told, *everything*? You tell me! Why was the village not reinforced? Why have not new tanks and new personnel carriers been sent to Tarjil? If you cannot tell me then say nothing.' Her mood swung: she was again the innocent. 'If he had tried to trap me, to take me, would you have shot me?'

'I try to keep my promises.'

'You know what they call me?'

'I imagine they call you *friend*.'

'He said that at Fifth Army they call me the witch.'

He set a fast pace back towards the village, and never looked behind him to see how well she followed.

Major Karim Aziz had come back to a place that was like home to him. It was old ground, familiar territory.

The driver had taken him to Tarjil. In the police station he had studied the maps, talked with the commanding officer, slept on the floor with his dog cuddled against him, and he had left the town long before dawn.

At first he had tracked north, towards the Little Zab river, shadowing the Arbīl–Kirkūk road, keeping in the lee of a ridge-line.

It was twenty-five years since he had first been posted to the region, and the fifth time that he had returned there. Nothing had changed except that trees he knew were taller, and the Victory Cities he skirted were more permanent and weathered, the hulks of abandoned personnel carriers more rusted.

He had slipped past a small gorge where a unit had been blocked in the al-Anfal operation, eleven years before. They had only been able to go forward after he had identified then shot the saboteurs' commander.

In the early morning, from higher ground, he had seen the track where three armoured vehicles had been ambushed twenty-one years before. He had been with the relief force that had driven off the bastards as they looted the vehicles, and they had found the bodies of the vehicles' crews; he could see the overgrown ditch beside the ochre hulks where he had vomited when he had seen the mutilation of the bodies.

By mid-morning he had looked down on a shepherd's hut of stone and corrugated iron from the same position he had taken nine years back. It had been the furthest point of the saboteurs' advance when they had swarmed south in the belief that the Americans would fly in support. The hut had been a night shelter for a reconnaissance group; with his Dragunov, he had shot their chief when he came out of the hut and stretched in the sunlight. The shot had been at the top of the Dragunov's range, one of the best he had ever achieved, and had made a stomach wound. In his mind he could still hear the screaming of the chief man as he lay outside the hut for an hour while none dared expose themselves to pull him inside.

By late morning he had reached a division of the shepherds' trails and he had gone to the west but, four years before, he had taken the eastern path on a forced march in the failed attempt to intercept the fleeing American spies who abandoned their Arbīl villa base. Everything he saw, every step he took, was as he remembered it. The ground had eroded but each footfall was an echo in his memory.

He took a position and settled. The dog had moved well with him. It ran when he scurried forward, slithered on its stomach when he crawled, lay motionless when he stopped, kneeling to scan the ground ahead. In the manuals it was written, by the Soviets, the British and the Americans, that a sniper must always be accompanied by an observer. In his long years in the army, Karim Aziz had not met a man he would have trusted sufficiently to accompany him; but he would trust the dog with his life.

The position he had chosen was amongst haphazardly shaped stones that offered him a clear view of the ground between the Victory City of Darbantaq and the town of Tarjil. Behind him were the tight-packed homes, the mosque's minaret, the faint outline of the communications equipment on the police station's roof. Further behind him, and barely visible, were the brigade's tents at the crossroads, the burning flame, and the conurbation of Kirkūk. Ahead of him was Darbantaq, five kilometres distant, with small smoke columns to identify it. Around him were the hills and valleys, and the silence.

Major Karim Aziz was at peace.

The peace came because he was far from Baghdad – from the pace and fumes, the noise and lifebeat of a city. He was anonymous in Baghdad, a pygmy figure. Even waiting endlessly on the flat roof with the Dragunov, he had never been able to gather up the sensation of power that was with him now. In the city he was one man against a million, one man against a regime, one man against an army. Here, it was hunter against hunter, a single marksman against a single marksman. It was his territory into which an intruder had strayed.

He looked towards Darbantaq across the slope of the valleys and over the swollen water-filled gullies. Bright green patches of ground, surrounded by yellowed grass, marked the peat marshlands. The dog growled softly, a whisper in its throat.

He was cautious with the telescope and he had draped a small square of grey cloth over the end of the lens glass. The sun beat down on him. If it caught the glass then his position was betrayed. He could see the roofs of Darbantaq, the smoke, and the personnel carrier skewed off the track leading to the village. Sometimes he could see figures moving between the buildings. At last light, with the sun sinking behind him, he would move closer.

He laid down the telescope, put it beside his rifle, and slowly turned his head. There should be no sudden movements to break the pattern of his camouflage. He slipped his hand back, ruffled the fur on the dog's neck, and felt the vibration of the growl. The work of an observer was to protect a sniper's back from attack from the flank or the rear. The dog lay facing away from him, and growled. It was on its stomach, head between its front paws, ears flattened, nose pointing the way for him.

There was a trellis of small valleys. One went north to south, another ran on a parallel line, and another east to west. He scanned each of them, and the further valleys, before he saw the movement that had alerted the dog.

A single man moved along on a herdsman's track at furtive speed in the second valley from him.

He reached for his telescope.

The man wore an officer's uniform. On the shoulders, magnified thirty times, was the gold-braid insignia of a ranking brigadier.

Of course, Aziz had checked with the regimental commander at Tarjil that no patrols would be out in the sector. A brigadier would not personally check forward positions, would not walk, and would not be alone. The man half ran and looked behind him as if pursued by demons.

He remembered . . . The brigadier in the communications centre of Fifth Army headquarters, and no reinforcements deployed, the lines of motionless tanks and personnel carriers . . . A demonstration of shooting power on a range. Two generals and a *brigadier* had come to the firing range and witnessed him accrue six hits from six shots at 700 metres when the probability of a kill at that range was listed as only 60 per cent. He saw that brigadier hurrying along the track on the valley floor. He lost him . . . Three weeks after the demonstration on the range he had received the invitation to a meeting. He had sat in the general's car, and the proposition of assassination had been made to him.

He was held in the tentacles of conspiracy. He heard the distant whine of a jeep's engine, and lay on his stomach, numbed.

'Did you see an army?'

'What sort of bloody army?'

Joe Denton had been standing with his bodyguards and the local men he'd trained, and was studying the fall of a well-grassed meadow between the village and the road. It was the best meadow available to the village, but the edge of the grass area was pocked with a small disturbance of earth, where the child had lost his leg. There should have been a wire fence round the meadow but some goddam greedy idiot from the village had taken the warning wire to corral his animals. The stupidity had cost a child's leg, and maybe even the child's life. It might have been a 72A, could have been a POMZ 2M, but it was most likely that a fucking V69 anti-personnel mine had exploded.

Denton was well paid by a British charity to clear old Iraqi mines, close to fifty thousand sterling a year, tax-free, but it was a bloody lonely life. Had it not been he would never have mixed in the UN club in Arbīl with a crook like Lev Rybinsky. The mud-caked car had pulled up on the road behind him.

'Joe, my friend, did you see an army led by a *woman*?'

'What are you talking about, Lev? The usual old crap?'

'You call me crap when you want cigarettes, Joe, when you want whisky? Hey, did you see a woman leading an army?'

'No.'

The car drove away down the road. Denton laughed mirthlessly: a woman leads an army in northern Iraq, and next week pigs fly. He thought of how many mines were buried there, at what depth, what density, and he started to draw a plan of the meadow.

'Did you see an army?'

'What if I did?'

'Was the army led by a woman?'

'And if it was?'

Sarah was at the co-ordinates given over a radio link because the message had said there were injured children to be met. The mud-caked car had stopped at the roadside behind the small convoy of pick-up trucks she had organized to make the rendezvous. The big fight had been to get the doctor to leave the clinic at Koi Sanjaq and come with her. She'd built the bloody clinic. That the doctor had a clinic to work in was bloody well down to her and Protect the Children funds – so, she'd told him he could bloody well get off his bum and come with her.

'I've got morphine.'

'Then hang around, Lev.'

'And I've got penicillin.'

'Make yourself comfortable. Is it that stuff you promised me weeks ago?' She laughed, a wild bitter laugh. The last load of medical supplies trucked across the border had been stopped at a road block by *pesh-merga* of *agha* Ibrahim's faction, and bloody hijacked. The lorry had been cleared out. The food had not been touched in the second lorry, and the third lorry with the building tools had made it through. She thought it often enough, that northern Iraq was the loneliest corner of the earth for an expatriate, which was why she knew Lev Rybinsky, and drank with him in the UN bar. If she had met the shit at home in Sydney, she would have looked right through him, walked right past him, and not noticed.

'What's her name, Sarah?'

'Meda.' Sarah saw Lev Rybinsky salivate, and his stomach quivered.

'Where is she?'

'Do I get the penicillin and the morphine?'

He was out of the car and scurrying to the boot. She thought him loathsome. He wore what she assumed was an Italian-made silk shirt, grubby, top button undone, the tie dangling loose, and a suit from Milan that was at least a size too small for him; the jacket wouldn't have fastened and the trousers' belly button was loose. The stubble on his face was creased by his jowl lines and the bald summit of his head glistened in the sunlight. He was repulsive but she needed him, as everybody did. He lifted two cardboard boxes from the boot and carried them to her. She saw that the donor labels had been ripped off. She didn't know whether they were from Protect the Children or another bloody charity. They were probably hers to begin with.

She smiled sweetly, and pointed. 'Up there. That's where she is.'

There was a slope and a distant clear-cut line of a ridge. Behind it were another three, softly hazy, barely visible in the high altitude. She'd hoped he'd gape and shrivel, but his pudgy face lit in triumph.

A line of men materialized over the nearest ridge. She put the boxes of morphine and penicillin in her pick-up, and Lev let her swig at the flask of whisky from the glove compartment of the Mercedes. She always needed whisky when the wounded were children. The column of men came down the slope with the casualties of battle.

One day each month a helicopter came to the eyrie in northern Iraq, collected Isaac Cohen, flew him back across the Turkish border to the base at Incerlik, and in the evening returned him to the isolation of his mountain home. On that one day he was debriefed by the Mossad officers stationed in Ankara who flew in to meet him. The contact was valuable and broke the impersonal monotony of radio intercepts – but even better was the chance to lie in a bath of warm water and to eat good cooked food. For a whole month he yearned for the comforts of that single day. The helicopter would not come for another twenty-four hours but already he was packed, ready for its arrival.

Haquim said, 'He is a snake, but a snake that has no venom. I asked him what was the price of the machine-gun, and he said it was a gift. I asked why he wished to travel so far to make a gift, and he said that the gift was proof of his friendship.'

Breaking the rule Haquim had set, Gus had been lying in the sunshine by the fence and cleaning the blister on his heel when he had seen the return of the men who had carried down the wounded. An overweight, elderly civilian was among them, carried on one of the litters that had been used for the casualties. Behind him more men carried a heavy machine-gun and ammunition on a stretcher. At the broken gate of the village, the man had slid heavily off the litter, wiped the sweat from his forehead and taken charge of the machine-gun. He had wheeled it into the village, grunting from the weight of it, and Haquim had met him.

'He is Lev Rybinsky, a Russian. He would not know about friendship. Everything for him is a negotiation for influence and financial gain. Where there is a closed border, he has access because he has bought the guards, he owns the customs men of the Syrians and the Turks and, perhaps, of the Iraqis. You want a tanker of fuel, he gets it for you. You want fruit from America, he supplies it. You want an artefact of antiquity from Nineveh or Sāmarrā, he provides it. Now, he comes to us with a gift of friendship and will not talk about a price.'

'It would have a hell of a hitting power.'

'At a range of a thousand metres it can pierce the armour on any part of a personnel carrier. Of course it is

193

useful, but I ask, what is the price? What does he want that we can give him?'

They watched.

The Russian dragged the machine-gun towards the command post, from which Meda emerged. He stopped, wiped an old handkerchief over his head and face, straightened his tie, then bowed elaborately to Meda. She was laughing, and he reached forward, touched her arm, as if to discover that she was real. Haquim turned away.

'You know, Gus, that we attack Tarjil tomorrow?'

'Yes.'

'You understand that to attack Tarjil we must come further down from the mountains?'

'Yes.'

'The real friends of the Kurds are not a man who brings a machine-gun – or a man who brings a sniper's rifle. They are the mountains. And now we are leaving our friends behind us.'

'What do I do at Tarjil?'

'There will be a briefing at dusk, then you will be told. Then, perhaps, I will be told.'

'Yes.'

'Where were you this morning, when you went with Meda?'

'Don't ask me because I can't tell you.'

He saw the beaming face of the Russian amongst the tight-pressed shoulders of the men and he heard Meda's voice. He saw the adoration of the men for her and the sunlight played on her mouth, which, in dark secrecy, had kissed the cheek of a senior Iraqi officer. Her hands moved high in emphasis, and they had shaken the hand of the officer. He sat on the ground and began to unwind the hessian bandage roll from the body of the rifle so that he could, again, enjoy the distraction of cleaning it.

The sergeant said, 'I am from Basra, Major, and my young brother is with me here, and my cousin. Will the saboteurs attack in the morning? It is good that you are here, Major, with your rifle.'

Karim Aziz turned away from him. He was still in shock from the extent of the conspiracy, and struggling to comprehend what he'd seen. His legs ached from the long day's walk, but the dog still bounded at his side. The darkness on the streets of Tarjil was broken by pockets of light from curtained or shuttered windows and from fires lit by the soldiers beside their bunkers. He had seen the gleam of confidence in the eyes of the men behind the sergeant as they noted his paint-smeared face and the heavy hanging camouflage smock, the rifle balanced in the crook of his arm.

An old man hurried from the shadows carrying a small can of heating oil, then saw him and blocked him.

'I am retired now, Major, but I was professor of the economics faculty of the University of Mosul. This is my home. My wife pleaded that we should flee south, I said the army would protect us. It is good to see you, Major, with your rifle.'

The man kissed his cheek and stumbled on into the darkness. In the last light of the day, before Aziz had turned, he had been close to the village of Darbantaq – four hundred metres from it – and had lain on his stomach with the dog beside him, and watched. He had seen her – the witch – once, but she was hemmed in by a crowd and was crossing, fast, the gap between a row of homes and the command post. He had watched as a paunchy European had brought a DShKM heavy machine-gun into the village. He had noted the way the men sat in quiet clusters, as men always did in the hours before they went into battle. He had seen a part of the body of the officer at the entrance to the command post, and had tilted his head to study the ground from which the shot would have come. He had found, at the sufficient elevation to clear the roofs, the scrape on the slope made by the sheep. He had trekked back, his mind in turmoil.

Wandering alone in the streets of the town that would be attacked in the dawn, confused and troubled, tugged between the extremes of loyalty and conspiracy, he had seemed to have become a beacon towards which the hope of frightened people was drawn.

'You are the master sniper, Major. Through the length of the regiment you and your skill are spoken of. We are not forgotten by Baghdad, Major, if they have sent you and your rifle. Shoot her! Shoot the witch.'

If he fought he would shoot against the conspiracy he had joined. If he did not fight, he would betray the trust of those who depended on him. He went slowly through the town, past the sandbag positions and cars that had been driven across the streets to make barricades, hugging the shadows and harbouring his torment.

The man had no face.

He lay against a rock, but had no face. Or he was in a ditch, or had tunnelled out a hide, or was back in trees, buried in shadow . . . but there was never a face to bring a character to the man.

The meeting droned on.

He needed to give a face to the man. He did not know

196

whether it was cold or carried warm humour, whether the face had charity or parsimony. He did not know whether the face of the man was bearded, moustached, or clean-shaven, whether it was topped with hair, whether the eyes shone without mercy or with kindness. The man had come north to find him and to kill him, and he could not give him a face.

Meda, with the map spread in front of her, talked, and the men listened.

He could not escape from his search for the face. In the morning the man would be waiting for him. He had come north to take one life. Gus heard not a word that Meda said. Nothing he had been told, had read, that he had experienced, had prepared him for the bleak certainty that a master sniper was at that moment making his preparations for the morning.

'Gus?'

All through the day he had been able to shut out the thought of the man, but no longer. He was drawn, a lemming to a cliff, towards Tarjil, where a fate of sorts awaited him. The chill was on his body.

'Gus, is that all right?'

Who would tell his grandfather, his father and mother? Who would tell Meg? Who would clear his desk? Who would tell Jenkins? And would they pause on Stickledown Range to remember him?

Meda snapped, 'Gus, are you listening? Do you agree?'

He pinched his nails into the palm of his hand. He asked quietly that she should run through it once more, so that he was certain he understood.

'It is a battle against a regiment. There is more to interest me than what you have to do.'

Haquim glanced sourly at him. 'I will explain it to him afterwards.'

When the meeting finished and the commanders fanned out into the darkness to brief their own small cabals of men, Haquim walked with him. He was told of a town of three thousand souls on flat ground just below the lip of a hill. In the heart of the town was the largest mosque, and beside the mosque was the police station, which was the headquarters of a regiment of mechanized infantry.

'The regiment has not been reinforced, *she* says. She does not tell me how she knows. If she is right then there will be a garrison of four hundred men, *if* she is right.'

Gus told him of the man without a face. Gus told Haquim, stampeded through the interruption, what the Israeli had said to him, and he saw the fury boil in the *mustashar*.

'We go in a line, because she says so. We do not feint to the left, avoid the predictable, then attack from the right. Our route is a straight line, and across the line is Tarjil, where a regiment is placed. They have defended positions. Tomorrow you will lie on your stomach. You are permitted to hang back. What of the men who have to cross open ground? What of them? How many will be killed? How many will live without arms, legs, eyes, testicles? Think of her, think of me, think of the men going against defended positions. Do not, Mr Peake, dare to think of yourself.'

Gus hung his head.

A column of men was coming through the gate of the village, loaded with weapons. He saw their tired, serious faces and wondered how many would survive the next day.

He found Omar beside the wire amongst a small mountain of old newspapers, kneading the sheets of paper together in a metal bathtub by the light of a hurricane lamp. The boy grinned happily at him.

'Show me,' Gus ordered.

Cheerfully, Omar lifted the pulped paper from the bathtub. Gus doubted the boy, in his cut-short life as a kid, had ever played with *papier-mâché*. Childhood had been denied him. The water splashed down the boy's arms and over his battledress and he held up the shape of a man's head . . . The face was without features.

'The cat, Mr Gus – while it dries, before we paint it – tell me about the observer and the cat.'

'Major Hesketh-Prichard wanted to write about the importance of the observer. He thought too much emphasis was given to the sniper, and not enough credit to the observer.'

'I am the observer, so I am important.'

'Don't interrupt. I thought you wanted to hear it. This young lieutenant of the Royal Warwickshire Regiment was watching a German trench that was thought to be disused and he saw this big cat. It was a tortoiseshell, orange and black and white, a fine well-fed animal, and it was sitting on some sandbags sunning itself. Many others had studied that section of trench, but the lieutenant was the first to see the cat and realize its importance. Rats plagued the British trenches as well as the German ones. The lieutenant decided that this fine cat could only belong to a senior officer, at least a major, and had been brought to the trench to kill the rats. If the cat belonged to a major then the bunker over which the cat was sunning itself must be a command post. The lieutenant spoke to the artillery and the next morning there was a barrage of howitzers, the bunker was blown up and all the officers in it were killed. That shows the importance of a good observer, Omar . . . Oh, Major Hesketh-Prichard said the cat survived, it wasn't killed.'

'I think tomorrow, Mr Gus, many will be killed.'

He looked at the drying features of the shape, which by the morning would have been given a painted face.

Chapter Eight

By the hurricane lamp's light, Omar daubed the dried face with paints liberated from the wrecked school building: grey, red and white for the flesh on the face, brown for the moustache and the eyebrows, a pink mix for the lips, grey and blue for the eyes.

When the paint set, Gus sent him to find a scarf in khaki or olive green, a good strong stick and a combat shirt. The boy disappeared into the darkness. Gus should have been sleeping, resting and regaining the strength he would need in the morning. He wondered if Meda slept, or Haquim. Beyond the wire, in front of him, the night held its silence.

While the boy had made a face and while he had told him how to paint it, he thought that a great game was played out, but that he was only a small part of it. The painted face was not that of his enemy, it was his own.

'So, I find the sniper . . .' a voice boomed, then a cascade of laughter. Gus peered back, and saw the Russian.

'I am told you are English. I bow to an English gentleman.'

'What do you want?'

'To pass the night hours in the company of civilization.'

Gus growled, 'Find it somewhere else.'

'Are you frightened?'

'I am *not* frightened.'

'Let me tell you, Mr Gentleman, about myself. Then when you have heard me with English politeness, I will ask the question of you again. I am from Volgograd, but then it had the name of our great leader, Stalin. I was two years old when the Germans came to Stalingrad. My father and my uncle fought there, my mother was in the cellars and basements with her baby son. It was a battle without etiquette or regulation, a fight for survival . . . Perhaps you believe, if this battle goes badly, you can still go back to the green pleasant land of England. There was no retreat for my father, my uncle and my mother from Stalingrad. Across the river were fifteen thousand troops whose military task was to prevent retreat – they shot those who fell back.'

'I have no interest in the battle for Stalingrad.'

'Listen to me. The battlefield bred the great snipers of history, and great sport for those who watched. Which would you prefer to see: a boxing fight, a race around a stadium, a football game, or two men with rifles hunting for each other? The sport at Stalingrad was to watch the duels of the snipers, and to bet on them – half a loaf on the Russian, a quarter of a chocolate bar on the German. The best of them were known throughout their armies. As soon as a sniper became famous he was tracked by an enemy who was also a celebrity . . . And you tell me you are *not* frightened. You are, Mr English Gentleman, already famous. The word spreads here, as in Stalingrad. Half a million men, in the third month of the battle, watched the fight to the death between the two master snipers.'

'Your story is not relevant to me.'

'You are famous. A man will have come because he has heard of your fame. The great duel was between Major Konings and Vasili Zaitsev. Zaitsev was a hunter from the Ural mountains, who had killed three hundred German soldiers in the battle for Stalingrad. Konings, a major in charge of the sniper section of the School of Infantry Tactics at Wunstorf, was flown into the battle from Berlin to redress the balance of death.

'Stalingrad was the pivotal battle of the war, Mr English Gentleman. You could say it was the turning-point in the history of the century, but at the very point of its fulcrum was the duel between Zaitsev and Konings.'

'Come on, how did it finish?' Beside him the boy had knotted the scarf around the papier-mâché head, rammed a stick up its throat and had buttoned a tunic across its neck.

Rybinsky smiled. 'You make a face of paper – an old tactic. For a full week Zaitsev took a place near where his friends, Morozov and Sheykin, had been shot, and he watched and saw nothing. Zaitsev took Kulikov with him as his observer, but they could not identify Konings' position. On the seventh day of the fourth week of the month after Konings had come to Stalingrad, Kulikov saw the flash from a speck of glass in the rubble of no man's land – a telescope or the sight on a rifle – but they could not see Konings. They used the old tactic, as old as the one you use. Kulikov raised his helmet on a stick. Perhaps Konings was tired, perhaps uncomfortable, perhaps he wanted to piss, but he made the mistake and fired at the helmet. If the helmet had only dropped back, Konings would not have exposed himself – but Kulikov screamed, as if he were hit. Konings' mistake was that the scream aroused his vanity. He thought he had killed Zaitsev. He raised his head to see his success. It was all Zaitsev needed . . . Are you frightened that you don't know whether you are Zaitsev or Konings?'

Gus pushed himself up. There was the murmur of voices behind him and the sounds of weapons being armed, and the squeal of the wheels that carried the heavy machine-gun. He said, 'I'm sorry, Mr Rybinsky, but I don't care to give myself that significance.'

'Is he there? Has Major Konings come from Berlin?'

Gus sighed hard. 'Yes. Yes, he has travelled. If you stick around, you'll have the grandstand seat.'

Gus and Omar joined the great silent column moving away into the night, and far ahead of them the bright flame burned.

Major Aziz sat in a doorway at the front of a hardware shop. The door behind him, and every other door in the town, was locked, bolted.

He looked down the street in front of him: like every other street in the town, it was barricaded and empty.

He sat with his rifle loose across his knees, fed biscuits to his dog, and waited.

Ken Willet took the key that was passed to him.

Ms Manning had planted her buttocks against the cleared desk. Her arms were folded across her chest and she gazed back defiantly at the source of the tirade that had been halted in its tracks, briefly, to offer up the key.

'I don't know what sort of pressure you people, spooks and whatever, have to endure, but if you think you're hard done by then try half a day in here.'

Around the cleared desk, telephones were ringing and two women were trying to stem a tide of chaos. Outside the office, in the wide tarmac yard, the giant lorries with their trailers were starting up and man-oeuvring towards the main gate. Each time the office door opened for a shouted query from a driver, the owner broke off from his lecture to Ms Manning. Willet had the safe door unlocked and pulled it back.

'If he was here, right now, Gus would be taking care of the Hamburg consignment, which is up the spout because the bloody Germans have filed the wrong customs declaration – can't be late because that lorry's got to get back, off-load, then be in Birmingham for a machinery pick-up for Milan – and in Milan there's a factory on short time because they haven't got that machinery, and I'm on a penalty if I don't meet the schedule. I've two drivers off with flu, genuine, not skiving, but I'm shuffling the others round so that our supermarket contract doesn't suffer. I've another lorry off the road with gearbox trouble, perishables to lift out of Barcelona, three lorries in the queue at Dover because the bloody French are on strike . . . and an empty bloody desk where my transport manager should be sitting.'

Willet took the papers from the safe, stacked them neatly beside his knee and began to read.

'I may own the bloody place, own the lorries, own the bloody overdraft, but I don't run this office. Be in hospital with a coronary if I had to. Gus runs it – or ran it until three weeks back. He said he wanted to go to Turkey with one of the drivers. That's agricultural equipment spares going out, and denim jeans coming back. Said he wanted to understand better the drivers' problems – but he didn't come back with the jeans. In Ankara, he off-loaded himself . . . God knows what he was up to, because he'd stowed gear under the seat that wasn't shown to Customs. He told the driver he'd make his own way home. I've not had sight or sound of him since.'

'What was the gear?' Ms Manning asked crisply.

Willet, on the floor with the papers, could have answered.

The owner snapped, 'It was a rucksack, the driver said, and a long carrying bag. The driver said it was camouflaged. It was smuggled so God alone knows what was in it. If Customs had found it, Christ . . . Didn't say where he was going, how long he'd be. The least of my problems right now. My problems are *pressure*, and no bloody transport manager here to sort them.'

'Good at his job, is he?'

Willet, shuffling through the papers, speed-reading them, didn't think she understood her capacity to sneer a question.

'Are you good at your job? If you're half as good at your bloody job as he is then my taxes are well spent. Course he's bloody good. Pressure doesn't faze him, not like me. There can be fuck-ups from bloody Edinburgh to Eastbourne, from Cardiff to Cologne, and he soaks them up. I don't get tantrums or shouting from Gus, I get the fuck-ups sorted. He doesn't bawl out the girls, doesn't shout at the drivers. He sits there, where your arse is, and sorts it. He does it on his own. Calm – just what I'm not . . . So, get out of my hair, and leave me to keep this shambles on the road.'

At the bottom of the papers on the floor was a sixteen-page colour sales brochure. Willet slipped it into his briefcase and replaced the other papers in the safe, swung the door closed and turned the key on it.

The owner didn't see them out. He had a telephone at each ear, the secretaries were trying to attract his attention, and a driver and a grease-stained mechanic were hovering at his shoulder. Willet followed Ms Manning from the dreary little office and they left behind them the confusion, and the girlie calendars sent out by the tyre companies.

'What a dreadful man,' she said.

'Pays the taxes, doesn't he, for our salaries?'

She gave him a savage, disdainful look. He wondered how she'd survive the slash-throat world of private enterprise. They paused as a juggernaut drove past them. The tang of the diesel seeped into his nose.

'We're wasting our time,' she said. 'We're wasting it on a damn fool idiot with a death-wish.'

'You're wrong.'

'Really? Then enlighten me.'

They were walking towards her car.

Willet said, 'We are not wasting our time. We are evaluating Peake's capabilities as a sniper. That's what we've been briefed to do and that's what we're doing. We are learning. We do not yet know what those capabilities are. If he doesn't have those capabilities, then yes, he is a damn fool, who will be killed. If he does have them, the horizons change.'

The sneer was back. 'One man? No way.'

They were at her car. Willet stood in front of the door, blocking her.

'A sniper can change the course of a battle – no other

soldier has so much influence. I'll tell you what a sniper can do. A brigade-size manoeuvre I was at on Salisbury Plain . . . the acronym is TESEX, that's Tactical Evaluation and Simulation Exercise. All the weapons have the capability to fire a laser beam, and every man has a device on his uniform that'll register the laser. A rifle shoots the laser and if there's a hit the device bleeps. With me so far? A brigadier, a high-flier, was in charge of the attack side of the exercise, been planning it for weeks, probably months. The defending force, commanded by a colonel with a proper sense of humour, pushed a sniper forward towards the brigadier's command post. It was going to be a three-day exercise and the brigadier thought it would notch him up to major-general level. Five minutes into the first of the three days, the sniper "shot" the brigadier. The old bleeper went . . . all the planning out of the window, all the promotion hopes dumped. The brigadier shouted, "This can't happen to me," but the observer controller told him it could and it had. He yelled and argued, didn't make any difference. "Do you know who I am?" was his last throw, and the observer controller told him, "Yes, you're a casualty and you're going into a body bag, *sir*." The attack failed.'

He stepped aside. She unlocked the door.

'It's a ridiculous story – just men playing kids' games.'

'Actual war, that's the same game. It's what he can achieve if he's good enough, which is why Peake is worth learning about. Cheer up, things are looking rosy: we're going to have a day at the seaside.'

'Do you have anything I should know about?'

Both of them were too long in the trade to posture a

courtship ritual, like peacock and hen; they wouldn't waste each other's time.

'What are you looking for?'

Isaac Cohen lay in the bath, his flabby stomach protruding from a sea of soapsuds. Caspar Reinholtz had seen the helicopter land, as it always did on that date of the month, had looked through the windows of his offices as the Mossad man went from the American living quarters to the bathhouse with a towel over his arm. The Israeli's controller would arrive at Incerlik in the next half-hour and then Cohen would be beyond reach.

'The woman, the advance, anything that I haven't got.'

'They took Darbantaq.'

'Figured they would.'

'And didn't give themselves the burden of prisoners.'

'Predictable.'

'Right now they're hitting Tarjil.'

'That's a nut you could break your teeth on.'

If their masters in Langley or Tel Aviv had known of the contacts between Isaac Cohen and Caspar Reinholtz there would have been an immediate order that they be discontinued. Relationships between the Mossad and the Agency were scarred by suspicion. But it was hard enough in the field without letting the bickering of their masters prevent a casual exchange of information.

'Tarjil wasn't reinforced.'

'That's taken care of.' Reinholtz sat languidly on the toilet seat beside the bath.

Cohen's smile of understanding widened. He used the sponge on his chest. 'The armour hasn't moved out of Kirkūk.'

'Tell me something new.'

'It'll be a difficult fight in Tarjil, Caspar, with or without fresh armour.'

'She's got to get through Tarjil or she's dead in the water. For the big play to start, she has to get all the way to Kirkūk.'

'It's a big play – am I hearing you?'

'Telling it frankly, Isaac, as big as it gets. It's her and the armour and the sniper?'

'He seemed a good guy, the sniper, I met him.'

'I don't think so, Isaac. I'm not talking about the guy in the column – I met him, too. This is very confidential. There's a sniper in Baghdad . . .'

'Do you have a name?'

'That is very sensitive confidential. I'd like to share on that one, but . . .'

The Israeli gazed into the American's eyes. 'Aziz? Major? Baghdad Military College? Chief instructor in sniping? Major Karim Aziz? Sorry, Caspar, he's not in Baghdad. He was transferred to Fifth Army three days ago. Is that important? I wouldn't want to spoil your day but doesn't that make a difference to your plan?'

The American rocked on the lavatory seat. His hands went up to his face as if to block out the news. His body shook. He stood and tossed the towel for the Israeli to catch and went towards the bathroom's door, his cheeks ashen.

'You could just say, Isaac, you spoiled my day. You've screwed it big-time.'

Cohen stared at the taps, heard the door open then close, and wondered whether the first strand of the big plan was unravelling.

* * *

210

For Gus, it was a simple shot. Any of the Sunday-morning amateurs on Stickledown Range would have made the hit.

In the hour before dawn, he had followed Omar to the house that was set back from the road into the town. It had been empty but the lights were on, there was still food on the table and toys lay on the kitchen floor. The cupboard doors upstairs were open. He thought the father had finally decided on flight after the children had been put to bed, and that the parents had packed frantically what they could carry with the children into a car.

He had gone up the stairs, led by Omar, and had wedged the pulped-paper head into the corner of the main bedroom's window so that the features would appear to gaze back at the town, and had put the binoculars on the windowsill immediately below the head. They had pushed aside the cover of the ceiling hatch, and levered themselves up among the rafters. Before first light he had dislodged a roof tile for the firing position, then removed a second tile for the telescope Omar would use.

Gus had stared down on to a battlefield swathed in grey mist. When he'd settled he told Omar to knock out a minimum of another fifteen tiles, and heard them slide crazily down to the guttering.

The house he had chosen was set in a wide plot. The ground was already dug and hoed and the first vegetables were sprouting. Beyond a low wire fence, against which children's bicycles lay, was the garden of the next house, which had a lower roof. A hundred yards further down the road a lorry was slewed across as a barricade. Then the houses formed close-set streets, and rising above them were the minarets and the dull, plastered façade of the police station, topped by a communications dish. In front of the police station, where the road widened, was another barricade of three overturned cars.

He had taken his aim. The range was four hundred yards. The flare was fired from behind them, arched over the rooftop, then burst above the first barricade.

Gus fired.

The communications dish on the roof of the police station disintegrated and its frame collapsed.

He waited.

It was as though he had thrown down a glove into the mud in the path of his opponent, or slapped the face of his enemy.

Paint flakes and metal fragments had fallen on him when the dish was hit.

There was a waist-high parapet on the roof of the police station, but at two of the corners there were higher sandbag emplacements that covered the road into the town and the two barricades blocking it. Aziz had chosen the centre point of the wall facing the road and, as he lay on his stomach, his view was through a rain-water gully. The furthest house from him, along the road, was held in the Dragunov's sight.

He had heard *crack* and, a second later, *thump*. The firing position was between 350 metres and 450 metres from him. First, down the road, he made football pitches in his mind, and counted four. There were two houses in the sighting distance, the nearest was lower and he did not believe offered the elevation to clear the parapet and still hit the communications dish. He

212

started his study of the further house. He was back from
the gully, offered no target. He made a further calculation from the vertical lines in the reticule of the sight
that were the equivalent in height of an average-sized
man, then the conversion between the height of a man
and the height of a window. The size of the windows told
him that the house was 400 metres from him. There was
no other building of sufficient height from which the
shot on the communications dish could have been fired.

He saw the painted head, and the binoculars.

He counted seventeen holes in the roofing where the
tiles had been forced away.

His eye never left the 'scope, and his finger stayed
with an infinite gentleness on the Dragunov's trigger,
and he spoke softly to the dog.

'He tells us that he knows we have come to hunt him.
Maybe the Americans told him or the Zionists, maybe
they picked it off the radio. He wants me to know where
he is. Do you find that peculiar, little man? It is an old
game. You put up a bogus target and the sniper shoots
it, and then you look for him, and you kill him. Very old,
and not even a good head. He does not have sufficient
respect for us . . .'

The machine-guns on either side of him had started
to fire. The battle was joined. At the edge of the circle of
his 'scope sight were the first running and crawling
columns of men closing on the furthest barricade. There
was an answering thundercrack, repeated, and repeated
again, from a heavy machine-gun and great chunks
came careering off the parapet wall. Had Aziz shifted
his aim fractionally, there would have been fine targets
among the columns, but his eyes were locked on the
seventeen holes in the house's roof.

*   *   *

He could see the men behind the barricade scurry
between different shooting positions. Two machine-
guns from the roof of the police station fired over the
barricades on the road, with lazy running tracers that
died among the two columns of *peshmerga* hugging the
ditches either side of the tarmac.

It would have been easy for Gus to knock away the
machine-gun crews on the police-station roof or to
devastate the defence of the forward barricade. He held
his fire. He searched for the sniper among the rooftops and the windows, the high points of the police
station and the minarets, the heaps of rubble and
rubbish beside the road. He saw men go down, some
poleaxed, some writhing, in the charge for the barricade.
He saw men he had hiked alongside, and eaten with,
washed with, slept close to – men with familiar faces –
stand and blast back at the firing from behind the
barricade, then throw up their arms like helpless idiots
and crumple. He saw her . . . She had a bandanna of torn
cloth around her head to hold her hair away from her
eyes, grenades tied to her body, and she carried an
assault rifle. She came out of the right-hand ditch and
ran low across the road towards the other side against
which the firing was most concentrated. She dived for
the ditch where the men were pinned down. He saw her
grab two, three, by their shirts and heave them forward.
She stepped over those who had fallen in the ditch, and
those who flailed their arms in agony.

He watched Meda's crabbing dash towards the barricade, and the firing slackened. He saw the soldiers
break. Again and again, her arm waved above her head
for the columns to come forward. Gus could have shot

several of the running soldiers, aimed at their backs, but he searched instead for the position of the sniper.

The battle was fought around him, but Major Karim Aziz played no part in it.

It was beneath him, beside him, but his focus was on the house. He watched the crude head in the upper window, and he scanned the missing tiles that were spread at differing heights along the length of the roof. From his elevated position, protected by the parapet, there were many targets he could have taken. At that range, he could have picked off enough of the *peshmerga* to have slowed, if not halted, the advance. He was trapped by the obsession to locate and kill the sniper confronting him. He could have given covering fire to the soldiers who ran back from the furthest barricade. The course of the battle was vaguely apparent to him in the bottom of the arc of vision through his 'scope. The dog shivered against his leg. He was comfortable within himself. If he had given the cover, he would have betrayed his position. He watched the house, waited for the chance, as the concentrated fury grew below him.

'Aren't you going to shoot?' Omar shouted.

'Search the rooftops, and don't show yourself,' Gus murmured.

Through the magnification of the 'scope, he watched the roofs. The sun was rising behind him and he hoped its low line would catch the glass of a rifle-sight or a telescope's lens or binoculars. Below, across the road, there was thickening smoke from fires started by the tracers, but above that grey carpet the roofs, where a sniper could have taken his position, were clear. The firing was a cacophony of noise, but Gus watched the rooftops.

'When will you shoot?'

'If I see him I'll shoot, but not until then.'

He was aware that a defence line held at the further barricade. At moments when his concentration wavered, he saw the soldiers milling behind the cars and in doorways, but he cut them out because they were distractions. Some days, when he fired on Stickledown Range, not the major meetings for which silver spoons were presented, there was chatter and laughter around him, *distraction*, but he had learned to ignore them and to concentrate only on his own shooting.

'You have to shoot!' Omar yelled.

'It's all about patience,' Gus said quietly. 'His patience and mine. The one whose patience goes first is the one who loses.'

He watched chimneys and television aerials and satellite dishes, windows that were slightly ajar, the flat roofs and the crenellated parapet of the upper part of the mosque's tower. He saw her, fleetingly, through the smoke haze at the lower extremity of his 'scope sight, emerge from a side lane to hurl a grenade towards the barricade, but then his eye wafted away and slipped back to cover the roofs and windows that were bathed in bright sunlight.

'If you don't shoot, I will!' Omar screamed. Gus ignored him.

He could have disrupted the defence of the barricade, could have shot the soldiers who lurched towards the far side of it with boxes of fresh ammunition, could have dropped the soldier who rose and fired from the hip as Meda made her last charge, hemmed in by her men, on the overturned cars. To have fired would have been to betray his position. There was no conflict in his mind. He realized that the boy had left him. He never took his eye from the 'scope sight, but he reached out with his trigger hand and felt the emptiness. Then his hand touched the discarded telescope. He thought he had explained it very clearly, reasonably, to the boy, why he did not fire. Then he settled again to resume his watch. He saw the wave of men break against the barricade, but the sniper still did not show himself.

The resistance at the barricade crumbled. The smoke swirled around him. More often now his body was spattered with the dust and rubble of the fractured concrete wall behind which he sheltered. He saw the movement at the door of the house and his rifle's aim edged sideways to cover it. The moment of opportunity had come, the smile played on his face. His finger rested on the trigger. Major Karim Aziz swore in frustration. A boy hesitated in the doorway, then ran for the ditch and the road. He was little more than a child and carried an assault rifle. He felt a surge of anger as his aim traversed back to the windows of the house and the roof's seventeen holes. His eyeline again shifted, away from the sight, over the barrel of the Dragunov, towards the charge at the barricade below him. He realized then the fate of the battle in which he had taken no part. When the barricade fell, the last struggle would start – for the police station. So little time was left to him. He shouted to the machine-gun crew on his right to fire on the house, rake the roof, flush the bastard. He watched the roof and the upper window where the head was displayed and waited for the bullet burst to impact on the tiles, to move the bastard . . . and he saw nothing. He

217

waited. He was shouting again, angry because his order was not obeyed, he turned his head. The machine-gun crew were dead, the blood from their bodies running in little merging dribbles. He heard the thunderous beat of the rounds from the heavy machine-gun firing on the main gate of the police station. They had died beside him and he had not noticed.

The streets on either side of the police station were filled with scrambling civilians in desperate flight, carrying bundles or sacks or bags, and some dragging children behind them.

He looped his backpack over his shoulders and crawled away towards the far side of the roof where the iron ladder led down to the vehicle yard.

He saw the commanding officer of the regiment charged with the defence of the town. The yard was thick with the choking smoke of fumes from two personnel carriers and five jeeps. The officer was running heavily towards the forward jeep, which faced the opened gates of the yard, burdened by his packed bags, a rolled carpet flopping under his arm.

Already in the jeeps were the second-in-command, the operations officer, the intelligence officer, the political officer, more bags, more carpets and pictures.

He raised his rifle, as the line spurted forward, and aimed at the coarse clipped hairs on the back of the commanding officer's neck, the sweaty stain between the shoulders, and fired.

The man slumped onto the bags and the rolled carpet, and the jeep was gone through the back gate of the yard. He ejected the used cartridge case, picked up the dog and climbed quickly down the ladder into the deserted yard.

218

*   *   *

The firing had died.

Gus eased himself up from his prone position and started to massage the stiffness from his legs.

Meda was on top of the barricade, balancing her weight on the door of the central car, and again, as she had before, she punched the air. He wondered how many times she had been seen over the open sights of the soldiers' weapons, how many times they had fired at her and, somehow charmed, she had escaped. She was the symbol, she was the witch. The men swarmed past her and fanned out into the streets on either side of the police station. Gus lingered at the firing position and watched as Haquim reached up and urged her down.

As he lingered, he hated himself. He waited, ready to shoot, because the sniper on the rooftops or in an upper window might still fire on her and give away his position. But she was down, safe and protected by the barricade.

He started to pack away his equipment, and the telescope the boy had left behind.

He had seen her.

He could have stood on a doorstep, snatched at a packing case from a shop, shot over the heads of the fleeing townspeople, over the emptiness of the street behind them, and over the *peshmerga* beyond the emptiness. He could have hit her as she stood on the barricade of cars.

He could have killed the witch.

And yet he had not considered it. He had known that, if he had fired, every weapon in the hands of the *peshmerga* would have been turned on him and on the flight of the defenceless in reprisal. He had joined the jostling panic of the escape.

He was engulfed in the tide, was swept forward. He held the dog close to his chest. He had been in a desperate flight before, and he disliked the disorder. In the Mutla Pass out of Kuwait City and at the bridge over the Tigris river, with the American tanks behind them and the planes wheeling above them, he had run for his life. The firing of the one shot, his contribution to the battle, did not cause him to feel guilt. The hurt, deep and personal, was that his waiting had not been rewarded . . . He was out of the town and among the column of civilians. He put the dog down so that it could run beside him.

He saw the disappointment and anger on the faces of those around him and could not tell them why he lived, why they should not have believed in him, or where he had been with his rifle.

The triumph glowed in her. 'We didn't see you, didn't hear you.'

He said dully, 'I was looking for their sniper . . . '

'What? Is that a joke?'

'If I had fired, after the shot against the dish, I'd have given my position to their sniper. I waited for him to make the mistake and —'

'Whatever you say, but make sure you clean it, Gus. There will be a jam because it was not cleaned. We needed you, so clean it.'

He walked away from Meda and rounded the barricade of cars. The bodies were against each other, the soldiers' and the *peshmerga*'s, locked against each other as if the final struggle for the barricade had been hand to hand. The stink was of opened bowels, spilled fuel and discarded cartridges. Haquim was folding away the box, Josephus, that had blocked the radio after the communications dish had been shot out.

'Why did you not shoot? Was there a malfunction? We have at least a hundred casualties. I waited for you to shoot – you could have saved so many of our casualties. You should not blame yourself. Anyone can suffer a malfunction.'

He strode on from Haquim, cursing his low expectations. He went towards the sagging gates at the front of the police station. There was an entry to the left, half blocked by a cart with a dead donkey still in its shafts, and saw the heap of uniformed bodies behind the cart, then the sudden movement as if a rat disturbed rubbish bags. It was Omar. Gus watched as the boy scurried over the bodies and methodically pilfered from them. First a gold chain ripped from a throat, then a ring wrenched from a finger, then a wallet snatched from an inner pocket, the blood wiped off it and the notes taken, a bracelet prised from a wrist.

Gus strode forward.

He stepped over the dead donkey and insinuated himself between the cart and the wall, and he kicked as hard as he could. He felt the shock wave ripple up from his boot to his hip. He kicked Omar off the bodies, and the boy cringed. He struck him with the butt of his rifle. The boy cowered against the wall and the brightness of the loot was in his hands, which were clasped across his face. Again and again, brutally, Gus battered the boy with his rifle butt. He brought blood to the boy's face, from his forehead and eyes. Blood was in the boy's nose, dammed in the wisps of his moustache.

Omar shouted through his hands, 'At last you have found, Mr Gus, a job for your rifle. Now you are *brave* with your rifle.'

He left the boy against the wall and walked on into the town.

Aziz looked back.

Behind him was the great straggling column of the survivors, men, women and children, civilians and soldiers, and further behind were the bags, sacks and bundles discarded under the bright heat of the afternoon's sun.

He remembered the first time he had gone to war, nineteen years old. His division of mechanized infantry, in support of two armoured divisions, had surged out of Jordan and over the frontier to support the battered Syrian tanks in their fight for survival against the Zionists. They had gone with high hopes, brimming confidence, and the Zionists had hit them at the village of Kfar Shams. Crouched behind the thin walls of his personnel carrier, he had witnessed the carnage of defeat in combat. They had limped home to Baghdad. His father had met him at the barracks. The nineteen-year-old had nursed the stench of defeat, but his father had declaimed that they were national heroes who had saved the flank of the Syrian army and protected Damascus from capture. It was what the radio had told the people but he had known the reality of the catastrophe. Then, the teenage Karim Aziz had carried no responsibility.

He walked on towards the brigade at the crossroads.

*   *   *

They were a force of liberation, but no crowds cheered them from the pavements.

The *peshmerga*, in gangs, kicked down the doors of homes, dragged up the shutters from shop windows, took what they could carry, and smashed what they had to leave behind.

No flowers were thrown down at them from upper windows.

He did not see Meda or Haquim. He thought that they would be far back at the barricades, where they would see nothing, hear nothing, know nothing of how the wave of freedom crashed over the town of Tarjil.

No flags were waved, or scarves.

A man was pulled, struggling from his home, thrown down into the mud of the street and a petrol can emptied over his head. There was the flash flame of a lighter as Gus turned and sleepwalked away. He turned his back on the sizzling death of an agent of the secret police.

A man, an informer, kicked his feet in the air. The noose at his neck was tied to an iron bracket above his shop. A shoe careered across the lane as the man kicked, and his women watched in silent, sullen hatred. Gus did not wait to see the death throes.

He walked right through the town. All about him was retribution and revenge. Far ahead was the empty road that stretched to the horizon where a small dustcloud marked the progress of the refugee column. He sat against a wall and the sunlight played on his face. He shut his eyes to forget what he had seen.

Chapter Nine

She was alone, friendless, far from home.

She sat on the bonnet of the pick-up and waited. She was angry, blamed the tooth – right upper molar – was tired and hot. It was rare for Sarah to feel sorry for herself, but she did that day, and the tooth made it worse. The doctor sat in his own pick-up's shade, parked behind hers, read a paperback, his Walkman earphones clamped over his head, being no bloody company. She wouldn't have trusted him with her tooth. The two nurses, local women from Arbīl, were in the cab of the third pick-up, fanning away flies and listening to a wailing singer on Radio Baghdad. Joe Denton, the sour little beggar, was a mile up the road, but what he did would make any bloody man sour. Her bodyguards and the interpreter were under a tree beside the road and sleeping.

She was a failure because she achieved a small damned part of nothing. Sarah could not have said truthfully that, in her time in northern Iraq, she had changed the lives of any of the communities with which she had worked. When she went, when they had found another high-principled lunatic to take her place, she'd be forgotten in a day. Her own high principles had long ago been battered out of her. Build a school, fill it with kids, appoint a teacher – a month later the school's half empty because the bloody Stone Age fathers won't permit education for the girls. Build a clinic, equip it, appoint a nurse – three months later the drugs have been stolen for black-market sale, and the nurse has been bought by a UN agency paying better money.

Her charity, Protect the Children, had a two-million-pound budget sloshing into northern Iraq, and the biggest single part of it was for the payment of the goddam loafing bodyguards who watched her, her colleagues, the warehouse, the offices and villas in Arbīl and Sulaymānīyah. And no bloody way they'd give up their lives to protect her if she was targeted by the Iraqis, or fell foul of an *agha*. It was all a bloody mess.

The reinforcements had arrived, spewed from a convoy of lorries, and had set off up the hillside towards the line of disappearing ridges. Sarah had known nothing of guns before she had come to northern Iraq. Guns were what policemen carried, holstered on their hips, at home, and were shouldered by the toytown soldiers outside the palaces in London where she'd au paired for six months. Now she knew about guns. She could have reeled off the names, calibres and qualities of all the weapons carried up the hillside by the reinforcements. She had also seen what such weapons could do. There had been a significant battle – she knew because the word had reached her clinic that she should go to the rendezvous point again to meet casualties. If so many reinforcements were going forward, a bigger battle was copper damn certain.

The previous evening, the meat had been tough,

stringy. Her tooth hurt. She might, God willing, only have loosened it; she might, her damn luck, have cracked the filling. To get a tooth fixed would mean a three-day journey out of northern Iraq into Syria, and then a three-day journey back. She didn't have a week to lose, not with more casualties forecast.

She saw the column clear the nearest ridge and start to wind down the slope.

She was trained as a paramedic. With her were a doctor and two local nurses. They did not add up to a goddam casualty clearing station. They had three pick-ups. Lorries had been available to bring the reinforcements, but had done an about-turn and disappeared, not waiting for the inevitable casualties. They were for her to clear up. Good old Sarah would cope, always coped.

'Tell me something new,' she muttered.

She started to try to count the litters being carried down the hill, then hitched herself off the pick-up's bonnet and marched, big steps, to the tree where her bodyguards and the interpreter rested in the shade. She snatched a pair of binoculars from her senior bodyguard's neck without bothering to ask and leaned against the tree to steady her view.

Sarah swore.

She had three pick-up vehicles, all fitted with carrying slots for stretchers. Three pick-ups could take eighteen casualties. With the binoculars she counted forty litters being carried down the hill, then snapped her fingers for the bodyguards and the interpreter to follow and walked back to her vehicle.

She knew what she needed to do and said where she wanted to be driven.

It was a short ride. Around two bends, along a straight stretch flanked by stone-strewn hillsides, past a clump of trees beside which wild flowers grew, and they came to the place where the two pick-up vehicles were parked off the road near to the small village of stone homes with iron roofing. Normally she'd have had time for the kids who ran to greet her. She tossed her hair back, and strode briskly through them, ignoring their expectant faces.

She saw Joe Denton. In the green meadow beyond the village were five lines of bright white pegs. Sitting in a small knot, short of the meadow, were his own guards and his own interpreter, and the local men to whom he was teaching his trade.

She thought him a miserable little man, but from what she knew of him it was typical that he would not allow any other man into the minefield until he had first been into it himself and made his evaluation.

He wouldn't have seen her arrival. Facing away from her, he lay on his stomach, his weight on his elbows, his eyes on his fingers. He wore a biscuit-coloured pair of overalls, but there was a heavy armour-plated waistcoat over his chest, shoulders and back. A helmet with a Perspex visor covered his eyes. Sarah had seen mines detonated often enough from safe distances, and she'd seen all too often the mutilations they made. She didn't think the waistcoat and the helmet would be of too much use to him if his fingers didn't get it right.

She knew about mines: they were a part of the education she had received in northern Iraq, were not on any curriculum in Sydney or London. Even from this distance she could see that Joe Denton was carefully unscrewing the top cover of a VS50. She knew about the

VS50: pressure on the pad in the top cover activated a firing pin into a stab-sensitive detonator, range of 24–30 feet. His hands were holding it and his eyes were nine inches from it. Purchasers of the product could tell the Italian factory whether or not they wanted a metal or a plastic plate inside it – a bastard for a de-miner to find and make safe, easy for a kid to step on. She watched as he unscrewed the top, the painstakingly slow movements of his fingers. He laid the detonator aside, then the disarmed mine. Bloody good – one down, about another ten million to go.

Sarah shouted, 'Joe – Christ, I am sorry to disturb you. It's Sarah. Please, I need a favour, like now.'

He didn't turn to look at her. He was crawling forward and spiking the grass in front of him, probing for his next target.

'Joe, I need help. Please.'

His voice came softly back to her. 'What sort of help?'

'There's a load of casualties coming back from the other side. I don't have the vehicle space. Can I borrow your trucks, and drivers, please?'

'Feel free. Bring them back.'

'You can spare them – great.'

'I'm not going anywhere . . . Wash 'em out before you bring them back.'

In the culture of Joe Denton, and she knew it, she was just a tree hugger. She was a stupid bloody woman, interfering, adding to the dependency culture of Kurdish villagers, achieving bloody nothing, like all the rest of the huggers, the aid-workers. He put down the probe and started to work with a small trowel, the same as her mother used in the garden at home. She never saw his eyes, but she could picture them behind

228

the visor. Very clear, and very certain, eyes that could have looked right through her at that moment.

God knows how, but they did it. They squashed, forced, pushed fifty-two casualties into five pick-ups . . . Not all of them would make it to the hospital. There would be more room for the survivors by the time they reached Arbīl.

In the late afternoon, when the stillness had settled, Omar found Gus, sitting against the low wall, gazing out over the slope of the hill that fell away from him. He saw the boy first, searching, then felt the glow of relief when the boy reached him. Behind the wall goats were penned, restless but quiet. He hadn't waved to the boy, or called to him, but allowed himself to be found. Omar's battered face showed his nervousness.

'I did not know where you were.'

'Didn't you?'

'I have been through the town to find you.'

'Have you?'

'Are you very angry, Mr Gus?'

'I am not angry, Omar, not any more.'

He could not have explained it to the boy, or to anyone he knew, how the early morning of the battle for Tarjil had changed him. The inner man was altered.

The boy squatted down beside him. 'I have to take, Mr Gus, or I do not have anything.'

'I understand.'

'Because I have no father to give to me, and no mother.'

'Yes.'

'Worse than not having anything is to have your anger, Mr Gus.'

The boy shifted up to be against Gus's shoulder. Back where he came from, because he was changed, none of them would have wanted to know him. The boy's sharp smell against him was mingled with the stench of his own body. They would not have known his eyes, which were brighter, colder, staring out from his paint-streaked face. His trousers were torn alongside the reinforcement strips at the knees, and the foliage knitted into the hessian strips of the gillie suit was old and as dead as the man they had known.

'They say your rifle jammed, Mr Gus.'

'Do they?'

'That you beat me in anger because your rifle jammed.'

He did not know where he could have started to explain to the boy, who had nothing, that it was wrong to steal from the dead. But if he had started, he would still have been the same man, would not have been changed. He thought that now there was no place for him to criticize the boy. He no longer had that right, or the inclination to exercise it.

'Is that what they say?'

In the far distance was the flame. He made the promise to himself that he would walk to the flame, and offer no judgements on the boy, and the men who marched with him.

'I told them, Mr Gus, that your rifle jammed.'

He sat in the last sunlight, which beat low against his eyes, and he slipped his arm over the narrow bony shoulders of the boy. He watched the flame burning close to the dipping sun. By comparison it was dimmer, less substantial. The boy wriggled and reached into his pocket, then took Gus's hand and prised it open. In a

230

small cascade the chains of gold, the bracelets, the dull rings and a thin wad of banknotes fell into Gus's palm. He let them drop through his fingers. They lay in the dried dirt between his legs.

He looked down at the tawdry chains and rings. The grey dusk was slipping over the sloped ground that ran to the high, spurting flame, gaining ascendancy once more.

Gus held the boy close, because again the boy had nothing. He thought of the sniper, the man without a face. To himself, he laughed, and wondered whether the sniper, too, with his own people, claimed that his rifle had jammed.

'I didn't fire because I did not see the man I came for . . . You dispute my orders? Then, please, immediately, call the barracks at al-Rashid of the Estikhabarat, and my orders will be confirmed to you. You ask why I did not fire on random targets. My skill is as a sniper, I am not an artillery officer, I don't play with tanks. You ask why I shot the commanding officer of the regiment. He was fleeing in the face of the enemy and abandoning his troops, he disgusted me. Myself, I was the last officer to leave the town. Do you have any more questions for me, General?'

The general would never countermand an order given by the Estikhabarat. Not even he would dare to take action against an officer who had shot down a coward.

'Did you see her?'

'I saw her.'

'But you did not have the opportunity to shoot her?'

He saw the general's sly smile, which invited him to

231

lay his foot on the mantrap. Major Aziz wondered where the brigadier was; he did not understand why, at a time of military movement and confusion, he was not in the communications bunker. He had not seen the brigadier at the crossroads, or on the road between the crossroads and Kirkūk. He thought that he stood among mirrors that distorted all of the images. He did not know who was his friend and who was his enemy.

He retorted, 'I could have shot her. If I had shot her a minimum of a hundred civilians would have been cut down in the counter-strike. You were not there, General, you did not see those people fleeing. If I had shot I would have condemned them. They are citizens of our republic, yes? They have the protection of our President?'

He stood in front of the laundered general. He could smell the scent of the lotions on the man's body. His own was streaked with sweat, the smears of camouflage paint dripped into his eyes and down his stubbled cheeks. The dust from his smock and the mud from his boots flaked to the floor around him.

The map was exposed on the table. At the centre of the map was the crossroads. The lines were drawn in bold Chinagraph from Kirkūk to the crossroads. It was what he understood. The lines were clarity. The mirror images were distortion. At that moment, if he had been able to telephone his wife, speak to her, explain to her, beg her for guidance, she would have told him that he was a simple man and that he should perform his duty. The mirrors twisted his perspective, made ugly his sense of duty. He had never known the mirrors before he had allowed himself to be recruited and gone to lie each night on the flat roof waiting to take his shot. The plan was explained.

'I lose a town for a few hours. I lose a Victory City for a few days, and here I destroy them.' The general stabbed his finger for emphasis on the map. Stained with nicotine, it rested on the ground between the crossroads and Tarjil, at the furthest point of the Chinagraph lines. And the question was silkily put. 'Do your orders permit you to fight there, Major?'

Aziz nodded and stumbled out of the bunker. In the last light of the day he went to find food for his dog and put behind him the images of mirrors that distorted simplicity.

'Hi, Caspar, had a good day?'

'How'd the shopping go?'

Luther was black, cheerful and had joined them four months before at Incerlik from time in Venezuela. Across the office space, Bill and Rusty were clearing their desks and shutting down their consoles for the evening. Luther was scheduled for night duty, and should have been sleeping in the day, but he'd caught a late ride into town. Three plastic bags were slapped down on the desk, which was dominated by the framed photograph of the guy's family. The packages, wrapped in newspaper, poked out from them.

'Went well. I got some good bronze stuff that'll look nice on the walls at home, and a couple of drapes, and a bit of jewellery for Annie that a little oily mother-robber swore was out of a Van grave – you know, the Ararat mountain and Noah story. But what the hell? It was a decent price.'

'Pleased to know that. I've had a poor sort of day.' Bill and Rusty were gone. 'Pull up a chair.'

Luther gangled towards him. The guy was tall enough for basketball. He sat. 'Sorry to hear that, Caspar.'

'I am talking about RECOIL.'

'You have my full attention.'

'I hate the Need-to-Know bullshit. There are three strands to RECOIL. I have the three, for my sins. Bill has one, Rusty has one, you have one.'

'I have one, correct.'

Bill was briefed on the movement of an armoured column, Rusty on the uprising led by a woman, Luther covered the plan's third element – the same in the Agency's posts in Amman and Riyadh, a three-way split for the watchers.

'Not any more. You had Major Karim Aziz and his goddam rifle down in Baghdad – but not any more. I hear, sadly on the best authority, that he's been deployed to Kirkūk.'

'Shit.'

'Aptly said, Luther. It's like a strand is cut.'

'Frankly, Caspar, are two strands enough?'

'Maybe, maybe not. I just don't know . . .'

The last time Caspar Reinholtz had known the quivering, gut-turning apprehension as a plan went to the wire had been three years before. Two strands then. The promise of a culvert bomb near to the Abbasio Palace to catch the motorcade, and a mutiny by the 14 July Battalion. The cars hadn't come, the culvert bomb hadn't been fired, but the battalion had moved on the Baghdad Radio transmitters and a heliport used by the President – poor bastards. The arrest, torture, mutilation, execution of a cousin had provoked a general to lead the battalion in mutiny. One strand hadn't been enough to carry the weight. The troops with their tanks had been massacred, the general had killed himself. That night, he'd written his report in frustrated anger, and known that, once again, the President sat in his goddam palace and laughed at a failure of American policy. He'd sent further reports of the round-up arrests, the hangings in the Abu Gharib gaol, and hated writing them because he knew they all reeked of failure.

'What I can tell you, if another strand goes, RECOIL is fucked sideways.'

'You've been here for ever, Caspar. How many times have we been to the brink, had a really good scene in place, had the Boss for Life in the sights, had all the players lined and ready to go, and seen it all go down?'

Not a week went by without his superiors pursuing him for details of the chance of insurrection, mutiny, treachery in Iraq that would topple the President, the Boss for Life. They waited at Langley, champagne on ice, for the day they could dance and sing on the man's grave. Every photograph of the President, out of Baghdad, showed the shit laughing.

'More times than I'd like to count, Luther. I have to play positive, it's what I'm paid to be, but if either of the other two goes belly-up, it's over. And I'm getting a bad feeling in my gut. That's why I've had a poor sort of day.'

A plan of mutiny must spread.

In the last days, before execution, it must breathe and move beyond a cabal of key conspirators whispering in secrecy. At a crucial moment of maximum risk, the plan must be shared if the recruitment of others is to be won and it is to reach critical mass.

The brigadier was a hard, tempered fighting man.

His staff car drove him past the sentries and into the compound of an armoured division of the Republican Guard. It was said, in the eddy of whispered rumours that passed amongst the chosen families of the regime, that the niece of the general commanding the division of the Republican Guard had been propositioned for sex by a nephew of the President, had declined the overture, and had been insulted. The rumour said the nephew of the President had called the niece of the general a 'barren useless goat'. When it happened and the drive south began, down the highway from Kirkūk to Baghdad, the brigadier's armour must pass through Tuz Khurmātū, the garrison camp he now entered.

He was without fear. As a battalion commander he had survived the ferocious battles to hold the Basra road against the Khomeini zealot hordes, coming at his bunkers in human waves. As a brigade commander, he had been widely praised by his peers for keeping his unit intact as a cohesive fighting force confronting the American 1st Armoured Division. No-one had ever doubted his courage or his tactical skill to his face . . . but no promotion had come his way. He should have had command of a division; he should have had the riches that were the reward of a divisional commander. The months had turned to years, the festering resentment had grown, and he had welcomed his recruitment to the plan. When it succeeded he would receive – it was promised him – the Defence Ministry. Also promised was a draft of one million American dollars.

He was saluted and ushered with deference up the

steps of the general's villa. If he had been a man who knew fear there would have been a slight crease of anxiety on the brigadier's face, because a sniper had been transferred abruptly from Baghdad to Kirkūk. Fear was not a sector of his character.

His boots beat on a marble floor, a door was opened for him.

The plan must be shared.

Joe Denton thought she'd probably done it herself. He walked round the two pick-ups with a surly stride. The seats in the front and the floor in the back of each vehicle had been hosed, scrubbed, wiped clean. Joe had heard the vehicles arrive at the roadside by the village, but he'd worked in the meadow until there was no longer light to continue. Then he'd crawled back along the peg-marked path that was cleared. It had been a slow day, but the pace was the same as every other. Beside the road was the return for his work. He had extracted and made safe fourteen VS50s and three V69s. Next week he would allow the locally employed de-miners to start, not before; he was not yet satisfied, from his own expert skill, that the mines hadn't shifted from the straight rows in which they had been planted. It would be at least three weeks before he could take a beer with the villagers and tell them they could use that meadow of best grazing grass. He finished the inspection of the vehicles.

'Thanks.'

'Thanks for loaning them.'

'Do you want something to eat.'

'Wouldn't mind – like to hear about my day, what I heard?'

'If you want to tell me,' Joe said gruffly.

237

They were as lonely as each other. Neither had a friend amongst the Kurds they worked with. They were both employers, there to maintain discipline, had the authority to dismiss their workers and take the decisions that mattered. Without friends they existed in a vacuum of trust. They had little in common other than proximity and loneliness. She was the blond, weather-tanned girl from a Sydney suburb; Joe was the straggly built one-time soldier from the west of England. No point of their cultures intersected. She needed company, and with bad grace he needed the same.

They sat under a tree.

Sarah said, 'We started with fifty-two casualties. There was every sort of wound you could imagine. We had brain damage, livers, spinal cords, stomachs, lungs, main arteries – we had the lot – and they'd only brought the worst. Christ knows about the people left behind. We started with them all squashed in. There was room when we finished the journey.'

She laughed.

He thought it was the shock that made her laugh.

'You know, Joe, when we finished we had them all bedded down in the pick-ups, nice and restful, thirty-seven when we reached Arbīl. We had dropped off fifteen. The ones I was with told me about the battle. There's a town called Tarjil over the ridges there and it was defended by a regiment, a whole bloody regiment. I'm not a soldier, Joe, but I would have thought soldiering is about watching your arse. They went frontal, up the main street. They ran against machine-guns – is it me or is that just dumb?'

Joe's hand slipped to her arm to stop her. He waved in the gloom towards his bodyguards and made a gesture of eating. They should bring some food. He touched her again to tell her that he listened. He knew about fighting. His experience of war was close second-hand, moving behind the combat troops in Kuwait and making safe unexploded ordnance. After the guns had gone silent he had been in the Iraqi slit trenches and in their bunkers, dealt with their ordnance, and seen the slaughter's end-game.

'I don't know how I'd be if I'd had half my guts taken away – maybe not too bloody happy. Not one whined. It's all for freedom. They say they have to fight for their freedom. Is that crap, Joe? There's this woman leading them called Meda, and she's told them about freedom. I don't suppose you've met her but I have, and they'd follow her wherever she goes. This morning, dawn, she took them to hell.'

He sat against the tree-trunk. She was beside him. He had his legs pulled up tight and his arms wrapped round them. His chin was down on his knees as he stared at the dark ground in front of his boots.

'God, I don't know what freedom is. No way I know what their idea of freedom means. The nearest I know about freedom is when my bloody contract here is finished and I get out and I've money in the bank to spend. Can you imagine, Joe, running up an open road into gunfire because that's the way to find freedom? There's a part of it that we're involved in, you and me, Joe. It's only a small part, but we're in there.'

He looked up sharply.

Sarah said, 'I took a letter from an old man. The old man, Hoyshar, is the woman's grandfather. The letter was addressed to an Englishman. I gave you the letter, you promised you'd hand it on. Did you?'

239

The memory of what he'd done, and thought nothing of, welled back in him. He nodded. He remembered what he had forgotten, the name on the envelope. He stared into her eyes and didn't answer.

She pressed. 'Moving that letter ensured our bloody involvement . . . Apparently some sniper came out here because of that letter. A guy from England, didn't have to. You know what they said, those guys who were wounded, with their guts hanging out, without arms, with holes in their lungs? The poor simple bastards say he is the best shot they ever knew, but they were hurt at Tarjil because his rifle fouled up and he couldn't shoot over them. He came because of that letter I gave to you and you moved on. No-one else came. After Tarjil they're going to hit a brigade camp, and then it's Kirkūk. And the daft fuckers think they'll win because of one sniper and the woman.'

'They'll be out of the mountains,' Joe said grimly, 'be in the open. The tanks'll put them through the mincer.'

'Makes you feel small, doesn't it? Involved but not able to help. Fucking small.'

'I just do my job. That's what I'm here for. Nothing more.'

Joe Denton, twenty years in the Royal Engineers, specialist in explosives, stared down at the shadowy pile of the seventeen mines he had made safe that day. In the backpack beside him, with his helmet and armoured waistcoat, were the seventeen detonators. If Joe, the corporal, had not been screwing the daughter of a Military Police officer on his last posting in Germany, if he'd not smacked the officer's chin when ordered to stay away from his little angel, he'd still be in the army, and would be without involvement.

'I'm thinking of all that shit going on out there, while all I do is sit back here and pick up the fucking pieces.'

The food was brought to them. They sat under the tree and the night settled around them.

'I had toothache this morning, Joe. What I saw today made me forget it. Toothache just doesn't compete. It's all in the mind.'

'My last war . . . What a hell of a way to finish.'

'Prizes, awards – hey, and rises. I hear cash registers.'

'You want to get killed, Mike? Try somewhere to get killed that people care about, Dean. It's the way the world works.'

They were still in Diyarbakir's premier league watering-hole, the bar of the Hotel Malkoc, huddled around a table by the window.

'It'd be the ultimate bow out.'

'I might get a professorship in media studies, out in the Midwest.'

'Don't kid yourself. People wouldn't even bother to look in the atlas to find where you were killed.'

It had been the end of another fruitless day of obstruction and failure, capped by a lousy meal. Mike, Dean and Gretchen had swapped their sob stories, and had moved on to the inevitable – the pull-out, the booking of air tickets – when the Russian had sidled up and greeted them as old friends.

'How did he know about us? I mean, how?'

'Because we talk too much, Mike.'

'That German, I say it myself, he is a complete sod.'

Gretchen pulled a face, her mouth curled in disgust. So, they had been talking flights out from Diyarbakir when the stiletto-thin German, Jürgen, had intruded into their group and made the introduction. The proposition had been put. The German and the Russian were behind them, leaning comfortably at the bar. Fifteen thousand dollars was the price.

'I'd be putting my reputation on the line, asking the office for a guarantee of five thou.'

'They'd crucify me if they paid up and he was a conman.'

'It's not the point. The point is the *danger*. Don't you see that? It's the danger of going in there, and nobody caring.'

'Then we'll just have to make them care,' Mike said boldly. It had been written of him in a television rag that he'd dodged more bullets than John Wayne. The image was there to be maintained. He twisted and waved to the Russian to join them.

Gretchen had her eyes tight shut. She grimaced. 'I can't quite believe it is actually true.'

'Actually true . . .' The Russian beamed behind her, then bent to offer the posture of confidentiality. 'You talk about the woman. Twenty-four hours ago, in Iraq, I was with her. I met her. You have the word of Lev Rybinsky. Look at my feet, look at my clothes, look at the mud. I walked across mountains to meet her, to be with her, and walked back. I am very sincere with you. The money is not for me, it is to open the door of the route to her. There is no profit in this to me. I have come to you because of my love for the freedom of an abused people. The world should know about her. For me, there would be no financial gain.'

'You'd take us?' Mike asked, breathily.

'Of course.'

'We'd see combat?' the American demanded.

'She is marching to Kirkūk and she will not stop. The storm is gathering – yes, my guarantee, you would see combat.'

'We would walk with her?' Gretchen queried nervously.

'You would walk beside her – for fifteen thousand American dollars – into a liberated Kirkūk. I regret I cannot drop the price. Did you know there was a foreign sniper with her?'

AUGUSTUS HENDERSON *PEAKE*.

4. (Conclusions after interview with Ray Davies (owner of Davies and Sons, haulage company) conducted by self and Ms Carol Manning – transcript attached.)

TEMPERAMENT: AHP is an intensely private individual, and is therefore probably best known by his employer. He has worked for the company all his adult life, starting as a teaboy/office runner aged 18, and rising to the position of Transport Manager. Much is made at the company of the stressful pace of the job – much is also made of AHP's ability to cope with that stress. Words used to describe his TEMPERAMENT are 'phlegmatic', 'patient' and 'calm'. They are the descriptions of a character most appreciated by instructors in sniper arts. Interestingly, the owner knew next to nothing of AHP's life away from the workplace. His shooting passion with the Historic Breech-loading and Small-arms Association was not

243

mentioned. He brought his partner with him to social events, the Christmas party etc., but his personal life was lived behind a closed door. However, importantly, it was made clear that AHP lacks a ruthless side to his character. (The example is minor but indicative of character.) He was unsettled when given the task of sacking a driver who was persistently behind schedule on trans-European journeys, and 'wriggled' over clear evidence that a second driver was claiming paid sick leave for a bogus ailment. The TEMPERAMENT is excellent for the role AHP has given himself, but I doubt he has the necessary 'steel' for combat. Also, without a long knowledge of MILITARY WEAPONS and MILITARY TRAINING, his chances of medium-term survival remain slim to non-existent.

Willet pondered on that last sentence.

He had found, each time he wrote his notes for Ms Manning's line manager, an increasing urge to talk up the positive character points of this man. The urge was based, and Willet recognized it, on a growing sense of jealousy. He believed that somehow, and in the most unobtrusive way, he was belittled by Augustus Henderson Peake.

He never moved without an order to do so. In his analysis, he was an automaton and a robot. But Peake had made his own decisions, had packed up and travelled on his own impulses. Willet would never be his own man, not now and not once he had left the military. From the jealousy was born knowledge and admiration.

The concept of a transport manager affecting the

course of a faraway war was laughable, of course, yet the worm of doubt ate at him. He remembered an old army video, shown to the sniper course at Warminster in monochrome, that had listed the sort of civilians who might have the required qualities. Not a transport manager among them, but . . . A *fisherman* can sit all day at a canal bank and not see his float go down: he has the virtue of patience. A *steeplejack* can climb to great and dangerous heights, knows his safety is in his own hands, that a false move will end his life. A *countryman* can shoot straight and move silently, is cunning and thinks ahead to anticipate the movement of his prey. A *clerk* can spend an entire day with columns of figures, has the priceless power of concentration that shuts out distractions.

All ordinary men, and all fashioned into killers by the instructors. That was the answer. Peake had the necessary virtues, but not the military weapons and tactics. Willet realized that what had started as a tedious, late-at-night instruction to pry into an ordinary man's life was turning into a search for the Grail.

He printed what he had written and phoned out for a delivery pizza. Waiting for it to arrive, he wondered whether he undersold that ordinary man, whether Peake could survive, whether the forces arrayed against him were too great and whether that enemy was closing in on him.

Late at night, another simple man – who knew only his chosen trade – went back to the war.

He had not taken the chance of a bath, or gone to the officers' quarters to eat, or telephoned his wife.

In Aziz's backpack was more food for the dog, and for

245

himself there was the filled water canteen, goat's cheese and bread.

He was driven in an open jeep towards the cross-roads, away from the flame. When next he saw her, whether there were a hundred or a thousand between them, he would shoot her. It was the decision of a man who craved simplicity. He would shoot her, over the heads of a hundred or a thousand, regardless of the consequences of a counter-strike, then go with his dog to hunt the sniper who opposed him. With the clean wind on his face, he thought that he had broken the distortion of the mirrors. He was well read. There were many books in English on military history in the library of the Baghdad Military College. If he wanted to learn their secrets, he had to have the language and over the years he had taken the chance to read textbooks, pamphlets and manuals of the British army. A book had told him of Claus Schenk Graf von Stauffenberg. It had troubled the simple soldier and, perhaps, had led him along the road of recruitment and mirrors. Stauffenberg had lost faith in his Führer, did not believe in a hopeless war. Stauffenberg was the bomb carrier and had failed, was shot like a dog in the hooded headlights of lorries. How was he regarded by those who lived and fought in Normandy and in the Russian marshes? The mirrors did not make him a hero but a traitor. To troops remorselessly retreating, Stauffenberg was the man who betrayed his fellow soldiers . . . He would shoot her.

He broke the mirrors in his mind, and after he had shot the witch he would hunt down the sniper.

Gus had slept, woken, started, and at that moment not known where he was.

'Did you dream, Mr Gus?'

'No. I dreamed nothing.'

He wiped his eyes with his sleeve. His hand dropped to the dirt beside his legs. The small, cold shapes of the chains, bracelets, rings, and the rolled notes were still there. The boy could have pocketed them in the darkness while he slept, and had not. He hadn't dreamed of home. Home was behind him. Home would not have understood that a boy thieved from bodies because he had nothing. The boy had not pocketed the trinkets and Gus felt a humble love for him, and couldn't have told them at home about that love. Far away, the flame burned at Kirkūk. Between him and the flame was the infinite spread of the darkness.

'Will you be angry again?'

'That's in the past.'

'Will the rifle jam again?'

'No, not this time.'

'It is what I said. The *mustashar* came with Meda. They wanted to talk to you about the rifle, but I would not let them wake you. I said that you had cleaned the rifle and it would not jam again. They wanted to hear it from you but I did not let them wake you.'

'Thank you.'

'Will you tell me, Mr Gus, a story of Hesketh-Prichard?'

He closed his eyes. He let the quiet seep against him. 'Right, yes . . . It's a story that Major Hesketh-Prichard tells about a man whose bravery and dedication he much admired – and that man was an enemy. The troops may have hated the enemy. Snipers weren't taken prisoner by those in the trenches, they were shot in cold blood there and then. But a sniper doesn't hate his opponent. There is respect for the skill of the other. He will try to kill him, hope to succeed, but there is always respect.'

'Please, Mr Gus, the story.'

'You're an impatient little sod . . . There was a big-game hunter, Jim Corbett – elephants and lions were what he killed before the war – he told this story to Hesketh-Prichard. Corbett always gave names to the enemy's snipers and he called this one Wilibald the Hun. Wilibald the Hun was credited with killing more than twenty British soldiers. For days they looked for Wilibald across the turnip field in no man's land but couldn't find him. There had to be a trick to make him fire when the snipers on the British side were all looking for him. On a cold winter's morning, with a frost over the field, they put up a heavy steel plate with an observation slit in it. He fired at the slit, shot right through it, but that wasn't Wilibald's mistake. The mistake he made, and it cost Wilibald his life, was to fire early on a cold morning. The gas from the rifle, when there's cold air and no wind, hangs for a few moments. It makes a marker. All the snipers fired into the gas. They went forward. Wilibald was in the turnip field only seventy yards from the British line, way out in front of his own trenches. He was covered in turnip leaves. He was middle-aged, very ordinary, rather fat, and he was respected for his courage and his skill . . . but Wilibald the Hun made the one mistake and that's all it takes.'

Chapter Ten

'The tanks will not be used,' Meda said.

A fire still burned in the roof of the police station's main block and the tang of the smoke caught in Joe Denton's nostrils. He had hiked blindly across the mountains all through the night; in an hour it would be dawn. Other than when he had smacked his girlfriend's father's face, he had never in his adult life done anything as stupid as leave the safety of northern Iraq and travel through the punched hole into government territory. The thanks he received were, he felt, bloody minimal.

'They will not use the tanks they have in Kirkūk.' She turned on her heel and stalked off.

Arrogant cow. Arrogant good-looking cow, though, none the less. Joe watched her, saw the firm roll of her hips as she walked away from him, and before that he'd seen the clean-cut lines of her chest where her blouse was unfastened.

Scattered through the police-station yard were huddles of men who waited without protest for her to find the time to come, hear their problems, talk to them. He had tried to help. He had joined a column of reinforcements, walked through the goddam night, unloaded the mines from the backs of two mules and believed he would be welcomed, thanked. On the hike across the high wilderness, Sarah had talked of the woman, said she was the last best chance, was unique, not said she was an arrogant cow. So, they didn't want his bloody mines . . . There had been an older man near to her, a pace behind her. When the woman had dismissed the chance of tanks being deployed out of Kirkūk, the older man had gazed to the heavens as though argument were pointless – and then had trailed away after her.

Joe settled himself against a truck's wheel and closed his eyes. Sarah had gone to the town hospital to get busy and executive and organize a convoy to take more wounded back north where they could receive better treatment. She knew where he was. He sat close to the heap of mines, cold, hungry, his pride punched. For her and her march south, he had broken the inviolate rule of the charity that employed him. He had taken sides. He had stepped off the lofty pedestal on which he was supposed to stand. He had only been a corporal in the Royal Engineers, but he'd learned enough about military tactics to believe that he would have been of some use to these bloody peasants.

'Godforsaken fucking place!' he spat.

'I thought you were sleeping.' There was a gravelly chuckle above him.

Joe stared into the darkness, blinked and saw the shadowed outline of the older man.

It came in a torrent. 'Don't mind me – I've only put my job on the line. I came here to do something that is almost criminal, to bring you mines. I've dug them up and now I'm offering them to you to bury them again.

Stupid or criminal, take your pick. I thought I was helping. But it appears I'm surplus to requirements.'

'You have our gratitude.'

'It's a hell of a way to show it. She—'

'She is what takes us forward.'

'She is an arrogant cow.'

'She is what has brought us here. I am Haquim, the *mustashar*. I am, if I am listened to, the adviser on tactics. You are a military man, Mr Denton?'

Joe said bitterly, 'Not an officer, not a bloody Rupert. Corporal, ex, Royal Engineers, if it matters . . .'

The older man squatted beside him. 'Would you know, Mr Denton, how – where – to lay mines for the maximum effectiveness, with an expert sniper, against tanks?'

'She said there would be no tanks.'

'That's what she said . . .'

Joe took a deep breath, as if it were a moment when his involvement firmed. 'Yes, I might be able to help you in that area.'

The older man unfolded a map, shone his torch down on it and pointed to the position of Fifth Army in Kirkūk and the crossroads outside the city. His finger traced a line on the route that linked them. He remembered what he had said to Sarah, a few minutes less than twelve hours before: the tanks would mince them. He was told what weapon the sniper carried, the calibre and capability of the ammunition the rifle fired. His face was close to the ragged map. Joe talked softly, carefully, asked for paper and a pencil, and for the man to give him a couple of minutes to think it through. He had an idea but it would be a betting man's throw.

By the time Haquim returned, he had drawn the plan.

Haquim folded away the map. Joe asked, 'Where's the sniper?'

Haquim shrugged.

'I need to talk to him,' Joe said. 'He's the one who has to get it right. If he doesn't get it right, and the tanks come, then everyone's toast.'

The crossing of the mountains was hard going. There were no lights to guide them and the German hissed a protest each time they kicked a rock or set a stone tumbling down from the path.

Four hours into their march the discipline was fracturing.

'God, what I'd give for a drink . . .' Mike whispered.

'A bed, a clean bed . . .' Dean murmured.

Gretchen soldiered on, her mind apparently elsewhere.

They heard Jürgen's guttural whisper for quiet. Did they not realize the density of Turkish army patrols?

'All right for that human fucking parasite, he's not carrying half a ton of gear.' Mike's cameraman, propositioned late in the evening, had flatly refused to take part in a night march over the mountains from Turkey into northern Iraq. Equally resolutely, Dean and Gretchen had declined to help Mike with the camera equipment. If they bounced a patrol they risked being shot out of hand in the darkness, or they faced arrest, thuggery, unpleasant interrogation, and a week's sojourn in Diyarbakir's military gaol. Significantly, the German, Jürgen, carried nothing.

They were at a narrow point in the path, which was good enough for low-life smugglers, but for the journalistic pride of London, Baltimore and Frankfurt it was hell. There was a cliff wall to the left, a loose-stoned track for them to walk on, and a precipice to the right. Each of them had an idea of the depth of the precipice: the last rock dislodged by Gretchen had slid from under her boot and fallen, fallen for an age before they'd heard its distant impact. The bastard Russian, back at the Hotel Malkoc, with a drink and a clean bed and probably a woman, would meet them in the morning. He'd said it was impossible for them to be hidden in a lorry for the border crossing. They'd walk – maybe get shot, or at least captured – and if they made it through he'd meet them.

'After we come back, I promise to do that swine proper damage.'

'*If* we come back.'

'Get positive, Gretchen – Mike, you'll have me to help you.'

The wind ripped at their clothes, the cold shredded them and all for a story about a woman leading a distant army, talk of freedom, the prospect of air-time and column inches. They held hands and made a chain, and stumbled on after the German. Holding hands was their small gesture to each other of solidarity – if one went over the goddam precipice they'd all go.

'Why are we doing this?'

'I am doing this, Gretchen, for my real-estate mortgage.'

'Anyone who does this, goes into northern Iraq and not for money, is an idiot,' Gretchen said solemnly.

He saw the man.

The dawn came slowly, layering the light across the ground. Before its arrival, Aziz had crawled for an hour in a network of rain gullies until he had reached a vantage-point where he could conceal himself and watch. It was the furthest forward he could go and he was settled beside the collapsed roof of rusted tin and the broken wooden frame of what had once been a shepherd's shelter. He could go no further forward because the ground ahead of him was scratched empty and bare by the wind. Not even his dog, resting beside his knee, could have crossed that ground and remained concealed.

The dawn had come from over the high hills to the left of the man. Beyond the wind-whipped, sun-scorched ground that stretched three times the range of the Dragunov was an isolated clump of rocks rubbed smooth by the elements. The man sat on the rocks and made no effort to conceal himself.

Aziz's eyesight, unaided, was not adequate, but with his telescope he could see him clearly.

As the sun rose, as the heat settled on the ground, his view of the man would become distorted, but the air at dawn was cold enough for him to see the man in sharp focus.

He understood why the man showed himself. It was a challenge.

Through the telescope, Major Karim Aziz watched the man who was his enemy. He saw the dirt and the dust that cloyed the overalls, and the confused tangle of the hessian strips, and he saw but did not recognize the shape of the rifle that was held loosely across the man's thighs. The face of the man was paint-smeared and daubed with mud, and there was a dark shadow of stubble over his cheeks and chin. Sitting on the rock with his rifle, the man seemed at peace.

Aziz knew from his experience of the battles against the Iranians that there were times when soldiers sought calm, as if at those moments the hate in them for their enemy died. Later, they would fight . . . they would stalk . . . they would kill. In the quiet, killing men looked for the faces of their enemy as if there was a need to prise away the masks, as if to find something of brotherhood. He could not reach the man. The flat, featureless ground between them prevented him from a hidden stalk and a single rifle shot, and the man knew it.

He was disturbed, could not lift away the mask – and, confused, could not make the brotherhood. The challenge mocked him.

Major Karim Aziz knew what he had to do. If he did not do it, the fear would take root. If the fear was in him, when the peace was gone he would not aim and shoot well. Fear was the true enemy of the sniper. If he did not answer the challenge, he would know his fear had conquered him. The strength of the sun was growing on his back and the dog panted beside him. In a few minutes, a little time, the heat would have settled on the ground and the clarity of his lens would subside to mirage and distortion . . . He thought of his wife, in the hospital, with the children who had no drugs – and he wondered whether this man, sitting at peace, had a wife. He thought of his children, in the school that had no books – and he wondered whether this man had children.

Aziz put his telescope back into his backpack and stood.

He walked away from the shepherd's shelter with his backpack looped over his shoulders and his rifle loose in his hands. Far beyond the growing shimmer as the ground warmed was the outline of the rocks, and he did not know whether, at three thousand metres, the man noticed his movement, but it was important to him that he had picked up the challenge.

He turned his back on the man and headed towards the road, Scout skipping beside him.

The next time he saw him, when there was no peace and no calm, he would kill the man.

'He's a champion, that's what you have to realize. He's a winner.'

Willet had told Ms Manning that they were going to the seaside. It wasn't strictly true. The industrial estate east of Southampton allowed them a slight whiff of the sea, but no view of it. The unit that had produced the brochure he'd taken from Peake's safe in the haulage-company offices was old, uncared-for and drab. It was anonymous: only the steel-plated door and the small heavily barred windows gave evidence of the factory's product inside. They sat in a small, untidy office and the walls around them were hung with photographs of weapons. The sales director, earnest and bright-eyed, a communicator, had told the outer office to hold his calls.

'He's *can*, *will*, *must*. I see enough of them, I recognize them. I call it being "the master of circumstances". It's about the ability to withstand pressure, and I'm talking about extreme stress.'

It was the unpeeling of another layer. Willet scribbled his notes, but Ms Manning gazed around her and studied the photographs. He thought he'd brought her to new territory, and her expression showed she thought it disreputable.

'Look, if Gus Peake had not decided to interest himself in firing a half-century-old sniper rifle, if he'd focused on the modern equipment, he'd be right up in the top flight of the Queen's Hundred. I'd go as far as to say that he'd be challenging for the Queen's Prize. Instead he chose the sort of demanding discipline that will not produce celebrities, but he's still the best at that discipline. He won't get a chair ride at Bisley, won't have a cabinet of display cups, but I'll wager he has a drawerful of spoons, if you know what I mean.'

Afterwards Willet would have to explain to Ms Manning about Bisley, about the annual shoot that was the showpiece for the year, the choosing of the hundred best marksmen for the last day's competition, and the lifting of the winner onto a chair so that he could be hoisted to receive the Queen's Prize as the band played 'See the Conquering Hero Comes'. He might tell her that in 1930 a woman had sat in the chair and been seren-aded . . . He cursed himself for allowing distraction to cloud his thoughts. It was why Ken Willet was not a champion and never would be, and why he'd failed the sniper course.

'I liked his mind management. He's very quiet. When he was down here he only spoke when he had some-thing to ask. Some customers talk the whole time, think that'll impress me. He's not afraid of silence. That's important – it marks a man down as one who doesn't have conceit.'

Ms Manning frowned. Willet wondered, after they'd gone, whether the pair of them, the investigators, would be dissected by the sales director to his colleagues – whether he and Ms Manning would be categorized as conceited or confident, or simply from a second division.

'Confidence and conceit are very different things.

Conceit is failure, confidence is success. A conceited man cannot abide failure and turns away from any area where he may lose. But a confident man thinks through the ground conditions then backs his intuition. Champions are confident, not conceited – that's why Gus Peake is a champion. I've known him for the last three years. You see, we make military and civilian rifles, so I go to Bisley. Target-shooting with modern rifles can be about as dull as watching paint dry – I usually wander over to the HBSA people for a chat and a coffee, it's how I met him. I'm not a friend, I doubt he has any, he didn't seem the type – but I've watched him shoot and talked through shooting problems. He has my respect. What's he up to?'

'You don't have to know that,' Ms Manning said coldly.

Willet cut in, offering a little truth for something more, 'He's in northern Iraq. It's a long story, doesn't affect you, but he's with a group of Kurdish tribesmen. He's gone to war.'

'It *might* just affect me. What he purchased from me was sale or return. I promised him a good price if he brought the kit back.'

Ms Manning asked, 'What did he buy?'

'Just so that there are no misunderstandings, he produced a section 1 firearms certificate, so he is quite entitled to purchase a bolt-action rifle, and it was quite legal for me to sell it to him. Obviously he's passed all the necessary user tests, he's a member of a recognized club, he's satisfied the police that he owns a secure gun box. Do you want to see what I sold him?'

Manning nodded. He swung round his chair and darted for a side door, leaving them at the table. She sipped her coffee; Willet reached for the last of the biscuits that had come on a plate with the coffee mugs.

The rifle was slapped down on the table in front of them. Ms Manning spluttered on her coffee.

It was a killing machine, she could recognize that, as Willet could. It was nothing about sport, but was for killing men. The butt, stock and barrel were painted a dull olive. It was tilted upwards by a fixed bipod, and the polished glass of the telescopic sight winked malevolently. The sales director didn't ask her, but picked it up and dumped it in Ms Manning's hands.

'That's it, that's what Gus bought. The grand title is AWM .338 Lapua Magnum. I say it myself, it's the best thing we make and the best sniper rifle that anyone makes, anywhere.'

Very slowly, bulging the biceps under her blouse, Manning lifted it to her shoulder. She'd tilted her spectacles up on to her forehead. Her eye peered into the sight, her finger was on the trigger. Willet wondered whether she'd ever held a rifle before. Her aim moved round the office, from the leave chart to the computer screen in the corner, from the computer screen to an American presented plaque, from the plaque to the window and wavered as a seagull flew close, from the seagull to Ken Willet's head and chest. It was the first time he had seen her grin in that way. She had the power, given her by the size, weight, sleekness of the rifle. He looked into the small, dark abyss of the barrel. She squeezed. He felt sick, his stomach twisting. She put the rifle on the table and dropped her spectacles back over the bridge of her nose.

'Don't ever do that again,' Willet hissed. 'Don't ever point a weapon . . .'

She laughed in his face.

'That's what Gus has taken. In the right hands it's a serious weapon. Sale or return, as I said. Am I going to see it back here? I suppose that depends on what he learned down in Devon.'

'You sat out there?' There was an accusing note in Haquim's voice.

'Yes.'

'Alone? Without protection?'

'Yes,' Gus said.

'Where you could be seen?'

'Where I could be seen.'

'For why? For what?'

'I can't explain.'

'You talk serious rubbish . . . Meda says there will be no tanks.'

'Does she?'

'If Meda says it the men will believe her.'

'Will they?'

'You think yourself amusing, Mr Peake . . .'

He was light-headed, as if drunk with alcohol.

As the sun had climbed Gus had tramped back to the outskirts of the town and to the low wall that penned the goats where he had left Omar. He had had to shout at the boy to drill home the instruction that he was not to be followed. There had been a purpose to his long, lonely walk, to evaluate the ground over which they would fight in the morning. He had sat on a rock and soaked the place into his body and his mind. He had wanted to test his powers of observation and to reckon out the camouflage he would need and to measure the visibility that would be available to him as the heat grew . . . He had known he was being watched. Gus had not seen him, but at one point there had been the flash of sunlight striking the prism of a lens. It was the knowledge that he had been watched from a great distance that induced the impertinence he threw back at Haquim. The *mustashar* sobered him, jolted him.

'Have you thought that you might be taken, Mr Peake? Not killed clean – captured, dirty.'

'No.'

'Perhaps that is what you should think. It is all a bluff. We must create an illusion of energy, strength. We have to go forward on a narrow thrust. Each step we go forward takes us further from the protection of the mountains. Tomorrow that protection is behind us. We are in the open. We go forward, and every step we advance we make the salient deeper and we expose the flanks. Do you know about flanks, Mr Peake? The most important thing is that they can be pinched. I put it very simply to you, when you make a salient with flanks you can be cut off, you can be surrounded, and squeezed. You wonder that I am worried? I carry the worry alone. *She* has no idea of the danger of encirclement. She has no military experience. Meda believes only in the certainty of her destiny, and she says there will be no tanks. I'm not asking for sympathy, but I have the right to demand that you do not make fun of me. She says there will be no tanks, but it is for me to consider whether she might be wrong. She does not ask it of me but I fear for her, for those who follow her, for myself, for you – if the tanks come and we are not killed cleanly.'

'I apologize,' Gus said quietly. 'I apologize sincerely.'

'You have to meet a man who has brought mines to

261

hear how a sniper should use the mines – if she is wrong and if the tanks come.'

Gus followed Haquim back through the town towards the police station to listen to another expert.

The brigadier was a strong man, and he shivered as he watched the tanks being armed and fuelled. He had shared, spread the conspiracy, and the promises were piled behind him. He had the promise of the witch and her *peshmerga* army, and the promise of the Americans, and the promise of men in Baghdad. But – and he knew the sort of promises that wafted around men committed to insurrection – there were always more promises. Never had sufficient promises been heaped behind the officers planning a *coup d'état*. With insufficient promises there was a short walk to the gallows. He needed the promise of the general at Tuz Khurmātū.

The huge tank shells, 125mm calibre, were being lifted into the hatches. The fuel lorries were alongside the leviathans, loading the diesel. In the morning he would address the officers of the armoured brigade and demand their loyalty to him as their commander, and the promises that they would follow him.

He would be a great man if the promises were kept, and a dead man if they were broken.

The brigadier could not shed the chill from his body as the sun beat down on him, and on his tanks.

Present at the meeting were all the male members of the general's extended family.

Inside the barracks compound of the Republican Guard armoured division at Tuz Khurmātū, the windows of the villa were curtained and the door to the salon locked on the inside. The mahogany-framed television set was tuned to a satellite channel from Germany and played promotional music videos, with the sound turned high. They were of the Sunni religion, and of the Dulaimi tribe. Their territory stretched from Fallūjah on the Euphrates river, across the desert wasteland to Al Qāim near the Syrian border. The Dulaimi tribe held second place in the regime's favours and trust after the President's own tribe, the Takriti. They were men hardened by an upbringing in the harsh desert territory of sun-scorched days and bitter night frosts. They were fighters. The sons, cousins and nephews of the general crowded the salon. They wore the insignia on their shoulders of armoured units, artillery, infantry and Special Forces. The general was the head of the family and they listened in silent respect, craned to hear what he said. He was known to his family and his tribe and his tank crews as 'the Hammerfist'. No man had ever doubted his courage.

He explained his dilemma. The general, the Hammerfist, told them of the visit he had received from a brigadier of Fifth Army in Kirkūk, and the proposition put to him.

Did they join the conspiracy, or did they destroy it?

To know of treason, and not to denounce it, was to commit treason. Should the conspiracy founder, should the brigadier be captured and interrogated, should he be broken under torture, should he speak of a meeting with a general that had not been reported to the relevant authorities, then the general too was a conspirator – and all of them who now attended the meeting in the villa's salon. There was no middle way.

If they joined the conspiracy and it succeeded, each of

them would be rewarded. If it failed, however, they would be hanged after they had been tortured. Faced with the dilemma, the general asked for advice as to which course he should follow. He could arm the tanks of his division, or he could pick up the telephone and make a call to the al-Rashid barracks of the Estikhabarat. Which?

The quiet clung around them.

Each man considered insults thrown at him by the regime, and benefits they had gained from it. They thought of the consequences to their families, pondered the reliability of the Kurds, and of an American promise to create a no-fly zone and a no-drive zone above the tanks roaring towards Baghdad.

Straight-backed, hands clasped behind him, the general – the Hammerfist – waited for them to make known their reaction to a devil's dilemma.

At brigade, at the crossroads, five miles north-east of Kirkūk, Major Aziz did what all soldiers do in the last hours before a battle. He cleaned his weapon and wrote a letter to his wife.

They were not dirty, but from habit he cleaned the bolt and the breech, the PSO-1 telescopic sight mounted directly above the trigger, the interior of the magazine, and then he wiped hard at each of the ten rounds of 7.62mm ammunition before returning them to the magazine. All around him, in the gathering darkness, soldiers checked their weapons. When he was satisfied that there was no possibility of a malfunction caused by dirt, he wound the loose rough cloth strips round the butt, stock, 'scope and barrel of the Dragunov.

Aziz found a place close to the command bunker where a small shaft of light spilled out from a narrow firing slit. Also, a part of his routine was to carry in his backpack a few sheets of crumpled writing-paper, with envelopes. He was hunched down so that the spear of light was on his raised thigh, where the paper rested. He wrote only a half-dozen lines. He had written the same letters many times, for fear of not saying goodbye, in Kirkūk, in Basra, and in Kuwait City. The following morning, or a week afterwards, each of those letters had been destroyed, ripped to shreds, because he had lived. He wrote of his love for her, and for the boys – they were jewels on which fell the golden sun – and he thanked her for the happiness she had given him. When he had finished he sealed the sheet of paper in an envelope, put her name on it and placed it in the breast pocket of his shirt, where it would be close to his heartbeat. If he were killed, if he died the next day, or the day after, he held the hope that the letter would be retrieved from his body, perhaps stained in blood, and that it would be taken back to her. Once it was in his pocket, the moments of self-doubt evaporated, the time for reflection was finished.

He slipped into the command bunker. It was buried in the sandy soil, roofed by heavy timbers that were, in turn, covered with bulldozed earth. There was quiet inside, as if the staff officers had already made their preparations. Aziz asked for the plan for the morning, and guidance as to where he and his Dragunov should be positioned. He explained where he believed the enemy's sniper would be.

*   *   *

Joe Denton's voice dripped at him – where he should be, how he should lay the mines, and how and at what point he should arm them.

The column had formed in the darkness outside the police station. Gus said that he understood the plan and thanked Joe for it. Denton reached up, caught at the hessian straps on Gus's shoulders and kissed his cheek, not wet but a brush of the lips against the stubble and the patina of dirt and paint, then turned away. He saw Denton climb into a truck beside the aid-worker. The headlights led a convoy of lorries away to the north; more wounded from the battle for Tarjil were being moved to safety. If he had been able to see the man's face, Denton's, then he thought there might have been tears in the eyes. It was Gus's duty to go forward, but not Denton's, nor was his the responsibility of a grand-father's friendship: he was the victim of destiny, but Joe Denton was not.

After the convoy's lights had slipped away into the darkness, he heard Meda's hectoring voice at the front of the column. When she paused for breath, there was the coughed, spluttered echo of approval. There was a last declaiming shout from her, an exhortation, and the answering bellow of loyalty.

Shuffling at first, but growing in speed, the column surged out of the town. There were no doors open, no upper windows unshuttered, no knots of civilians to watch them go. It was as though they had come as liber-ators and left as a conquering army of occupation. He remembered the tide of vengeance that had ac-companied them. The tramping feet of the column marched over the place where the tarmacadam had been scorched, and under the doused light on the lamp-post over which the noose had been hooked. He walked with Omar and the four men carrying the grain sacks that held the mines. Whether they were liberators or occupiers was the judgement to be made by the people who did not wish them well. Their judgement hammered him. If they were victors they would be liberators; if they were losers they would be occupiers. It hammered him because the people of Tarjil had branded them, sunk the fire into the flesh, as *losers*. No man or woman would shout support for a loser and wish them well. Dirty, fetid, the column left the town and its darkened, empty streets.

Gus thought the mood of the town, its judgement, had caught many of the *peshmerga*. It was not until they were out of the town that the men began to sing. Again and again, with the deep power of their voices, the refrain of the anthem was howled into the night. It was the sound of hungry wolves that came in winter from the high ground to stalk beside barricaded homes in search of food. It was the sound of a predator. Omar sang with them, a high shrill note, as if to prove his adulthood.

'What do they sing?'

He could not see the boy's face in the darkness.

'We are the *peshmerga*, brave heroes of
    Kurdistan,
We will never lay down our arms,
We fight until victory or death.'

Gus grimaced. 'That's bloody cheerful, Omar.'

'We are not frightened of death, Mr Gus. You cannot be frightened of death or you would not have come. We have the power, we have Meda . . .'

Gus marched on. It was strange to him that the bold words Meda had used in the town to the *peshmerga*, and the repetition of the anthem, demonstrated a willingness to face death. He had seen her with the aid-worker when he had been receiving the instructions from Joe Denton. He wondered if Meda had shown the flesh wound to her, whether it had been dressed again, whether it was poisoned or clean. His blister hurt but the pace of the march did not allow him to slow and hobble. It seemed a lifetime since he had last slept decently or eaten well. He thought the civilization of an old life was being steadily stripped from him.

When they were well clear of the town, when no torches were used, when they moved in thin moonlight, the singing died. Haquim had been along the line and demanded quiet. A discipline had settled on the column. Gus wondered, in the quiet broken only by the scrape of weapons' metal and the tramp of feet, if the men thought of home and families – or were their minds as empty as the wolves', the predators'? His own mind, except for the pain of the blister, was void of emotion.

Haquim materialized from the milky darkness. They had reached the point where Gus, Omar, the men carrying the mines and the *mustashar* would break away from the main march towards the crossroads. Meda was beside him.

Meda said, sarcastic, 'Do you need a chair to sit on?'

'I'll send down for room-service and get a beer.'

'You will be comfortable away from the real work, fighting.'

'I've a good book to read.'

She was brittle, contemptuous. 'There will be no tanks.'

'Then I'll enjoy my beer and get on with my book. It'll be a pleasant day out.'

She flounced away, strode off up the column, and in a moment was lost among her men. It was a bad parting. If either of them did not survive the day ahead, the last memory would be of contempt and mockery. The column was going south, but the small group edged to the east and started the big loop that would take them to where Joe Denton advised they should be. Omar led. He had no compass, and had never crossed that featureless, dark-shrouded ground before. He had only been shown on the map but did not pause or look around him. Gus thought it the innate genius of the young dog-wolf.

The boy stopped, crouched, his arm held back, hand open, demanding their total stillness and silence. Gus heard the approaching sounds, the wind over dried leaves. They were huddled together, low on the open ground as the sounds grew closer. At first it merged with the night then, clear in the moonlight, a great caravan passed them. Sheep, men, goats, women, donkeys, children, dogs, all slipped by, never wavering in the path of their journey. Gus was awestruck at the simplicity of what he saw. A nomad tribe on the move, as they had whispered over the ground at night in the time of Cyrus and Salah al-Din Yusuf, nothing changed, secure against the predators, the newer dictators and demagogues. Maybe they had heard, as their forebears would have, that a battle was to be fought, and they moved on. Their dark line passed. As the sounds faded into the night, Omar started out again.

An hour later, they were near to the road, the bridge and the glow of the sentries' cigarettes. The iron-hooped sides of the bridge were lit by the lights of the patrolling armoured personnel carrier.

The sacks with the mines were dumped on the scraped earth beside the road.

Haquim said, 'If the tanks come, if she is wrong, only your skill can save us.'

'I can do my best, friend, but I do not know whether my best is enough.'

'I do not ask for more. Let us pray to God she is correct, that the tanks will not come . . .'

'Then I'll sit in my chair with a beer and a book.'

Haquim hit him hard on the arm. Gus thought that the old soldier equally disliked contempt and frivolity. Haquim was gone, and with him the men who had carried the sacks. He was alone with the boy. The embankment of the road towered above him. He watched the personnel carrier reach the bridge ahead, then reverse and turn, its searchlight spearing the flat, barren ground. They were deep in the ditch below the embankment when it returned, and the searchlight's beam was far above them. They tracked away from the bridge to a place where the embankment was lowest, and Gus armed the mines, while Omar scratched the holes for them.

The burden crushed him. They depended on him.

There were many who saw him go.

The logistics officer in the command bunker, puzzling over the reasoning behind the decision to withdraw two of the three infantry battalions to Kirkūk and even more about the complex manoeuvre to achieve it at night and in secrecy, saw him kick himself up from the chair where he had dozed, hitch on his backpack, sling his rifle, call his dog and go out into the night.

The logistics officer called after him, 'Hit the bastards, Karim, hit them so they scream.'

The sentry ran from behind the sandbag wall and wrenched open the wood-framed wire gates. He was about to scurry back to the security of the sandbags when he realized that the officer stood erect as if no danger could confront him. He saluted clumsily. The officer thanked him, as if he were a friend, and he walked through the gate with the dog. His bulky over-suit dripped with fresh grey mud, and the same mud was embedded in the dog's coat. The sentry saw him unhook his rifle from his shoulder, then hold it loosely across his body as he slipped through a pool of light and away into the shadows. He knew the bandit army coming towards them was led by a woman; it was said, in the tent where he slept when not on sentry duty, that bullets could not harm her, that she was the devil's child. He thanked his god for sending the officer with the big rifle who went to break the magic of the witch.

While Isaac Cohen, Mossad man, slept in his eyrie, the wind-bent antenna sucked down signals, which the computers decrypted.

He slept without a care.

Chapter Eleven

The brigadier, dressing in the darkness before dawn, had selected his best uniform with the medal ribbons of three decades of military service. The orderly had made a fine job of polishing his boots. He had chosen to wear his brigade's scarlet cravat, which hid the heave in his throat. In the shining holster on his webbing belt was his service pistol, loaded and armed. His heart pounded, dinned in his ears, and he did not at first hear the shout from his orderly, a man he would trust with his life.

While he had slept, men had flown north from Baghdad, had come in secrecy to Kirkūk.

He had rehearsed his speech, again, while showering, shaving, dressing. Ahead of him were the opened double doors to the briefing room. He had tried twice, the evening before, to make secure telephone contact with the general commanding the armoured division to the south, but had failed. That had not distressed him. Since the American bombing and the imposition of sanctions, secure communications were haphazard, replacement parts rarely available. He heard the shout repeated, but his mind was far away in the detail of his speech.

All of the officers of the brigade, equipped with T-72 tanks and BMP armoured personnel carriers, would now be waiting on him in the briefing room. He had served with the older men, the more senior, most of his adult life. The younger men were the sons and nephews of officers, now retired from active duty, whom he had fought alongside in the Iranian, Kurdish and Kuwaiti wars. The brigadier believed the senior and junior officers owed primary loyalty to him, not to the regime. His speech, practised alone in his room, would appeal to that ingrained loyalty. The shout and the running feet were a barely noticed distraction as he approached the double doors.

From the Kirkūk military airfield, the men had been driven to Fifth Army headquarters, had taken an office behind a steel reinforced door, had established a radio link to the al-Rashid barracks and had prepared to talk to him about loyalty.

The brigadier paused at the double doors. He heard the scrape of chairs as the officers were ordered to stand. He smoothed his hair, and his tongue flicked at his lips. In no battle he had fought, and the medal ribbons on his chest showed there had been many, had he felt such gut-wrenching tension. Had the brigadier been a gambler, a dice-thrower, he would have been better able to control that tension – but he believed in loyalty. They stood in ranks in front of the lectern he would use . . . A fresh tension intruded on his thoughts. He had instructed the technical officers and NCOs to work through the night, to scavenge and cannibalize, to get the maximum number of the brigade's fighting vehicles to combat readiness. The tanks and personnel carriers made an imposing parade-ground army but spares were at a

273

premium. The speech returned to his mind, melded with the repeated shout and the drum of approaching feet.

The first moments of his speech, the first words they heard, would be the most important. He steadied himself. He would say, decisively: 'Officers, friends, our brigade is a family. A family stands together – a family will make the supreme sacrifice in blood. In the history of this family, united by selfless dedication, this is now a time of critical importance. The loyalty of this family is to the proud and honoured state of Iraq, not to the criminal clique that has for too long abused this family's trust. Today we are given, by God, the chance to rid our beloved people from the rule of the felons, which has brought misery down on us . . . ' The shout and the foot-fall were clearer. The doors would be locked behind him. If there was a weasel complaint from any officer, he would draw his pistol and shoot dead the callow bastard who made it.

'Brigadier, please, there is a call from Tuz Khurmātū – the general commanding the Republican Guard armoured division. He must speak with you personally – a matter of national security.'

He needed the support of the general commanding the Republican Guard armour at Tuz Khurmātū. He gestured to his second-in-command standing beside the lectern – two minutes.

He did not see his orderly's face. He was led from the corridor on to the parade ground where the mainten-ance teams sweated under arc lights over the tanks and the personnel carriers. There was the roar of revving engines and choking clouds of diesel fumes. He did not see the tears of betrayal running on his orderly's face. He was led into a small brick building with high barred windows and through an opened steel reinforced door. In a bare room, on the the wood table, the telephone was off the cradle. He snatched it up.

He said hoarsely, 'We are about to move, in an hour we move. Do I have your support?'

He recognized the voice on a crackling line. 'You are a traitor. I am a servant of the President. You are a traitor and will die like a traitor – like a dog.'

The pistol barrel was against his neck. In the moments before his arms were pinioned, he struggled to get a hand to his holster and failed. When his arms were pinioned, when his service weapon had been taken, when the cotton hood was over his head, the beating started.

In his own leisurely fashion, and after an untroubled night's sleep, Isaac Cohen began his day. He shaved with an old blade that barely scraped the stubble from his cheeks and chin, sluiced his body in cold water, dressed in faded jeans, a T-shirt, two sweaters and worn sneakers, ate an apple and a carton of yoghurt, flicked the pages of *Maariv*, which he had read the night before, made football small-talk with the commander of the Turkish troops who guarded him, and went to the building that housed the computers.

At the door, the key to the padlock in his hand, he looked down over the land lightening in the dawn.

There was snow on the highest peaks, and the deeper ravine valleys were still in black shadow, but the first shafts of the sun caught the lower hillsides beyond the mountains. With binoculars, if he had steadied himself against the door, he might have seen the brightness of the flame that burned at Kirkūk, but he did not have his binoculars. Below him, over the crag faces, an eagle glided, hunted. He blinked and unlocked the padlock. He seldom lingered at dawn or in the middle of the day or at dusk to strain his eyes and look over the falling ground. The eyes that mattered in the life of Isaac Cohen, that gave him vision, were in the dishes and the loosely slung aerials and the antennae that were riveted down on the roof of his communications den.

Inside, with the murmur of the machines for company, he filled, then switched on his electric kettle.

When he had made himself instant coffee, he would use the eyes that bored deep across the lands he could not see, and scan the decrypted messages the computers had gobbled in the night.

Later, where his own eyes could not see, the computers would give him a clear view of a fighting ground. He had done what he could, was now no more than a spectator, but he thought of them as he started to read the overnight radio traffic and he whispered a short private prayer.

AUGUSTUS HENDERSON *PEAKE*.

5. (Conclusions after interview with Brian Robins (sales director of AI Ltd, rifle manufacturers) conducted by self and Ms Carol Manning – transcript attached.)

ABILITY: As a marksman, AHP is as good as any. He has the ability to shoot under all conditions and can absorb the stress of competition. He is regarded by this source as a WINNER. He has the

276

inner steel that prevents him from accepting second best as an adequate outcome.

KNOWLEDGE OF MILITARY WEAPONS: AHP has wisely purchased the most complete sniper rifle on the market (paid in cash, £3,500).

He has travelled to northern Iraq with an *AWM .338 Lapua Magnum*. The rifle has a maximum range of 1,200 yards to 1,400 yards. The AWM has greater range and hitting power than the standard AW using 7.62 NATO ammunition, and is more manoeuvrable and covert than the heavier AW50 version.

The AWM is classified as a 'basic' weapon. It is not sophisticated; fewer technical problems in rugged terrain and battlefield conditions. The armour-piercing rounds, Green Spot ball, give the AWM a versatility not present with more conventional sniper rifles. It can kill personnel, but will also destroy equipment. It has the penetrative power, using FMJ (Full Metal Jacket) rounds, to be used successfully against a variety of targets – ammunition dumps, grounded aircraft, radar installations, bunkers and armoured vehicles (with the sniper in an offensive or defensive mode).

The AWM creates COMBAT POWER. It can degrade key equipment and gain psychological battlefield advantage.

Before that morning in the sales director's office, Ken Willet had never seen a sniper's rifle the size and power of the AWM .338 Lapua Magnum. When he had tried, and failed, the course at Warminster, he had used the Parker Hale weapon, which was smaller, lighter and did not have the capacity to fire the armour-piercing bullet. What had been aimed at him by Ms Manning was a rifle altogether more deadly than anything he had himself ever handled. He was confused. Was a professional's weapon in the hands of an amateur or an expert? With the confusion came the problem. His adult life was steeped in the lore of the military. He had been taught to believe that only the men who made a total study of military tactics and were subject to military discipline could achieve results in a military theatre of operations. If the reason for his confusion was valid then he might just have wasted the last dozen years of his life. Could an amateur, a transport manager in a haulage company, gain the same combat successes as a professionally trained sniper? He was too tired to find the answer, to end the confusion.

When he went to bed the dawn was coming up. But he could not sleep. Inside his mind, thundering and reverberating, was the roar of tank tracks.

'Keep clear of officers and white stones.'

'What, Mr Gus?'

'Major Hesketh-Prichard would have known that – it was the advice given by sergeants to fresh troops in South Africa. The British army was fighting there a hundred years ago.'

'Because officers get shot?'

'Correct, Omar, and because the sniper uses landmarks, any light-coloured stones, as points for measuring distance.'

'Why do you tell me?'

278

'Everything in the skill is old, everything we do has been done before, everything is learned from the past . . .'

Gus was deadened by tiredness. It was only something to say to help him to beat it. Inside the thick material of the gillie suit he was cold because of the tiredness. He felt a sickness, a scratching in his throat, from the cold and the stink of the goats. In front of them was the raised roadway leading to the bridge. Beyond the bridge the road led on to the defended crossroads. On the road's far side, dead ground to him, the embankment was steeper than the incline facing him, and at the far side of the bridge the river's banks plunged down to a morass of boulders. When the tanks left the road they must turn towards him, then drive towards the one place in the riverbed where the banks were shallow and the stones smaller – if they were to reach the crossroads.

Gus had not slept. He had marched back from the road, said whispered farewells to the men who had carried the mines and helped Omar to bury them. Tracking back over the open ground to find the firing position, he had then dug out the small trench in which he now lay. The light was coming, spreading over the desert landscape before him. His eyes roved over the markers. Wedged against rocks, hooked on to strands of rusted barbed wire, caught against old fence posts were scraps of newspaper and torn plastic bags. Each time he had placed the newspaper and the bags he had remembered the distances of his stride. There was nothing random in their placing: they were his white stones. The goats had been Omar's idea. They had bleated in the night; they were the missing peg to be slotted in the plan.

The light was coming and Gus heard the first distant popping of small-arms fire. He tried to sound calm but his teeth chattered.

'Remember what I said. Keep clear of officers and white stones.'

Against the scratching of the goats, he heard the boy's quiet laughter. 'Are you very frightened, Mr Gus?'

'Go away, and take those foul stinking creatures with you.'

The light was growing; the popping of the guns had become a rattle. The boy whistled and thwacked his stick on a goat's back, then the hoofs and Omar's light tread drifted away. The first golds of the morning caught the ground, flickered on the newspaper pages and the plastic, and Gus tried to remember each distance he had paced out in the darkness. It had been the boy's idea to steal the goats and then to go forward with them. He lay in a shallow trench covered by the sacking in which the mines had been carried, and over the sacking was loose dirt and small stones. Away to Gus's right, the shooting was persistent and no longer sporadic.

Haquim had said they depended on him – if the tanks came. He had a role. Far to his front, where the incline rose to the roadway, was a scene as old as the warning of officers and white stones: a goatherd boy sat and watched his beasts. Gus wriggled his hand under his gillie suit and found the water bottle at his waist. He reached forward, emptied the precious water onto the ground under the end of the rifle barrel, and made a mud pool – that was old, as old as Major Herbert Hesketh-Prichard.

Somewhere, out there, was the sniper sent to kill him.

*   *   *

The water dribbled into the ground. Little rivulets ran
from the point where he poured and disappeared. Then
he tipped the last of the water from the bottle into the
palm of his hand and let the dog drink from it.

Major Aziz lay in a scrape in the dirt and readied
himself. The letter with his wife's name on the envelope
was against his heart, but she was nowhere in his
thoughts – obliterated, along with his children.

The position he had taken was forward of the crossroads and a full 500 metres to the right flank of the route
he reckoned they would use when they attacked. The
first skirmish had begun. In front of him was the criss-
cross of the machine-guns' tracers, and the blast of
mortars.

When they made the encirclement, the tanks would
be like a crude fishing-net that scooped up the majority
of a catch but which let part of the shoal slip away.
His target – he had agreed to it – was the witch. She
would be at the forefront of the charge on the trenches
and bunkers at the crossroads. He estimated she would
pause to regroup her strike force at a distance of around
300 metres from the wire perimeter of the brigade positions. She would have her men around her, would be
close to the roadway, and she was his target.

They would not charge against the wire unless she
was there to goad them, urge them onwards.

He saw the first men in the advance. The sun beat on
his back and he felt the rhythmic pant of the dog's
breathing against his thigh. He wished he had more
water for the dog, but the wetted ground under his rifle
barrel was more important. A hundred metres ahead of
him, on a branch, he had placed a torn-off length from

281

the cotton scarf knotted around his head to prevent sweat running to his eyes. It hung limply and there was no need to make adjustments for wind deflection. The bullet was in the breech, the rifle armed, and his finger was beside the trigger guard.

He looked for the witch and waited.

'I am about to fight a battle.' The general spoke with frayed anger. 'What will handicap my fighting ability is distraction. What I tell you, you will find no treachery with me or the men who serve under me.'

'It was never suggested.'

'You will find only loyalty and dedication to the President.'

'Treachery is a plague.'

'There is no sickness with me or the men serving under me.'

He had been called from his room. He had been told that officers of the Estikhabarat had arrived in the night from Baghdad. He had been informed that his armoured brigade commander was under close arrest. With four subordinate officers, each carrying loaded side arms, he had marched to the briefing room. He had lectured the officers. He had stood at his full height in front of them. 'We fight for our President. We go to battle in the name of the Ba'ath Party. We protect the integrity of the Republic of Iraq.' He had spat on the floor then drawn his pistol and fired a single shot into the spittle. While the smell of the cordite hung in the air, he had said, 'If any of you wish to follow the traitor then I will first spit in your eye then shoot it out. Are there any who wish to proclaim their loyalty?' There had been an answering shout, at first hesitant, then raucous: 'We fight for our

282

President, our Party, our beloved Republic.' He had briefed them, dismissed them.

'Allow me to explain the tactical plan.'

'It is right that you should do so.'

'There are no traitors here,' the general said defiantly. He would have said that the brigadier, the Boot, the man with big feet, was his friend. He did not know whether his protestations of loyalty were believed. 'Traitors should be shot.'

'Of course. The plan?'

Some would have stayed with his friend, and with the fists and the clubs; only the most senior would have come to the command bunker. The most senior would have no trust for him.

He pointed to the map. 'I have a holding force, a battalion, in brigade base at the crossroads. Their task is to delay the advance of the woman and her people. We seek to persuade them that the position is weakly defended, to give them encouragement to mass and cross open ground. I send an armoured column forward, to encircle and to destroy. The rabble will be in the open, without cover. They will be destroyed by the tanks.'

'How many tanks?'

'Six.'

'Why six? Why not twenty-six, or forty-eight?'

'Six tanks because that is the number that are in working order, plus a reserve of nine, plus seven more that have faults but are nearly serviceable, out of forty-eight. There are forty-eight on the parade ground for inspection – but there are six tanks plus the reserve that are fully operational. Check for yourself.'

The calm voice asked, 'How would you recognize

that the contagion of treachery runs deeper than you now believe?'

'If we do not encircle them, crush them, that would be evidence of treachery . . . Do I have permission to issue orders, to make the killing zone?'

The man from the Estikhabarat smiled, and nodded.

The life of the general, and he recognized it, hung on the capability of six tanks of the T-72 class, with nine more in reserve, to encircle and destroy a force of peasant tribesmen caught in open ground. He gave the order.

Gus heard the guttural thunder from down the road, towards the ever-burning flame.

It was like Stickledown Range on a perfect day, clear vision, no wind.

The thunder began as a murmur, and grew.

On a perfect day at Stickledown the sun never shone so brightly that the target was distorted in a mirage, the rain never lashed, the gales never blew.

The murmur was a rumble.

The perfect day was a mindset. The champion isolated himself in a bubble cocoon. When he shot well, at the limit of his powers, Gus never sweated, was never wet or cold.

The rumble was a roar.

For that perfect day, he was not tired, not hungry, not cold, not frightened. He went through the routine, as he would have done on any of the perfect days at Stickledown Range when he fired at the V-Bull to win a silver spoon. His breathing was good, relaxed. His eyes were clear focused, not blinking. His body was loose, the muscles not tensed. The rifle was firmly against his shoulder.

The roar was the thrash of a club on a drum.

In the aim of the rifle, through the telescopic sight, was a goatherd, a mere boy. The boy ran around the goats and seemed not to know what he should do as the animals milled on the raised road in the path of the advancing tanks. Joe Denton had told him that a T-72 tank weighed 38 tons and had a maximum road speed of 39 m.p.h., and the boy with his goats was on the road and in their path. They might slow, they might shoot, they might drive straight through and over the goatherd and his animals. The boy seemed, in panic, to run round and round the goats as if he did not know how to drive them off the road. Gus thought the boy was quality. He took his eye from the 'scope and looked back along the road.

They were bunched close, a sea of dust around them. The clanking of the tracks pierced his ears. They were squat, low profile, painted in a dirty sand yellow, and the main armament barrels protruded out ahead of them. In each of them, he counted six, a man stood in the turret. They were bellowing leviathans, closing on the boy and his goats, as he ran round and round the frightened flock. The soldier in the turret of the lead tank waved, gestured for the boy to jump clear.

He settled again with the rifle. They were not going to slow for the boy and his animals, they would crush them. Gus neither hated his enemy nor felt any remorse at what he planned. His mind was clear, as on any perfect shooting day. The lead tank appeared in the edge of the circle of his 'scope. In the sight's centre, at the

T-junction of the reticule lines, was the boy and his goats.

The boy fled, the goats scattered. The boy dived down the incline and into the ditch. Gus could see the tops of two of Joe Denton's mines that had been obscured behind the goats.

The lead tank, its engine thundering, squirmed on the narrow elevated road to avoid the TM-46s that were Joe Denton's gift, but there was nowhere for the driver to go. Gus saw a thunderflash of light, then smoke and the climbing debris of a tank track, and heard the scream of its brakes. The lead tank lurched across the width of the road, stabilized and stopped.

The second tank rumbled into the lead tank. To Gus, the leviathans seemed to couple.

He had his target.

At the intersection of the 'scope sight's lines was the head and chest of the machine-gunner, reeling from the impact. The second tank's tracks were climbing as if to straddle the lead tank's body, and the gunner clung to the edge of the hatch for support.

Gus did not hear the noise. On Stickledown Range, he never heard the noise of voices and other rifles' reports. He fired the shot and, as the bullet reached the target, jerked it up, he was sliding the bolt action back, ejecting and aiming again.

In a lithe loose movement, Omar climbed out of the ditch, scrambled up the incline and jumped. He cleared the spinning wheels of the tracks of the second tank and stumbled onto the superstructure of the brute. He reached at his belt; his arm seemed to rise as if in a gesture of triumph, and something small dropped from his hand into the cavity of the hatch through which the machine-gunner had slumped. Gus had no image in his mind of a hand grenade bumping with a death rattle to the iron floor of the darkened hulk then rolling to a stop beside or under the buried seats of the driver and the main armament gunner; did not consider that moment of terror in the cavern as the brief seconds of the grenade's fuse frittered away.

His aim was on the third tank.

It was predictable. He did not see the little puff of grey smoke that followed the explosion in the second tank's bowels, nor the first licks of flame from the body of the lead tank; nor did he see the boy leap down and run to the ditch.

The third tank had stopped, then – coughing diesel fumes – swung in a crabbing gait towards the safety of the incline. It was a frantic thrashing creature seeking its escape down the incline. Through the 'scope, Gus saw the sheets of newspaper and the scattered shreds of the plastic bags hanging from the wire and the old fence post. The wind had not risen. He had no need to alter the windage turret.

Gus had never, in his shooting life, attempted anything so difficult.

The beast yawed on the rim of the incline. Below the turret, in the shadow of the flange that fastened the gun to it, was a strip of bright glass. The 'scope showed him every rivet in the metal around the glass and the smears across it. The glass was wider than a man's forehead and as deep as the forehead of a bald man. He breathed, sucked in the air, let it slip, held it, then fired. He had a good, sharp view because there was no dust thrown up from the mud earth under the tip of his barrel. The tank lurched over the incline . . . It was a moment of

Gus's childhood. Like a small boy's birthday party. Short trousers, grey ankle socks, school sweaters, and the birthday game of Blind Man's Buff . . . The tank was blind. Perhaps the armour-piercing bullet had hit the side flange of the driver's vision aperture and frosted it; perhaps the bullet had driven through the glass and was a small molten core of lead flying without control around the the interior of the tank and through the bodies of the driver, the gunner and the commander; perhaps the driver's face was lacerated by a mist of glass fragments . . . Little children, blindfolded, groped for each other, tried to find each other, and did not know where they were . . . It was the greatest shot that Gus Peake had ever attempted. The tank engine cut. Below the incline, the beast was blinded. He did not think of the dark horror that little children felt when they were blindfolded, or in the interior of the beast of the three men who were sightless.

He watched the fourth tank. It was as Joe Denton had said it would be. The tracks screwed across the road then dipped down the incline into a dense duststorm. There were new spurts of dust and thick black smoke as the tracks lumbered across the ground where the mines were laid. The beast was crippled.

They would be screaming now, Joe Denton had said, into their radios. They were halted, bunched and hurt. Some no longer had the power to manoeuvre, some had lost the power to see. With the best shooting of his life, Gus had made a hell for them and there was no-one to cheer him as there would have been on a perfect day on Stickledown Range.

He fired at the join of the open turret hatch of the fourth tank and the impact rocked the metal flap and tilted it down. The machine-gun on the sixth tank was rotating fast towards him. Joe Denton had said that the machine-gun beside the turret could be fired from inside the hulk. It was his perfect day. He hit the machine-gun itself, the box holding the ammunition beside the breech, and watched the spray of the tracers igniting.

Omar rose out of the ditch. The boy carried the last of the anti-tank mines that had not been buried beside the road. Omar ran beside the tracks of the fourth and fifth tanks in the line, under the jutting main armament barrels that swirled round towards the source of their prickling pain and past them. The sixth tank had started to reverse. The boy ran along its length. The two big guns fired, dreadnoughts marooned in shallows, and the shells howled far beyond him. The boy was behind the sixth tank as it slewed back towards him, then Gus saw him falling and rolling back down the incline and his hands were empty. The rear tank detonated the mine. The broken track rose in the air and fell into the black cloud.

Joe Denton had said it could be done.

On the far side of the road the incline was too steep. At the front and the rear the road was blocked by the hulks. On the near side of the road, down the incline, were the mines. The trap was sprung.

The tanks put up smoke. Little canisters flew in the air, arched, fell back and burst. A wall of smoke protected them. He did not consider the panic of the men immured in the hulks. He wondered if – in that autumn fog he had known so well in Hampshire as a child, blinding and constricting – Omar crawled over the superstructures of the beasts and looked for cavities into which to squeeze grenades.

Gus had fired the greatest shot of his life and there was no applause and he didn't care.

When he saw her first she was beyond the Dragunov's range.

She was in the 'scope, but at that distance he would not have had a better than fifty-fifty chance of a hit. He always told the recruits at the Baghdad Military College whom he'd taught to snipe that a prime virtue was patience, and a prime defect was to shoot too early and give away position.

She was smaller than he remembered her. She was with a group of men and her head bobbed between their shoulders. The group was close to the road, dragging the wheeled heavy machine-gun. There was a girlish twist in her hair that fanned out behind her when she ran then fell back on to her narrow shoulders.

The dog shifted suddenly beside his leg. He turned, annoyed, and saw the fly settle on the dog's nostrils, then dance away. He swatted at it.

She was slight, but still able to reach up towards a big brute of a man, heavy and bearded, and push him forward. She ran. There was heavy firing from the crossroads, but she was charmed. The group followed her, caught up with her and crouched, then she ran again. Major Karim Aziz, a veteran of combat, understood. Without her the men would hunker down in cover and ditches and fire wildly in the air, but not expose themselves. She shamed them. Who could hide when a girl, a woman even, exposed herself and ran forward? Steadily, as she went forward, Aziz tracked her through the 'scope. When, in his slow track, the sight reached the length of cotton scarf then he would have a shot with a

290

95 per cent probability of success. He had no doubt that his patience would be rewarded – the shot, fatal or incapacitating, would be sufficient to halt the advance.

The sniper was not with her and that was a niggling irritation to him. Sometimes he strained to hear crack and thump, but the rage of gunfire was too great for him to identify the sniper. He was comfortable, almost tranquil – except when the bastard fly was at the dog's face and the animal squirmed. He checked his wristwatch. In ten minutes the T-72 tanks would reach the battleground, turn it into a killing zone. He had time enough. Within ten minutes the woman would have reached the line that ran from the barrel of the Dragunov, past a length of cotton material hooked to a discarded branch, to the ditch beside the road.

She was closer to the line, with youth, almost a prettiness, about her face. With short, darting sprints, she was edging nearer to the line he had made. There were more men around her now and more often she was hidden behind them. If a mortar fell close to the group, if the shrapnel splayed, he would be cheated . . . The dog shifted and he flicked his trigger hand over its head.

There was an older man, limping, who caught the forward group. He watched the argument between the woman and the man. Maybe he told her that she should be further back, that she was too precious to be so far forward; maybe she replied that she alone could lead the rabble to the crossroads. He smiled to himself, mirthlessly. He knew the older man would lose whatever argument was played between them. She was approaching the line, but not yet at it, and he waited.

He had waited ten days, fifteen years before, in the front-line rubble of the Iranian city, Susangerd, had watched for the mullah who galvanized the defence of the town. A big man, in a black robe and always wearing a flak jacket, a dark, tangled beard below horn-rimmed spectacles and a paint-scraped helmet, who had evaded him for ten full days. On the eleventh day he had shot the mullah; by the evening of the eleventh day the greater part of the town had fallen. He had not fired a single shot before killing the mullah; but that one shot had achieved more than a thousand artillery rounds. If he could wait ten days, he could wait ten minutes.

She was up, running.

The men scrambled after her. He saw some go down – he prayed he would not be cheated – he saw one slide backwards from the heavy machine-gun but another took his place. She ran with a loose freedom and the men scurried after her. She dived forward. It would be the last resting-point before the final surge towards the wire and the bunkers. He could hear above the gunfire blast the roar of shouting men. He heard one word, yelled again and again over the force of the bullets' splatter, 'Meda . . . Meda . . . Meda . . .' They came in a swarm behind her.

Through the 'scope, Aziz saw the length of cotton scarf he had hooked to the fallen branch. For a moment, his eye came away from the sight and his glance rested on the parched, cracked ground under the rifle barrel. He should not have given any water to the dog. All of his water should have been poured on to the ground under the tip of the barrel . . . He was aiming . . . The dog moved again.

He had her upper chest in the crosshairs of the sight. Once more a fly danced over the nostrils of his dog.

He had the unfastened second button of her shirt as

292

his target. The fly crawled over the nostrils of his dog.

He breathed deeply, began to exhale, then caught his breath at its fall point, and started the steady slow squeeze of the trigger. He was rock steady, and squeezing. The dog snorted and jumped and careered against his leg. He fired.

Because he had shared the water there was a dirty dust puff under the barrel tip, and he could not see the travelling flight of the bullet. He did not know whether it would go high or low or wide, but he knew in that moment that he had missed her.

He wrenched back the bolt, and tried to settle to fire again. He did not curse the dog. The head of a man three feet from her, to the left and above her, split apart. There was violent movement. Men fell over her body, but the older man, a veteran like himself, had binoculars up to his eyes. He knew the older man was a veteran because the man's arm waved immediately, pointed to the puff of dust, identifying his position.

The bullets of the heavy machine-gun, with tracer, surged towards the shallow trench in which he lay. He did not swear at the dog or hit it, but instead pulled it under his body. The bullets, 12.7 calibre, beat around him, spattered up the dirt and stones over him. The ground around him seemed to explode. He closed his eyes. He thought of his letter. He was deafened by the onslaught. Aziz had never before fired at a target to kill, and missed. He pressed himself down into the ground, as if to bury himself, and felt the throbbing beat of the dog's heart against him, and he wondered if the letter would be retrieved and delivered.

When he looked again, through the 'scope, a torrent of men was running through the line. He could not see the woman, the witch, but he heard the shout of her name.

'Is that what you're telling me?'

Caspar Reinholtz had been called from the USAF wing of the base at Incerlik. He had been with the intelligence and photo recce officers, plotting the flight paths for the following day. The signals were coming in from State and Defence, and the maps were out that covered the road between Kirkūk and Tuz Khurmātū, and then the main highway south to Baghdad. Rusty had found him, come panting to the door of the deep bunker where the big computers were, and the hushed voices, and the pools of bright light. Rusty had said that the Israeli was on a secure link.

Cohen yelled at him down the link, 'That's what I'm getting off the traffic, Caspar.'

Reinholtz repeated the brigadier's name, spelled it letter by letter, twice, and the name of the armoured unit at Fifth Army that he had commanded . . . He had run as fast as he could back to the Agency's compound in the young athletic tyro's wake. A Brit commander had once told him that officers should never be seen to run. He had panted past the reinforced hangars where the attack aircraft were being armed and fuelled to enforce no-fly and no-drive zones. A promise had been given: no Iraqi aircraft would be permitted to fly against the brigadier's column when it headed down the road to Tuz Khurmātū; no Iraqi armour would be permitted to drive on an interception course against that column. He had staggered breathlessly into his office, and waved the kid away, told him to go find Bill.

Cohen told it simply, 'It's what the traffic says. The

first signal was in the night – al-Rashid to the local hoods of the Estikhabarat – four senior men flying to Kirkūk, and the brigadier to be under no-show surveillance. The second signal was Estikhabarat in Kirkūk to al-Rashid, the guy was in the bag and the evidence was stacking up. You talked about a "big play", Caspar . . .'

'I did.'

'I thought your "big play" might be affected.'

'Your kindness overwhelms me, Isaac.'

'Do you wish you didn't know?'

'I'd like not to believe it.'

Bill was in the room. He gestured for him to sit. He felt it like a pain that was personal.

The voice was soft in his ear. 'Hey, Caspar, if your "big play" is affected, *please*, this is serious, please do not include a source when you get down to sending signals.'

'I hear you. Maybe, some day, I can return the gift of some really fucking bad news to you, Isaac. Don't misunderstand me, I am grateful, but I feel like I've been hit with a baseball bat.'

'If it's still relevant, the ground force is hitting the brigade at the crossroads out of Kirkūk and going well. They've destroyed tanks. Your friend, the sniper . . .'

'Not relevant.'

'Keep smiling, Caspar.'

'Have a happy day, Isaac.'

He heard the static. He laid down the secure telephone. Bill sat quietly in front of him, would have heard what he said and would be allowing him time to collect himself. He stared down at his desk. Promises had been made, and with the promises had been the expenditure of millions, goddam millions of dollars – for nothing. The bastard, the Boss for Life, laughed. The Boss for Life might just have heard of Caspar Reinholtz, might have been told of Caspar Reinholtz by the low-life of the Special Security Service or the General Intelligence Directorate or the Military Intelligence Service, might have known enough of him to make the laughter personal.

He lifted his head. 'Where were you, late summer of '96?'

'Kicking my heels, Rome.'

'I was in Arbīl.'

'I know that, Caspar – Arbīl, when it was bad.'

'When we made promises, spent the money, recruited like we were here for ever, and ran.'

'You still carrying scars?'

'Till the day I die. We ran from House 23-7, Ain Kawa Street, in Arbīl. We ran so fast, with our pants down, that we left behind the computers and the sat-phones and the files. Can you imagine that?'

'It doesn't help, Caspar, to dredge what can't be changed.'

'For four years we'd recruited, been the flash guys in town. We'd been free with the high and mighty talk – we were believed.'

'It's the past.'

'We left people behind to be butchered. We made it easy for the butchers. They could tap into our computers, decode the sat-phones to learn who we talked to, read the files. Good people, brave people, bought the bullshit we gave them, and their reward was that we left their names for the butchers . . . We gave it a couple of years, let the weeds grow on the graves, and came again with promises.'

'Is it that bad?'

'It's the time to be digging more graves.'

'The Boot?'

'Arrested, poor bastard.'

'That's kind of unfortunate.'

'Yes . . . Get me Langley, probably better if I have a speech rather than a text link . . . There were three strands. Two strands might carry the weight. I only have one strand of thread left.'

He would talk to Langley. Langley would talk to State and Defence. Defence would stand down the attack aircraft, order the bombs and missiles unloaded, the fuel siphoned out. He would talk to Langley, then get the message to the young woman, a true goddam heroine, that it was over and she should get back where she belonged, to her home in the mountains. It was over.

It was not a sophisticated interrogation. No attempt was made to win the man, no bogus offers of clemency were offered.

They beat the brigadier, the Boot, near senseless, and when he drifted into unconsciousness, they threw buckets of fetid water over him. Then they beat him again.

There was no gag in the brigadier's mouth as he sat pinioned to the heavy chair, but he never answered their questions, or screamed, or begged.

The senior man from the Estikhabarat stood in the doorway of the command bunker as the general gave his final orders.

He instructed that the reserve force of nine T-72 tanks was to move north from Kirkūk, within a screen of personnel carriers, to recover the initial armoured force that had been deployed. A defensive line was then to be made south of the bridge. The brigade position at the crossroads was to be abandoned and the troops there should withdraw as best they were able. Concentrated artillery fire was to be put down on the road north of the crossroads to hamper the enemy's reinforcement.

It was little, and it was late.

The general believed that his career of distinction had been broken by a sniper who had outwitted him. By his own words he had given a definition of the evidence of treachery . . . His orders were broadcast on the radios linking the units.

The senior man from the Estikhabarat beckoned to him. There would be more of them in the corridor outside the bunker, and more on the steps.

Rather casually, so as not to create alarm among the staff officers round him, he dropped his hand to his holster, drew his service pistol, held it for a moment beside his trouser leg, then pulled it up, poked the barrel into his mouth, and squeezed the trigger.

They were at a road block.

'All my fucking life, from the first fucking war I went to, to the fucking last, I am fucking blocked by ignorant, fucking illiterate peasants,' Mike said.

'What's killing me is that the goddam money is in that fucker's pocket,' Dean said.

They sat on the road beside the wheels of the Mercedes. The Russian had left them. He'd flashed greenbacks, their bloody greenbacks, he'd been allowed through the block after he'd paid off the thugs there. He'd hitched a ride on a jeep mounted with a machine-gun, and no doubt lost a few more of their

298

bloody greenbacks. He was long gone up the road.

'To be so near to a story and not to be able to touch it, that is very, very painful,' Gretchen said.

'Is there anything more fucking depressing than being stopped at a fucking road block, with the fucking story in sight?'

'When your wallet's empty, no.'

'But, there again, no story is worth being killed for.'

There was a distant thud of artillery fire and a long way ahead were palls of hanging smoke. The men at the block grinned venomously and repeated that it was too dangerous for honoured visitors to go up the road. They were into the third hour at the road block, and the second hour after the Russian had left them.

'Do they know who we fucking are?'

'Perhaps the fat crook only told them who we used to be.'

'We are nobody, we represent people who do not care.'

Each of them, caught the wrong side of the road block, knew what they were missing. They could hear it and, with it, fifteen thousand dollars burning up.

'I bet nobody's told the bitch that she could be leading tomorrow night's news.'

Mike and Dean and Gretchen smoked, chewed gum, ate melting chocolate, did nothing, waited.

The sun was not yet at its zenith, but it was already the end of a perfect day.

Gus and Omar watched the line of tanks and armoured cars fan out beside the road. They were among the great glacial smoothed rocks of the riverbed. He could have fired again but he had long learned on

299

Stickledown Range that a perfect day could not be repeated so soon. With the tanks and armoured cars, toys in the distance, were cranes to drag clear the disabled T-72s . . . He imagined the spitting anger of the unit's commander when he found the handkerchief scale of the minefield, and the slightness of the mantrap. He wondered also when he would next see Joe Denton – if ever – to talk him through it, and thank him. Away to his right, a straggling column of soldiers crossed the bridge.

As he crawled up from the river and started to walk away towards the crossroads, the shivering began in Gus's body. He lurched and might have fallen, but the boy caught him, supported him.

When the shooting had died, and the anguish of trying to protect her, Haquim took some men and went to search.

There was little for him to find.

He stood beside the discarded marker, the scrap of cloth draped over the branch. If he had looked for it in the battle, from the ditch beside the road, he would not have seen it. If he had seen it he would have thought it had been blown there on the wind. It was a short link with death, her death.

His knee hurt fiercely, but he strode on briskly away from the road and from the hanging cloth.

The single discarded cartridge case caught his eye when he was almost upon it. It was a shorter link with death, Meda's death. Behind it was a shallow depression in the ground in which a man's body could just have been concealed. In front of it was a plate-sized piece of cracked earth with a small gouge in the centre of it. It was a new form of warfare for him. Her life, all their lives, hung on a scrap of cloth that he had not seen, and the amount of water poured onto the ground under a barrel tip.

There was nothing more to find. Haquim left the watered ground, the cartridge case and the strip of cloth behind him – and reflected that one sniper had lost a battle, and another sniper had won it.

Willet woke.

The dream had been a nightmare. He was sweating. The last moments of his sleep, while the nightmare was rampant, had pitched and tossed him in the bed . . . He was the sniper, lying in a shallow ditch covered with sacking and earth. He was deafened by the clanking rumble of the approaching tanks. He was screaming for help from his mother and from Tricia as the crushing tracks came closer. He was trying to crawl from the ditch, under the great shadow of the tank. He was pulped, mashed, by the tracks, and his mother did not answer his screams; neither did Tricia.

He sat on the bed, shook, then staggered to the small bathroom and flushed cold water over his face.

He turned on the radio to find that statistics were running riot: home owners' mortgage rates were being lowered by a half of 1 per cent; waiting lists for hip-replacement operations were up by 3.25 per cent; truancy in a school serving a sink estate in the north-east had risen by 5 per cent; travel companies reported that bookings by retired 'greys' going after spring sunshine in the Mediterranean had increased from the previous year by 9 per cent; the government's popularity had dipped by 1 per cent . . . Life was about fucking percentage points. Life was about money in the pocket, non-critical illness, loutish kids, holiday breaks, and the rulers' ratings. It was not about Mr Augustus Henderson Peake or his rifle in combat against tanks. Money, ailments, kids, holidays, politics were the spider's web that constricted Ken Willet's life, and the lives of everyone he knew.

He went back to his computer. He felt a deep resentment for Peake, the transport manager who had broken free of the web. He could not have done what Peake had, gone into combat. His innermost thought, which he would not share: the survival of Peake would belittle him, the professional soldier.

He typed briskly.

MILITARY TRAINING: This interview, however, failed to provide evidence of the necessary expertise in utilizing to the full the AWM's capability. I can imagine situations where AHP will gain short-term successes. Without the necessary training, I would believe it unlikely that AHP can influence any important combat situation. Excitement, battlefield adrenaline, commitment are insufficient substitutes for extensive training under the guidance of experts.

I continue to rate medium-term survival chances as slim to non-existent.

Willet shut down the machine.

He pulled his road atlas off the shelf and looked for the best route to south Devon.

Chapter Twelve

'Do you know that you stink? I hear that you are a tank killer.' The Russian stood over him.

Gus lay on the sandy ground, his head on his rucksack, propped against a jeep's wheel. The boy was sitting cross-legged beside him. The jeep was a few paces inside the wide circle of men. Some squatted, some crouched, some stood, and they held their weapons and watched. In the centre of the circle with Meda, with the maps, were *agha* Bekir and *agha* Ibrahim. The great ring around them listened in silence to the bickering between the warlords, and the interventions of Meda as she stabbed her finger at the maps. Each time the Russian spoke there were concerted grunts and hisses from the *peshmerga* nearest to him, protests at his voice, but he ignored them.

'I hear that you and the boy stopped an armour column, but you still stink. You should get yourself a bath or a shower and some soap. You smell like a carcass out on the steppe, in summer, a rotten carcass . . . She is saying she will take them into Kirkūk tomorrow, and they are arguing about whose fighters should lead the attack. They are shit.'

303

The shells still whined overhead and hit the road to the north. Gus could not, for the life of him, understand why the order was not given to target the crossroads. He thought that three thousand men made the circle, and she was in the middle of it with *agha* Bekir and *agha* Ibrahim. One salvo would be enough. *Agha* Bekir and *agha* Ibrahim had come in separate convoys, had run the gauntlet down the road, with escorts of jeeps and pick-ups. He watched the body language. If one agreed, the other disputed it. Sometimes she threw up her arms and sometimes, to their faces, she cursed them.

Rybinsky said, 'She is saying that she will take them into the headquarters of Fifth Army tomorrow, and they are arguing about whose foot should be first through the gate. That's the sort of shits they are.'

The two *agha*s sat on metal-framed deckchairs. She was between them, on her knees, with the maps held down by stones. Gus watched them, animated in distrust or sulking.

'You know what she said? She said she'd tie Bekir's left foot to Ibrahim's right foot, and they would go into Fifth Army together – then she'd tie Bekir's right foot to Ibrahim's left foot, and they'll go into the governor's offices. Look at the hatred behind the smiles, because she's leading them where they cannot lead themselves. And she's a woman, that is very painful for them – on that they are united, the one thing. And they have a very great fear of Baghdad, but if they get to Kirkūk they will be famous in Kurdish history. They want to believe her, but still they have the fear.'

She had ripped the bandanna from her forehead, and her hair hung loose. She gripped their ankles, above their smart polished footwear. With a decisive movement she tied her bandanna around one's left leg and the other's right. She stood. She held out her arms as if to demonstrate to the circle the unity of their commanders. Above the whistle of the shells and the rumble of the detonation, there was a creeping growl of approval.

'It is always the same with army commanders, the jealousy. I know, I was in the army. I was in Germany, in Minsk, I was in Afghanistan – always commanders of men have an envy. Then I transferred to Strategic Nuclear Forces. I was at Krasnie Sosenki guarding the SS-25 intercontinental ballistic missiles – perhaps one was targeted on where you lived, worked. The only thing good about Krasnie Sosenki was that it was not Chechnya. I left, I walked out six years ago. I had not been paid for eight months, so I went my own way, into import–export.'

Gus saw Haquim on the far side of the circle. There was a great sadness in Haquim's eyes. He was squatted down and his hand cupped his ear so that he could hear better. If he survived, came through, he would tell his grandfather about Haquim and about a boy who climbed onto the hulks of tanks. There would be much to tell his grandfather, but import and bloody export would not be a part of it.

'In import–export in Kurdistan, I have no competitors. I have the market. That is why I am here. For me there is a big opportunity. These are a very unsophisticated people: for a percentage they will sign anything. Around the Kirkūk oil fields there is chrome, copper, iron, coal. I will get the licence to exploit the wealth of Kirkūk – an honourable financial agreement, of course. Then I can retire . . .'

She was back on her knees, very close to them and

their tied ankles. He watched the softness of the movement of her hands and the persuasion in her eyes. He
could not look away from her, and neither could the tied
men. He knew it, he would follow her where she led.

'Do you know Cannes? Do you know the South of
France? I would like a little apartment over the harbour,
with a view of the sea, when I retire. I have never been
there but I have seen the postcards. I think an apartment
over the harbour in Cannes is very expensive. Are you
a rich man, tank killer?'

There was a bank account that had been emptied, and
a job that he had walked out of. Three days before, or it
might have been five – because those days now slipped
by unnoticed, merged with each other, and he no longer
knew the day of the week or the date – the mortgage
payment would have been triggered, and would not
have been paid. Perhaps Meg used her key, came in,
sorted his post on the mat and made a pile of the brown
envelopes, but her teaching salary was not enough to
meet the gas, electricity, tax and water. In terms of the
life he had turned his back on, he was as destitute as
the men who crowded shop doorways, when the light
fell and the businesses closed in Guildford's high street,
with blankets and carton boxes. He had nothing but his
rifle, the kit in the rucksack under his head, and his love.

'What do they pay you for killing tanks? Five thousand a week, dollars? No, that is not enough – ten
thousand a week? Will you have a bonus for reaching
Kirkūk? What's the package, fifty thousand?'

It would not have happened unless she had done it.
She took *agha* Bekir's hand and *agha* Ibrahim's hand. She
held their two hands up high, so that each man was
jerked off his chair and the handkerchief and the

306

umbrella they held were dropped. Slowly, so that every man in the circle could see it, she brought their hands together, and the fingers clasped. The great circle bayed their names. It was a moment of power. The men kissed . . . Gus thought that the next day he would stand in Kirkūk.

'She is fantastic. She is incredible. I think she is a virgin. I, myself, would trade in all that package, fifty thousand dollars, to take away that virginity. Would you? I tell you, tank killer, if you want to trade in the package then you should first find a bath or a shower, and some soap. I wish it were me – I think I have to be satisfied with the licences to exploit the chrome at Kirkūk, and the copper, iron and coal.'

Gus closed his eyes. If he had not shut his eyes, lost sight of the Russian's leering face, he would have hit him.

'I suppose I've been expecting you – someone like you and like the lady.'

The sergeant sat on a camping stool. The rain drove in from the west and the sea. The slope of the Common ran away and up in front of him. His binoculars were up to his eyes, never left them, as he scanned the gorse, dead bracken and heather.

'I was expecting to meet you. That's why I asked for you by name,' Willet said.

It had been a dreadful drive down from London. Two coned-off roadworks on the motorway and the start of the Easter holiday had snarled the traffic. He and Ms Manning hadn't talked much, and mostly he'd relied on the radio for company. When they had finally turned off the road south of Exeter and reached the guarded main gate of the Commando Training Centre – Royal Marines, they'd been eighty minutes late for their appointment. A pleasant-faced major had met them, given them coffee, accepted Ms Manning's grudging apology, then shaken his head in puzzlement and said, without equivocation, that he'd never heard of Augustus Henderson Peake – and, anyway, it was quite impossible for a civilian to receive the advanced sniper training conducted by the Lympstone base. Ms Manning had sworn, and Willet had proffered a name.

'Does this drop me in the shit?'

'I wouldn't have thought so, Mr Billings, I wouldn't have thought there's any call for that.'

The major had driven them out to the Common. The rain came from low cloud that settled on the ridge a thousand yards or so from where Sergeant Billings sat. There was little to see and Ms Manning stood back, with the major, and had opened a brightly floral umbrella. Willet crouched beside the sergeant and watched the observers, who stood like old fence posts in the dead foliage on the slope and waited for Sergeant Billings to direct them. Willet had seen no movement, and he'd been passed a pair of binoculars, until the sudden murmur of Billings' voice into a pocket radio sent the left-side observer tracking fast into a clump of flattened ochre bracken. The weird shape of a man in a gillie suit, covered with bracken sprigs and heather, emerged from under the observer's feet.

'Wrong mix of camouflage – he rushed it,' Billings mouthed. 'Too much bracken when he was in the heather, too much heather in the bracken. Shouldn't have used bracken until he was out of the heather. He's failed. Actually, he's lucky. If he'd been in the field and I'd been the counter-sniper, he'd be dead.'

'How long was Peake here?'

'Three days.'

'Is that long enough?'

'It was all the time Gus had. Yes, it was long enough.'

'Doesn't seem long.'

The failed sniper, who would be dead if he had been in the field, tramped miserably towards them.

'That jerk's been here a month, great on the written stuff, useless on the practical. It depends where you're coming from. Gus was coming from the right direction, Gus had my dad to teach him, like he taught me. Dad understood ground, understood the animals he stalked . . .'

'I was told he was a poacher, your father.'

'What the landowners called him, and the magistrates. Dad could have got up close enough to undo your bootlaces. He told me he was going to northern Iraq. It was about his grandfather, he said. I remember his grandfather, a good old boy, but Gus's father was crap. He said my dad was a bad influence – but at least my dad might just keep him alive . . .'

There was another murmur into the radio and the right-side observer plunged off into a low gorse thicket and identified the target, spotted through the sergeant's binoculars at 624 yards. Again Willet had seen nothing.

'What was his mistake?'

'He's got hessian net over the lens of his 'scope. He let the net get snagged in the gorse. I saw the lens.'

'So, he's dead.'

'Failed or dead, take your pick. I spotted Gus morning and afternoon the first day, morning and afternoon the second day, morning on the third day, and each time he was closer to me. The third afternoon, I didn't get him. What I can say to you, Mr Willet, it would take a real class counter-sniper, as good as me, to bust Gus.'

'Why did you help him? You put your career on the line, your pension with it. You were in flagrant abuse of Queen's Regulations. Why?'

For the first time, the sergeant's eyes flicked away from his binoculars. He had a strong, weathered face and piercingly clear eyes. 'It was owed him, because of his loyalty.' The eyes were back to the binoculars. 'I had a debt to him because of his loyalty to Dad. You called my dad what the landowners and the magistrates called him, a *poacher*. A poacher is a thief in the eyes of those turds. He got sent down, my dad did. He was locked up in Horfield – that's the gaol at Bristol – for three months. Mum and I, we hadn't any money, we only got to see him twice. The first time, my dad was pathetic. They might just as well have put him down as cage him. He was a free spirit, had to have the wind on his face, had to be out in the pissing rain. I cried all the way home and Mum wasn't much better. The second time he was brighter, changed, and he said that Gus had been to see him. My dad thought he had plenty of friends before they locked him up, but Mum and me, and Gus, were the only ones who visited him. He'd taken the day off school, told his teachers he was going home for a family funeral, but he hitched rides up to Bristol and saw my dad. All the other *friends* had turned their backs on him. Not Gus. That's loyalty. He wouldn't run out on you. He never saw my dad again . . . We moved and Dad was dead within the twelvemonth. Why? To me, loyalty is important. It's the mark of a true friend, when you're down the back's not turned. What's he doing there? Will he make it through?'

'I don't know.'

Behind them, the major called out that he was taking Ms Manning to the shelter of his car. Willet seemed not to feel the rain dripping off his face. There was another failure, another death, another soldier tramping disconsolately forward after his position was identified. He told the sergeant that he would make damn certain that no blame accrued to him for helping the civilian, Augustus Henderson Peake, understand the trade of killing, and surviving.

'What else did he learn here?'

'I took him into the library, showed him what we had on sniping and signed them out in my name. In the evenings, off camp, I got the specialist instructors to meet him. There was Sergeant Williams who's into dogs, because dogs are big for snipers, that's tracker dogs. Sergeant Browne is weapons maintenance, Sergeant Fenton is camouflage, Sergeant Stevens is the top man for the tactics of using the AWM Lapua Magnum against armour, communications and helicopters. Sergeant—'

'Did you say helicopters? You mean gun-ship helicopters?'

'It's not a cake-walk he's gone on, Mr Willet. That's why I passed him on to an old friend. Whatever they throw at him, he won't back off. It's a powerful thing, loyalty.'

He'd sent the signals first, then steadied himself and opened the secure voice link to Langley.

Caspar Reinholtz was alone in his office. The overall picture that he would share with the disembodied voices on the link was not for Luther, Bill and Rusty to hear.

He allowed few interruptions. The inquest would come later, a commission of inquiry, but his job now was merely to put flesh on the bones of another disaster in Iraq. Beside the receiver for the link was a sat-phone he would use as soon as he had finished with the link.

While he spoke, however hard he tried to cut her from his mind, the picture of the young woman was in his thoughts.

The great circle was tighter around *agha* Bekir, *agha* Ibrahim and Meda, but held at a respectful distance.

Gus heard the warbling pulse of the sat-phone, heard it because the men in the circle were quiet as they watched the feast of celebration. The chairs had been pushed aside and a rug laid out for the dishes of lamb and rice, and spicy vegetables. He knew what they ate because the scent of the food drifted across the open space of the circle. He sat against the wheel of the jeep and the boy was crouched beside him. The sat-phone cried to be answered. They would eat later, with all the men in the circle, then be briefed, then march in the dusk towards distant Kirkūk and the flame. The persistence of the sat-phone was silenced.

Gus watched idly. He saw *agha* Bekir put a dripping piece of meat in his mouth, hold the receiver to his face, and chew while he listened. Gus saw the sea-change.

The face clouded. Where there had been a wary smile there was now a concentrated coldness. The lines were back on the features. The boy had seen it and seemed to squirm; the murmur of voices in the circle was stilled and quiet laughter died. *Agha* Ibrahim was passed the sat-phone receiver and grains of rice slid from his fingers as he took it. He too listened, his face darkening, then threw the receiver away from him. Meda scrabbled on her knees across the rug, tipping aside food bowls and pots, and snatched it up. Gus heard her furious scream, and then she too dropped it. They were all on their feet. *Agha* Bekir was shouting to one side of the circle, and *agha* Ibrahim to the other, as if some strange apartheid divided their forces, and Meda was a small, spinning, yelling shape between them, and the rumble of the voices in the circle was confusion.

Every emotion of anguish was on the boy's features.

'What do they say?'

The boy piped, 'They say it is finished. Meda will not believe them . . . They have the courage of sheep . . . They say it were better that it had never begun. Meda says tomorrow she will take them to Kirkūk. They say there is no air cover, that there is no mutiny in the Iraqi tanks, as they were promised. They say they are going home.'

Meda gripped their clothes in turn. She was ferocious in her attack, and she pleaded with them, but neither would catch her eye, as if they dared not, as if they feared her reproach.

The boy said, 'They say that if they go now it is possible the revenge of the government will not be so great. The Americans' promises are broken, they say they will never see Kirkūk. Meda says there is a place in history for them. They are worse than sheep when wolves come.'

For a moment, she hung on to the men, but they pulled clear of her. *Agha* Bekir and *agha* Ibrahim shouted their orders at the sectors of the circle. Meda was pleading with their men.

313

The boy's passion was squeezed from him. 'They say they are taking their men with them. Meda says she will be in Kirkūk in the morning, on her own if no man will follow her.'

On each side, the circle parted to allow the departure of the chieftains. Gus sat against the wheel of the jeep and held the big rifle across his legs. He felt a sense of calm because it was still a part of his perfect day.

Great shuffling columns of men passed her. She gazed on them with contempt. Gus saw the men who had used the wheeled machine-gun abandon it and walk on. He saw those who had run to the wire with her at the Victory City, and those who had gone down the road with her towards the barricade at Tarjil. A few broke the regimen of the columns and dropped down to sit in the dirt at her feet. He saw the big cars spurt away with their escorts of pick-ups and jeeps, and clinging in the back of one of them, amongst the men with guns, was the Russian. So, the bastard turned his back on licences for chrome, copper, iron and coal – and a small bitter smile hovered at Gus's lips. He saw Haquim go to Meda, argue with her and try to pull her away, but she pushed him from her and his weight went on to his injured leg. He slipped to the dirt, and crawled away in his humiliation. Many went and only a few were left.

'What are you going to do, Mr Gus?'

'You should walk, Omar, you have a life to live.'

'What are you going to do?'

'Perhaps go and find something to eat.'

'I cannot leave you, Mr Gus.'

They hugged each other. They were the transport manager and the urchin thief, and they clung to each

314

other, were tied to each other as tightly as the chieftains' ankles had been.

'I am honoured to meet the sniper who does not fire.'

'Do you wish to hear my report, Colonel?'

The new man, flown in from Baghdad, was rake thin. His uniform was immaculately creased and the medal ribbons on his chest were a kaleidoscope of colours. Major Aziz knew his name and his face from the photographs in the newspapers. The photographs always showed him at parades standing a pace behind the President. He wore the flash on his shoulder of the brigade of Amn al-Khass, the unit of the Special Security Service tasked with the protection of the President. It was predictable that a new commander would seek to belittle the men over whom he had authority, to demonstrate his power. In his filth, tired, hungry, Aziz stood loosely, not at attention, in the command bunker, and the dog lay in the dirt from his boots.

'How many rounds have you fired, Major Aziz, in defence of our positions?'

'I have fired once. I missed. Sniping is not an exact art, as you will know, Colonel. Do you wish to hear my report now?'

'Perhaps your mind was resting on your duties as a kennel-boy. Get that fucking animal out of here, then clean yourself up, *then* make your report.'

Aziz had come back across the dried riverbed, and rejoined the road south of the bridge near to the raised embankment where the engineers still worked under floodlights to recover the last tank, and where the sappers had cleared the last mine. He had been given a ride back to Fifth Army. Then he had been told of the fate of the brigadier, the Boot – and of the general's suicide. As he'd walked across the open ground towards the command bunker, he'd glanced at the squat cell block, and he had thought of his family. Where he stood, the floor of the command bunker was scrubbed clean except for the dirt from his boots, but they had not been able to remove the blood spatters from the ceiling.

'Were you at Susangerd, Colonel?' He spoke quietly, as if in casual conversation. 'I do not remember seeing you at Susangerd, nor at Khorramshahr. We did not meet, I think, in Kuwait City. Were you operational in al-Anfal? I look forward to hearing of the rigours of staff work in divisional headquarters.'

He saw the flush in the colonel's face. Officers looked away. The recklessness was like a narcotic.

'Forgive me, Colonel, my memory played a trick with me. I have fired twice. I fired at the woman and I missed. At Tarjil I fired at the commanding officer – and did not miss – because he betrayed the soldiers under his command. He was running away. I am prepared to kill any officer, whatever his rank and whatever his position of influence, if he betrays the trust placed in him by the army and, of course, the people of Iraq. Do you want to hear my report, Colonel, or do you want me to go back to the war?'

He bent and ruffled his fingers through the hair at the nape of the dog's neck, then he looked up at the blood on the ceiling, and the sight of the small, barred windows of the cell block hooked his mind.

'Make your report.'

Major Karim Aziz spoke of what he had seen. From a good vantage point, with enough elevation for him to look down a slight gradient into the camp, he had settled with his telescope, and the dog had been beside him. He told of the arrival of *agha* Bekir and *agha* Ibrahim, then of their abrupt departure. He said that a large proportion of the force of the *peshmerga* had followed after them in general retreat, but the woman remained at the crossroads with no more than three hundred men. He predicted an attack in the morning because he could see no other reason for her to stay. He described what he had seen in a flat monotone, and where he would be in the morning. He finished, saluted, called for his dog and shambled out of the command bunker.

The brigadier, the Boot, was a proud man but it was hard to have pride when lying in the corner of a cell in the piles of his own excrement and the pools of his own urine.

Maybe they rested, maybe they had gone to Communications to talk with the al-Rashid barracks, maybe they had left him to agonize on the future facing him before death.

The pain racked his body. There would be many, now, who would have heard of his arrest, knew that he faced torture, and who shook in the fear that he would name them.

Pride was the only dignity left to him. If he broke under torture, screamed out the names, then the last of the dignity would be taken. He heard the stamp of feet in the corridor, and the slide of the bolt. In the cell's doorway, he saw the faces of the men who would try again to steal his pride.

He watched the *mustashar* hobble towards him.

There had been more than three thousand men at the

crossroads, and now there were fewer than three hundred. One jeep still waited, with the engine turning.

Haquim winced as he bent his knee and lowered himself to sit beside Gus.

His voice was dried gravel under tyres, and sad. 'You should go now. You should walk with me, Mr Peake, to the jeep, and sit with me and leave. You have done what you could.'

Gus looked into the eyes without light and the mouth without laughter and could hear only the sadness.

'You can be proud that you came and that you tried to help. You are not to blame that the force against you is too great and the force with you is too small. It is the story of the Kurdish people. No man can call you a coward . . .'

'May your god ride with you, Haquim.'

'Do you think I am a coward, Mr Peake, or do you think it is the anger because she does not listen to me? May I ask you, has she made her apology to you for being wrong about the tanks? Has she?'

'It is not important.'

'She believes to apologize is to show weakness. The stubbornness is a death wish. She will neither apologize to you, nor accept that a march on Kirkūk with so few is like a death wish – for her and for everyone who goes with her.'

'I wish you well.'

'The spell of her holds you . . . and you think of me as a coward. I cannot run fast enough to be with her and to shield her. I have no reason to be here, to go into Kirkūk, to die under the light of the flame. I was not always a coward.'

'I will remember you as a good and true friend.'

318

'Listen to me. It is important, if I am to live with my-self, that I tell you of the days when I was not a coward. I was a junior officer of artillery. For five years I was with an artillery regiment in support of the ground forces defending the Basra road. We were safe, we had deep bunkers to go into when the Iranians shelled us, but in front of us were our infantry. There was as much barbed wire behind our forward positions, where our infantry were, as there was to the front. They were trapped there, peasant boys, and behind the barbed wire were minefields to prevent them breaking and fleeing from the attacks. Behind the minefields were security troops to round up the deserters and shoot them. They were fodder for the cannons of the Iranians. At the end of the fifth year that I served there, in the heat and with the smell of death, I went alone in an evening into the marshes to see if I could find a forward position for an artillery spotter. I found them. They were all Kurds. They were from Arbīl and Rawāndiz, Dihok and Zākhō, and there was one from the moun-tains near to my home at Birkim. I saw their terror of me. They thought I would call for security troops. My own blood, little more than boys, of my own people. I took off my badges of rank and threw them into the water. When the day ended we started out. I took them home, Mr Peake. We walked for a month, always at night. There were eleven of these Kurdish boys, and I led them home to their mountains. We moved in darkness and hid in the days. We stole food, we avoided the road blocks. If we had been seen or cap-tured, we would have died before firing parties or on the hangman's rope. I brought them out of the marshes and across deserts, through fields, around cities, in the heat and in the cold. I delivered them, each of them, to their homes, to their mothers, to the mountains. I was not always as you see me now . . .'

'May your god go with you and watch you.'

'Should I tell you when I fought with the rearguard when the Iraqis came in the Operation al-Anfal – the name was taken from a *sura* in the Koran, the chapter that describes holy war against infidels – that name was used to legalize the murder and rape and looting of Kurds? Should I tell you how I fought to win time for the refugees in 1991, after the Coalition's great betrayal? They will see what you have done against tanks – they will fly against you with the helicopters . . . I want to be with my children. I do not want to die for nothing.'

The tears streamed on Haquim's face. Gus took his grimy handkerchief from his pocket, wiped them away and made smears on the other man's cheeks.

The handkerchief was wet in his hand as he watched the jeep leave, watched it until it was small then gone into the mist that was thrown up at the cooling end of the day, and he thought of the helicopters.

They saw the cars speed through the road block with their escorts, then came the bigger column of lorries, pick-ups and jeeps, laden low with men.

'What's going on here? The fucking yellow bastards are running!' Mike exploded.

'Looks like the stakes have gotten too high,' Dean whined.

'It was madness, we should never have tried. Expensive madness!' Gretchen cried.

The dust from the wheels of the column spattered over them. The faces of the men told a story of defeat.

'I haven't seen her,' Gretchen said.

'Probably long gone, probably gone to wash her goddam hair,' Dean said.

'I'll wring her neck with my own fucking hands, if I ever get sight of her,' Mike said.

The Russian came and spilled down from the back of an open vehicle. They swarmed around him. He shouted that it was a matter beyond his control, that the war was over, finished.

'Where is she?'

He did not know. Maybe they cared to go and look for themselves, to walk down the road through the artillery bursts and search for her. Himself, he was leaving. He reached into his back pocket and heaved out the bulging roll of banknotes, unwound the elastic band holding the roll tight, and threw the notes high in the air for the wind to catch. He let them scrabble for them.

The cheeks and jowl of Lev Rybinsky quivered in misery. 'Your loss is that of a distant cousin, a mere story – my loss is that of a son. I have lost the chance of gaining the licences to exploit the minerals here. If you want to go and look for her then go. I am leaving.'

When they had collected all of the money they climbed into his car and joined the tail of the long column heading north towards the mountains.

The drone was in his ears. He had his back to the road but it was bad for Joe Denton to try to work while he was distracted. Over his shoulder, on the road, was the grind of the vehicles. The minefield was more difficult to work in than he had expected. A part of the meadow had a shallow dip in it, from long years of winter rain. The soil had been pushed by the rain flow to the side, and had buried the tripwires of the V69s. The Italian ones were the most dangerous of all the mines he cleared, and particularly dangerous when the tripwires were buried. The killing range was a radius of 27 yards. When the tripwire was touched – and the tension in the buried wires gave them a hair-trigger condition – the initiator charge hurled the V69's core vertically upwards to a height of 18 inches above the ground, then a restraining wire detonated the core, throwing out thousands of tiny metal cubes. If he fired a V69 then the helmet with the visor covering his face would be lacerated, and his protective vest would be shredded. More than any of the mines he worked on, Joe detested the V69s: too many times he had seen the child amputee who had wandered out over other meadows to pick flowers, and men and women who had gone to round up cattle herds and now limped on crutches, or to harvest apples from orchards and now wore the hideous lifeless artificial legs. Clearing the long-laid mines was not work for a man suffering distraction.

All the time the approaching drone had been in his ear he had been excavating the lie of a tripwire with a trowel and a slim metal probe. He stopped, caught his breath and watched the column on the road, then crawled back along his cleared channel between the pegs.

The lorries, pick-ups and jeeps lumbered along the narrow track. He saw the faces of many men, quiet and without passion. He stood at the side of the road, scanned those faces and looked for Gus.

At the end of the convoy was a mud-spattered Mercedes, then came Sarah's two pick-ups with the bright new paint of Red Crescents on the doors and bonnets. Joe waved her down. He saw casualties on stretchers in the vans, but they were not full – and yet the army retreated.

'What happened?'

She was tough, old Sarah, the one who liked to say she'd seen everything misery could throw at her, and she gibbered.

'They took the crossroads. The Iraqis fell back, damn nearly gave it to them. She was wrong, she – the woman, Meda – promised there would be no tanks. It was a trap, the soldiers fell back and left the *peshmerga* out in the middle of a killing zone, with the tanks to do the killing. Your sniper – and your mines – together they stopped the tanks. The pick-ups would have been full, and some more, if your sniper hadn't listened well to what you said. The casualties stayed minimal . . . They should have been going for Kirkūk tomorrow morning, but the warlords called the whole bloody thing off. They've quit and taken their people with them.'

'Have you seen him?'

Sarah said, 'Most didn't, but some stayed – that's what I was told. The some are the misfits, the useless and the thieves, what the warlords don't have on their payroll. She hasn't come out, and he's with her.'

'How many are left, to go to Kirkūk?'

'What I was told, it's around three hundred.'

'Then they're best forgotten,' Joe said. 'You won't see them again. When you forget, it doesn't hurt.'

The pick-up pulled away. He saw that she bit her lip. The dusk was coming on, and he went back, so carefully, into the minefield to collect the gear he had left there. In the morning he would finish with the buried tripwire.

*　　*　　*

He had lain a long time on his bed, until the darkness blacked out the beaming smile of the President on the wall in front of him.

Alone, but for his dog, his sense of duty burdened him.

Major Karim Aziz tried to analyse the priorities of duty. Was his first duty to his wife and children, and their safety? Was it to the soldiers who would stand at barricades in the Kirkūk suburbs and fight the woman and her remnant force, regardless of their own future? Was his supreme duty to the great and historic people of Iraq?

If his duty was to his family, he should slip away, drive in the night to Baghdad and take them as fugitives on the hazardous journey to the Turkish or Iranian frontiers. If he failed they would all be killed. If he succeeded he abandoned his duty to the soldiers at the barricades, and to the people of Iraq. Duty was his life, the prop on which he had leaned for so long. He drifted close to exhausted sleep. The dog snored contentedly on the mat by the far wall. Above his duty to his family and his soldiers and his people was the image of the sniper – faded at first, then clearing – sitting and watching and mocking him.

The thought of the sniper caught him. He tossed. His hand found the shape in his breast pocket of the letter written to his wife. He shook on the bed. His chance to fulfil his duty lay upon the courage of the wretch in a cell. The wretch would know of him, could denounce him to staunch the pain. His duty was to confront the sniper. It was his supreme indulgence to crave the aloof, alone, personal battle with the sniper – if the wretch gave him time.

He pushed himself off the bed. With his Dragunov, his backpack and his dog, he went out into the night – past the dull lights illuminating the cell block – to find the woman who would lead him to the sniper, if he was given the time.

'Still here?'
　'Yes.'
'Not running?' A chuckle whipped her voice.
　'No.'
'Should I apologize?'
Gus said calmly, 'Not necessary.'
'Apologize because my judgement was wrong?'
'The tanks came, you were wrong.'
'But you, the hero, stopped them,' she taunted.
'I did what I could.'
'If I don't apologize, if my judgement was wrong, why do you stay?'
'I don't think I could explain.'
He had not moved all day. He had allowed the tiredness to seep from his body into the ground. He could not see her face, but the strut of her body was in bold outline above him and the bulk of her seemed greater because her hands were set on her hips. It was Gus's own small piece of defiance that he had sat all through the day and into the evening darkness against the jeep's wheel. If she wanted to come to him she could; if she did not, he would not go in search of her. Small fires were burning and around them were little clusters of men, some in earshot and some beyond. In the middle of the night he would move. Haquim had talked of helicopters . . . Omar had left him, and sometimes he saw his slight silhouette drift close to the fires then disappear. He

thought the boy craved the company of adult fighters, as if that took away his youth. He was sorry that the boy had stayed.

The anger rippled in her. 'I did everything for them, and they gave me trifles. At the moment I needed them, the swine – Bekir and Ibrahim – turned away from me because the final victory has to be earned and is not set in stone. When I am in Kirkūk . . .'

'What will they do when you are in Kirkūk?'

She snorted. 'Come, of course, what else? Come to take the rewards for what I have done for them.'

'Yes.'

Gus jacked himself up. He used the butt of his rifle to push himself off the ground, and he hitched his rucksack onto his shoulder. He took her hand. He wondered if she would fight him. He took it loosely, then tightened his grip to jolt her forward. She dug in her heels, but his grip was the same as when he held the rifle ready to shoot, firm and strong. As Gus took the first strides she held back but with each step he jerked harder, and after the first strides she accepted and walked beside him. They went past the sentries, sitting and smoking cigarettes, out into the black darkness beyond the perimeter of the crossroads camp.

'Where are we going?'

'Towards Nineveh,' Gus said.

'That is more than a hundred kilometres, and backwards.'

He said patiently, 'We are going where we can imagine we are at Nineveh.'

'If we could reach it, and we cannot, all we would find are old rocks and old stones.'

'It's where it began – it's why I am here. It started at Nineveh.'

'That is rubbish.'

'We are going towards Nineveh.'

He led and she no longer fought him. They walked away from the wire and left the flickering fires behind them. They were under stars and a thin moon's crescent. From the time he could sit on his grandfather's knee and smell the stale whiff of tobacco on his breath, he had known of the palace, and the friendship made there. Deep in the memory of childhood was the story of King Sennacherib who had died 2,680 years ago, when the same stars and the same thin moon made a pallid dullness of the ground, and the same stars and moon had watched over the friendship of men now aged. Grafted in his mind, from the days when he could first read, were the pictures in the books of the throne room in the palace and the bas-reliefs and the shallow outline of the excavated city gates. There was a figure in relief that he remembered above all, a crouching archer. In an album of faded photographs, two men stood outside a tent, posed beside a car, larked in the ruins, knelt and helped the archaeologists: one was tall and wore an open shirt, and a wide-brimmed hat, ludicrous baggy shorts and battered sandals; the other was shorter and seemed heavier in the folds of the long-tailed tribal shirt and the shapeless trousers, with curled unruly hair under a cloth wound as a turban. And the same quiet, the same stars and moon had blessed that friendship, at Nineveh.

'There were stories and books and pictures, but it was too far away to be real. There were letters sent to my grandfather, by your grandfather, but they had no value, no context in anything I knew. Then I came with him to the border. We found his friend, and we found you. You never cried. All around you was screaming and weeping, despair. You had just buried your brothers. You hung back, somehow apart from the misery around you. I had never seen before, have never seen again, a young face of such determination. You were not more than a child, you never spoke, but I saw your face. Whatever else in my life goes on past me, that face is always with me . . . I may not be good with words, but I am blessed for having known you, given me from old men's friendship. Do you think we are close now to the old men, near to Nineveh?'

'I think we are.'

'I came because that face, without tears, enabled me to dream and to dare.'

He sat on the ground. He pulled her down beside him. A shell whined high over them and exploded in the distance on the road. He felt the light wind, medium strength but coming on to fresh, on his face, and she shuddered. He hesitated, then slipped his arm over her shoulder. Gus knew it was not the cold that made the shudder in her body. Together, his arm around her shoulder, they could dream, dare. He pulled her harder against him, her shoulder under his, her hair against his cheek, her hips against his, her thigh . . . She cried out in pain. She was so strong, so proud, so bloody obstinate, and he had forgotten. He took the torch from his pocket. He did not speak. He pushed her back onto the dirt, and his hand went to her belt. He unfastened it and dragged down her trouser zip. He heaved the trousers down and shone the torch onto her thigh. The dressing was gone, and the edge of the wound was reddened and angry. Maggots moved in the centre of it, between the weals that marked its limits. He saw the wriggling life of the maggots. He crouched over her thigh, smelt the dankness of her, and very carefully began to pick each of the maggots from the wound. She did not cry out again. He poured water from his bottle over the wound and washed away the newest of the flies' eggs. He did not criticize her for not having had the wound dressed, for not having stolen the time of the aid-worker at Tarjil while she'd worked to save the worst of the casualties. He loved her because, under the bombast of her conceit, she would never put herself first, and never complain for fear that her strength was diminished. He made the wound clean. He switched off the torch, lifted her buttocks, drew up her trousers and zipped them, then fastened her belt.

He did not think it was necessary to fumble for words to explain why he had stayed. He saw the great flame burning and beyond it were the roofs, minarets and the high buildings of Kirkūk. He could dream and he could dare, because of her. He kissed her. It was a slow, awkward kiss, lip to lip, mouth to mouth, the kiss of teenage children in wonderment.

They walked back into the camp, away from Nineveh.

She called briskly for a briefing meeting in fifteen minutes, and the shyness was gone from her.

There was a jeep parked near to one of the fires and Gus saw Haquim beside it.

Haquim said, 'As you could not leave her, neither could I, though it was the act of a fool to come back.'

'Why?'

'To be with her, and to tell you about helicopters . . .'

'You didn't have to come back – I know about helicopters.'

'And to shield her, to keep her safe from herself.'

Gus settled comfortably against the jeep's wheel. The boy brought them coffee. Only when he drank it did he lose the taste of her mouth in his, but still he did not forget.

Chapter Thirteen

Away to the west, the flame burned, an isolated beacon beyond the myriad lights in Kirkūk.

They went fast over flat, open ground. If they looked for cover, went forward at a crawl, they would not make their schedule. If he had not believed in her, he would have turned.

The route, Omar leading and Gus a pace behind, would take them in a great arcing circuit around the city's lights. Going hard, Gus could not avoid kicking loose stones and sometimes stumbling into small ditches. He took on trust, too, the boy's skills and the sharpness of his hearing. He had known at home, as a child, out with Billings, the night flight of the hunting barn owl and learned its skills, the sharpness of its hearing as it phantom-glided in the new plantations, listening for the movements of tiny voles and shrews. He thought the boy had the skills and hearing of the owl. The schedule allowed no slack. His own stride was heavy, scuffing the ground, but the boy was as silent as the owl when the old poacher had showed it him.

It was two hours since they had left what remained of the main column. There were isolated lights to their left, lamps over a fence, a roving searchlight from a silhouetted watchtower, and a dull glow from the tightly packed homes. Omar's route would bring them between the fortified village and the more distant spread of Kirkūk's brightness.

He heard a shrill cry.

Omar never wavered from the route, as if it carried no threat to them.

The crying was pain, that of a rabbit in a snare.

A track crossed the dark ground ahead and linked a Victory City to Kirkūk. The sound of the crying grew, but the boy did not slow.

They came to the track, crossed it, stepped down into the ditch on the far side of it and Gus straddled the source of the crying. The woman was a black shadow shape. The thin moonlight fell on the beads of her necklace and caught the irregular shape of her teeth, the lines on her face, made jewelled rivers of her tears.

The men were dumped in grotesque postures in the pit of the ditch. Omar, ahead of Gus, shuddered – as if ghosts crossed his soul – and the woman's cries turned to a ranted anguish. The smaller body wore a Hard Rock Café T-shirt, but the motif was stained in black blood. The moonlight caught the lustreless eyes of the heavier man. She shouted at them as they went by, and after them as they hurried away. Her shouts seemed to hang in the night air like a thinning mist. They went on until they no longer heard the sound.

'What did she say?'

'I do not think you wish to know, Mr Gus.'

'Tell me.'

In his mind were the bodies, perhaps her husband and son. The face he had seen was aged with suffering.

332

He told himself that it was right to go on, not give sympathy and help. He heard Omar draw in a great gulp of breath, then the whisper of his voice.

'She went into the fields the day before yesterday and she found wild flowers. She brought the flowers home. She is a widow and she lives with her son, her son's wife and her grandson. She put the flowers in a jar that had been used for storing jam. She set the jar and the flowers outside the door of her house. She told the people who lived near to her that, yesterday, they should collect flowers as a celebration because the woman, Meda, was coming to bring them freedom. The soldiers did nothing because they, also, Mr Gus, believed that Meda was coming. Then they heard that the *peshmerga* had turned, had gone back to the mountains. They are survivors, Mr Gus. They denounced her, her son and her grandson as followers of the witch. She said the whole village walked with them, abusing them, when the soldiers took them out of the village and shot them. She curses Meda. She says that if Meda had stayed in her own village, in the mountains, then she would have her son and her grandson. She wanted us to bury her son and grandson . . . Are you better for knowing that?'

His heel hurt worse, his body ached with tiredness, there was the growing pain in his eyes from peering into the darkness and, ceaselessly, his stomach growled for food. He, too, had put his trust in her. They walked on. The sling of his rifle bit into the flesh of his shoulder, freshening the sores of the rucksack's straps, and he welcomed it.

The boy pleaded, a child's voice, 'Tell me, Mr Gus, a story from Major Herbert Hesketh-Prichard.'

He should have remained silent, should have

concentrated on his footfall, but there was rare fear in the boy's voice. He should have been thinking of the schedule, and the helicopters.

Gus said softly, 'Major Hesketh-Prichard wrote that the best scout he ever knew was an American called Burnham who fought as an officer with the British army in the war against the Matabele tribes of Rhodesia in southern Africa, and that was more than a hundred years ago. He was awarded the medal of the Distinguished Service Order by the Queen. He was a small man but always very physically fit. He had good hearing and strong eyesight, and his sense of smell was remarkable – as sensitive as any animal's. His finest achievement was to go with his rifle through the entire Matabele army, alone, past their sentries, past their patrols, right into the centre of their camp. In the middle of the camp he found the tent of their leader, M'limo, and Burnham shot him dead. Then he was excellent enough in his fieldcraft to go back through their lines to safety. He was the best . . .'

'It is a good story, Mr Gus.'

'Only the best, Omar, can go through the lines, kill the heart of the enemy, and go back to safety.'

'But the fault was with the Matabele people who did not protect their leader.'

'Fail to protect the leader, Omar, and everything is wasted.'

Their stride quickened in the cloak of darkness. The minutes of the schedule given them were slowly being eaten away.

His mind was made up. It was not duty that drove Major Karim Aziz, but vanity.

In the night hours he searched, as he had many weeks before – a lifetime before – for a vantage-point.

Because he had fought before in the streets, cellars and sewers, Aziz knew the pulse of a city at war, but that night the mood of Kirkūk perplexed him. He would have expected the city's people to have retreated behind barred doors and shuttered windows, that every shop would be padlocked and closed, that the street sellers would have gone to the shanty town beyond the airfield. But the lights burned out over the wide boulevard streets of the New Quarter, and there were still cars and commercial trucks on them, with the tanks and personnel carriers. The cafés, too, were doing trade, and at the pavement tables men sat in thick coats and smoked, drank and talked.

He knew she must come at dawn, and the sniper with her. With a small force, she would have gained a toehold, or at least a fingernail grip, on the centre of the city where the big buildings of the administration were sited. If she were not coming then she would have joined the long, dusty convoy he had seen retreating from the crossroads. Vanity was his spur, as it had been when the troops had cheered him after he had shot the mullah many years before. The same vanity, not duty to his family, his army and his country, had sent him on the hunt for a vantage-point that would have given him the shot of a lifetime on the flat roof with the view of the door of a villa. The vanity obscured the image of the brigadier in the cell block from his thoughts.

He strode away from the governor's house and the gate into Fifth Army headquarters. He was certain that she would attack down the width of Martyr Avenue towards the house and the headquarters. He was refreshed by the rest on his bed and he had eaten bread, a little cheese and an apple. The dog was close to him. It was a week since he had shaved. The dust and mud clung to his boots, his trousers and his smock; the backpack, perched high on his shoulders, was grimed in filth; but there was brightness in his eyes, and in the lens of the sight mounted on the stock of the Dragunov. When he passed the cafés, the men stopped their talk, lowered their cups and held their cigarettes away from their mouths as if drawn by the sight of him. He walked towards the outskirts of the city, and visualized the battle and the part he would play in it . . . She would make the punch down the six lanes of Martyr Avenue, with a small diversionary assault on the parallel 16th July Avenue that was four lanes wide. The helicopters would be up and over them, would scatter them. She would be in a doorway, or in the flood-drain in the centre of Martyr Avenue, but if she were to lead, she must show herself.

There was a doorman at the entrance to the last block of apartments on Martyr Avenue. He walked past the man, who bowed his head, the dirt from his boots flaking on the lobby carpet, and climbed the stairs. He emerged onto the roof and stood in the shadow of the water tank.

Aziz looked out over the vista beneath him. Behind him, on the far side of the city, was the glow of the lights of the airfield from which the helicopters would fly. To the side, set in a shambles and without pattern, were the pinpricks of the Old Quarter. In front of him was Martyr Avenue, the barricade and two tanks with personnel carriers behind them. Beyond Martyr Avenue were two neat lines of apartment blocks, then the sharply illuminated length of 16th July Avenue. When he swivelled further he could see the plaza outside the governor's house, and at the end of it was the floodlit gate to Fifth Army headquarters. His search for a vantage-point was completed . . . But he was too high, the elevation was too great. For a moment longer, as if he had earned a little of its luxury, he let the night air play, cool and cleansing, on the stubble of his face and the dirt. Then he whistled for the dog and went back to the staircase, down three flights of steps.

The door on the second floor had no nameplate. He rang the bell, kept his finger on the button.

A bolt was drawn back, a key was turned. He saw a momentary joy on her face, then the shock. Without explanation, Aziz pushed her aside, kicking the door shut behind him with his heel.

She wore a loose housecoat and fluffy slippers. There was make-up on her face but insufficient to hide the crow's feet lines at her eyes and mouth – his wife, in his home, did not use cosmetics because they could not be paid for. She had blond, short-cut hair, but the stems were grey-black below the platinum. He went through the living room, past the chairs and tables and lamps – more expensive than they could have afforded to buy – and into the soft-lit bedroom. There was a big bed, with pink sheets and blankets, and a padded headboard, such as he and his wife had never slept in. He pulled aside the drawn curtains and stepped through the French windows onto the balcony. He could see the edge of the airfield perimeter, the Old Quarter and the barricade at the end of Martyr Avenue. Through the apartment blocks was a clear view of long sectors of 16th July Avenue. It was a corner apartment and there was an additional balcony off the living room from which he would be able to look over the square outside the governor's house and the gates to Fifth Army. He went back into the bedroom, and gazed at the photograph in the frame on the dressing table.

The face smiled above the uniformed shoulders.

It was the face he had seen, cold and evaluating, when he had fired on the range and in the mountains too. He picked up the photograph of the brigadier. The face, bloodied and scarred, was now in the cell block. His hand shook as he laid the photograph face down on the dressing table.

'You know him? He is very kind to me. To me, he is a gentle man . . .'

He told her to close the bedroom door and switch off the light.

'He did not come last night. I thought, just now, that you were him . . .'

When the room was darkened, Aziz dragged back the curtains and fastened them at the sides of the window. He went to the bed, ripped off the pink coverlet and threw it onto the balcony.

'I am from Malmö in Sweden. I have been in London, Paris, Nicosia, Bucharest, Beirut, Cairo and Baghdad, and now I am in Kirkūk. I am very lucky to have found such a kind and gentle man at the end of my road. I suppose that he is busy with the situation – but you know better than me that he is important.'

He settled himself down on the coverlet, used it as padding so that the hard tiles of the balcony would not stiffen his legs, reduce the circulation and harm the accuracy of his shooting.

'And he has told me that soon he will be more important . . .'

He told her to leave him and to take her photograph with her. The peace of his mind was fracturing. He watched for the woman and the sniper. Because he had put vanity above duty to his family, his life depended on the man in the cell block.

'We should go in one group.'

'No, we must be in small groups,' Meda said.

Haquim smacked his knuckle into the palm of his hand. 'We need to be a fist and punch with firepower.'

'We should be water running through fingers, in groups of twenty, no more.'

'Strength in numbers is our only option,' Haquim persisted.

'We should attack from all angles so they do not know where to find the heart of us.'

The men, 280 of them – fewer than the number needed to take the Victory City, far fewer than the number who had charged the defences at Tarjil – stood in a tight, mesmerized circle around her and Haquim. It was as if she held them in a noose. In the moonlight, he saw the adoration in their eyes. He knew some of them as thieves, and some of them as beggars. Some were so old they could barely run and others were so young they could not have done a day of man's work in the fields. The best men, the men on whom the *mustashar* would have depended, had gone back with *agha* Ibrahim and *agha* Bekir, as he had . . . but, unlike him, none of the best men had returned. They would be slaughtered, all of them – her and him – when the helicopters flew. He

339

thought she had sacrificed the life of the Englishman, used an old loyalty, sent him on the long march against the helicopters and killed him.

'You're wrong.'

She laughed in his face. 'I am right, always right. You are wrong, always wrong.'

'It is madness.'

Haquim heard the hostile rumble in the throats of the men around her. He fought for their lives and they did not recognize it. She danced on him. Everything he had achieved in a lifetime of soldiering she danced on, as if it were worthless. He had told the Englishman of his long march across the country when he had brought the peasant boys back to their homes, and at least the Englishman had listened with respect. He had held the pass with the rearguard so that the refugees could reach the safety of the frontier; without value. He did not dare to look into her eyes for fear that she would entrap him, too . . . but he would lay down his life to protect her.

'You should not be frightened, old man. We are not frightened, nor Mr Peake. Trust me. We are two hundred and eighty. We are in groups of twenty men. We are in houses, gardens, alleyways, yards, not in the roads where they have barricades and tanks. They will not have the helicopters to search for us because Mr Peake will not be frightened. We are going forward. You will sleep, tonight, in the governor's bed, while I direct Kirkūk's defence from the governor's office.'

'If you get to the governor's house, how long do you think you can hold it?'

'Until they come, a few hours, it's all we need.'

Still, Haquim did not dare to look into the light of her eyes. He rasped, 'Who comes?'

'It is because you are frightened, old man, that you are stupid . . . The pigs will come, of course. Bekir and Ibrahim will come – all of the *peshmerga* will come. They wait a little way off. They need me to give them courage. When I am in the governor's house they will have the courage and come. It will happen.'

At last, reluctantly, Haquim looked into her face. The sneers and taunts had gone. He was responsible. He had heard talk of her, gone to her village, listened to her, believed in her, promised her grandfather that he would watch over her, had taken her to meet *agha* Bekir and *agha* Ibrahim, and he had watched the little army swell. The smile caught him as surely as the barbed hooks the children used when they caught fish off the dam of the great Dukan reservoir. He took her hand. There were grenades on straps against her chest. He placed his hand, with hers inside his, on the metal of the RG-5 fragmentation grenade that was closest to her heart.

'If I am with you and believe you will be captured, then I will shoot you. If I am not with you, and you will be captured, *please*, please, I beg it of you, pull the pin.'

Against the wire that stretched either side of them, limitless until lost in the darkness, Gus used the binoculars and confirmed what he already knew. The range was too great – they had to go through the wire.

So little time . . . A jeep passed, idled into his view and he was close enough to it to see the faces of the soldiers. There was a tumbler strand a foot above the ground into which the mesh wire was buried, another at the waist height of a standing man, another at the eyeline of a man at full height and just below the stretched coils of razor

341

wire. They began, frantically, to dig with their hands at the dry soil.

There was a growing smear of grey-gold light behind the faraway mountains.

Three helicopters were on the bright-lit apron, slug beasts; he had been told they would be the Russian-built Mi-24 gun-ships, and if they caught her in the open with anti-tank missiles, rockets and the rapid-fire machine-gun, she was gone, and it was finished. He dug, ripped his nails, scraped the skin from his hands.

The tankers backed away. The crews, in loose-fitting flying-suits, were walking round the beasts, approving the fitting of the ordnance stowed under the wings.

They had reached the bottom of the wire, but the deeper earth was harder, drier. The boy used a knife to stab into the ground and Gus scraped it back behind him. The light was growing, the time was slipping away. The hole widened. The boy hacked down into the earth and Gus shovelled it aside. He should have been resting, should have been calm and with the chance to watch for wind variation over the expanse of ground between the fence and the apron area where the helicopters were readied to fly. The boy, eel-like, wriggled down into the hole and then began to chop at the soil on the far side of the wire until it sprouted up as if a maddened mole made the tunnel. Omar was through.

Gus heard the whine of a helicopter engine starting and saw the first lazy turns of the rotors.

He tore off a hessian strip from his suit and gently looped it over the lowest of the tumbler strands.

As he passed the rifle through the cavity, the boy took it. He crawled into the hole and stuck. Omar dragged at his shoulders. Gus was stuck fast. He saw only the dark-

342

ness of the hole . . . If the tumbler strand was disturbed the sirens would blast, the jeep would come, and the helicopters would fly . . . His head burst out into the light.

The pitch of the engines rose.

They crawled, together, on their bellies towards the helicopters.

AUGUSTUS HENDERSON *PEAKE*.

6. (Conclusions after interviews with personnel at CTCRM, Lympstone conducted by self and Ms Manning – transcripts attached.)

MILITARY TRAINING: The normal duration of a sniping course would be 3 weeks, AHP was given 72 hours (less minimal sleep time) of concentrated Fieldcraft and Tactical training. It is possible he would have absorbed a considerable amount of what he was told, shown and briefed on, but at best the knowledge will remain superficial. Also, he has been educated in procedures that would be adopted by a regular army where he would be provided with all necessary support. AHP is not in such an environment and will be operating alongside irregulars of doubtful quality.

TACTICAL TRAINING: AHP, at CTCRM, received specialist advice from 5 sergeant instructors – but I consider that given by Sgt Stevens, MM, to be the most important. Sgt Stevens served in northern Iraq in 1991 in the Safe Haven operation for Kurdish refugees, and therefore had a first-hand knowledge of the terrain; he stressed to AHP that the further south the irregular force probed, so would increase the technical superiority of Govt of Iraq forces. Emphasis was placed on the use of the AWM Lapua Magnum rifle's armour-piercing capability against helicopter gun-ships, and the need for bold and imaginative counter-measures against such a threat. (The fact that AHP is a civilian, not hidebound by standard military procedures, leads me to believe that boldness and imagination would be expected from him. KW) In the use of such tactics, the LOYALTY spoken of by Sgt Billings would probably cause AHP to push home an attack in situations where his personal safety is directly threatened.

Willet paused, his fingers lying limply alongside the keyboard. He wanted to push himself up from his chair, go to the window, pull back the curtains and open it. He wanted to shove his head out into the night air and shout over the roofs and the streets, over the crawling cars and the last stragglers going home from the clubs, to throw his voice far beyond and far away. He wanted to be heard by a man who sat huddled in the warmth of a gillie suit, who held the long barrel of the rifle, who waited for the dawn.

He wanted to yell, 'Turn back, don't be a stupid bastard . . . Walk away. It's for nothing . . . Come home, come back to where people love you . . . Live a life, a fucking boring life, but live it . . . Be like me, be a bloody coward, be like me and find an excuse to turn . . .' He knew that if he screamed into the emptiness of the night, he would not be heard.

Willet began, again, to type.

The binoculars told him the lead helicopter was 670 yards in front of him, the second helicopter was 705 yards from him, and the third helicopter in the line was 740 yards from his aiming position.

The windsock beside the control tower hung lifelessly against the flagpole. Gus had the range and did not need to concern himself on windage deflection.

The helicopters shuddered in line as the engine power grew.

If such a beast was his target, he had been told where it was vulnerable and where the Mi-24 was protected by armour plate. The earnest Doug Stevens had laid the sheet of paper on the table among the spilled beer and the ashtray's garbage, drawn the outline of the beast, scribbled in the shaded areas where it was armour-plated, and highlighted the parts where, if it were hit, it could be killed. A technician scrambled up the side of the lead helicopter, and the pilot's hatch door was opened. Might be a fuel gauge playing up, or oil pressure, might be the navigation system. The pilot, high in the forward end of the fuselage, was protected – on the drawing on Doug Stevens' paper – by armour and a bulletproof glass canopy, but his door was open and lit by the high lights.

Gus fired.

Flat on his stomach, the boy close beside him, Gus watched the vortex of the bullet's passage through the dawn air.

The technician fell back, dropped away from the

ladder. At the same moment, the pilot slumped. The core of an armour-piercing bullet would then have careered on inside the cockpit and struck glancing, spinning blows against the armour that was supposed to keep a bullet outside the womb in which the pilot sat, but not inside.

He heard the boy squeal in excitement, but his eyeline had moved on. He raked back the bolt and his fingers felt for the elevation turret of the 'scope. He twisted it the minuscule correction of one half-click.

The sides and the underpart of the fuselage of the Mi-24 were protected, Doug Stevens had said, but the gearbox in the mounting under the rotors was not. Stevens had said that Special Forces and spooks had trained the Afghan mujahedin to shoot down from the valley's cliffs on to the gun-ships' superstructures. They wouldn't have heard the shot in the second and third helicopters, but they'd have seen the technician fall and the statue posture of the ground-control man with his outstretched signal batons.

Gus had a window of seconds: such an opportunity would not come again.

He fired at the gearbox of the second helicopter, immediately below the outstretched sweep of the rotors. Metal parts dropped away.

Bolt back, cartridge case ejected, and the sweep of the 'scope towards the third of the beasts. It was already lifting. He could see the pilot secure inside the casing. It rose, tilting away from him and he lost the sight of the gearbox below the rotors. He locked his aim on the blurred shape of the vertical tail rotor. He sucked in a breath, exhaled, caught the last of the air – and held it.

Gus fired three times, at 740 yards mean distance, into the spinning shape of the third helicopter's tail rotor.

He did not hear the boy's shout. He did not see the jeep, at the distant end of the wire, reversing and turning. He twisted up onto his knee, caught at the boy's collar, and pitched him back towards the wire. Then Gus was running.

There was no longer a pain in his heel, an ache in his body and exhaustion in his eyes. Gus ran for his life and the boy stampeded beside him. If he had not hung the hessian strip on the wire he would have lost precious moments, finding the hole under the wire.

He threw himself down into the hole and the boy pushed, levered him through the gap. Then he was running again, weaving, gasping for air, bent low. Behind him, the pilot of the third helicopter fought an unequal battle with his machine and lost.

The immediate goal was the airfield's rubbish tip where the crows, startled by the gunfire, wheeled and screamed. The secondary goal, when the piled rubbish tip covered their backs, was a dried river gully. The final goal, far ahead, was to link with Meda and the attack.

Machine-guns had started up, but without a target.

Only when he was in the gully, when the pain, the ache and the tiredness surged back to him, did Gus bleat his question.

'Can they fly?'

'You killed them, Mr Gus, they cannot fly.'

They ran on down the gully, as the dawn lightened. It was, Gus thought, the decisive day of his life, the day he had dreamed and dared, but there was nothing of the taste of her in his mouth, just a dry dusty film.

The attack went well, made good ground – at first.

They had advanced in silence through ditches, drains,

347

through gardens and small vegetable fields to the edge of the city's limits. They had scurried, crawled, run from shadow to shadow, in their small groups, and waited for the signal.

The report of the first shot, then the second, then the third, fourth and fifth, had come muffled to them across the breadth of the city, and before the sound of the fifth shot had died there had been the blast of the heavy machine-gun and the rip of its tracers – the signal.

The assault on Kirkūk was like that of mosquitoes on an ailing man. The weight of a man's hand might fall on a biting insect, but in that moment of distraction another mosquito bit and drew blood. The barricades, with the tanks and personnel carriers in support, were ignored. Martyr Avenue and 16th July Avenue were empty. The attack was through the yards, homes and alleyways of the Old Quarter. When gaps were plugged, new points of weakness emerged. Pockets of resistance were cut off, left isolated.

To those in the Fifth Army command bunker there was no coherent pattern to the attack: as the radios from the forward positions shouted for help, the officers trained in defensive warfare at the Baghdad Military College did not know where they should stiffen the line. And they had no serviceable helicopters. Inside the safety of the bunker, as the counters were moved remorselessly back over the map towards the red circle marking Fifth Army headquarters, the first doubts – anxieties – had surfaced. The defence line would not have been stabilized, however temporarily, if the colonel had not ordered a killing zone of fire to be put down on the Old Quarter. Mortars, machine-guns, rocket-propelled grenades hammered the small homes of those who were expendable.

In the smoke, noise and chaos, Meda sought to restore the impetus of the advance. In an alleyway between a panel-beater's shed and a cheap clothes shop was an abandoned jeep with a machine-gun mounted and the belt of ammunition lying in the breech. She must show herself, and goad her small groups of separated fighters to press on. She must be everywhere. Without her, and she knew it, the advance would stall. They had come through the yard and into the panel-beater's shed. The roof was ablaze. The door was destroyed. Four men were close to her, Haquim was somewhere behind. If she was to be everywhere, she needed the jeep.

He peered into the maelstrom of smoke and fire.

Many times he had seen the little darting movements of men, emerging and disappearing, but it was harder now to see them because of the smoke's pall.

With his old trusted patience, he waited for her to show herself.

He lay on the pink coverlet, his circulation good, his stomach comfortable. He had not fired. He had seen soldiers try to surrender and had watched as they were engulfed, knifed. He had seen, also, a young officer castrated and left to writhe on the ground smearing a spray of blood from his groin onto cobblestones. He had seen three soldiers who manhandled away a wounded colleague shot in the back at close range – but he had not fired.

He had no doubt that the time would come when he would see her.

Major Karim Aziz sensed that a line formed. It stretched across the Old Quarter, its median point at a range of 450 metres, and he adjusted his elevation for

349

that point. The smoke helped him, its billowing spirals told him the wind factor was minimal, but that was outweighed by the greater problem of its interference with his vision of the fighting ground. That median point was an abandoned jeep. Once he had taken it as his point, he tracked along the line on either side of it, slowly, so that the view through the lens would not distort.

It was a blurred movement at the extremity of the lens.

First he saw the figures running from the collapsed doorway and jumping into the jeep.

A man was bent over the steering wheel, reaching down, magnified, desperate to start it. Another man, turbaned, bearded, swathed in ammunition, was behind the mounted machine-gun. Only when the jeep jerked forward, when her body was thrown back against the support of the front passenger seat, did he see her.

The jeep had moved forward, then it was reversing, then it was lost behind a swathe of smoke. He could not follow it, but he had seen her face. He felt a great calmness. He had seen her face and the anger at her mouth. He wondered if she doubted herself, if she knew that it was over, not how it would end, but that it was finished.

The jeep emerged from the smoke, and Aziz's finger made the intuitive adjustment to the elevation turret, one click, an additional 50 metres of range, watching as it swerved to the right at a tight junction.

He saw the jeep, her face, the driver's, the shop behind them from which flames licked, as the steering was wrenched hard over. He could not hear the distant scream of the tyres, or the blast in his ears as he fired.

Strangely, slowly, the jeep toppled over after it had

350

crashed against the wall. For a few moments, a seeming eternity, it was supported by the machine-gun and there was a gap from which the gunner and the driver scrabbled to free themselves, but then the mounting on the machine-gun collapsed: the jeep rocked and was still but for the spinning wheels. His finger was on the trigger, slight pressure. He watched for her and did not see her. The gunner, delirious with shock, ran. The driver twitched and died.

He recognized the older man running forward from the ditch at the crossroads. He could have shot him – afterwards he would be unable to analyse why he had not fired on him as he limped forward and tried to lift the upturned jeep alone. He watched him stagger away, heaving for breath, then cup his hands to his mouth and bellow at the fire and the smoke for help.

No help came.

The man tried again to lift the jeep, and failed. A mortar shell exploded a little distance beyond it. He could not hear the singing of the shrapnel at that distance, but he saw the man blown over and begin to crawl away on his stomach. He knew that she was under the jeep. Through the 'scope, he fancied he saw tears on the man's face.

Aziz walked from the balcony into the bedroom. The dog was asleep on the pillows. He called it. He crossed the living room. He did not look at the old whore from Malmö who had reached Kirkūk, the end of the road. She was slumped in a chair with the bottle beside her and the glass in her hand.

'Will he come? Will he come tonight?'

He went down the stairs, pride coursing through him. He had made the most important shot of his career.

*　　*　　*

She was trapped, in darkness. She had heard Haquim's shouts: he would have gone for help. When the jeep had overturned she had covered her head with her arms, and now she could not move her arms and her legs were wedged. The weight of the grenades pressed against her chest. She could not see and could not move, and the stench of the fuel engulfed her. She knew that Haquim had gone for help because she could no longer hear him, and the shooting was fainter. She thought that the men must now be near to the governor's house. When the firing moved away people would come from their houses, where they had sheltered, and they would help to lift the jeep and free her.

Time passed, slipped away from her. She did not know how long, could not see the hands of her watch. Gus would be searching for her now. She tried to remember the touch of his lips. Gus had killed the helicopters, as he had promised he would. He would come to find her.

There was no firing. If the men were near to the governor's house, she could not understand why she could not hear the firing. There were voices, the scrape of boots.

She heard the grunts and the curses. The jeep was lifted. She blinked in the narrow shaft of sunlight and a post was pushed under the jeep's door, as if to prop it while they took new grips. They should hurry. She would lead the last assault on the governor's house. She did not know how they could have gone so far without her.

The jeep rolled back. She clung to the seat as it was lurched over, felt the relief of freedom until she

352

saw the ring of soldiers and the guns pointed at her.

She remembered what Haquim had said . . . She was slumped in the seat. Her fingers, awkward, clumsy in the moment, groped for the ring of the pin on the grenade that was closest to her heart. A rifle butt smacked into her face and she was dragged clear of the jeep.

There was an officer behind the soldiers who cradled a big rifle like Gus's, and who wore a smock like his gillie suit. A dog sat disinterested beside his boots. He watched as she was searched, as the grenades were stripped from her chest, as her tunic and blouse were ripped open and dirt-grimed hands patted the skin of her breasts, waist and thighs, and lingered though they found nothing. He turned and walked away.

A family had come out from the door of a house. They wore their nightclothes – grandmother, parents and children. The soldiers held her so that the family could spit on her in turn.

It had taken Haquim a full fifteen minutes to make contact with one of the groups, to extract them from a close-quarters fire-fight, to organize them, to bring them forward towards the upturned jeep. From 200 metres, through the drifting smoke, he saw the family spit on her, then saw her hustled away.

As the word of her capture spread, the attack stalled. The line sagged, then broke. An ordered retreat became the rout of a rabble. By the time they reached the city limits, many had thrown away their weapons and run.

In his life as a Kurdish fighter, Haquim was familiar with defeat – but none hurt him harder than this. The immediate goal was to cross the barren open fields, to leave the fires in the Old Quarter behind them and the flame of Baba Gurgur, and reach the high ground. They had no friends but the mountains. He had heard her say: 'We will sacrifice everything that we have – our lives, our homes – for Kirkūk.' His back was turned on her but he could not forget that last sight, Meda small and without defence, hemmed in by the bodies of the soldiers.

He stumbled on, in his personal agony, towards the safety of the hazy blue line of the high ground.

'What do you hear, Mr Gus?'

'I hear nothing.'

'What do you *not* hear, Mister Gus?'

'I don't hear anything.'

'Mister Gus, you do not hear the shooting.'

In reverse and faster, they were making the same arced march as in the previous night. Away to his left was the pall above a part of the city. For several minutes Gus had been aware that the shooting was finished, but he had said nothing and pressed on, had harboured it to himself. He wondered how many minutes it had been since the boy had realized that the shooting – far away, distant but clear – had died. He was a sharp little beggar and Gus thought that Omar would have realized before himself that it was over.

He said savagely, 'Absolutely correct. There's no shooting.'

'If they had reached the governor's house, then there would still be shooting.'

'Correct again. You are, Omar, a fount of bloody wisdom.'

The boy looked simply into Gus's eyes. 'If there is no

354

shooting they have broken the attack. They have retreated.'

'Tell me something I don't know.'

'We did what we were asked to do. As we had killed the tanks, we killed the helicopters . . .'

'I doubt that it's anybody's fault.'

Three hundred yards ahead of them was a low cairn. He could see it clearly. If there had still been the sound of shooting, the stones would have been the marker for them to swing left, towards the city, and join the push into the Old Quarter. She hadn't, but Haquim had planned for failure. If the attack failed, Haquim had said in a hushed voice that she should not hear, at the marker they should turn right, go east, towards the sanctuary of the high ground.

They reached the cairn. They did not need new markers as they went east. They followed a wavering line of discarded mortar shells, rocket-propelled grenades, backpacks, ammunition boxes, and the wheeled heavy machine-gun that the Russian had brought in exchange for the prospect of licences for mineral extraction.

He did not think Meda would have turned, but he said nothing because the boy, also, would have known that. His lips were sun-scorched and without feeling, and there was only the taste of dried dirt in his mouth.

Her head hit the jamb of the door as she was dragged into the cell block.

She was taken into a corridor, then the hands released her. She swayed, staggered and was pushed forward down its dull-lit length. The men lining the sides of the corridor kicked at her, or punched her, as she walked.

Two doors were open at the far end. If she held her hands over her face she was kicked in the belly; if she protected her belly, her face was punched. She reached the first of the open doors. Hands grabbed her hair and her shoulders and twisted her so that she must look inside the cell. It was hard for her to recognize him.

He lay on his side, slumped against the far corner. The high ceiling light, above a close wire mesh, shone down on the blood on his face and the pools of urine on the concrete floor. Before she had met the brigadier she had told Gus Peake that he should shoot her if she walked into a trap, and Haquim had told her that if she faced capture, she should pull the pin of the grenade hanging over her heart. She was pitched through the second open door, heard it clang shut behind her. Where were the *peshmerga*? Where was Haquim? Where was Gus Peake?

She sat on the floor of the cell, her knees drawn tight against her chest, under the high light. She heard no answers, only the brutal crack, and the thump again, as the bullet had struck the jeep's driver.

Soldiers held him on their shoulders, carried him across the square, past the governor's office, through the gate and into the compound of Fifth Army headquarters.

He was saluted, waved to, cheered.

His dog trotted alongside.

Aziz felt the exhilaration of pride and just before he was set down at the entrance to the command bunker, he punched the fist that held the Dragunov rifle into the air. At that hour, Major Karim Aziz was the hero. He told the men gathered around him that, later, he would go and search for the sniper who had humiliated the armour and destroyed the helicopters. He would hunt him down, they had his word. The colonel came from the bunker, clasped him, kissed his cheeks, told him that the remnants of the bandits were now in flight, and promised that the President would hear of his success. He said that his one bullet had achieved more than a brigade of tanks and a flight of helicopters.

Faces pressed around him, glowing in trust and admiration, but looking up beyond the men he saw the shadowed cell-block windows.

LIBRARY: Sgt Billings withdrew from CTCRM Library the under-mentioned works:

The British Sniper – Skennerton.
Notes on the Training of Snipers, 1940–41 – Ministry of Defence.
Scouts and Sniping in Trench Warfare – Crum.
With British Snipers to the Reich – Shore.
Sniping: Small Arms Training, vol.1, 1946–51 – Ministry of Defence.
Sniping – Idriess.
Sniping in France – Hesketh-Prichard.

All these works were read by AHP. They are old and deal with historic conflict situations, but the methods of sniping have changed little.

SUMMARY: I believe AHP will perform well when going forward but, through 'doing well', he will increasingly attract attention once all elements of surprise are lost. I am not yet satisfied that he has the necessary knowledge of ESCAPE AND EVASION when the going gets harder. He has chosen to embark on a journey of great complexity and extraordinary danger, and the

357

LOYALTY factor may well deny to him the knowledge of when to turn in retreat. I rate his chances of survival in the medium term as slim.

Willet watched as Ms Manning read his report. A rare smile spread across her face. 'I see you're cracking up.'

He was tired, and he bit. 'What exactly do you mean?'

Her eyes flashed. 'Slim – chances of survival in the medium term – not *non-existent*. That's progress. My God, Augustus Henderson Peake, Esquire, would be happy to know that Ken Willet has changed his bloody mind, if only by a quarter of a crank. These books he read, they seem to come out of the Ark.'

'Not everything in this world is glitzy and new. Real things, things of value, aren't achieved at third hand, by damned remote control. We've tried to fight at a distance, high-tech, no casualties – good stuff for television but useless for getting things done. If you want to get things done then you have to put your life on the line. You bin the computers, you go body to body. He'd have known that because the sergeants would have told him. It was important for him to read the old books.'

'Steady, young man, steady.'

'Myself, if I'd gone where Peake's gone, I'd have wanted Hesketh-Prichard in my knapsack. It's about cunning, deviousness, courage, ruthlessness, the skill of killing . . . It's also about old-fashioned virtues. The trouble is that an old-fashioned virtue is *loyalty* and, at war, loyalty is a killer. "Slim" may not be realistic, I grant you.'

Chapter Fourteen

'You saw it?'

Gus stood over Haquim. They were under a great overhang of rock where the wounded were sheltered from the sun, and where the survivors crouched silent, beaten in fear.

'Yes.'

'And you did nothing?'

Haquim was the only target available to Gus. He had known she would not retreat, and had presumed she was dead. When they had reached the rendezvous, gone into the grey light of the shade, moved through the wounded in search of Haquim, Gus had expected to find a slight, shrouded figure, with the head hidden. It had not been conceivable to him that, while a man of them was left standing, they would fail to retrieve the body.

Haquim, pathetically, shrugged. 'I did what I could.'

'Which was nothing.'

'Don't insult me.'

'You did nothing – it's the truth that insults you.'

'I gathered a group of men. I went back. I saw her taken away. I could do nothing. I would have given up lives . . .'

He saw himself far ahead, in the distance of time, in his grandfather's kitchen making coffee, with the photograph on the window ledge above the sink, and explaining in stuttered words that Meda had been captured, abandoned, that he himself had not protected her. He played the bully.

'Well done, I congratulate you. Because of the risk involved you abandoned her.'

'More would have been killed.'

'You owed it to her to have tried.'

'I am a *mustashar* with responsibility for my men's lives. I cannot give up lives for a gesture.'

'I hope you can live with it.'

He did not know how he could live with it. He had kissed her and there was no longer the feel of her lips on his, and no longer the taste of her. He had nothing by which to remember her – not a bandanna, a handkerchief, not even a soiled field-dressing that carried her stain. In one week, she had come to mean more to him than anyone he had known in his life, and he owned not a single trifle of her. For the first time, Haquim lifted his head, stared back into Gus's eyes, and bit back. 'I am not frightened of the weight of responsibility . . . There was nothing I could have done.'

'Live with it and sleep at night with it.'

'If you knew more of war you would not abuse me. The lesson of war, as I have learned, is that you do not throw away what is most precious, *life,* like empty cigarette cartons. Life is not to be wasted. Can I tell you something?'

'Another damn excuse?'

'The soldiers held her before she was put in the truck, so that a family could confront her. Each of the family

360

took their turn to spit on her. To you she was the symbol to follow, and to me – against all my judgements. For you she was romance, for me she was a vehicle that gave a small chance of success. For them, those she claimed to speak for, she was a vision of evil. That was the last I saw of her, with their spit on her face.'

He heard his own stumbled answers to the confused persistence of his grandfather's questions. He saw the steady gaze, and honesty, of Haquim. He bent down, squatted, and reached forward to take the wearied, grizzled face in his hands.

'How was she?'

'That is an idiotic question.'

'Tell me how she was.'

'The arrogance had gone from her. You saw it, when she contradicted me, the arrogance that each time she was right, and I was wrong. You saw her cheapen my experience – how many times? She was not a fighting woman but a pinioned girl. She was no longer tall, she was small and afraid. She was not a leader, she was ordinary. When they held her, and the family spat on her, she was without value.'

Gus crawled into the darkest corner of the overhang, and lay on the ground. The power of the rifle was in his hand, but that, too, was without value. His face was to the rock, where he could not see the wounded; he saw nothing but the bewilderment of his grandfather, and heard nothing but his grandfather's questions, and the thought of her fear was a blow to his heart.

In the early evening, a cloud passing over the face of a full moon casting a shadow, Commander Yusuf reached the headquarters of Fifth Army.

He had the right to be tired, but fatigue was not apparent in this slight, wire-framed man. He had been driven, with his escort, from Basra where he had been engaged on pressing business, but the business in Basra took second place to the developments in the north. It was said of him that, above all, he was a family man, and liked nothing better than to be with his grandchildren, to indulge them, sit them on his knee and tell them stories, stroke their hair with neat-boned fingers.

The title 'Commander' was self-given. He had no rank in the echelons of the army, nor the need of it. His authority ranged over the lowliest, most humble of soldiers in the slit trenches facing the Kuwaiti border, and over the most senior generals of the High Command. He was a man who hunted for signs of dissent against the regime he served, who searched night and day for evidence of treason. There were few of any status in uniform, from bottom to top, who would not have shivered at his arrival in the camp where they were based.

Commander Yusuf saw himself as a shield behind which the regime and, above all, the President could feel secure. The work of that shield was torture. The same fingers that caressed and smoothed the hair of his grandchildren were equally adept in the arts of inflicting crude pain on those who were assumed to be enemies of the state. He was always busy. His work left little time for him to enjoy the youth of his grandchildren. He was rarely at home. His life was lived at pace because the twin threats of dissent and treason were ever present. Before he had been in Basra he had been in Karbalā, before Karbalā he had been in Ar

362

Ramādī, before Ar Ramādī he had been in Ba'qūbah. Because he would be among the first hoisted up under any conveniently close lamp-post if the regime fell, he devoted his waking hours to the search for dissenters and traitors.

He had the appearance of a junior functionary, the look of a man who organized railway timetables or administered a minor section of a hospital, as he carried his briefcase from his car and walked to that part of the compound that housed the section of the Estikhabarat. It was said of him, in bitterness, that where he came the birds no longer sang.

He sat alone in a far corner of the mess. He had turned the high-backed chair round so that he faced the drawn curtains of the window and the wall.

An orderly had brought Major Karim Aziz a plate of bread and cheese, an apple, a glass of milk, and had asked if he wished to drink whisky. He had declined. He shared the bread and cheese with his dog, and gave it the apple core. He was sipping the milk when Scout growled. Then Aziz heard low voices and the shuffle of feet on the carpet behind him.

He shunned company because the earlier elation was gone and he thought himself a man who had been cheated. The force of the *peshmerga* was in flight. The former brigade position at the crossroads was re-occupied. At first light, the next morning, units of Fifth Army would move back into Tarjil, and by the afternoon probing patrols would have reached the Victory City of Darbantaq. By the end of the next day the narrow corridor would have been emptied of the saboteurs. The chance to hunt the sniper – one to one, skill to skill, eye to eye, bullet to bullet – was lost to him.

The growl had become a snarl.

He stared at the curtain and the wall and imagined the man tramping back towards the distant mountains, walking in a ragged column bowed by defeat. He would be gone in the morning. There was no work for him in Tarjil or at the Victory City. And then the future hit him. The future was . . .

The snarl was a yelp of pain.

He started up in his seat and his sudden movement, as he twisted to look behind him, knocked the table and spilled the milk. A small man, older than himself, with flecked, cropped grey hair and a complexion of extra-ordinary smoothness, was crouched by the back legs of the chair. Aziz had not heard his approach. The narrow, fleshless fingers of one hand held the skin at the nape of the dog's neck, while the other played gently over the fur on its head. His uniform of drab olive green had no rank insignia on the shoulders and no ribbons on the chest. In his breast pocket was a neat line of ballpoint pens, as though he were a bureaucrat, but he held the dog with expert power so that it did not dare to struggle, and stroked its head as if it were a child. Four men stood behind him, sweat staining their armpits and blood spattered on their tunics and trousers.

The dog quivered.

'I am Commander Yusuf, and I am honoured to meet the sniper who has delivered to us this misguided peasant woman. I almost feel sympathy for her because she is not more, not less, than a plaything for others. It must be comforting to be able to shoot with such accuracy even when the target is a person of so little worth.'

'Would you let go of my dog?'

'I call her "worthless" – do I offend you? I assure you that offence is not intended. There are some here who believe she was of importance, but I do not share that opinion. It is the mark of our Arab society that some of our heroic forces feel demeaned by fighting against saboteurs led by a *woman*. It is an affront to their dignity and manhood that a woman should better them in combat.'

'You are hurting my dog. Please, let go of it.'

'They call her a witch. It is understandable. A witch has supernatural powers. Our heroic forces wish to offer her such powers as an excuse for their own failure, and their own treachery. She will be a victim, and it will give me no pleasure to hang her, but that will be necessary to satisfy the simple minds of our soldiers. I need to know from her only the extent of the treachery of officers who betrayed their trust. Then she hangs. The officers, Major Aziz, concern me.'

He listened to the purring voice. He had never met the man before, nor seen him, but had heard the name. It was whispered in the corridors of the Baghdad Military College, at the headquarters of the armies, and in the command posts of divisions and regiments. It was said, in the whispers, that none who faced him in the cells, whatever their courage, could resist the persuasiveness of his interrogation techniques.

'I have no interest in those who betray their trust. I am a soldier, I do my duty. Would you, please, release my dog?'

'I watch, Major Aziz, for the trail made by the belly of a snake and I follow the slime of that trail. The trail leads me, always, to the nest of the snakes. When the nest has been found, it is best to pour petrol into its hole and set fire to the petrol. The snake is a creature of treachery. It is discovered where least expected, then it must be followed, then killed . . . I am honoured to meet a man who knows where his duty lies.'

As he stood, the hand released the nape of the dog's neck. The dog, coiled like a spring, hurled itself at the man's ankle and bit hard. Commander Yusuf did not flinch, did not cry out. He seemed to watch the dog for a moment as it worried at his ankle. The strength of his kick was sufficient to break the hold of the dog's teeth and propel it against the wall below the drawn curtains, where it fell back gasping.

'Why should your dog regard me as a threat, Major Aziz, when all I offer it is kindness?'

The brigadier was on the floor of his cell, crumpled, finished with perhaps for an hour. The door was left open so that he could hear everything from the adjacent cell. He could not see through the open door because his eyes were closed by swelling, nor could he feel the rough concrete on which he lay because his fingers were numbed by the pain from the extraction of his nails. He was the Boot, a man credited with brutal strength and fortitude.

He had not yet broken, not yet given names.

The brigadier knew of the reputation of the little puny bastard with the voice that was never raised, and with the thin-boned fingers that had held the pliers. The reputation said his patience was great and failure was never accepted. He had tried not to cry out, even when the pain ran like rivers in him, because to cry out was to weaken her as she waited for them to return to her cell. He heard sometimes her whimpered cries, and once he heard her scream, and he thought that they burned her. What they had done to him, what they now did to her, was as nothing to the agony that awaited them both if they did not break, because the bastard's reputation was for a refusal to be beaten.

When he had seen her first, she had been vibrant and so patronizing of him – but his ears heard her fear and the eyes of his mind saw the cigarettes ground out on her, the fingers prising into her. And when she had cried, screamed, weakened him, they would come back to his cell. He did not know how long he could last, but he knew that when he broke, others, now trusting in his courage, would follow him into the dark cells to await the coming of Commander Yusuf.

Isaac Cohen heard the radio transmissions as they were decyphered by his computers.

He felt a crippling weight of sadness. She was not one of their own, but the grief was as acute as if she had been.

In Tel Aviv, there were old men of the Mossad, retired and gathering now in the pavement cafés on Ben Yehuda, who had spoken of that pitiful and helpless sadness when the news had leaked of Elie Cohen's capture in Damascus and of his execution in Simiramis Square. So much power at their disposal and none of it able to pluck out a patriot from a cell and from the gallows' platform . . . There were the veterans of the Agency, whom he had met on Washington visits, who had spoken of that same burden of sadness when the news had filtered through of the taking in Beirut, and the subsequent death, of Bill Buckley – and a greater power had been worthless.

He remembered her as she had been when he had seen her in the mountains: certain, confident, at the edge of conceit, dismissive of his help. The torches had played on her eyes, and he had known why men followed her. He wanted to remember the certainty, the confidence, because then he did not imagine her in the cells of Fifth Army. The old men that he'd known had said to him that when Elie Cohen was in the cells in Damascus, they could not sleep, rest, laugh, make love to their women, could not live. He would talk to the sniper when the remnant army straggled back and hear how it had happened, and he might curse him for allowing it to happen . . . He was not the lapdog of the Americans. If his sadness permitted it, he would call them in the morning, but that night he would think of her, and say a prayer for her.

Gus asked, 'Will you go to see the old man, Hoyshar, for me?'

'I will.' Haquim's hawk eyes beaded on him.

'Tell the old man everything that has happened.'

Haquim nodded.

'And he should write about it, and what he writes he should send to my grandfather.'

'I will do what you ask – but I tell you, Mr Peake, this death wish will achieve nothing.' There was a choke in Haquim's voice.

The column had begun to march away. The wounded were carried on the strongest men's backs and on litters. Over Haquim's shoulder, Gus could see the long straggle of the fighters. They were slow going, at the start, but he thought that when they sniffed the fine air of the high ground their pace would quicken, and they would have the goal of home to stretch their strides.

Gus said, 'I am grateful for your advice, and I want your forgiveness.'

'For what?' Haquim asked gruffly.

Simply said, 'For the insults I heaped on you.'

Their hands clasped, locked, the gnarled, blistered hands of the older man and those of the younger man. Gus could see the laid-out lights of Kirkūk and the silhouettes of the higher buildings, the towering flame that had been the unattainable target. It was about respect, which was precious to him.

Haquim said, 'There is a remote possibility that I can save her. I have to attempt it, but I have little time.'

Their hands slipped apart. Haquim leaned over Gus and whipped his fist against Omar's face. That, too, was about respect. Then he was on his way. Gus thought that a lesser man than Haquim would have turned, hesitated, waved a final time, but there was no such gesture. There was no stolen moment for the softness of sentiment. He watched Haquim hobbling away into the fading light to catch the tail of the column.

Gus twisted towards Omar and said, 'You can still go . . .'

Stubbornly, his face lowered, the boy shook his head.

'There is a life for you, stealing and thieving and pilfering, looting from the dead, there is still a chance of a life for you.'

'Major Herbert Hesketh-Prichard always needed an observer.'

Gus's voice shrilled in the dark space under the

369

overhang, into the infuriating calm of the boy's eyes:
'You can go, damn you, and feel no shame. You can run,
reach them, and live.'

He watched the column merge into the gloom. For
Gus, it was like the breaking of a linked chain, which,
while secure, led to Hoyshar and on from Hoyshar to
another old man, and from his grandfather to his
parents, his woman, his work and the long weekend
days on Stickledown Range. But the column had disappeared into the last traces of grey light and he could
no longer hear the shuffling of their boots, or the scrape
of the litters. A chain was broken, but new chains were
fastened. There would be chains on her ankles; a chain
held him to her, a chain held the boy to him. He snatched
at Omar's tunic top, caught it at the collar, wrenched the
boy up then pushed him hard away from him, away
towards where the column had gone. The boy sat
beyond his reach. Gus picked up a stone and hurled it
savagely at him, then another. They scudded past the
small body with his patient, staring eyes.

Gus shouted, 'Go, you little bastard, and live! Thieve
from the dead and the wounded. I don't need you. I
don't *want* you. Head away out of here – do as you're
bloody told! Go.'

His voice, trapped by the overhang, boomed around
him. He threw one more stone and hit the boy's
shoulder. He saw Omar wince, but any cry was stifled
and the boy did not rub the place where the stone had
struck.

'We are all not happy, Mr Gus, not only you.' Then
the cheek came, and the grin cracked across the boy's
smooth face. 'Did you fuck her?'

Gus shook his head, slowly and miserably. He could

not remember the taste of her or the feel of her. 'I kissed her, I loved her.'

'We all loved her, Mr Gus, not only you. Please, tell me a story from Major Hesketh-Prichard.'

Gus jerked his back straight. He recognized that the argument was ended, settled. The link to the past had gone with the column. They would be in Kirkūk by dawn.

'No man's land – where there were shell craters and fallen trees – was the best place for observers, where they were most valuable, and any unit with an aggressive commander always tried to dominate there. An intelligence officer with the 4th Battalion of the Royal Berkshire Regiment called Mr Gaythorne-Hardy thought it was necessary to know the exact layout of the German defences on Hill Sixty-three at a place called Messines. There was no point going at night across the four hundred yards of no man's land because at night he wouldn't be able to see the plan of their trenches and their defences so he went in daylight. It would have taken him hours to cross the open ground, and all the time the German snipers and sentries would have been watching it, but he was good enough in his fieldcraft to get right up to the enemy wire, to learn everything there was to know about their position. He was under their noses, but they did not see him. Getting there, learning, was of no value unless he was able to return safely to his own lines and report what he had seen. That was much harder, and he would have been tired. More difficult to crawl away than to go forward. But Mr Gaythorne-Hardy had the skill. From what he had seen, the enemy's trenches could be targeted more effectively by the artillery and our snipers had a better chance of killing

Germans. Major Hesketh-Prichard thought him one of the best.'

'Not as good as me.' The smile swept the boy's face.

'Of course not.'

Then came the puzzlement that creased lines at Omar's mouth and eyes. 'Why, Mr Gus, are we staying?'

Gus said, a hoarseness in his throat, 'Because it is owed her.'

'What can we do?'

'Something, anything is better than nothing.'

He heard the scream as he walked across the compound to find the telephone, the same scream as a goat's when it is tied and held and first sees the knife as the guests gather for a wedding feast.

At the steps of the building that dealt with Fifth Army's victualling, there would be an empty office and a telephone.

The sentry at the main entrance saluted, unlocked the door and admitted him. The screams would have been heard by the sentry and by every soldier, every non-commissioned officer, every officer in the compound. If the screams destroyed the brigadier's resolve, if the Boot broke, then any man in the compound whose name stumbled from his lips was doomed. His own name would end the pain, would still the cries.

The clerks who filled the order forms for Fifth Army's meat and rice, vegetables, fruit and cooking oil had all returned to their barracks. He walked along a half-lit corridor and into a darkened room. He did not switch on the light but groped towards a desk. He found the telephone. The arrival of the torturer had precipitated his course of action. He had lain on his bed and fashioned the plan. He could not abandon them. There was a dialling code that circumvented the switchboard operators and provided access to a direct line. She was distant, faint.

'Leila, you must listen exactly to what I say, and do it.'

He could hear the television playing behind her, the babble of the children's voices and her mother's. She said she was listening.

He was wary of the security of the direct line. 'Leila, are you listening? Don't interrupt. I am leaving Kirkūk in the morning. I have the chance to take a short holiday. You remember that four years ago we camped with the children? I wish to do that again. You will pack what is necessary and meet me at Sulaiman Bak on the Kirkūk road.'

She said that the weather forecast on the television had warned of freezing nights, and she did not think the conditions were suitable for camping with the children.

'You should pack clothes for four days, and the children's best boots. From Sulaiman Bak we will take the road for Kingirban and Kifri, then we will find a place to make a camp.'

She said that tomorrow was a busy day at the hospital, that it was impossible for her to find a replacement at such short notice – perhaps later they could camp, when the weather improved.

'As you love me, Leila, do as I say. Meet me at Sulaiman Bak. We have to take the chance being offered here.'

She said that Wafiq had an examination at school in

the morning – had he forgotten? And Hani was playing football for the school in the afternoon of the day after tomorrow – had he forgotten that, too? Karim Aziz could not know if the line was routinely monitored, whether it was already listened to. He repressed the desire to shout and block out each of her reasoned excuses for not leaving Baghdad.

'Leila, it is the best chance we have of a holiday with the children. There will always be busy days at the hospital, many examinations and football games. Pack tonight, be on the road early. It is important to me.'

She said that it was her mother's birthday two days after tomorrow – had he forgotten that, also?

'Be there, I beg of you. Bring tents, warm clothes, food. On the Kifri road there is a fuel station, about a kilometre from the Kirkūk road. I ask little of you. It is about the love that I have for you and for our children. It is the chance of a short freedom. It is for us. Please, be there . . .'

She said that it was difficult. Aziz replaced the receiver. He knew she would be at the fuel station. They had been married too long for her not to be there. He walked out of the building and across the compound, ringed by high lights. He was beyond middle age. She was plump and wide at the hips and her youth had gone. They had only each other, and their boys. He heard the cry in the night. He wondered if the torturer would need to sleep, would go to a cot bed to rest, wondered if the torturer's need to sleep and rest would win him the time to drive south to a fuel station eighty-five kilometres away and meet those he loved, take them towards Kifri then strike out for the *jebel* ridge, and cross the lines. He knew of many who had failed to find an unguarded track, and he had heard of a few who had successfully crossed the lines and then been captured by the *peshmerga* and handed back to the soldiers at an outpost for a cash reward. The wife he loved tolerated the regime in helpless resignation, never complained at the shortages of equipment and drugs in the hospital, merely stoically endured. The children he loved went to the school, believed implicitly what their teachers told them of the evil of Iraq's enemies, stood each morning facing the smiling image of the President and chanted their support, were proud that their father served him. He would tell them, on the road beyond the fuel station, that their tolerance and pride was a fraud. He would lead them, as fleeing refugees, towards the patrols and the strong points and he did not know whether they would curse him.

He settled on the floor of his room, in a corner where he faced the door. The dog was on his lap and the rifle in his hands.

The screams continued, and he knew the torturer did not yet sleep or rest behind the barred windows of the cell block. If his name was given he would hear the stamping footfall in the corridor and the door would burst open . . . What hurt him most, sitting through the night, watching the door, was that the sniper had turned, gone back, had in some way cheated him.

'He was cold, trying to focus, but wasn't doing it well because he was too tired.'

She had driven, and Willet had navigated. In her small car they had bumped up a dark forest track on a shale and chipstone surface, weaving amongst the ruts, following the crude painted arrows in the headlights. It had been a good drive down from London until they'd turned off the main road and onto the forest track. Willet had folded away the map. She had snapped twice that she was damn certain she was going to get Resources to pay for a car wash, but he'd sensed – and it was new – a staccato excitement in Ms Manning. He'd wondered if plain little Carol had been to a place like this on a Security Service training course and found fulfilment. Willet himself had not sploshed around on Survival in deep wet woodland for more months than he cared to remember. The rain had come on more heavily, was sluicing over the windscreen, when the lights had found the blurred image of the little camp of tents.

'I had a small group here then, merchant-bank people,' Dogsy said. 'I told Peake I'd give him as much time as I could, but he'd have to muck in with them, get into line in the queue.'

The rain had eased since they'd arrived at the tent camp. There was a small square of canvas over a low, smoking fire. A London-based insurance company, a corporate giant, had sent five men and four women out into the woods, into Dogsy's care, to learn self-esteem, self-help, self-control. On a spit of stripped hazel over the fire was a skinned rabbit, and Willet thought that it wouldn't be much short of midnight before the bloody thing was heated through, half cooked, and ready for eating. They'd done abseiling over a torrential river gorge before finding the rabbit in a snare they'd set the day before. Line managers and regional directors, bright-eyed and sharp, they took it all as serious fun, as the people from the bank would have done. The fact that Willet was from the MoD, and Ms Manning was out of

376

the Security Service, hadn't fazed Dogsy, and the two new arrivals were sat down in the circle round the fire as if they hadn't any rights to privacy.

'What interested me, I reckoned that the young 'uns from the bank would welcome a fellow sufferer. They made the effort but Peake didn't let them close . . . They didn't take to him, and he rejected them. If you know what I mean, they rated him as just a wannabe. He was trying too hard. He didn't laugh, didn't joke, like that was beneath him . . . I've seen that sort before. When I came out of the marines and transferred into the Regiment, I was put on the recruit-induction programme. Most of the recruits were too bottled-up, the type that fail. It's a character problem. A few like that get through, but you know the way they'll go. If they slip into the Regiment then, at first, they think they're going to save the world. Saving the world means killing. Killing gets to be a habit, makes a man lonely, isolated. Killing becomes addictive, can't be given up.'

The rain pattered on the small awning over the fire. The young people, sodden wet and mud-spattered, watched, listened. Willet understood why Gus Peake had not let them near. They would be going back to baths and champagne, client investments and pension funds; they would be thinking of themselves as the fucking chosen ones. Dogsy Jennings, ex-Marine, ex-instructor in the Regiment, played to his bloody gallery. Willet thought that the chosen children, the money crunchers, would return to their City world, complacent and important, and laugh for a month at what they'd heard around the bloody smoking fire, and believe they'd fucking well achieved something in getting wet for three days and eating rare rabbit.

'What did he learn from you?' Willet asked, without grace.

'Escape and Evasion. That's what old Bill said he needed – Billings, that is, a good mate – but what I told him might just have been a waste of time, mine and his.'

'You're ahead of me,' Ms Manning said quietly.

'If you've set out to save the world, gone on a killing spree, then you may hang around too long. If you're around too long, you lose sight of the way back, you don't get the chance to escape and evade. He's gone walking in northern Iraq, right?'

Ms Manning said, 'There's a revolt, a tribal uprising. I suppose the target is the city of Kirkūk. The Iraqi Fifth Army is based there.'

There was a whinny of general laughter from the group around them. That would have made their bloody evening, and the week ahead when they were back at their desks, God's fucking chosen children, and playing with investment figures and exchange rates on their bloody screens before heading down to the wine bar.

'Then I have to hope he knows when to quit,' Dogsy said. He was a big man, with long gorilla arms and a well-trimmed moustache. A top-of-the-range Land-Rover was parked behind the tents – Willet could have wept because in his imagination the exhausted Gus Peake sat around the same damp fire and heard the patronizing bastard talk Escape and Evasion, and heard the same laughter ripple from his audience. 'Do you know how long he's been in combat?'

There was a flicker in Ms Manning's voice. She said crisply, 'Maybe a week, or a few days more.'

'It has to be a stampede for that sort of thing to

378

work . . . He'll be killing every day. The killing would be so frequent that he loses count – how many, how often – and he won't be in a structure where anyone orders him to stop, quit. He'll be a changed man. Should he get out, those who knew him before won't know him – might not, when they meet him and see him, *want* to know him. He'll be a new man, and it may not be a pleasant sight. He didn't tell me what he did, his old life.'

'He was a transport manager . . .'

It was like a joke to those around the fire. Willet hated them. The giggles wafted across him.

'. . . in a provincial haulage company,' Ms Manning persisted.

A ponderous smile played at Dogsy Jennings' face. 'There's your answer. Should he come back, he's hardly going to be able to slip his feet under the desk and start again to move lorries about, like nothing's happened. He'll have taken a dozen men's lives, if he's any good. If he's brilliant as a marksman, it could be twenty men's lives, thirty. Any jerk who's arrogant enough to think he can change the world won't just switch off after one dose of it, he'll have to find more causes, more bloody crusades. I read men. It's my job to get under the bullshit of human nature. I didn't like him.'

'Didn't you? Why not?' The sneer rasped in her voice.

'I didn't like him, Miss, because that sort craves to belong. Got me? Whatever the motivation, he can't belong out there, and if he gets back he can't belong here. I did my best with Escape and Evasion because that's what old Bill asked of me – but any road I didn't like him. I don't like men who go looking to be bloody heroes.'

'What about loyalty, important things like freedom, heritage? What about sacrifice?'

Willet saw Dogsy's wink. The circle chuckled. The smoke eddied across the rabbit's carcass. Ms Manning pushed herself up then rubbed the damp off her backside and Willet saw the anger in her face.

'Come on, Ken,' she said. 'Let's leave these creeps to their silly bloody games.'

He followed after her, past the tents and the Land-Rover and back towards the track where her car was parked. He hadn't thought it could happen, that her emotional commitment could be made to Peake and his rifle. Dogsy Jennings' words seared in his mind. 'He won't be in a structure where anybody orders him to stop, quit . . . Should he get out, those who knew him before won't know him . . . He can't belong out there and, if he gets back, he can't belong here.' He thought she'd been magnificent, and he'd tell her.

She reached the car. Her eyes blazed at him, and she spat her words. 'When you write this up, do me a favour, leave out all that pompous crap about survival chances. Spare me that shit.'

They moved in darkness, in total silence, towards the lights and the flame.

The boy led. Gus had given Omar authority over his life and safety. They went at a steady pace past patrols that he had not heard but the boy had. They crossed roads along which personnel carriers cruised, and the boy found the hidden ground into which they could duck as the searchlights roved over the ground, and he would not have sensed where the shallow earth scrapes offered them that protection. When there was a ditch into which he would have stumbled, the boy gently held his hand and guided him. Where men, talking softly, guarded their goats, they slipped by and the boy had read the wind so that they did not alert the goatherds' dogs.

They went towards the lights where the chains held her.

Chapter Fifteen

Early each morning an elderly corporal, with a driver and an escort of two riflemen, collected the packages of urgent, sensitive material for Fifth Army flown into Kirkūk from the capital.

Although he had lost an arm in the defence of Basra fifteen years earlier, his birthright from a tribe that gave unquestioned allegiance to the regime ensured that a position in administration was available to him for as long as he wanted it. His daily routine was the run to the airfield, the collection from the Antonov transport plane, the drive back into the centre of Kirkūk, coffee and cigarettes, then the government's newspaper, then a game of dice with matchsticks as the stakes, a meal, a siesta, then a gossiping evening with other corporals, the ironing of his uniform, the cleaning of his boots and bed. He had little cause for complaint – and it was safe. All the other corporals in administration could expect to be transferred every two months, for a week, to the forward strong points in the hills to the north, but not him. His disability protected him.

When the jeep slowed to a stop at traffic lights, one of the few sets working in Kirkūk, on the wide carriageway into the city from the airfield, the corporal's orderly life was ended. A single shot, fired at great range, exploded into his head and the remnants of bone, blood and brain peppered the body of his driver.

They were running.

'Where next?'

'Doesn't matter where – anywhere I can aim from.'

Omar led and Gus followed. The low shafts of sunlight threw deep shadows in the narrow lanes between the shanty-town of haphazardly built shelters on the edge of the city. Men, women and children, just risen from their beds, scattered as the wraithlike figures pounded past their homes.

When the dawn came he was so tired.

Major Karim Aziz dragged himself up from the floor as the first light seeped into the room, and felt his forty-five years for the first time since he'd come to Kirkūk as the aches, pains, stiffness ran through his body. He had not slept but had watched the darkness and the ribbon of light under the door, had listened for the boots. The cries and screams had come, not often, in the long hours and he had known that the torturer was tireless.

He packed his few belongings, scattered across the floor, down into the belly of his backpack.

Leila, too, would now be filling the boys' rucksacks and telling them that an examination at school did not matter and a football match was unimportant. She would have telephoned the hospital and lied that she was unwell. Perhaps already she had told her mother, shuffling in slippers in the kitchen, that there would be no party to celebrate her birthday. Through the night he had wondered when he would tell her of their future.

He put the last of the dog's biscuits on the floor and they were wolfed down.

The future, in the darkness hours, had been nightmarishly with him. It might be a patrol on the ceasefire line between government territory and the Kurdish enclave; on his own, without difficulty, he could evade the patrols – but he would not be alone, he would be with his wife and his sons. It might be capture by a warlord's men, and the Estikhabarat would pay fifty thousand American dollars for him to be returned to them, bound and blindfolded, across the line; on his own, with his rifle and his dog, he could fight his way through the danger of capture – but he would not be alone. Should he succeed, it might be the stagnant life of an exile without money in the embittered Iraqi communities of Amman or Istanbul; on his own, perhaps, he could burrow into the tawdry life of the exiles he had read of in the newspapers and heard of on the radio and exist – but he would have responsibility for his wife and children, who would be lost flotsam. Soon she would be on the road north.

He folded the dog's rug and put it into the backpack.

At the petrol station, or in the car, or when they started to walk, he would tell them. He would say that he was a traitor to the President who smiled with warmth at him from the photograph on the wall, that he had sided with the enemies of the President. He would say that all the struggle of their lives was for nothing because he had betrayed it. In the night he had shivered because of what he had done to those he loved.

The dog was by the door and waited for him.

In his mind he had seen – again and again – the shock spreading on their faces at the petrol station, or in the car, or when they started to walk, as they learned the future. The worst of the nightmarish thoughts had been of her clutching her children to her, turning and abandoning him . . . It had been his vanity on the range when he had shown his shooting skills. It had been the massage of his conceit by the silky words of the general, in the car cruising at night beside the river in Baghdad, telling him that he, above all men, had the marksman's expertise.

The dog bounded into the corridor, he closed the door of the bare room and wondered if the President still smiled.

He walked out into the compound.

Men were coming from the shadowy shape of the cell block.

He saw them rubbing their eyes in exhaustion, flexing their fists as if they were bruised, wiping smeared mess off their tunics. But the slightest among them walked briskly as if he had not missed his sleep.

The piping voice sidled across the quiet of the compound. 'You are leaving us, Major? Take with you my congratulations.'

He said hoarsely, 'I accept them, I am grateful . . . I am a simple soldier, I did what I could.'

'I never met a *simple* soldier. Have a good journey back to Baghdad.'

He tried to ask the casual question: 'Your own work, Commander, is it nearly done?'

'Near, but not yet there. A few hours, and this preliminary stage of my investigation will be completed . . . but the trails of treachery run far. You have my assurance, simple soldier, that I will follow the trails wherever they lead . . . Enough of me. Are you disappointed that your triumph is not total?'

'I do not understand you.'

'You were sent to kill a sniper, a foreigner – and you did not.'

Aziz blurted, 'He is beyond my reach.'

'Have a good journey, and be assured that those who take responsibility for the security of the state will not rest while traitors live.'

Aziz heard the dog's low angry growl, flicked his fingers nervously to it and strode out towards the administration building, where he would find a driver to take him across the city to the military car pool. While he walked he felt the small narrow-set eyes on his back, following him.

The soldier stood at the road block.

He was nineteen years old, a conscript in a mechanized infantry unit. The road block was behind him. He had been detailed by his sergeant to wave down the cars, lorries and vans for inspection. He was from a poor family in Baghdad, and his move to the basic training camp before going to Kirkūk had been the first time in his life that he had been away from his mother. He hated the army's food and hardly ate. He was ghostly thin and his stomach churned as he held his rifle and directed the traffic into the lane where the drivers' papers could be looked over. He was a lonely youngster, shunned by his colleagues in the barracks hut because the loneliness caused him to wet his bed most nights of the week. Behind the road block, workmen were digging a trench in preparation for the repair of a blocked sewer. The smell was foul but, more importantly, the piledriver the workmen used to break up the tarmacadam had obliterated the sound of a single shot fired half an hour earlier a full kilometre away. He was thinking of his mother when he died. Against the noise of the vehicles' brakes and gear changes and the hammer of the piledriver, none of the men near to him heard the crack of the rifle's report or the thump of the bullet's strike. The soldier subsided, as if the strength was gone from his legs, and blood spilled from deep holes in his chest and his back.

The orderly paused at the back of the truck.

On the flat-bed was a heap of black rubbish bags. He lit a cigarette. The ebony crows were waiting for him, flapping their wings as they strutted on the bags he had brought earlier in the week to the dump, and cried raucously at him. Each morning the orderly cleaned the quarters used by the officers of an armoured unit based at Kirkūk and collected their rubbish in the bags along with the food they had not bothered to eat the previous evening. It attracted the crows, but the brutes could wait while he enjoyed his cigarette. The orderly was from the desert region, near to the small town of an-Nahiya, close to the Syrian border. There were no mountains in that region, but he enjoyed those moments when he could smoke a cigarette and admire the high ground beyond the city. There was the same emptiness, and he blinked into the sun rising over the faraway ridges. He was particularly cheerful that morning: his time in the army had nine days to run and then he would be on the slow bus back to an-Nahiya where his father kept a road-side coffee shop. The orderly did not realize that by standing and dragging contentedly on his cigarette he made a good target for a distant marksman. As he fell backwards the crows screamed and rose in a moment of panicked flight over the heap of rubbish bags.

They moved again, fast.

'Why, Mr Gus?'

'Because, Omar, they are available.'

'I do not complain, Mr Gus, but they are not officers, not commanders. They are not helicopters, tanks, communications . . . Why?'

'They wear the uniform.'

The boy shrugged. They went through yards, over fences that sometimes collapsed under them. There would have been many inside their homes or outside sweeping away dirt or hanging out clothes to dry who saw them. But those who were inside looked away and those who were outside hurried back through the doors and locked them. They were not in that part of the city where Party members lived, or functionaries of the administration, but where people valued their lives and believed the best preservation was to see, hear and know nothing. The boy carried the Kalashnikov assault weapon, and Gus held hard on to the stock of the big rifle as he ran. As the sun rose, they careered on, hunting for the next position from which he could find a target wearing the uniform. And gradually the pattern of the boy's route led him towards the heart of the city.

He arrived at the military transport pool.

Major Karim Aziz thanked the driver curtly, hoisted up his backpack and the rifle's polished wooden box. The dog ran beside him as he walked to the pool office. He gave his name and his rank at the desk, and demanded a self-drive car for his journey back to Baghdad. His name was known, his reputation had moved quickly. Surely, for the major, whose expert marksmanship was responsible for the capture of the witch, there was a place on a flight south to Baghdad?

'I wish to drive and I want a car immediately.'

Beyond a closed door, behind the desk, he could vaguely hear the military radio net. He could not distinguish the messages, only the babble of activity.

Forms were produced from below the desk, and carbon sheets. With two fingers, a clerk laboriously typed his name, his rank and his destination. He fidgeted impatiently. He was asked if he wanted coffee, but irritably shook his head. He paced in front of the desk, and perhaps that increased the clerk's nervousness and the errors; the papers and carbons were torn out of the typewriter and the work began again. When the typing was complete the papers were passed to him. He scrawled his signature on them, and they were taken from him into the office where the radio was . . . By now, Leila and the children would have left home, would be on the road towards Sulaiman Bak.

An officer, a major's insignia on his shoulder, overweight from a life spent welded to a desk, came from the inner room.

'I am honoured to meet you, Major Aziz. Did these fools not find you a chair?'

'I don't want a chair, I just want a car.'

With a flourish the officer countersigned the papers. 'I apologize that I can only provide a Toyota, Major. As soon as it is valeted, fuelled, it will be at your disposal.'

'Forget the valeting, give me the keys.'

The officer smiled smugly. 'You are an expert at

marksmanship, I am an expert at running the motor pool of Fifth Army. You have pride in your work, Major, and I have pride in mine. No car issued to a distinguished officer will leave this yard until it has been correctly cleaned and prepared. We are both proud men, yes?'

'Just get it done.'

He started to pace again. The officer hesitated, then said uncertainly, 'I am assuming, Major, that you have not been beside a radio for the last three-quarters of an hour.'

'I have been getting here, in bad traffic.'

'You do not know of the killings?'

'What killings?'

'Three soldiers have been shot dead in Kirkūk in the last three-quarters of an hour. A corporal on the airport road, a soldier at a road block, an orderly taking rubbish to the dump. Not important men, Major, not officers.'

'Perhaps the remnants of the saboteurs from yesterday are still holed up, hiding.'

'Each without any warning, each from an unseen rifle, each with a single bullet.'

She would be on the road coming north. She would be driving with their sons, and with her trust in him. Behind him was the cell block. He had thought the sniper had fled back to the mountains, beyond reach. He remembered the sun-hazed mirage of the man sitting on the rock at too great a range for the Dragunov. If she did not have trust in him she would not have taken the car, loaded it, and driven north.

'Get the fuelling and the cleaning done quickly. I need to leave.'

*　　*　　*

She heard him cough, then hack the spittle from his throat.

Meda was sprawled in the furthest corner of the cell from the door. She heard him, then the long painful wheeze.

She twisted, each slight movement hurting her, and heard the gasps. She lay on a foul-smelling bed of old straw in a sleeve of stained cotton. She had not heard him so clearly before, but the last time they had brought her back to the cell, as she fell to the concrete floor, she had found that the bed had been moved from the left side of the cell to the right. Close to her face was warmth, a wet heat. Against the back wall of the cell, under the high, barred window where the dirt filtered the light, was a channel in the concrete, where water could run out when the floor was sluiced. The warmth and the heat were from urine dribbling out of a hole in the wall beside her head.

Her mouth was close to the drain, and the stumbling flow of his urine.

'Are you there?'

'Where else would I be? I am here.' From the drain came a black, shaken chuckle, not laughter.

'Can we survive?'

'We have to survive.'

'For how long?'

'For as long as God gives us strength.'

'Can we be saved?'

'Only by death.'

She trembled. Between the interrogation sessions and the smiling soft-skinned face phrasing the questions with care in the intervals between the beatings and the pain, she had thought of home. She had summoned the image of the village, the orchards in blossom, the smell of food cooking and of wet wood burning, the children bringing back armfuls of wild spring flowers, and of old Hoyshar reading to her from the books of military history that had been left for him by his friend, esteemed brother Basil, children playing and shouting – but she could no longer find the image. All she had left were the words coming through the narrow drain hole and sighs as if the effort of speaking each word brought a worse pain.

'When does death come?'

'When they have finished with us – for you earlier, for me later.'

'Can you not tell them something, a little?'

'If you start, you weaken. Then it is not a little but everything.'

'If you are strong?'

'Today men pray for my strength that they can live.'

'How do you make the strength?'

'By thinking of those I love.'

'May I be loved by you, because I am frightened.'

'We will love each other, child and father . . .'

She closed her fist. She reached into the hole, pushing her hand, wrist, forearm, into it. She felt the feathery brush of the cockroaches' legs on her skin. In the rough hole, with the creatures on her, her arm shivered, but she thrust it deeper, to the elbow. She felt the coarse close-cut hair and thought she touched his neck, and he started at the touch and let out a small cry because he had moved suddenly. The big, hard hand took Meda's. Her fingers were in his. She felt the wetness of his lips on her fingers, on the palm of her hand that had been burned with cigarette stubs. It was as if she reached beyond her cell, beyond the fences and walls, beyond the city, through the drain towards a freedom. It was not a father holding a child's hand and kissing it, it was the hold and the kiss of the man she loved. She was alone with him, given strength, watching the same stars as shone over Nineveh and Nimrud . . . Gus would come for her, take her back into the night, to freedom, and she would feel again his lips kissing hers.

'He will come and save me.'

'No-one will come. The only safety is death.'

'I have to believe it.'

'If you believe it then you will be weak. Be strong, give me strength.'

'You were my enemy.'

'I am all you have, you are all I have.'

'I will be saved . . .'

Meda tried to drag her arm back from the drain hole, but she could not. He held her hand with the firmness of desperation.

'She is only a girl, a peasant. We are responsible.'

Etiquette said that Haquim, already offered coffee in a thimble china cup and sweet biscuits, should have taken the chair, upholstered in royal blue, and sat opposite *agha* Ibrahim and engaged in polite talk before gently steering the conversation towards the reason for his visit. He was incapable of such courtesies. The coffee remained untouched on the low table, the biscuits uneaten. He roamed the salon room, beating out a stride, then turning and gesticulating with his finger for emphasis. The room had been the principal lounge of the hotel that had once been a retreat for the privileged of the regime when they came north to escape the heat of Baghdad's summer; it was now the commandeered residence of the *agha*, and the old opulence was maintained. Haquim's boots, as he pounded backwards and forwards, scattered dried mud on a hand-woven carpet.

'She had dreams, delusions. We played on her simplicity. We have a duty to her.'

The *agha*'s eyes followed Haquim. The only evidence of his mood and inclination was in the eyes. The hands were still, did not fidget. The mouth was set, expressionless. But *agha* Ibrahim could not hide the message of his eyes. Haquim was heard out in silence, but knew he had failed. Nothing would be done, a finger would not be lifted. As he spoke he seemed to see her in the cell, just as he had seen her in the village, just as he had seen her in the charge of the Victory City and on the stampede towards the town of Tarjil, and the rush along the ditch beside the high-built road to the perimeter defences at the crossroads. Because of what he saw, and the memory of the way she trapped him with innocence and certainty, his voice rose.

'She took you to the outskirts of Kirkūk. You saw the flame of Baba Gurgur. When you turned, it was a betrayal of her. History will curse you, and the spirit of your father and your grandfather, if you abandon her.'

The passion of the veteran fighter went unanswered. No man, certainly no woman, spoke to *agha* Ibrahim with such disdain. Haquim thought that the call would already have been made on the satellite telephone to the palace offices in Baghdad and that there would have been the protestations of loyalty; but it would not be admitted. He thought he shouted to the wind.

394

'I beg of you, use the communications you have. Call them and plead and bargain with them. Offer them what they want.'

Perhaps, if he had wished to, the *agha* could have saved her. If he had picked up again the satellite telephone and begged, pleaded, perhaps her life could be returned to her. Perhaps, for a quarter or half a million dollars, of the customs tolls exacted by the *agha* for permission for lorries and tankers to cross his territory, her life could be won. The slight shrug told Haquim that nothing would be done, that the interview was terminated.

'She did it for you. She risked her life to bring you to Kirkūk. Your indifference shames you.'

He had expected nothing more and nothing less, but it had been his obligation to try. He would drive from Arbīl to Sulaymānīyah, and if the answer was the same he would go back to the mountains, to his village, to forget. He stamped out of the salon room.

The soldier in the watchtower at the fuel depot was high above the traffic on the nearest street.

He had heard two shots fired with thirty minutes separating them but, and he checked his wristwatch again, the second shot had been eighteen minutes before. The soldier strained to hear another shot but it was harder now because a mullah called the faithful to prayer and the chant billowed out from the loudspeakers in the minaret tower of the mosque closest to him. In the watchtower, he was dismayed at not being able to respond to the mullah's call – he was from one of the few Sunni families in Karbalā where the treacherous Shi'a were in the majority. Being of the minority sect in that city, he gave total support to the regime, its troops, police and security agents – his family might be butchered with knives in their beds in the night. He had reported hearing the shots, shouted it down to his sergeant, but he could not locate them. From his vantage, he scanned with binoculars across rooftops, upper windows and street junctions, but saw nothing that threatened him. The call had reached a crescendo when the binoculars were driven back into his eye sockets by the armour-piercing bullet and the top half of his head spiralled down to the ground close to the boots of his sergeant, who supervised the refuelling of a lorry.

The back marker in the scrambled patrol crouched at the corner of an office block.

The patrol was one of many that had been hustled out of the barracks and were now scattering beyond the inner city and reaching the outer suburban blocks. He was back marker, on the young officer's insistence, because he was the most intelligent soldier in the platoon, and he understood that it was a position of trust. He had a place offered him at the university in Baghdad for the study of chemical engineering when his army service was completed. He detested the army because it took him away from the laboratories and pitched him amongst illiterate peasants. It was an indication to him of the officer's regard for him that he was given the role of guarding the safety of the men ahead of him. He heard, over his shoulder, the officer's shout for the patrol to move forward. It seemed idiotic that he did not know against what force they were deployed. Twice, patiently, he had tried to ask the officer to explain for what or whom they searched, but each time the officer's attention was on the peasant soldiers. He stiffened in his crouched position, ready to follow the patrol, to track backwards. His eyes were on the far side of the street, on the windows and a flat roof with aerials and TV dishes. He had not been told that, to protect the patrol and himself, he should be watching roofs and windows that were a full 700 metres away from him, and far beyond the range of his assault rifle. There was no pain, only the blow against his chest, and then the swift collapse onto the pavement. The back marker heard, for a moment, the officer's call for him to follow, and saw a man emerge from the office block and stand beside him, his face wide with horror.

The military policeman was holding up traffic to let a column of armoured personnel carriers through the junction.

He enjoyed the authority given him by his uniform – and his authority was about to grow. In the breast pocket of his tunic was a typed sheet of paper, signed by his captain, informing him of promotion from corporal to sergeant to take effect from the first day of the next month. Everything about the military policeman's bearing was proud. As the first of the personnel carriers thundered past him, he raised his arms and held back the civilian traffic. The previous day, he had been at one of the barricades on the edge of the Old Quarter where the bastards from the mountains had been blocked. He had not seen the witch herself, but the convoy carrying her to headquarters had raced past him with horns blaring and sirens calling in triumph. He hoped they would hang her, high and soon, and that he would be there to watch it. There was a great confusion in the city that morning and he had heard that riflemen were scattered in Kirkūk, but he knew little of the detail other than that there had been five fatalities. When he fell, bludgeoned down onto the road, his upper body sprawled under the wheel of a personnel carrier whose driver felt only the slightest bump.

'How far do we go?'

   'Close enough for her to hear.'

   'Hear what, Mr Gus?'

   'Hear that I haven't abandoned her, Omar.'

   'How does that help?'

   'I hope it gives her strength.'

   'Is it to help you, Mr Gus, that you are killing?'

They were closer to the city's heart and heard more often the drone whine of the armoured vehicles on the main routes, and the shouts of patrols. They were at the back fence of a villa's garden when a woman yelled. He saw the blotched face at the upper window and she clasped her hand at her mouth as if to stifle herself, and her dressing gown gaped open. Gus understood. The woman yelled because she saw two figures of a bygone age, primitives, filth-encrusted and armed, camouflaged, tracking across the end of her garden. She would waddle from the window to the telephone. The boy went over the fence first, vaulting it easily, and Gus followed.

   As always, the moment before the yell, the boy had bared him. He was glad not to have to answer Omar's question as they ran down the alleyway.

He stood in the doorway.

   The officer looked up, saw Aziz, smiled obsequiously. 'I promise you, Major, it will only be another two, three minutes, and the car will be ready.'

'What does it say on the radio?'

'There is great chaos, Major. I do not mean it disrespectfully but the men on the radio are running around like headless chickens.'

He hissed, 'What does it say?'

'Patrols, cordons, lines, and the new casualties. For myself – and I am not a hero as you are, Major – I am happy to be here and organizing an efficient—'

'How many new casualties?'

'There are three more – a soldier at the fuel depot, another on patrol, a military policeman. There is a hunt but they cannot find the sniper, he shoots one time at a long distance then moves. Ah, your wait is over, Major.'

The officer gestured. Major Karim Aziz turned and saw a soldier driving a small saloon car to the front of the building.

'I am happy to have been of service to you.'

Beyond the car was the jeep that had brought him from the headquarters of Fifth Army: the driver was sprawled behind the wheel, dozing in the morning sunshine. He would be beyond the grasp of his sergeant and would hope to while away the rest of the morning before returning to duty. The man offered himself, challenged.

At the desk, Aziz took the typed sheets of paper and tore them in half. The dog followed him from the building. He carried his backpack and the rifle's box to the jeep, opened the door, and punched the driver awake. As they sped out of the military car-pool yard he was already unfastening the clasp locks of the carrying-box of his rifle.

* * *

'I'm not looking back – I never want to see that fucking place again,' Mike said.

'No way, I'm happily waving goodbye to the land of broken goddam dreams,' Dean said.

'I think we should never have come, never have believed in the nonsense about that woman,' Gretchen said.

They walked away from the roadside and the big Mercedes. None of them had thanked Rybinsky. They followed the German, Jürgen, up the winding path that led to the ridge, and above that ridge were three more, and beyond all of the ridges were the mountain peaks. Each carried their own personal bags but, as a gesture of comradeship and democracy, the camera gear was shared between the three of them. They would climb in daylight towards the border, then rest, and under cover of darkness make the dangerous crossing into Turkey. Their heads were down: neither of the men or the woman were used to failure. Each, in their own way, grunting with the exertion of the steep trek, expressed the bitterness that went with failure.

'I'll get a radio spot,' Mike said. 'I'm going to crucify this fucking bullshit place, and the woman, if she ever existed.'

'I reckon she existed, but only as a myth in these people's minds,' Dean said. 'Being realistic, we're talking about a foot soldier at best.'

And then they were quiet, struggling to climb, and behind them was the bright yellow Mercedes and the ever falling panorama of the ground.

'What do you want?'

'For, God's sake, Joe, I want to talk.'

'Talking seldom helped anybody, Sarah.'

'Because I can't help, that's why I have to talk.'

'I might not listen.'

'They caught her. She was captured . . .'

Joe Denton knelt in the rich grass. There were now eleven lines of pegs running the length of the meadow, and he had just begun to work up the second of them. From the pattern of the laying of the mines he had calculated that he could clear a little more than half of each line in a single day's work. It annoyed him that she was there, distracting him. She had been up and down the road all day looking for any straggling survivors of the final battle in Kirkūk to make it over the hills and ridges. Most had come the previous evening, but she had found six, burdened by two grievously wounded men, early that morning, and had ferried them to hospital. They'd been the last. He looked at her. She was sitting awkwardly on the pick-up's bonnet. It was dangerous for him to be distracted.

'Doesn't that concern you?'

'Predictable. What concerns me is a thousand V69s, then another field of them, and another.'

'You helped.'

'And sometimes my stupidity amazes even me.'

'That's not Joe Denton. Joe Denton cared.'

'I did what I could. Sorry, Sarah, but she's not my problem. Your problem. You think you can do something, you can't. Get a look at the map. The map says this is fucking Kurdistan. It is an unforgiving place and when we, outsiders, try to do something we fall on our bloody arses. We think we are important, interfere, but we don't affect events – we go home. I am busy. I am clearing twenty-five V69s a day, tops, so there are only another ten fucking million left. That's why I'm busy. You don't want to talk, you want a shoulder to cry on – like all the other huggers. Go and find the sniper, go and have a cuddle and cry with him, give him a good ride before he flies back home to tell his war stories in the bloody pub. Go away, because I am busy.'

'Can't.'

'Can't what?'

'Can't do anything like that.'

'Try harder – close your eyes and think of the beach, Sarah, think of where you bloody belong.'

'He didn't come out.'

'What? Is he dead?'

'He stayed behind, to "do something".'

She slid off the bonnet of the pick-up. She slipped into the passenger seat beside the driver, in front of the bodyguards. He stared in front of him, at the line of pegs, as the pick-up drove away. He was glad that Sarah hadn't asked him what would happen to the woman in Kirkūk because he would not have lied to her. He was a long time staring at the line of pegs. After the sound of the truck had gone, drifting away in the bare hills, he began again to probe for the next of the buried V69s and to feel for the tripwires and for the antennae. He tried to shut from his mind the sniper who had stayed to 'do something', but he could not because he didn't know what could be done.

AUGUSTUS HENDERSON *PEAKE*

7. (Conclusions after interview with Dogsy (*sic*) Jennings of Corporate Survival, Hereford, con-

ducted by self and Ms Manning – transcripts
attached.)

ESCAPE & EVASION: AHP, by sharing a course
with a management team of bank officials, will
have received a minimum of training and advice
on survival tactics should he need a fast and
improvised retreat from the theatre of operations
– I emphasize *minimum*. But Jennings classified
him as a 'crusader' and I believe such a mental
attitude would lead AHP to hang around after
the last bus has gone. His E&E tactical
knowledge, as gained from Corporate Survival,
would be wholly inadequate.

SUMMARY: I rate his chances of survival in the
medium term as . . . WHO BLOODY CARES? The
bank officials didn't; Dogsy Jennings didn't; why
should I? He made his bed. His conceit is to go
where ORDINARY, DECENT and EXPERTLY TRAINED
men would not dream of going. His arrogance is
his involvement in a cause from which GOOD,
HONOURABLE and CAREFULLY PREPARED men
would turn away. AHP demeans us all. Will he
survive? I don't give a damn. Will I ever meet
him? I hope not. Where he has gone, what he has
attempted, makes me feel second-rate . . .

The bell rang as Ken Willet's fingers rippled on the
keyboard. He was losing control, his eyes were misted
and he could not see the screen clearly. As he stumbled
across the room he glanced at his wristwatch. It was
mid-morning; he still wore his pyjama trousers. He

scratched at his bare armpit, then opened the door.

Carol Manning stood on the mat and rolled her eyes in mock astonishment. She was holding a bottle of wine. She walked past him. Tricia refused point blank to come to his flat, said it was a tip and stank, said that if they ever married and he didn't learn to clean his act up then he'd have to sleep in the coal bunker. Carol Manning was in the centre of the room and he saw the mischievous grin on her face.

She said his desk at the Ministry had told her he'd called in sick, the wine was Australian chardonnay, and cheap.

She said where they were going the next day.

Ken Willet shambled into the kitchen to find a corkscrew and to wash two glasses. When he came back into the room she was standing over the screen. She handed him the bottle and went on reading. He hadn't seen her laugh like that before – and her eyes sparkled. He pulled the cork. He would, of course, have deleted the SUMMARY. His head dropped, as if humiliated. He poured the wine. She turned, and still there was the sparkle and the laughter.

She said, 'I thought it was a good time to get pissed up – any objection? You know that feeling, a cold comes over you, something you can't touch, can't see, but something desperate's happened and however hard you scratch your mind you don't know what it is – know it? Something awful? I felt that, so I'm going to get pissed up.'

She emptied her glass and he refilled it. He apologized for what he had written.

'No cause to – it's the truth. You hate him because you're jealous. He's ruffled your self-bloody-esteem. It's

404

taken you long enough to catch on that he's brilliant . . .
Where's that bloody bottle? Got me? Brilliant . . .'

A medical orderly peeled from the cab of the marked
ambulance and ran towards the casualty.

He recognized the particular fist of death, the small
entry wound and the large exit hole. That morning, he
had seen a similar wound on the body of a soldier at a
road block and another at a rubbish dump. He was not
easily unnerved. He had served as a field medic, a
stretcher bearer, in the marsh battles to hold the line
against the Iranian hordes, and he had been in Kuwait
when the bomb loads had fallen from the American
aircraft. He could accept the random death handed
down by unseeing artillerymen, machine-gunners and
air crews, and the horror they left behind. But this was
different somehow. The chill gripped him. At the road
block and the rubbish dump, and here at the corner of
an office building, young soldiers had been specifically
identified as targets. He seemed to see the bodies magnified in the telescopic sight that would have prised into
their lives in the moment before death. Fear, the first he
had ever experienced, ran loose in him. A crowd stared
vacantly as he felt the corpse's neck for a pulse and
found none. The crashing blow to his back pitched him
forward so that he toppled onto the body, and then the
blackness came.

The sentry clawed open the heavy steel-plate gate at
the main entrance to the headquarters of Fifth Army.

On the gate, being a man with alert ears and eyes, the
sentry knew of the stalking death spreading without
pattern across the city. He had heard on the squawking
radios and from the shouts of officers that a sniper was

at work and firing indiscriminately. A dozen times in the last hour he had dragged open the gates, allowed foot and mechanized patrols to speed out of the compound and had heaved the gates shut. But, and it would be fatal to him, he did not know the locations in Kirkūk at which seven soldiers had died; had he known, he might have appreciated that each killing brought the marksman closer to the gate he guarded. The sentry was a big man, from a family of stonemasons working in quarries beyond As Salmān in the desert quarter, and he would go back to the heavy equipment, the heavy hours, the heavy rocks when his army duty was completed. He had broad shoulders above a wide, muscled body, and his very size, too, would be fatal to him. The sentry pushing shut the gates made a fine target, and did not know it. A slimmer, slighter man would have escaped. The bullet, by small miscalculations, was fractionally low and fractionally wide, and caught the sentry in the back at the extremity of his rib-cage, then it yawed and sent crippling shock-waves up to the lungs and down to the kidney and liver. He was on the ground, his blood smeared on the gate he had been pushing shut. He screamed for help, but was not answered by men cowering behind the half-closed gates.

'Were we close enough?'
   'She would have heard.'
   'It is enough?'
   'It is enough because she would have known.'
   'Can we get out now?'
   'We can.'
   'You have seen sufficient – Mr Gus, the tourist – of the sights of Kirkūk?'

'No, when it is necessary I will return.'

'For her? Fuck you, Mr Gus. You're mad.'

'So that she knows she is not alone . . . With you, Omar, or without you.'

'Without me you are dead,' the boy spat scornfully.

They ran from the open concrete floors of the uncompleted apartment block. Twice they were seen and erratic shooting followed them. Without Omar's intuition, gathered from thieving and fleeing, Gus would have blundered into the closing net of patrols and into the path of the personnel carriers that criss-crossed the city.

'Mr Gus, have you been helped?'

In the space of almost two hours he had probed into the city and fired eight shots. He had felt no remorse as he saw the vortex of air and the speck of the bullet speeding towards a chosen target, a man doomed because he was available and wore the uniform. He had felt only a brutal anger he had not known before. They went through ditches, gardens, yards, sewer-pipes, on their stomachs or running. They left behind them road blocks, checkpoints, house searches, cordon lines of soldiers, blundering chaos, and the anger never abated.

He shouted, 'If this gate is not opened immediately, you bastards will answer to me with your lives.'

With a full swing, full force, Major Karim Aziz kicked the steel plate of the gates. The screams of the soldier filled his ears. The wounded man, drowning in his own blood, flapped the ground. 'Open the gate and have a stretcher with you, or I will have all of you cowards hanged before the night's out.'

He went back from the gate and crouched over the young soldier. Behind him the square and the road leading towards the office and apartment blocks had emptied. There were troops in firing positions, down and finding cover. He sensed the terror all around him, created by a single man who fired the bullets. He cradled the soldier's head. He could not have ignored the challenge. He heard the gate scrape open. The sniper's trademark was on the bare chest of the soldier where, frantic to kill the pain, his fingers had torn away the tunic and shirt buttons. In the well of the blood was a cleanly drilled entry-hole. As the stretcher-bearers sprinted from the safety of the gate, he lifted the soldier and noted the exit pit large enough to take two field-dressing pads to cover it. The soldier was taken from his arms, thrown down onto a stretcher, and stampeded inside. A single man who made such fear was an opponent worthy of him. There was a small glint on the tarmacadam below the gate that caught his eye. On his hands and knees he crawled to it, picked it up. In his palm was the misshapen piece of lead antimony crushed by the impact on the gate. It had been cased in cupro-nickel when it was recognizable as a bullet. He gazed at it for a moment, then dropped it and thought of his wife, who would be in the car with their children, trusting him . . .

He walked across the square towards the side-street into which the driver had swerved the jeep. He found the man half hiding under the vehicle, stood over him, exposed, and gave the instruction that his backpack and the box should be returned to his old room.

With his rifle in his hands, his dog beside him, Major Karim Aziz stood in the centre of the square and stared up the length of the road at a thousand windows and a hundred roofs.

She heard the boots and the dragging slither as if a weighted sack were brought down the corridor, and the weight collapsed beside the darkness of the drain hole. The door slammed and the boots receded. Her mouth was beside the hole.

'Did you hear it?

'I heard only their questions – and I did not answer. I had the strength . . .'

'Did you hear the shot?'

'You had given me the strength, your love . . .'

'He was there, with his rifle. He is coming.'

'Give me your hand . . . No-one is coming, only death. Give me your hand, I beg you.'

'I heard the shot . . .'

'A man makes a gesture, clears his conscience, then goes . . . Only I can help you, child, only you can help me.'

She put her hand, her wrist and arm, back into the drain.

Chapter Sixteen

His family would be pulling into the fuel station – hot, tired, fractious and looking for him.

Major Karim Aziz came out of the medical unit. The gate sentry might live and he might die. He was escorted by a doctor who thanked him sheepishly, and explained again, uselessly, why a wounded man had been left in the road to bleed without help. The doctor said that the sniper had made a corridor of fear that ordinary men did not have the courage to enter. The doctor wheedled congratulations at the major's bravery, but Aziz walked on and left the man babbling behind him. He had a fresh, urgent step as if a reason for living had again been given him.

The boys would be spilling from the car and complaining to their mother; her temper would be short and she would be barking at them.

He was walking towards the command bunker when his name was shouted from behind him. He walked on, but his name was called again in a thin, nasal voice. He stopped, turned slowly. He thought that Commander Yusuf, the man who was said to harbour an obsessive love of his grandchildren, was breaking again for coffee or for biscuits. There were more blood spatters on the tunics and trousers of the brutes with him; they would not have changed into new uniforms because it was part of the terror they strewed around them that the pain they inflicted should be seen in the bunker and in the officers' quarters.

'You came back, Major.'

'I had thought my duty here was finished, Commander Yusuf. I returned when I realized that was not the case.'

'You are a sniper, Major,' the torturer said, with distaste. 'You understand the psychology of this cowardly killing.'

Aziz stood his ground. 'The man who came into Kirkūk this morning was not a *coward*.'

'Soldiers without military significance were butchered – a fox amongst chickens. Is that not the work of a coward?'

'I came back to shoot him but he is not a coward, Commander. He is no more a coward than the man who, in the name of the state, tortures and mutilates the body of a defenceless prisoner.'

His words died. The men around the commander, the heavy-set, cold-faced beasts, stiffened, and he saw the menace in their eyes, but the commander laughed. The dog bared its teeth.

'Is he, Major, as much a hero as yourself?'

Major Karim Aziz said quietly, 'He is a brave man, Commander, but I am also certain that it requires great courage – in the name of the state – to *interrogate* a bound captive.'

The eyes watching him were amused.

'Come.'

The commander took his arm, gripped it with his narrow fingers. The hand was against the body of the rifle that he carried loosely in the crook of his elbow. The dog scampered warily beside him, and the brutes made a phalanx behind him. He thought he was as much of a prisoner as the wretches in the cells. His vanity had made him turn.

Pacing around the petrol station, she would be telling the children their father would come soon and wondering where he was.

He did not try to break the grip of the fingers. He was led, taken, into the building used by the Estikhabarat. The boots stamped in rhythm behind him. He was brought into a room that was fragrantly scented with air-freshener, and there were flowers on the table. He saw a desk with papers from files piled on it, and beside the files was a framed photograph of the commander sitting on a sand beach with near-naked children beside him. On the far side of the room a tape-recorder's spools turned, and another of the brutes, headphones on a shaven skull, sat at the table and wrote busily. Aziz was offered an easy chair and settled into it. Did he want coffee? He shook his head, but asked if water could be brought for his dog.

The commander walked to the tape-recorder and threw a switch. The sound burst into the room. As if confined in a minuscule space, a guttering, hacking cough came from the speakers, then a slow moan of pain.

'Be strong. We are together. Together we are strong.'

'I told them nothing.'

He heard the wheezed words of the brigadier, the Boot, and her small, timid voice. He stared expression-

412

lessly ahead of him. The commander had lit a cigarette and was glancing with studied casualness at the front page of the regime's morning newspaper.

His conceit had brought him back, and his wife and his children were waiting, would now be anxious because he was late meeting them.

'They ask me, always, who gave me my orders – which officers? The Americans? The pigs, Ibrahim and Bekir? I can tell them nothing because the pigs and the Americans gave me no orders. I have not told them of when we met . . .'

He forced himself to listen to the whispered, frightened, hurt voice.

'I have told them nothing. If it were not for your strength I would have broken . . .'

'Hold my hand tighter.'
   'I hold it and I love it as if it were my family.'
   'Hold my hand because I am afraid.'
   'When you are close, with me, I can survive the pain.'
   'How long can we last?'
   'Long enough, I pray, for others to escape.'
   'What was your dream?'
   'I was told I would be the Minister of Defence.' There was the bitter whinge of his laughter, and the slight motion in his body would have hurt him, because he moaned again. 'I was told I would be a great man in the new Iraq. I was told . . .'

The pain of his gasp sighed in her ear. She felt the grip of his hand slacken and wondered whether he had drifted towards unconsciousness. The comfort she had felt when she had heard the single shot – the faraway crack and the close-by thump – were long gone. In a wild moment of excitement, she had thought that a crescendo of firing would burst around her, and that there would be the fear-driven cries of men in the corridor as they ran and, in the delirium of her terror, she had seen the cell door open and he would have been there with the rifle and would have caught her up in his arms and carried her from this hellish place . . . But there had been only the one shot and it was long gone, and she had cursed him for not coming, for being safe.

'Hold me, you have to, hold me.'

'I am holding you.'

She felt the tightening of his fingers on hers, as if she had brought him back to the living, as if she were not alone.

'Hold me because I am afraid, and have nothing to tell them.'

'What is your dream?'

'To be in my village, to be a woman, to be free.'

'Without you, I cannot protect them, buy them their time to escape.'

Through the conduit of a drain hole between two holding cells, the brigadier of the staff of Fifth Army and the peasant woman from the mountains knotted their fingers to give each other strength.

The voice seemed to fail, then rise again.

'I was to be paid a million American dollars for taking the armoured brigade south from Kirkūk.'

'I was offered nothing. What would I do with a million American dollars?'

'I would have put you on the lead tank – washed you, cleaned you, carried you into Baghdad.'

'Then I would have gone home.'

The commander gestured for the switch to be lifted, and the silence fell on the room. His smile was easy, affable.

'Major Aziz, it is standard to allow prisoners in adjacent cells the opportunity to communicate with each other. There is a drain between them, and a microphone in it. Prisoners who believe they have successfully resisted interrogation always betray themselves when they have been returned to their cells – we learned it from the British, it was their procedure in Ireland. I am surprised that it has taken them so long to find the culvert. It is because we hold her that the sniper, this butcher, has killed so many, yes?'

'I think it was to tell her that she was not forgotten – and to expiate his shame that he did not or could not protect her.'

'The sniper is your target?'

He said simply, 'It is important to me.'

'I have finished with her. Is she of use to you?'

'She will be hanged?'

'Of course – she is a witch. Our brave soldiers ran from her. She is talked of in the bazaars and in the *souks*. It is necessary to hang her.'

Cold words. 'She should be hanged in public tomorrow morning at the main gate . . .' He said how the gallows should be built. He thought of his wife and children at the petrol station, angry and fretting for him. He thought of the brigadier, the Boot, denied the strength of the grip of her hand, and the names that were secreted in his mind. He thought of the sniper who would be drawn from a hiding place by the sight of the gallows and the peasant woman standing under the beam.

415

The moth would be drawn to the flame. If a moth flew too close to the flame the wings were singed, and it fell. But he was – himself – walking towards a flame and if he was burned he would fall, and if he fell then he was dead. And there had been the great flame burning above the oilfield outside the city that had drawn her fatally nearer. The flame burned for all of them, bright and dangerous, beckoning them.

A young man, walking back to his village near Qizil Yar, west of the city, had been knifed and his body thieved from. The young man who had thought himself fortunate to find work in Kirkūk, cleaning the tables in a coffee shop, had stayed on in the evening to see a film at a cinema. He had been stabbed in the back, killed, and his identity card stolen. Before his body was cold, while it lay in a road drain and the first of the rats sniffed at it, the identity card was presented at the outer road block on the main route into the city.

In the next hour, the identity card was presented three more times, studied by torchlight, then the beams switched to a young man's face, and Omar was waved on.

He was the observer in the tradition laid down by Major Herbert Hesketh-Prichard. Everything he saw was remembered: where the tanks were, and the blocks, and the personnel carriers parked in side-streets with the radios playing soft music from the Baghdad transmitter he remembered.

He was another grubby, dishevelled young man with unkempt hair padding the pavements of the city. There were many such as him, drawn to Kirkūk in search of subsistence work. He attracted no attention from the soldiers who were only a few months older. He passed among them, drawn forward towards a distant hammering, nails sinking into wooden planks.

Omar knew he was close to the place where she had been taken. He had heard the *mustashar*, Haquim, describe the place to Mr Gus and make the excuses. He slipped from the wide main street that led towards faraway arc-lights, the sounds of hammers beating on nails, and drifted through shadows in the narrowed lanes of the Old Quarter. He could smell the burned wood of homes that had been fired in the fighting. There was a line of buildings where the walls were marked by desperate bullet lacerations, a small square, muddy roads leading from it, and a broken wall into which the jeep carrying her had crashed. There was a panel-beater's shop where men worked to the light of oil lamps. It was as Haquim had described it. He saw an open door beyond the panel-beater's shop, closer to the wall; through the door a family gathered in a dully lit room and watched the television. There were old men, young men, women, children, in front of the television. The *mustashar*, Haquim, had said a family had come from their home and had spat into the face of Meda. He would have liked to have killed them, rolled a grenade through the door or sprayed them with an assault rifle on automatic, but that was not the work of an observer as written down by Major Hesketh-Prichard. He slipped again into the shadows until he could see the lights of the wide street.

The orphan child of the aid agencies, the plaything of American soldiers, the carrier of ammunition for the *peshmerga*, the thief from the living and the dead, the friend of Mr Gus had no fear when he was close enough

417

to see the high gallows being built by supervised labourers outside the barricaded gates of the headquarters of Fifth Army.

'Which direction does it face?'

'To the front, towards the wide street.'

'Can you see it from the side?'

'There are screens at the side of canvas. You can only see it from the front, from the wide street.'

'But above it is open?'

'No, Mr Gus. It is covered by a roof of more canvas. You cannot see it from high, not from the side, only from the front . . . Why do they do it so complicated, Mr Gus?'

'So they can dictate where I will be.'

The sweat of the day's heat had cooled long ago on his body and the night wind now insinuated the chill into him. The blister was worse on his heel, aggravated by the charge out of the city after the killings. He had the last of the plasters from his rucksack on the wound and the ache of it was inescapable. When the sun had gone down, the stiffness had gripped his shoulders, pelvis and knees, and he had not slept until the boy returned.

'They do that, the roof and the sides, because of us?'

'Because of me, not you. You have done your work, Omar. If I want to see Meda brought out, see the rope put on her, see . . . I have to be in front, because they have covered the sides. I cannot be high, because they have made a roof. They hope to restrict me so that it is easier for them to find me. A man never had a better observer, but it is finished for you – you should go.'

'Without me you would not even get into the city.'

'It is not your quarrel.'

'Do you say that she is only yours, Mr Gus, not mine?'

418

'I want you to go.'

'You are nothing without me – Major Hesketh-Prichard was nothing without his observer. Even he said so.'

As he had waited for the boy to come back he had gone through the checklist he had been given so long ago. Mechanically, in the darkness, by touch, he had cleaned the breech and felt the firmness of the elevation and deflection turrets. He had tightened the screws securing the telescopic sight, he had massaged the lenses with a cloth, and had wiped each of the bullets of .338 calibre before loading them into the magazine and slotting it back into the rifle's belly. He could no longer conjure the faces of those who had been important to him so long ago. At each stage of the checklist she had been in his mind, and he had tried to remember the taste of her kiss.

'Afterwards, will you take me with you? Will you take me to your home?'

Gus let out a low, involuntary chuckle. 'Ridiculous.'

'Why is that ridiculous?'

'Because . . .'

'I am your friend here. I can be your friend at your home.'

He could not see the boy's face but he sensed the smarting resentment . . . Yes, he could take him home. The boy could sleep on the floor and each morning he could go out into the handkerchief-sized garden at the back of the block, lower his trousers, squat and defecate. Maybe he could thieve the silver spoons from the drawer. Yes, the boy could go with him to work, could sit in the office and be bored witless and look at the wallets protruding from the inside pockets of the jackets

419

draped on chairs and the women's handbags with the purses displayed. Yes, he could take him up Guildford's high street on a Saturday morning. He could watch the snake-like movements of the boy's hands and see his pockets fill. Yes, he could take him to the pub. He would try to intervene in time to stop the flash of a knife if a lout or a yob laughed at the boy's appearance. Yes, the boy should see Stickledown Range. He could lay the boy on the mat beside him and ask for him to call the distance and wind deflection and know they would be right. Gus reached out in the darkness and his hand found the thin shoulder. He gripped it hard.

'I would like to sleep now, Omar, and I want you to wake me when it is time to go.'

'I sort of sat on it, Caspar. I don't like to be a harbinger, the bringer of bad news. And I'm sorry for it.'

'I heard it on the radio, Isaac, on their news bulletin. You have nothing to apologize for.'

'They're going to hang her in the morning.'

'Jesus – I didn't get that from the radio.'

'They're going to hang her in the morning – they've told the Party faithful to ensure a good attendance.'

'Jesus Christ.'

'Did you hear about the shooting?'

'No.'

'There was shooting in Kirkūk this morning. You recall the marksman with her?'

'I remember him.'

'After she was taken, the rest of her people came out, all except him. He stayed. Kirkūk this morning was like your Dodge City, Caspar. He shot at least seven soldiers

420

before he backed off – long-shot stuff, one bullet for one man.'

'Why would he do that?'

'You met her, Caspar, you saw her. She'd twist a man's head. It could only be a futile gesture of his commitment to her . . . I have to believe he cannot turn away from her.'

'Isaac, maybe he should have gone to the Agency's school. We major in courses on walking out on trusting idiots.'

'There are PhDs on it at the Mossad. You are not alone on the excellence of walking away. Of course, there's nothing that he can do for her.'

'Isaac, I appreciate your calling. Appreciate the advance warning. I won't sleep much tonight. She was good and feisty – those bastards in Arbīl and Sulaymānīyah didn't deserve her. And we didn't. I hope she knows he stayed when no other fucker did. Shit . . . I have a paper to read so I'm up to speed to entertain a serious asshole who'll be here about the time she's dangling . . . Goodnight, Isaac.'

He cut the link. He reflected that there might just be a job vacancy, or two, or three, in the classified advertisements of the Baghdad newspapers.

Wanted: HANGMAN. No previous experience required. Expertise not necessary. Successful applicant must be prepared to work long hours. Good career prospects.

The paper had come in two hours earlier and had clogged thirty-two seconds of time on the secure teleprinter. It took thirty-two seconds to transmit the latest piece of Langley optimism, and the plan on the paper would give work for years to a hangman, or two, or three . . . He was so goddam tired. He started to turn the pages of the paper – and in a few hours, as she was hanged, a shiny-faced man would step off the shuttle plane from Ankara and would be expecting Caspar Reinholtz to be similarly breezy and cheerful, to say that it was the best plan ever conceived for the toppling of the Boss for Life. He was hunched over his desk, the words in front of him bouncing uselessly in his head.

First Phase: A core group of 250 Iraqi exiles would be trained in sabotage techniques by US Special Forces. *Second Phase*: A further 2,000 exiles receive eight weeks' basic military training. *Third Phase*: Twenty groups of twenty men infiltrate Government of Iraq territory to blow up power lines and disrupt internal transport. *Fourth Phase*: More men are pushed across friendly borders and set up a liberated enclave. *Fifth Phase*: The overthrowing of the regime of the Boss for Life.

It was always that simple and they always sent the plan on ahead of its author so that a dumb field officer, a Caspar Reinholtz, could not plead the need for time to study it. It would be considered *defeatist* to tell the author that the plan was a piece of crap.

A plan was dead. Long live the plan.

The woman, Meda, would hang in the morning and a new thesis of liberation was transmitted to Incerlik.

There was work for one hangman. There would soon be work for many more.

Maybe the man coming in on the shuttle would shake the lethargy out of Caspar Reinholtz's system, and maybe he would not. But, maybe, the man on the shuttle on the last leg of his journey from Langley should be congratulated for a new refinement of warfare: combat by fucking proxy. Maybe Caspar should grip his hand and slap his shoulder and praise him for digging out a plan where someone else did the fighting for America and faced the noose. No-risk fighting, no casualties going home in body bags to Arkansas or Alaska or Alabama, no mothers trying to be brave as the caskets went down into good Virginia or Vermont earth, because the poor bastards getting killed were proxy soldiers and didn't count.

Rusty came into the office, and brought coffee with him.

'There's a call for you, Caspar – the green phone. It's London – been cleared by Langley. They want to talk to you.'

'What about?'

'About that sniper. Do I say you're available or not available?'

He thought of the man he had met, and the big rifle, of the man who had not turned, not walked away, of the man who did not know the fucking rules.

'I'll take it.'

Long before dawn, while the stars and the moon's crescent still watched the city, the first of the crowd came, intent on gaining the best places. Those who had risen earliest, or who had not been to bed, pressed against the barrier behind which a solid wall of soldiers stood. They came at first in a dribble and would arrive later in a growing mass. Confronting them, above the soldiers, was a wooden platform on which was set a low chair. Above the chair and below a solid crossbeam was a dangling rope with a waiting noose that swayed gently in the light night wind. The same wind rippled the canvas sides of the scaffold and flapped the roof above the crossbeam. Because of the cold, those who had arrived first were well wrapped in thick coats and some carried blankets to drape over their shoulders. Music from transistor radios would help to pass the time before daybreak, and later coffee vendors would come. Warm plastic cups would be passed over heads, money would return on a reverse route, and there was a buzz of talk. Away behind the crowd, stretching into an infinity of dull street lights, was the length of Martyr Avenue. They came to see the death of the witch, but none of them who surged onto the weight of the barrier knew why there was a roof over the gallows and side screens around it.

He sat on the balcony, the night caressing his face. Her warmth was against his back. The dog nestled against his legs. Major Karim Aziz let the conceit play in his mind, and shield him from the future.

'Did you see him?' the woman asked.

'I saw him.'

He had been thinking of trophies, the heads that hunters set on walls. It would be talked about. Young men, not yet old enough to know of war, would gather in the quiet of barracks' corridors and speak of a duel to the death. He had wrapped the obsession around him, a cloak against the night. He had not thought of the brigadier, the Boot, with the nails torn from his hands, the blood seeping from the flab of his face, the burns of electrodes and cigarettes on his body, the names hidden in a tortured mind.

'Was he well?'

'I saw him very briefly.'

424

'He will be tired – I tell him he works too hard. Will I see him when they hang her?'

'I think not, I don't think he will be there.'

The bell had woken her. She had come to the door with a light in her face that was washed out when she had seen he was not her lover. He had gone through to the bedroom balcony and squatted down with his dog. He could see up the length of Martyr Avenue. He had no plan of what he would do afterwards. The duel was the present, and the anticipation of it, like some narcotic, overwhelmed him. She had come outside, sat on the cold tiles of the balcony, and leaned her back against his.

'Are you from Kirkūk, Major?'

'Baghdad.'

'You have a wife there?'

'In Baghdad, yes. She will be sleeping now – she will have had a long day.'

She would have waited for him from the middle of the day through to the end and then, cursing him, she would have ordered the boys back into the car and she would have driven back down the long road to Ba'qūbah, and then on to Baghdad and home. She would have thrown the packed bags into their room and the children's bedroom, and gone into the kitchen to make a meal. Later, because he had not met her at the fuel station, the door of their home would be sledge-hammered open and the house would be defiled by the boots of strangers. He had made a choice and he lived with it.

'And children?'

'Two sons. One has an important examination at school today, and the younger one has a football match tomorrow. They are fine boys.'

425

'And proud of their father?'

'I have to hope so.'

The boys would have sat sullen and quiet in the car during the journey home. They would not have understood why their father had not come or why they had made the journey in the first place. Perhaps their mother would have attempted to turn their mood with talk of school or football, and perhaps she would have spoken of the importance of their father's work. Perhaps she would have said nothing, bitten her lip and blinked into the blazing lights of the oncoming lorries going north. When the door was broken down, when their mother was beaten by the strangers, when the house was stripped and searched, his sons would be told that their father was a traitor. His choice was dictated by his vanity.

'Why are you here, Major?'

'To kill a man.'

'Because he is your enemy?'

'No,' he said absently.

She pressed, 'Because he is the enemy of the state?'

'Not the reason.'

'Because he has hurt you?'

'He has not hurt me.'

All he knew of the man was from the one distant sighting, distorted by the mirage over the open ground, and always beyond the range of the Dragunov. He knew nothing of him. He did not know where the man had come from, or why he had travelled, or of his life. After he had killed the man, he would not stand over his body and pose as a hunter would over the corpse of a bear or a wolf or a leopard, but he would kneel in a moment of reverence and hope they shared a god, and close the lids

426

of the dead eyes. Then, and only then, he would think of afterwards.

'How do you know he will come?'

'He will come, he has to. He is a driven man, as am I. We are equals. I respect him, and I believe he gives me respect.'

His eyes traversed the many windows of Martyr Avenue, and the roofs, and he waited for the dawn.

Three hours before first light Gus and Omar started out and headed for the glow of the street lamps and the flame.

'She did not know her place. She treated me as if I were inferior. In front of many who could watch and listen she behaved as if I were subordinate to her. I tell you, Haquim, even if I had influence, if I was listened to in Baghdad, I would not lift a finger on her behalf. But that is idle talk because it's not the truth. She is, and you know it, beyond reach. It is my duty now, as a leader of my people, to protect them. I will fulfil my duty, I will negotiate with the President. I can do nothing else. She deluded you. Go home, forget her. Go and sit in the sunlight in front of your house, and put her from your mind. You will excuse me, I am tired, I wish to go to my bed.'

'You disgrace yourself if you do nothing.'

'She climbed too fast.'

The *agha* Bekir rose from his chair. The silk robe swirled around his body. Behind the sweet words and the wringing hands, Haquim could see detestation for the young woman who had taken him to the edge of Kirkūk. His feet, snug in light embroidered slippers, slid across the floor towards the inner door. Haquim thought the bastard would sleep well.

He felt old, weary, and the dusty uniform clung to his body. The double doors behind him were opened silently: the audience was concluded.

Haquim went out of the building and into the night that had fallen heavy on Sulaymānīyah. His last effort for her had won no reward.

He drove away towards the dark lines of the mountains where the air was clean, where he could still dream of the city that had been their goal, and the flame.

Meda walked into the cell, the door rattled shut behind her and the boots went away down the corridor.

She had been woken, taken to a room where harsh lights burned, read a statement from a typed sheet of paper, then wheeled round and marched back to the cell. She was alone, and when the boots had gone there was only the quiet around her. She sagged to her knees, crawled to the hole, put her mouth close to it and whispered, in a small voice, that she was to be hanged at dawn. She asked for him to hold her hand till dawn came. She heard his laboured breathing. She reached with her arm deep into the drain but in a moment of respite he slept and did not take her hand. She did not shout into the hole to rouse him, did not cry for him, because she thought it would be cruel to wake him. It was many hours since she had heard the rifle fired, and she looked up at the high window where the stars were and she did not know how long it would be until the light dismissed them.

'My colleague, Dr Williams, did most of the talking and I did most of the listening. Fred, that's Dr Williams, wanted a witness. Fair enough – it's not every day a civilian comes in off the street to learn about the Iraqi armed forces. It could have been a can of worms for Fred if he'd turned out to be a mercenary, looking for kicks from killing people, so I sat in.'

It was still dark outside the building. Ken Willet could hear the chatter in other offices of the early-morning work of the cleaners, muffled by the Hoovers. He knew the block, Centre for War Studies, from his own years at the Royal Military Academy, but the psychiatrist had not been there at that time. Rupert Helps had pleaded a busy day, a first lecture at 8 a.m. then a filled, sacrosanct diary, and an evening engagement. Dr Williams was at NATO in Belgium for the week, but the psychiatrist had heard – on a routine visit to the Commando Training Centre at Lympstone – of the interest in Augustus Henderson Peake and had offered his help. Willet would have bet that Rupert Helps would have run bare-foot over broken glass to *help*.

Ms Manning asked, 'What did Dr Williams tell him?'

'I didn't listen that closely – Fred's the expert, you see. We hear it every lunchtime in the mess, his views on the Iraqi armed forces – myself, I think he's slightly over-rated. Anyway, a résumé to give an idea of the usual lecture. The Iraqis are a defensively minded and central-ized military machine. Faced with the unexpected, they will be slow to react because middle-ranking officers are not able to take field decisions. So, at first, they can be caught out, lose ground and positions. Once they've steadied their nerve and had orders from on high they are efficient. That was the germ of it – a sudden attack will make early advances, then there will be a regrouping, consolidation, counter-attack . . . then reprisals. I don't think he'd thought of that. He was jolted. I'd wager my shirt on Fred having the right appraisal of that scenario, but it is pretty obvious. The insurgents – Kurds, yes? – would go through villages and towns, and think they were a force of liberation, but God help the poor bastards who cheered them. It's the same through history – do you know your 'Forty-five rebellion? The Young Pretender marched south and took Carlisle, Lancaster, Manchester, and idiots cheered him to the roof, but they were backing a loser. There's always some nasty little creature who remembers who cheered the liberators loudest, who is going to dangle from a rope when the tables are turned – there were a great number of hangings in those northern English cities when the Highland army retreated . . . Back in Iraq, the same is true – the reprisals would be brutal. He went very quiet, like the wind was out of his sails. Fred told him about the terrain he'd be in, a little about how to cope with hunger, thirst, lack of sleep, heat. Then I chipped in.'

'What exactly was your contribution?' Willet asked drily. He had taken a fast and certain dislike to the psychiatrist. Perhaps it was the time in the morning, dawn not yet on them, perhaps it was the man's flamboyant bow-tie of vivid green and primrose yellow, perhaps it was the long hair gathered at the back of his head with an elastic band.

'If I'd reckoned him a mere psychopath, I'd have stayed quiet.'

Willet persisted, 'What would interest a psychiatrist like you?'

Rupert Helps beamed, and preened pleasure at being asked for his expert opinion. 'He's not a rounded man.

430

I assessed him as an innocent, rather juvenile – a child, unwilling to grow up and shed a world of romance, but *decent*. You with me? Peter Pan syndrome. The talk of reprisals was the give-away.'

'Sorry, but you haven't told me what your contribution was.'

'I told him to forget it. He should nurse his own problems and ignore other people's difficulties. I said he should put himself first.'

Ms Manning gazed into the psychiatrist's face. 'Did you expand on that opinion?'

'You know—'

'No, certainly I don't.' Willet thought she was a cat, about to pounce, ready for the kill. 'Be so kind as to tell me.'

'Well, because he seemed to be searching for fulfilment, I suggested he should push at work for promotion, never said what his job was. I didn't gather that he was in a very meaningful relationship – he could put more effort into that. He should find a hobby and develop it further. He could move home, get a garden, have a larger mortgage and therefore self-inflict the pressure to earn more through greater endeavour. If he needed to do good works I told him to drive at weekends for the elderly or the sick . . . I was trying to help. Did he go?'

She said brutally, 'Oh, yes, he went, completely ignored you.'

'Has he survived?'

The steel was in her voice. 'We don't know. We have very little access to intelligence from that region. Tomorrow I have a meeting at which I may find something out. Isn't there more to living than work, loving, hobbies, mortgages, charities? Shouldn't we rejoice that one man, alone among the dross, climbs towards further horizons?'

'You don't understand.'

'What don't I understand?'

'If he survives, he'll be damaged. He won't win, can't. Should he make it back, he'll be a damaged, altered man. I was just trying to help, damn you. He can't win, and it will all be for nothing – dead or damaged.'

She rose imperiously, 'Thank you. Perhaps that's a worthwhile sacrifice. Come on.'

Willet followed her out. They passed a column of cadets starting out on a cross-country run.

'The pompous bastard didn't even offer us coffee, gets us out of bed as though he's the only one with an important day, and no bloody coffee,' he said. 'Well done for putting him down, laying him out on the floor like that.'

'Don't patronize me.'

It was a brilliant dawn of ochre and gold and red thrown up from behind the mountains in the west. The dawn was a flame to which two men were drawn.

432

Chapter Seventeen

'Will you send my body back to the mountains?'

The commander seemed to ponder that last request. They were in her cell, the door open behind him. He seemed to think on it as if he were slightly confused. He had taken no part in the stripping of her military clothes, and army boots, and had looked to the ceiling when she was naked, before the smock of white cotton was lifted over her head and her arms were threaded into the sleeves. She was calm, stiff and awkward but he had heard on the speakers in the office the mewling of the wretch in the adjacent cell and he had heard the last faint words of comfort she had given him. Most men, officers in the army, asked for a cigarette and panted on it before it was taken from their mouths, discarded on the cell's floor and they were led out. The cigarettes lay on the floor half-smoked, still burning by the time the execution had been completed. He would not have admitted to being a man invested with cruelty, but he was keen on the bureaucracy entailed in his work as a shield to the state.

He looked into Meda's face. Her hair was held close against her head with a cloth bandanna. He could understand why men had followed her. If the shield he held was lowered, if the regime became vulnerable, if he – himself – were about to be led out, he would not be given an opportunity to make a last request. There would be sons, fathers, uncles and nephews, cousins of those he had sent to their deaths that the regime might survive, crowding around him and kicking, punching, spitting. No cigarette would be lit for him before he was lifted up under the lamp-post or the telegraph pole. He thought of what she asked. If the regime fell he knew what would become of his beloved grandchildren. It was her very calmness that disturbed him.

He answered her quietly, 'I promise your body will be sent back to the mountains . . .'

'Thank you.'

'. . . when your family have paid the price of the rope.'

There was a titter of laughter from the men who held her and fastened the thong on her wrists behind her back. He had sought to destroy the calm, but her eyes were unwavering and beading into his. He saw the contempt, and understood better why men had followed her – and why *agha* Ibrahim in Arbīl and *agha* Bekir had not lifted the telephone and pleaded with Baghdad for her life. He broke the hold of her eyes and looked at the wall where other wretches had written their names and the dates on which they had been taken from the cell, but noticed that she had not bothered to do so.

'It is time,' he said brusquely. 'Move her.'

They took her out quickly and her feet, in plain plastic sandals, scraped the floor. They dragged her from his sight.

He heard her cry out in the corridor, 'Be strong,

friend, be brave. Remember those who depend on you . . .'

He thought that one of the escort would then have clamped a hand over her mouth. He heard their boots and the scrape of her sandals, then the squeal of the unlocking of the cell block's outer door and the clang as it was shut again.

There was a deep, limitless silence around him. He stood alone in the cell and the walls seemed to close around him, the ceiling to slide down on him. He saw the high window, the grime on the glass that repulsed the brightness of the low sunlight, and the bulb that burned dully above the protective screen of wire. An hour before he had come to the cell to see her stripped, dressed in the white cotton smock that was too large for her, made for a man, which had been soiled with the excrement of the last traitor whose bowels had burst as he had kicked under the rope, he had been telexed from the al-Rashid barracks. A general of mechanized infantry, commanding a division, had crossed the Jordanian frontier and had reached Amman. A brigadier of anti-aircraft artillery defences, and two colonels of the Engineer Corps – with their families – had fled their homes. A colonel in an armoured regiment had driven his car into the cover of trees beside the Tigris river, sealed the windows, squeezed a pipe on to the exhaust and was dead . . . There would be others, there always were. A few escaped, but others stayed, believed it was possible to disguise their guilt from him, the shield of the regime.

The quiet burdened him, and the emptiness of the cell. Her calm had made the silence that seemed to crush him. He could not escape the gaze of her eyes. He felt the

435

weakness at his knees and he would have fallen had he not reached out and steadied himself against the door of the cell. He had seen many men taken from the cells, and afterwards he had gone to the home of his son and sat the children on his knee and told them stories or played with them with their toys on the rugs, but that morning he was far from his son's home and his grandchildren. He staggered out of the cell and leaned, breathless, against the corridor wall.

Commander Yusuf heard the crowd's voices. She would be on the ladder to the platform of planks. She would be seen. His composure returned as the silence ended with the shouts, jeers, yells of the crowd outside the gate.

He stood by the closed cell door. 'Do you hear it?' he murmured, in his soft singing voice. 'She is alone, as you are alone. She is beyond help, as you are beyond help.'

'One one six zero.' Omar was looking through the binoculars.

'One thousand one hundred and sixty yards, check?'

'That's what I said, Mr Gus.'

He had never fired at that distance. The furthest target on the Stickledown Range was at a thousand yards. His finger made the final adjustment to the sight's elevation turret. At its maximum height in flight, the bullet would be on a line that was 135 inches above the aiming point, then it would drop.

'Wind isn't so strong, maybe three to five miles per hour at our point, coming from the side. From smoke, between the office and the apartment block – four two zero yards – it is more strong, five to eight miles per hour. At three-quarters distance, by the governor's house, it is again as strong. I can see from the flag there.'

'If the flag's on top of the building that's too high for trajectory, doesn't count.'

'I know that, Mr Gus. The flag is from a window balcony, at *her* height.'

'What is it, at her?'

'It is again more gentle, from the side.'

The bullet, at that range, would be in the air for the time it would take to speak, not gabble, two phrases of seven syllables each. 'Point three three eight ca-lib-re. Point three three eight ca-lib-re.' He must allow for wind deflection at the muzzle point when the velocity was greatest, then twice more during its flight . . . Two clicks of deflection on the windage turret. Before the wind straightened it, the bullet would fly on a course that was initially eighteen inches to the left of the target.

'Check.'

He thanked God that the wind at the muzzle point was not moderate but gentle, not fresh and not strong. He could not see her. Men were clustered around her. The reticule lines of the sight were on the noose. There was no traffic on Martyr Avenue and he sensed the swelling quiet of the crowd, who had jeered as she was led out but now stood in hushed silence.

Then, two of the men in dun olive uniforms bent in front of her, and he thought they pinioned her legs. She stood so still. He breathed in hard, filled his lungs, and waited for them to lift her feet onto the chair.

The commander was outside the cell block. He had no need to be there, he could not have counted the number of executions he had witnessed, and with minor variations they were all the same. The quiet had drawn him

437

out of the block. He did not know why the Party men, the Ba'athists, did not lead the cheering and shouting. He could see her through the open gates, small and hemmed in by big men, below the noose. He looked hard and expected to see her back and shoulders quiver, but her head had not dropped. Away past her was the length of Martyr Avenue, and then the foothills of the mountains. He saw the hands grip her body, to raise her, and he turned away as if he had no stomach for it.

There were open windows with curtains flapping in them, roofs with lines of washing, the shadows thrown by water tanks, and the dark recesses in unfinished buildings where the sun did not penetrate. Using the magnification of the telescopic sight, Major Karim Aziz roved over the windows, roofs and the skeletal sites.

When the first light had peeped over the high distant ground he had sent the woman inside. He was calm. He had made the necessary calculations. For the sniper to have a view of the scaffold, between the side screens, he must be on Martyr Avenue. As he had requested, the street below him was blocked with armoured cars. It was, and he had paced the distance, 525 metres from the balcony to the scaffold. The sniper must be further back, but Aziz did not believe the man would trust himself to shoot at a greater range than 850 metres. He believed himself to be within 325 metres of the greatest prize his life had yet offered him.

There was no sound to distract him. Not a car moved on the street, not a hawker cried out, and the great crowd was stilled as if it held, guarded, its breath. The quiet was good and brought him the peace he needed.

He knew they had led her out, the crowd had told

him, but in the quiet he did not know whether they had lifted her yet onto the chair. He could not turn to see. It might be the flash of light from the rifle's sight, or the brief brilliance of the firing gases, or the dispersal of dust on a window sill. He thought the target would be the hangman. It would be the sad and stupid gesture of a man demented by helplessness to shoot the hangman. The gesture would leave her, in terror, on the platform for another minute or another five minutes before an officer had the courage to crawl forward, lift her, set her feet on the chair, the noose on her neck and kick the chair. To shoot the hangman would not help her. He had no complaint, as long as the sniper fired and, through firing, exposed himself.

There was a low moan from the crowd, wind on wire, and he thought they lifted her. He stared through the sight at the windows and roofs and the open floors of unfinished buildings.

She was on the chair.

Hands steadied her.

She stared ahead of her, across the crowd and up the length of the street. He wondered whether she looked for him.

He let the breath slip. His words were silent. 'Don't move. I am here. Don't move your head. My love . . .' He squeezed gently on the trigger.

This was not Stickledown. He was on the third floor of an unfinished office block facing down the Martyr Avenue in the city of Kirkūk. He was in the bubble where it never rained, was never too cold and never too hot, and the wind never freshened. The boy was beside him but he no longer knew it.

A hand reached up for the noose. Her head was still, and he thought she heard him.

Gus Peake fired, as if he were on Stickledown Range, at the centre of the V-Bull of his target.

'Kill her . . . Kill her . . .'

He watched the speck of the bullet and the early-morning air burst away from it.

'Kill her . . . Kill her . . . Kill her . . .'

When he could no longer see the bullet, he saw the buffet vortex of the air.

'Kill her . . . Kill . . .'

His lips made the fourteenth syllable as her head pitched apart.

Gus lay with the shock of the rifle burning in his shoulder and closed his eyes to shut out the sight of what he had done.

He had heard the bullet go past him.

It was part of the discipline of Major Aziz that he did not twist his body to follow the path of the bullet to see what target it had hit, or if it had missed. The moment after he had registered the crack of the bullet's supersonic flight, he heard the thump. Through his 'scope sight he studied the windows and roofs that were between 300 and 350 metres from him, but there was nothing. His search covered two or three seconds. He did not believe that the shot had been fired from closer than 300 metres, but there was that instant nagging suspicion that it had been loosed at a greater distance. His viewpoint, magnified and centred on the cross-lines of the Dragunov's sight, raked up the length of Martyr Avenue, over office windows and apartment balconies and more roofs. There was so little time. Beyond the office housing the Oil Company of Iraq, beyond the block with balconies and flower-pots, beyond the office of the Agriculture Ministry (Northern Region) was a construction site of concrete floors and reinforced steel pillars, open to the winds.

He would have tracked on with the sight had it not been for what he saw from the lowest point of the sight's circle – the workmen.

The workmen – and his mind raced to the calculation that they were a minimum of 1,000 metres from the scaffold – were the sign. A gasp of exhilaration slipped his lips.

He found them in the 'scope at the moment the tableau broke. There were four of them, day labourers, the fetchers and carriers of the cement blocks, the men who placed the crane's cable hook onto the steel beams, but the crane was idle and the operator had gone with the architects, surveyors and supervisors to see the hanging. Perhaps the workmen were Kurds and not willing to watch the slow, strangled death. They were on the first floor's bare plateau of concrete. They had frozen at the proximity of the shot. When he saw them their shock was fading and they cringed down, then looked up. It was what men anywhere would have done if a rifle was fired close to them, above them.

He had found his man.

Aziz grabbed his backpack, stampeded off the balcony and into her bedroom. He careered into her, flattened her and ran for the door. The dog scampered beside him. He charged down the staircase of the block. The man, too, would be running, but he would not have a wide staircase to go down, three steps at a time, but would be groping for a loose, swaying ladder. He burst

441

out of the building and ran up the pavement. He never looked back towards the scaffold. It was a panting sprint but the adrenaline gave him speed and the dog was always a couple of metres ahead of him, as if doing the work of a pacemaker. He passed soldiers in a doorway, ignored them, and was crossing the further traffic lanes of Martyr Avenue as a personnel carrier swerved to avoid him. In his youth, in spiked shoes and shorts, he could have covered the distance in seventy seconds. Now he was middle-aged, and there was no crowd to cheer him towards a tape. He had the weight of the back-pack hooked on one shoulder and the awkwardness of the rifle in his hand, but the scent of the chase was with him. He reached the palisade of planks fronting the construction site, heaving and fit to vomit, a minute and a half after the single shot had been fired.

The man would be coming off the ladder, would be weaving between stacked heaps of pipes, blocks and cables. At the back of the site, he would be running, for the plank wall or the wire fence, whichever was there. Aziz ducked along the side length of the palisade, covered with fly-posters and exhortations from the Party, and reached the corner of the wall.

The alleyway was empty. Facing the high chain-mesh fence were little lock-up businesses, all closed because their owners had gone to the execution. Three hundred metres down the fence, a boy appeared on the top and rolled and fell. From his run, Aziz could barely stand. He trembled with the effort. The boy saw him, covered him with an assault rifle, but did not fire. The man followed him. For a moment his weight was hooked on the top of the wire and then he dropped down.

Aziz thought the boy had shouted something to the

442

man, who looked up. He would have seen Aziz at the corner of the palisade and the fence. He was a big man and the sunlight threw gaunt lines on his face that was cream-smeared above the stubble. He wore the big sniper's smock. He seemed to measure the scale of the threat of Aziz at the corner of the palisade and the fence, then to reject it as an irrelevance. The boy caught the arm of his smock, pulled him across the alleyway, and they were gone.

Still heaving, trembling, still trying to draw air into his body, Aziz could not have fired. It would have been a wasted shot. He could no longer run but he pushed himself to trot forward.

He reached the point where they had come down off the fence. He was very careful now that he should not contaminate the scuffmarks made by their boots and bodies as they had dropped down. He gestured for the dog to sniff at the broken soil beside the wire, and cooed his encouragement.

'Find them, Scout . . . Hunt them, Scout . . . Search, Scout, search . . . Find them.'

His faith in the quality of the dog's nose was total. The dog led him into an entry between the shuttered businesses, and then into a maze of shallow streets. They would have run. He did not need to. He walked briskly after the dog. He would follow his dog, wherever it led, until he had the chance to shoot. Repeatedly, from his dried lips, he whistled for the dog to slow so that it was not too far ahead of him, but the dog held the scent.

They were in a storm drain and ahead was light. Omar had found it and brought them into Kirkūk through it, bypassing a checkpoint. They were crawling in the drain and could hear cars close by and the thunder of lorries and personnel carriers. In places they were on their hands and knees, but when debris clogged the tunnel they crawled on their stomachs. At the end, where the light was, when they emerged, they would be beyond the city and the open ground would be in front of them all the way to the hills. The spirit had gone from Gus. He had no sensation of success, no pride in having made the calculations correctly for what anyone would have described as a supreme shot. Near the end of the tunnel, when he was lagging behind the boy, Omar turned, caught his coat and wrenched him forward. His hands slithered on the drain's floor, his head went down and the foul stale water was in his mouth. He flailed out at the boy. They had not spoken – other than the boy's shout for him to hurry when he had fallen from the top of the fence – since he had fired.

As if believing Gus hid behind an excuse, Omar rasped, 'You missed.'

'I did not.'

'You hit her, you missed the hangman.'

'I wasn't aiming at him.'

'You fired at her?' He heard in the darkness of the tunnel the bewilderment of the boy.

Gus nodded tiredly.

'Do you tell me the truth, Mr Gus? In fifteen seconds, half a minute, or five minutes, she was dead.'

'She was my target,' Gus said.

'Why – if she was dead?'

Flat words, without emotion, leaden words. 'So that she died at the hand of someone who loved her, and not

444

theirs. In our time, not their time. It's why we came back . . . The only thing I could do.'

They reached the tunnel's end. The bright light washed over them. Two hundred yards away, in Gus's estimation, to the right was a raised road on which were personnel carriers and troops jumping down from trucks. The drone of a helicopter was overhead. There was open ground then rock-strewn cover, but that was a mile distant. The boy crawled forward and Gus followed him.

From the side of his mouth, the boy whispered, 'I thought it was to shoot the hangman. I do not understand, and . . .'

'I don't ask you to understand.'

'. . . and, I do not think Major Hesketh-Prichard would understand.'

The body had been dragged into the compound.

The commander had seen the wound that had scattered the blood and tissue, brain and bone. Already the square in front of the gallows platform was emptied, and the work had begun to dismantle the scaffold. He was asked by one of them who had taken her out, who had the debris of her head on his tunic and picked laconically at it, whether the body was to be sent home, and he said it was to be buried, the grave not marked, and that a chainsaw was to be brought to the cell block.

Commander Yusuf went into the block and the door of the cell was unlocked. He stood against the wall, in silence, as the men with him began to kick the brigadier's prone body. Until the chainsaw was brought, he asked no questions.

*   *   *

The dog was in the drain.

While he waited for the dog to emerge, Major Karim Aziz saw the personnel carriers manoeuvring on the raised road to drive down on to the open ground. He stood tall, so that he would be seen clearly – and he would be known – and waved them back. The personnel carriers, with their heavy engines and stinking fuel fumes, would distract his dog when it emerged from the tunnel and would disturb the scent. He fluttered his handkerchief to the crew of the nearest circling gun-ship helicopter, pointed to the far distance in the west, and the beast veered away. He had no intention of sharing the chase.

Looked at casually, the ground ahead seemed flat, featureless, and without cover. Nothing was casual when Major Karim Aziz studied ground. There were shallow gullies worn away by the winter rain. One of the rain channels would lead to the tunnel's mouth. He waited for the dog to show itself.

The troops from the trucks on the raised road were forming, under their officers' orders, the line of a cordon behind him. He gestured that they should stay back. He slipped down, sat on a low rock, and watched for the dog.

He did not think of his wife, who would now be at work in the hospital, or his sons; he did not think of the brigadier in his cell, without a hand to hold, who knew his name. Far ahead of him, scurrying and hidden in the network of rain gullies, was the man he hunted. The bright heat of the day beat down on him, the ground shimmered and distorted his view, but for once his own eyes were not so important because he had the nose of his dog.

Away to the left, the dog came into view. It shook a rainbow of water off its coat. He whistled for it to sit.

An officer stumbled, puffing, across the dirt ground.

Aziz said curtly, 'You do not come within a thousand metres of me. You are spectators. He is mine.'

He went to the dog and praised it. Without the dog he would not have known where to search. At the mouth of the tunnel he could see the smears where their wet bodies had crawled, and bootprints.

The dog led and he followed.

They had reached the rough ground, where there were rocks, wind-stunted trees and low thorn bushes. They had cover now and could go faster. Sometimes they crawled and the sharp flinty stones worked rips into the padding on his knees and elbows. Sometimes they ran helter-skelter from rock to bush to rock to tree to rock, then paused while the boy made the fast, intuitive decision as to where their next immediate target point was. Gus's heel hurt worst when they ran, and the pain of it rivered in his boot and up his leg. The boy looked back each time he paused in a shred of cover, but Gus did not. He was aware of a deepening frown of concern on Omar's forehead, even though he said nothing.

Gus did not look back because he would have seen the sprawl of the city's suburbs then the high buildings jutting up, then the forest of faintly drawn antennae at the headquarters of Fifth Army. Hidden behind the sprawl, past the buildings, below the antennae, were the gate, the gallows and her.

In his aching tiredness, in the pain, he was aware of a remote but occasional piercing whistling, as if a hawk hunted behind him and called its mate. It was like the cry of the kestrels he had watched with Billings, the poacher. He did not look to see if a bird of prey worked the ground behind and below him. His attention was on the escarpment ahead and the little ribboned ravines set in it. After they had cleared the escarpment they would be on the high ground of the hills, and each nearer and higher hill they climbed would bring them closer to safety, and further from her. He wondered if the bird, the hunter, watched him as he struggled to keep the boy's pace.

It was theatrical but always effective.

A prisoner was in pain, and the resolve was slipping. The commander had never known it to fail. At the far end of the cell block's corridor, the cord was pulled and the two-stroke motor of the chainsaw coughed to life. The motor was revved viciously as it was carried towards the open door of the cell. The roar of the motor filled the corridor and hammered into the cell as the saw's teeth raced on the sprockets.

A prisoner would not know whether they would start at the toes or the fingers, then move to the ankles or the wrists, then lop off – as if a prisoner were no more important than an overstretching pear or mulberry tree – the knees or the elbows.

The kicking was over, and no question had yet been put.

Two men held the brigadier with his back to the wall that faced the door and held his head so that he would see the arrival of the chainsaw.

The commander had never interrogated a prisoner who could shut his eyes as the chainsaw was brought down to the corridor and into view through the open cell door. He stood against the furthest wall from the brigadier – as if that, too, were a part of the theatre – so that the blood spurts would not soil his uniform.

It was in the door.

Now, he asked the question. 'With whom did you plot? With which snakes did you collaborate?'

The arm was held out and the brigadier tried to make his hand into a fist, but the men prised open his grip and exposed his fingers. The chainsaw was carried closer.

The name of a general – but the commander shrugged, dissatisfied, because he knew the general was already in Amman. And closer . . . The name of a brigadier and the names of two colonels. They were posted as missing and were hunted. The teeth were an inch from the hand. The prisoner was screaming. The name of a colonel, but that was inadequate because the colonel had gassed himself in his car.

Held very delicately, as if it were a scalpel in an operating theatre, and not a chainsaw with a half-metre blade, the teeth brushed the skin of the brigadier's knuckle and the blood careered up.

'Please, please . . . the *sniper* . . .'

Two fingers had fallen away. The shriek was drowned by the noise of the saw's motor, but the commander did not raise his voice.

'Which sniper?'

'The *best* sniper . . . He is . . .'

It was always the risk, when the chainsaw was brought to an older man, that the heart would fail. The commander never heard the name of the *sniper*, the *best* sniper. As the third of his fingers dropped away, the brigadier convulsed and his head sagged back.

'Cut him into pieces, send him home. Charge them, his family, two thousand dinars for the fuel.'

His soft footfall slithered away down the corridor.

Major Karim Aziz tracked relentlessly after the dog, whistling every few minutes for it to wait for him. He thought that the man, this stranger who had come into his country and given him this ecstatic opportunity of triumph, sweated because the dog had a strong scent to follow.

And the man was tiring, and limping.

The sun was scorching hot above him, but was starting its slide. His own shadow was no longer at his feet but lay behind him. The escarpment, towards which the dog led him, would give the opportunity for him to shoot. Far behind him, in their wide line, the soldiers followed. Each time he whistled the dog sat and waited for him to reach it. Then he fondled the fur at the nape of its neck, whispered sweet things to it, and let it bound away on the trail.

When he stepped over slight seeping springs that would have been small torrents in winter and dried out in full summer, he saw the bootprints of the man, and the slighter prints of the child guide, who did not concern him. A man not near to exhaustion would still have been on the balls of his feet, but the prints were heavy, and one was favoured. He had not seen them yet, but he would have the chance to shoot when, riddled with the heat and tiredness, they scaled the crevice gullies of the escarpment. The man and his guide would be at the foot of the escarpment an hour before the fall of day, and then the chance would be given him. Before dusk, he would have the man in his sights.

The message was transmitted to Baghdad, to the al-Rashid barracks.

Commander Yusuf knew only of key personnel in the armed forces when their files were handed to him and he started to probe their lives.

Who among the best marksmen serving in the army was considered supreme? Who had the ambition to crawl into the nest of snakes? Who could, with devious cunning, live a double life?

There was a profile in his mind of this marksman rated as the best. He did not yet have the paunch of middle age, he was vainly conceited and would boast of his shooting skill. He sought out the company of high-ranking officers and enjoyed the privilege their company brought him. He was married into a powerful tribal group that provided access to the élite . . . From his long experience of smelling out traitors, the commander always believed that he could paint their portraits.

He settled in his chair and closed his eyes, and thought of the love of small children, and did not notice that outside the window, in the compound, the shadows lengthened and that the room around him darkened, and he waited comfortably for the answers to be sent back to him.

The sun's orb – bloody and red – teetered on the ridge of the escarpment.

When they reached the base of it, where the rock faces rose up from the rough slope of trees and bushes, Gus pleaded, 'Can't we stop? Can't we rest?'

451

The boy peered past him, then snatched at his smock and pulled him into the deep shadow of a crevice.

'Can't we stop – if not to rest, just for water?'

'We have to climb, Mr Gus, we cannot climb in darkness – no, I can, you cannot.'

'I have to rest. My heel . . .'

'Climb.'

'Omar, I am not a bloody goat. I don't spend my bloody life on bloody hills. I need rest and water.'

Gus looked into Omar's face. The eyes gazed away over his shoulder. He heard the faint whistle, the distant kestrel, and he saw the savagely cut frown on the boy's forehead. He turned, took the line of the boy's sight down through the rocks and trees and bushes, and saw the small glimmer of white. He raised the rifle and peered into the telescopic sight, but his shoulders shook with exhaustion and it was hard for him to focus on it and recognize it. The reticule lines in the sight were blurred. For a moment, before the shudder in his body jerked the aim away, he saw a sitting spaniel. It was a dog like Billings had had, always at his heel; a dog like the gentry used for picking up shot pheasants in the fields around the vicarage. Far below the dog, at three times the range of his rifle, was a slow-moving line of soldiers. The soldiers did not threaten him. He tried again to aim the rifle and find the dog but could not hold the stock steady – and he failed again even when he leaned against a warm stone face for support.

'How long?'

'The dog has followed us since we left the tunnel, near to the road.'

'All bloody day, then.'

'It has followed us and behind it is a hunter. He

452

whistles for it to stop, so that it does not come close to us.'

'Why didn't you bloody well say?'

'What would you have done, Mr Gus?'

'I'd have shot it.'

'You could not shoot the sky,' Omar snapped at him. 'Get on, climb. Climb fast.'

The boy had led them to a point where a fissure split open the escarpment wall, and the angle of the sun above the ridge created a darkness in the cranny. Gus understood the boy's skill in spotting the fissure from a great distance and leading them to it without detour and a search. There was a hundred feet to climb and the angle of it allowed him to crawl up. Stunted tree roots and heathers in the fissure made good holds and good boot-rests . . . He remembered what the Israeli had said, a long time ago, a lifetime. The hunter was a sniper, the sniper was Major Karim Aziz, who travelled with a reputation. He remembered how he had waited in the roof at the town and watched for him. He had forgotten the man until he had seen the dog. It was a lifetime back to when the Israeli had warned him of the sniper, as far back as his home and his work and the friendly firing on Stickledown Range. The past, the sniper, surged back into Gus Peake's life. His mind was rambling. The past was before he had killed Meda, and before he had kissed her. The voice of the boy drilled into him.

'You have to go over open rock. I cover you with shooting.'

At the top of the fissure was a smooth stone with lichen patches. He would be silhouetted, without the protection of the recess when he went over it, before he reached the safety of the ridge.

He heard the whistle. He did not know how he had been so stupid as to think it was a kestrel.

'Hurry. Be quick, Mr Gus.'

There was a blast of firing, on rapid, below him. He reached up, caught at the top of the stone, the lichen making his grip slip, and he sagged, then grabbed again, heaved himself up and over and into the light of the low sun. The boy was firing to distract the man who travelled with a reputation. His boot scrabbled to find a fresh foothold, his rucksack snagged – and he was over. He lay for a moment on smooth wind-scorched grass, and the panic caught him. The boy had exposed himself to draw the attention of the hunter. He wriggled round, lay on his stomach with the weight of the rucksack and the rifle pinioning his shoulders and reached out, over the rim, to catch the boy's hand.

Far back in the rocks, trees and bushes, caught by the last of the sun, he saw the flash of the glass of a 'scope. The boy had his hand. At that moment, the sniper would have a clear view of his head and Omar's back. He pulled the boy towards safety.

The boy shook. The weight of the boy was in his hand. The crack rang in his ears. He dragged at the boy's wrist. He heard the thump.

Gus pulled Omar over the ridge, the boy screamed, and then the quiet fell around them.

AUGUSTUS HENDERSON *PEAKE*

8. (Conclusions after interview with Dr Rupert Helps, consultant psychiatrist at Centre for War Studies, RMA Sandhurst, conducted by self and Ms Manning – transcripts attached.)

IRAQI ARMED FORCES: (From briefing given to AHP by Dr Frederick Williams, Senior Lecturer, as recalled by Helps.) Because of centralized command & control systems, the Iraqis will be slow to respond to initial attacks. Once initial surprise has been lost, the Kurdish irregular forces will face a tough experienced enemy that will quickly roll up their advance. A fighting retreat will put AHP in maximum danger of death or – worse – capture. It would provide grave embarrassment to Her Majesty's Government should AHP be taken alive and subjected to a show trial.

AFTERMATH: In the predictable 'roll up', there would be inevitable harsh reprisals against Kurdish civilians. This was pointed out to AHP; he may not fully comprehend the scale of such reprisals before he sees them, in retreat, at first hand. They will shock him and weaken his resolve to escape.

HELPS' ANALYSIS OF AHP: A romantic, decent and immature individual, and quite unsuited to the rigours of mercenary warfare . . . He should have stayed at home. He will have achieved nothing of value.

SUMMARY: A sane man would have rejected the emotional nonsense drip-fed to him by his grandfather. It is to be regretted that others – the rifle manufacturer, Royal Marines instructors, the freelancing 'Survival' expert, the lecturers at

RMA – co-operated with this lunatic idea . . .
They have all contributed to AHP's likely death
or possible capture. Isn't any man better off
when he's chasing after job promotion, searching
for a more satisfying sexual relationship,
pursuing hobbies, increasing his mortgage, and
offering himself for good works? Isn't he?

He had never been adept at the use of sarcasm. Rather
desperately, Ken Willet wanted to shrug off the envy he
felt. He wondered if, ever, he would walk up to this man,
take his hand and wring it, hold it, shake it – but he
didn't think he would have the chance.

By the time Dean returned from the travel agent's office
to confirm their flight out the next morning, Mike had
the drinks on the table. There was a beer for Mike, a
bourbon on the rocks for Dean, and a brandy sour
for Gretchen when she came down. They were both
showered and shaved, and wore the faded safari jackets
with all the pocket pouches for pens and film canisters
that were their uniform. Upstairs their bags were
packed. Because it was unlikely that they would meet
again, here or anywhere – because the world moved on,
Mike was retiring from the combat field, Dean's editors
no longer cared about little wars in remote corners of the
world where nothing happened, Gretchen's magazine
wanted glamour without misery – it would be a
nostalgic evening. There would be a good session, long
in the bar and late into the dining room, and each would
tell the familiar cobwebbed anecdotes, josh each other,
laugh on the same cues, and be a little thankful that it
was over.

Gretchen came into the bar. She was still in her drab, dust-coated trousers and sweat-stained shirt, her face and hair unwashed since the trip into Iraq, but her eyes were red and her cheeks smeared as if she'd wiped away tears.

'What the hell . . . ?'

She said faintly, 'Just tuning the radio, when I was running the bath, caught the Baghdad station, didn't mean to . . . They hanged her in Kirkūk this morning . . . They did it in public . . . They called her a traitor. The radio said they hanged her . . .'

'You mean she was real?'

'Real enough to be hanged in public, in front of a crowd outside Fifth Army's gates,' Gretchen stammered. 'She actually existed, and we didn't believe it.'

'That is some fucking story.'

'She led an attack into the city. She was captured, and tried by a military court. She was hanged – we doubted her – she is dead.'

'OK, OK, it's not fucking personal.' Mike had his notebook on the table. 'I can get radio on this.'

'You're going to get radio, I'm going for the front page.'

'Let's go, let's fucking hack it,' Mike murmured. '"The Kurdish people have lost today the brightest symbol of their heroic fight to rid themselves of the yoke of Saddam Hussein's terror. The symbol was a Maid from the Mountains, whose brief life was ended by public execution on a gallows in the centre of the Kurdish city of Kirkūk." How are we doing?'

'Going great . . .' Dean took it up, scribbling on his own pad. 'Para two . . . "Known only by her given name of Meda, this illiterate peasant girl had led a small force of courageous guerrilla fighters in a desperate attack against the might of Saddam's military machine. She was hanged in front of a huge weeping crowd, rushed to the gallows to forestall a rescue attempt." End para.'

'Para three . . . "Kurdish warlord, the veteran fighter *agha* Ibrahim, said this evening, quote, I feel that I have lost a daughter. Not only me, but the whole Kurdish nation is in mourning. She was a wonderful example of the supreme bravery of our people. She will not be forgotten. She has, today, lit a flame that will never be extinguished, end quote." I think that's reasonable licence – they'll never know.'

'It's bullshit, but reasonable bullshit. Last para, "Your correspondent had the privilege of meeting this remarkable young woman, deep inside Iraqi-held territory, a few hours before she launched her last attack against overwhelming odds. She told me, quote, I want only the freedom of my people. I appeal for American – and British – help, end quote. Slightly built, stunningly beautiful, wearing a red rose pinned to her tunic, she slipped away to fight and to die." That's it.'

They drained their drinks, asked Gretchen to get the next round in and went to their rooms to telephone. They were each in time, and grateful for it, to instruct their editors to bin the earlier pieces of shit they had sent before descending to the bar. It would be seventy-seven seconds for the radio and four paragraphs for the paper. It might get transmission and into print, and it might not – who cared?

It had been a fine shot, into the sunlight and with the elevation making the distance hard to judge, but he knew that he had missed his target.

He had waited until the darkness fell, then had sent the dog up the fissure, scrambling and dislodging stones, and had climbed himself. He had only had half of the head of the man, at an estimated distance of 520 metres, to aim at and he had hit the child.

He had heard the scream and, at the top of the escarpment, his fingers felt the clammy wet pool of blood, which he could not see.

He set the dog on the trail. There would be more spots of blood and a good scent for the dog.

As the night thickened around him, carrying the boy on his shoulder, Gus plodded forward towards the darkest line that was the mountains.

Chapter Eighteen

There was no emotional bond between Major Karim Aziz and the dog, Scout. He recognized the animal as a tool of his trade, less important than the old Dragunov, more important than his own eyes and ears. As the years had passed since he had picked up the abandoned, hungry puppy in Kuwait City, his sight had lost its edge and his hearing become more cluttered. Just as it was important to him to maintain the rifle to the highest possible state of perfection, he kept up an ever more rigorous training schedule for the dog. The affection he gave it was merely to guarantee its efficiency.

At first the dog had been a companion against the loneliness of his work, then he had started to recognize the potential qualities held in its twig-thin body. By the time he had gone north four years earlier, when the Kurdish saboteurs were pushed off the plains and hills into the mountains, he had understood the abilities of the animal.

It was ahead of him in the darkness.

He could list the qualities and abilities, and exploit them. The dog was inquisitive, intelligent, energetic and brave. Its low profile as it moved enabled it to see skyline silhouettes that he was unable to spot. Its hearing located movements, clothing against equipment or boots through mud, that were quite inaudible to him. Its nose was crucial, several hundred times keener than his own. Once Scout had found a scent – in the air or on the ground – a chain was established that was almost impossible for a fugitive to break.

He had made a study of scent: the strongest was given by sweat from the human body, the product of physical exertion and stressed tension. Unseen and unheard, hidden by darkness, the man ahead of him carried his wounded guide, and there would be exertion and tension that could not be disguised. Aziz did not believe the man would have been so careless as to smell of shaving lotion or cosmetic sprays, but there would be oil on his rifle and that, too, would leave a signature for the dog to follow. On the ground there would be disturbed dust, broken grass and earth scraped by a skidding boot, which Aziz would not see but which the dog would find. Beyond the range of his vision, the dog would scurry on a seemingly erratic course, with its nose down on the ground and then with its head up to sniff the evaporating scent in the air, which was special to the night and hung low in the chill of darkness.

The moon was up, and the stars. If Aziz had stepped out of a lighted building, he would have been blind, but his eyes were now accustomed to the blackness around him. He never saw the man he followed, but he kept the dog within his short horizon. The pace of the fugitive surprised him but he never doubted that Scout would hold the chain linking him to the man. Many times he slipped on smooth stones and stumbled into the secret dips in the ground, but he maintained his advance.

Aziz assumed the man knew he was followed and had by now registered the whistles, and he thought that, as the night hours elapsed, the man's exhaustion would grow and he would seek to lose the ever-present tail, but he had faith in his dog.

Later, as the burden became heavier and the man more desperate, Aziz expected to see the signs of evasion, but he did not think the man could trick his dog.

He was walking more slowly, but every few minutes he heard the clear, distant whistle.

Gus carried the rucksack, the rifle and the boy. He did not know what his rucksack weighed, but the rifle was fifteen pounds, and he guessed the boy was 125 pounds. The rucksack was on his back and the sling of the rifle was looped over his neck so that it hung down on his chest. Omar was draped over his shoulder. He did not know how long he could go on with the burden. He fell twice, but the boy never cried out, and each time Gus staggered to his feet and pushed forward.

The whistle was an infuriating constant, never closer or more distant.

The boy would tell him, in a small, weedy voice, which way he should go. He thought it extraordinary that, unschooled, Omar could read the moon's passage and the lie of the stars, and know when he was off course. Those he had met at the commando training centre, and the man who ran the survival school for the arrogant bastards and bitches on corporate adventure, would have needed state-of-the-art Magellan positioning handsets and readings off three or four satellites.

462

Omar guided him. Without the boy he would have blundered in circles. If the boy died on him then the dawn would come and he would be short by miles of the safety line.

The whistling tracked him.

They had talked to him about dogs at the commando training centre, and he scanned in his mind for the memory of what they had said. What he had seen of it, at last light, the boy's wound was high in the chest. There was only one. The bullet had not exited. The bleeding was also inside the boy, oozing from the wound against the rough cloth of the gillie suit . . . They had told him that water was the key to breaking the scent trail.

'I have to find a stream, a lake.'

'Go right.'

'Are you sure?'

'Can you not smell the water?' The question seemed to bubble in the boy's throat and Gus knew the lungs were damaged.

'I can't smell anything.'

'Go right, and you will find water.'

'Then we go away from the line – you have to be sure.'

'There is water.'

Each step hurt. Each breath was harder to find. Each jolt scraped the pain from the blister on his heel, merged it with the ache in his limbs and the emptiness of his lungs and the numbing pressure on his shoulder. Each pace was worse. He heard the tinkle of water running on stones.

'Can you go on, Mr Gus?'

'I can go on.'

He could go on because he still had the chance to live, and did not have a wound without an exit. He could go on because he had only the blister, the ravaged muscles and the burden, not a squashed rough fragment of lead in his body. He had to throw off the scent, lose the dog. He slipped down into a narrow stream and went against its flow. The stones under his boots were smoothed, as if greased, and the whistle was away to his left. The stream took him into a small lake. The ripples were illuminated by the moonlight on the water and he waded close to the bank. The water was cold heaven on the pain of the blister.

The boy's voice croaked in Gus's ear. 'I am cold.'

'I'll do something about it when I can.'

'I am not frightened, Mr Gus.'

'No cause to be.'

'You can leave me and have a better chance.'

'I would not leave you as I could not leave her.'

'Tell me a story, Mr Gus, from Major Hesketh-Prichard.'

His voice, however quiet, would carry in the darkness, but so would the sounds of his movement through the water.

Gus whispered, 'I always liked best the story of when they searched for Wilibald the Hun . . .'

Over and over again, Commander Yusuf read the reply from Baghdad, and the name of a 'simple soldier'. The man had been in his hand, but the hand had opened and the man had slipped away from him.

It was dangerous for a servant of the regime to be wrong.

He went to the door of the inner room and opened it. They were vulgar thugs, still wearing the same blood-spattered uniforms, and there was a near-emptied bottle of whisky on the table and filled ashtrays. He would not have allowed any of them to touch the sweet innocence of the grandchildren he loved. He had been fooled by a simple soldier with a record of distinguished combat in Kurdistan, along the length of the Iranian border and in Kuwait. When he had met him, he had seen nothing of ambition, cunning, access to the élite or vanity, and he could be blamed for opening his closed fist and allowing the supreme sniper in the ranks of the Iraqi army to walk away from him.

'The marksman, Major Aziz, where is he? Find where he is.'

They were drunk. They leered back at him. Could it wait until the morning? They were slumped in their chairs.

He walked to the table and kicked it over. The fury blazed in him. The whisky dribbled into the rug, the cigarette ash clouded them, and they cringed away from him. If the order came from a higher authority, they would carry the chainsaw towards him, and his hands.

'Now. Find him *now*. Where is Aziz?'

He went back into his room and dictated his instructions over the telephone to the night-duty staff at the al-Rashid barracks in Baghdad. It would be a bad night for him, he thought, and long.

He had stood by the high stretch of the water while the dog had searched the bank, careered between rushes and rocks and then had picked up the scent again.

It had been a predictable ploy, but he thought that the man had done well to find the water in the darkness, and he marvelled at his endurance. Aziz understood why the man pressed on in desperation.

465

If he had not had the burden of a casualty, and not felt the responsibility to carry the casualty back, then the man could have gone to a rocky outcrop and hidden himself and waited. The dog would have pointed to him, but the man would have given himself the chance, at dawn, when the light flickered across the ground, to search for his tracker and shoot and rid himself of the pursuit. But the man carried a casualty – the child guide – who was in need of medical attention if his life were to be saved. He thought that the fugitive must be a fine man: only a fine man would have accepted the responsibility of the casualty. He had met hunters, who went after deer, boar and wolves, who spoke with gruff awe of the evasion skills of the beasts they hunted – but the respect did not stop them stalking, killing.

Three or four kilometres behind him, a speck of white light climbed, then burst and fell. It was his link with the world he had left behind him, the struggling line of spread-out, wearied soldiers, making a rallying-point for the line to contract and come together for the rest of the night. He would not rest, not sleep, nor would the man he followed.

It was difficult, because of his tiredness, for Aziz to concentrate, but it would be worse for the man with the burden . . . He could respect him, and still kill him . . . To stall the tiredness he worked through the checklist. They had tried the water, and only delayed the dog. They could not climb up or down vertical rock to break the scent because the man could not do so with the casualty. They could not scale a tree, then crawl along a branch, then jump. The man could not run steadily, no sweat and no deep bootprints. He was going lethargically over the checklist when the dog came back past him.

He froze.

The darkness seemed tight around him. On the checklist was the circle back. He did not know how close they had been, so tired, to each other. He could not know whether the man and the burden had been fifty paces from him, or two hundred and fifty. Had they passed each other? Had the man seen him, and hesitated? Had he made a silhouette, and had the man reached to unhook his rifle from his shoulder, and had the moment then passed? The dog worked over two loops. Could they have shouted to each other? The circle back was predictable. Could they have blundered into each other?

By going into the water, and the circle back, the man had tried each of the principal evasion tactics. They had been used and had failed and the dog now tracked along a straight, true path – as if the man struggled in desperation to reach the ceasefire line, with his burden, before dawn.

'Did you tell me the story of Wilibald the Hun?'

'I did.'

'Can you tell me the story of Mr Gaythorne-Hardy of the 4th Battalion of the Royal Berkshires?'

'How he crawled in daylight to the German wire at Hill Sixty-three, Messines? I did.'

'I must have slept – please, tell me the story of the cat.'

The lake water sloshed in his boots but he had lost too much time to stop and empty them, and wring out his socks. He thought that the boy lapsed into and out of unconsciousness. More time had slipped away in the long circle back. Once, the dog had scurried on the loop run and he had seen its grey-white coat in the moon-light, but the scent had held its attention and it had gone by him. Once, too, he had seen a straight standing figure – a tree-trunk, a rock, the hunter – and he had held his hand over the boy's mouth to shut out the wheeze of his breath and the bubble in it.

There would be no more attempts at evasion. Omar had given him the star that was his guide. He had failed to break the track that the dog followed. It would be the same star that had watched him and Meda, the same star that had been above his grandfather and her grandfather at the ruins of Nineveh. He lurched on. It was darker now behind him and the gathering clouds obliterated the washed-out light of the moon.

'What has our father done?'

She could not answer her younger son's demand for an explanation. Men swarmed through the house. She knew what he had done because they had shown her the papers dug up in the garden. She had been shown plans of the city's north-west sector, with a ruler-straight line drawn from the outline of an apartment block to the outline of a villa, and with sentry-points arrowed and road blocks circled. She sat at the table in the kitchen with her mother, who wept, and her father, who held his head in his hands, and her sons, and watching over them was the barrel of a machine-gun. She had told the men of her previous day, the drive to the fuel station on the Kingirban and Kifri road outside Sulaiman Bak; they had written what she said. She had told them that her husband had said she was to bring boots for rough walking and food and a small tent; they had pointed on a map to the ceasefire line within an hour's drive of the fuel station. The kindnesses he had shown her over many years were now forgotten, and the intimacies. She told them, flat-voiced, how he had been away from her bed every night in the week before he had been ordered north, and of his distraction and nervous temper. Quietly – as her home was searched, stripped, she chased survival for herself, her parents and her children. She denounced him. She heard her elder son cruelly respond to the question.

'Our father is a traitor . . . I hate him, as you should . . . Our father deserves to die.'

His family were not in his thoughts.

He whistled again for the dog to wait.

Each step was harder. The hours were crawling away but he could sense no end to the night. Aziz had had to crawl on his stomach from a bog into which he had strayed. Those had been nightmare moments. The sinking mud had clung to his legs, higher than his knees, and he had only been able to use the one hand to claw his way free because the other had held the rifle clear of the filth of the bog. He could have died there, exhausted, watched by the dog, unable to pull himself out. The nightmare had edged towards panic before he had been able to get a grip on a stone at the edge of the bog and lever himself out. He did not think of his family, but the panic had surged because he had thought he would not fire the Dragunov again. Everything in his life, which might have ended in waste in the bog, was preparation for the long hunt of the fugitive and then the long shot on the target.

Aziz looked more often now behind him. He watched for the encroaching mass of cloud. It had not

469

yet reached the moon's half-light, which enabled him most of the time to avoid the bogs and the stones, and to see the dog ahead of him, but twice he had heard the thunder peal and once the ground had been lit by a sheet of lightning. In its flash, he had seen the man perhaps half a kilometre ahead. It had been a fleeting glimpse. He had seen the weight on the man's shoulder and the narrow outline of the rifle barrel stretching up past the hooded head. The man had not taken advantage of the moment to look behind him, and had trudged on, bent under the burden. He already had respect for the man's skill – the shooting, the fieldcraft and the dedication – but Aziz did not understand why the man had not dropped off the burden, laid it down, put a handgun or a grenade in the child's fingers, and moved faster and freer.

The bog's mud, clinging to his boots and his trousers, further slowed him, as the clouds closed behind him. The panic of the struggle to escape the bog was replaced by a new fear: of the clouds and the rain that could wipe out the scent the dog followed.

He murmured, 'Is that what you are hoping for, friend, the rain? Do you hope that the rain will cheat me? . . . How do you find the strength – in the name of God, where do you find it? If the rain does not come you will have to turn . . . You understand, friend, that it is not personal? I believe that a man such as you, a man I respect in all sincerity, would know that it is not personal . . .'

There was no past in his mind and no future. There was nothing of his family, and nothing of his own salvation. The present ruled him, was each slow step forward, and the bounce of the dog ahead of him, the struggle to hold the pace, and the glimpse of the burdened man in front of him, the massing of the clouds behind.

'It is the last ridge, Mr Gus.' The voice was beside his ear, quiet.

'Say that again.'

'It is the last ridge.'

A coal-black line was ahead of him and above it was the grey mass of the mountains. He had not noticed the dawn come. The whistle was in the air some way behind him. He did not know how far he had gone in the night hours, how many miles of slopes, screes and muddy pools he had climbed and crossed. He had lost the pain, killed by his tiredness.

'He is still with you, Mr Gus.'

'He is still with me.'

'To shoot you, Mr Gus . . . I am so cold.'

'We must keep you awake. It's time for another story.'

The wind gusted abruptly onto his back. It seemed to knife into Gus's shoulders, through the weight of the rucksack and the dangling legs of the boy. The wind went from moderate strength to fresh to strong . . . He would take the boy home. There was no clarity in his thoughts, and no clutter of passports, visas and immigration. He would take the boy home and put him in the spare room, find a chair for him at work, walk him on Saturday mornings in the high street, and drive him on a Sunday to Stickledown Range . . . The rain blustered on to his back. He would teach the boy to read the pennants that marked the wind on the range and the boy would call the deflections for the alteration on the windage turret of the old Lee Enfield No. 4, Mark 1 (T), and would lie beside him on the mat. The lightning split the skies around him – he did not look back because he knew that he was still followed – and the thunder boomed in its wake. With the boy beside him, he would win the silver spoons.

The rain came hard and sudden. He thought it had come too late, then heard again the whistle and headed towards the last ridge.

It was his agony: 'Why does he follow me?'

'You are the best, Mr Gus. If he kills the best then he is supreme. He follows you so that he will be the best.'

'Is that important? Does it bloody matter?'

'I think it mattered to Major Burnham, Distinguished Service Order, in the Matabele war, to be the best.'

Gus staggered towards the dawn and the last ridge, the rain and wind lashing at him. Beyond the ridge would be the valley with steep-set sides, and beyond the valley would be another climb, then safety. He was lurching drunkenly towards the ridge and the dawn.

'According to Major Hesketh-Prichard, the American – Burnham – was the greatest scout of that time. His finest achievement was to go through the entire Matabele army to shoot their leader, M'limo . . .'

'Can I say something personal, Caspar?'

'Be my guest. Shoot.'

In the darkness, under a buffeted umbrella, Caspar Reinholtz walked the shiny-faced man back to the shuttle for the flight to Ankara.

'There are people at Langley – this is not easy for me – who doubt you, Caspar.'

'That's their privilege.'

'Don't interrupt, please, because this is, was, a problem for me. They say that Caspar Reinholtz went native, had gotten himself emotionally involved.'

'Is that what they say?'

'Had gotten more Kurdish than the Kurds, had lost sight of our aims.'

'Do they say that?'

'They told me that you, Caspar, would dump shit on the new plan. I want you to know that I am going to kick ass when I get back, and tell everybody, whether or not they want to listen, that you are on board and could not have been warmer and more supportive of the new concept.'

They were at the steps of the plane, shaking hands, while the rain spattered up from the apron. At least the bastard would have a turbulent roller-coaster ride, with his balls in his mouth, hanging on, thinking of Mother. He had not mentioned her, dead, or the sniper, missing, or the fuck-up that was RECOIL. With any luck, the bastard would be tossed from one side of the plane to the other.

Caspar smiled. 'Do you know what Will Rogers said?'

'What did Will Rogers say?'

'He said, "We can't all be heroes because somebody has to sit on the kerb and clap as they go by."'

'I like that – good for a seminar. I appreciate the hospitality and I appreciate that you're not wallowing in what's gone, that you're right behind our plan. You're a good and valued warrior, Caspar, a true Langley man.'

The man ran up the steps of the plane.

'Have a good flight,' Caspar shouted after him.

In those last hours, he could have said that the plan was a piece of crap, that it was a coward's no-risk plan, and he, too, would have been on the shuttle out to

Ankara. He had whitewashed it, said it was a fine plan. If he had been on the flight there would have been denied him the small chance to meet the sniper, go with him to a quiet corner, and hear how she had died – maybe put some flowers somewhere. He knew he owed it to her. The same rain, the same storm, over those goddam mountains, would be driving on the man who had seen her die. He wanted that chance.

Trudging and stumbling, falling, dragging himself to his feet, kicking his stride forward, following the dog, Major Karim Aziz did not consider that he might have turned back . . . To have turned back was to face the past and the future. His concern, going forward, was to keep the rifle under his smock so that the working parts stayed dry. To stay awake, to be aware, to keep going forward, he recited the specifications of the Dragunov. *Cartridge*: 7.62x54R, including 7N14 AP. *Operation*: gas, short-stroke piston, self-loading. *Weight*: with PSO-1, 4.3kg. *Length*: 1.225m, with bayonet-knife, 1.37m. *Barrel*: 622mm. *Rifling*: 4 grooves, rh, 1 turn in 254mm. The statistics helped him as he moved towards the ridge where the dog sat and waited for him. They were slow, grinding steps. The raincloud scudded over him. Far behind him, a Very light was fired, and he knew that he, too, was tracked, that the line of soldiers had kept pace with him, that they had not halted for the night. The soldiers were his past and his future and, to blot them out of his mind, he dipped back into the comfort of the specifications. *Muzzle Velocity*: 830m/s. *Max Effective Range*: 800m–1000m. *PSO–1 Telescope*: 4x24, 68mm eye relief, 6deg field of view. The cloud lay on the ridge in front of him, grey on black, and the rain ran on his face, the thunder clapping at his ears.

He heard, ahead, a great bellowed scream, an anguished cry of impotence, before the gale carried it beyond his hearing.

'Does it go badly for you, my friend?' Aziz muttered. 'It goes badly for me. I respect you for what you have done, it is sincere respect, because it is harder for you than for me.'

Gus had known it since he had reached the ridge over the valley.

He had paused, gulped for air, wiped the rain from his face, tried to stand against the force of the wind, and known the boy was dead. He had laid him down, smaller – as if life was weight – and he had rocked and howled into the last of the night. The rain spat on the boy's face and ran rivers into his staring eyes. He could have left him there for the dog to find, and the man; he could have left Omar and won himself precious time, because the man would stop and circle the corpse, then go close and examine it. He picked up the boy and heaved him again over his shoulder. Omar had said that the pit of the valley, under the ridge, was the ceasefire line beyond which the man would not follow.

It might have been a shepherd's trail he found, or a track used by wild hill goats. The rain sheened its surface. He went down the path heavily, slipped clumsily because he had the boy on his shoulder and the rifle to keep dry. Other than the occasional rumble of thunder and the spatter of rain on him there was a great silence that not even his boots or the tumble of small stones broke.

There had been a moment when he had felt grief, but it had gone. He moved more easily with each descending step as if, again, the freedom were given back to him. The boy was dead, and she was dead: the burdens were lifted. If he survived, he might have time to mourn.

In the pit of the valley he had the rush of the swollen stream to guide him.

Gus found a big flat rock, hewn smooth by a millennium's torrents, and laid the boy's body on it.

He paddled in the water around the rock and arranged the body so that it lay on its back. It no longer had a meaning to him. The arms hung loose. He did not think that the rain would cause the river to rise enough to dislodge the body.

On the far side of the stream, as he started to climb, he heard the distant whistle.

There was no pain in his body, no aching, no hunger or thirst.

An hour of darkness was left him. Gus scrambled up from rock to rock, stone to stone, catching at stumpy bushes that took his weight.

He could have gone on, he had the strength. He could have reached the ridge on the far side of the valley, could have left the man and the dog far behind him.

Halfway up the slope, he crabbed off the path. He moved slowly on his side and carefully, without the awkwardness of his descent, worked to lodge himself between the stems of the bushes so that he would not crush them.

When he settled he took the rucksack from his shoulders, wrapped his one towel from it around the length of the rifle, and then, with his penknife, he started to cut short sprigs of bilberry and dead bracken from around the place he had chosen. When he thought he had sufficient he began to hook them into the straps of hessian that the women, an age ago, had sewn to the suit.

All the while, the rain relentlessly beat down on him.

'I'm George. Very good to meet you, Carol. It's not often enough that we have the chance to share snippets with our sister service. And you're Ken, right? Ministry of Defence? Very pleasant to meet you.'

He stood and shook their hands. There was a gushing charm to the greeting that Willet thought worse than insincere. The Security Service would be lesser beings, and Ministry personnel would be primitives. The security staff at the building's main entrance had directed them to the bench on the embankment. Willet had been rather looking forward to gaining admittance to the secure sanctum of the Secret Intelligence Service, something to gossip about when he was back at the Ministry. But no conference room was offered them, no opportunity for rubbernecking the interior. They had been told they were expected at the fourth bench, going east towards the Festival Hall on the river's south-side embankment. George had been waiting for them, and was lighting a cigarette as they approached.

'I hope I don't have to apologize for meeting you out here, but it is a nice morning and I always say the view of the river is delightful. It's not that I'm a fresh-air freak but we have a Fascist correctness inside. Can't have a little puff indoors. I was once on night duty, dying for a gasp, and I crawled underneath my desk and lit up. I was right under the desk but the bells still went, and the gauleiters came charging in . . . Now, how's the young man doing? Is that what you want to know? I don't mean to be rude, far from it, but is Augustus Peake any concern of yours?'

'We think so,' Ms Manning said.

Willet challenged. 'If a British passport holder, with a bloody great rifle, is tramping around northern Iraq – with the consequences that entails – yes, it is a legitimate concern.'

George was fifty-something. He wore a loose cardigan that had been knitted for him, Willet thought, by a woman who had overestimated his size. He had a blotched face and thinning hair, and he coughed on his cigarette. It was early in the morning, bright and cold, and the wind came up off the river. Office workers, hurrying to be in before nine, strode meaningfully past them, and were interspersed with joggers pounding along the embankment. Willet hadn't thought to bring a coat and shivered. He thought making them use a public bench was the height of rudeness, and calculated.

'I come out here about three times a day and the river's sights never fail to fascinate me . . . It's all over. I'll backtrack – and what I tell you is American material because we don't have the resources to be on the ground there – and start with the march. It lasted a little more than a week and, like most of the Kurd expeditions down from the mountains, it ended in tears. The serious fighting involved some initial successes, then a suicidal raid into the city of Kirkūk – that period spanned five days. He's a transport manager, you know, with a small haulage company and I would say it is fair to assume that they've been a long five days.'

'But he survived?'

478

The moment after the cigarette's ash had fallen on his tie, George threw away the butt and lit another. Willet waited for his question to be answered, stared out at a small tugboat going downriver towards Parliament, dragging a line of barges. He thought it was a rotten damn place to be discussing the nothing chances of Gus Peake's survival.

'No news, in this case, may be good news. What I can say, we do not know either way. Most of the force that retreated from Kirkūk with their wounded made a successful return to the ceasefire line. He was not among that group. On the other hand, had he been taken by the Iraqis, if he was in their custody, we would probably have heard by now. I have to assume that Augustus Peake is currently in a no man's land and legging it back, like a hare with a thorn up its bum, towards safety. That's what I'd be doing, but I'm not him.'

'There's a woman.'

He gazed at her, then sniggered, '*Cherchez la femme* . . . When was there not a woman? Excuse me, please, my dear, I don't mean offence. Yes, there *was* a woman. It's all in the bailiwick of the Americans, you understand, and tied to their obsession with removing that man who's been in their faces for so long. Quite a simple plan really – triple-pronged. The President is assassinated . . . an armoured unit in the north mutinies and drives south . . . A woman is a useful symbol of equality, modernism and leads a tribal force into Kirkūk. It was a grand idea, but it didn't work. The President is alive, the unit didn't mutiny, she's dead. Dispiriting, really.'

The cigarette was gone, thrown after the previous one. There were pigeons gathering near them, as if they expected a feast of bread, not smoking butts. A destitute woman, carrying a cider bottle, swayed optimistically towards them but was waved imperiously away. Willet thought they were like the trustees after the death of a childless widow winding up her estate without the charity of respect.

'How did she die?' Ms Manning asked.

'Quite a pretty woman by all accounts, and charismatic ... It's confusing. What is clear, a sniper was sent from Baghdad to counter Augustus Peake. That sniper disabled the woman's transport during the fighting in Kirkūk and she was taken prisoner. The death is what's confusing. The Iraqi news agency is saying she was hanged in public, but rumour in the city has it that she was shot at very long range moments before the rope was put round her neck. She's dead, that's what's relevant, she's out of the picture ...'

'"Long range" – did Gus Peake shoot her?' Willet asked.

'I really wouldn't know, I wasn't there. Who would you trust for accuracy? The rumour mill in Kirkūk or the INA? It's not much of a choice if you're looking for reliability ... Eight years ago, in the uprising after the Gulf War, Kirkūk was held by the Kurds for a few days, then the army pushed them out and the citizenry fled to the mountains. Many died there, starvation, cold. They're back in Kirkūk, those people, older and wiser, chastened. They turned out in big numbers to see the execution. Look, city people rarely fight, they leave it to the peasants in the hills, they watch to see who is going to win. The word is, and it's probably sentimental twaddle, that the crowd did not jeer and abuse her as the Party hacks would have wanted; they watched her die in complete silence. That's promising, for the future. Mythology comes from death, and mythology – martyrdom – is something we can work on.'

'What exactly does that mean?' There was threat in Ms Manning's voice but the man chose not to recognize it and puffed at his newest cigarette.

'Obvious. You can't stand still in this business. Mythology, out of martyrdom, can sire insurrection. Policy, as laid down by our revered masters . . .' He waved, a gesture of contempt, towards the towers and façade of Parliament across the river. '. . . dictates that we seek insurrection in that awful little corner of the world. The word of the hour is "proxy". Other people do the dirty work, get the shit on their boots, follow the myth of a martyr, and we achieve – at minimum cost – the aims of our policy. Please, my dear, don't look so squeamish.'

Willet interjected. 'Are you telling us that there were two snipers in Kirkūk – and one of them was Gus Peake?'

'That is a fair assumption.'

'How long ago?' A hoarse question.

'Twenty-four hours. Probably while I was sitting here yesterday and poisoning myself . . . Do you know about snipers?'

'I failed the course.'

'Bad luck. My father was a sniper in Normandy, 1944, but not a very good one. I rang him last night, to get a viewpoint. What he said, about the best of them that he'd met, they're proud, solitary and élitist, and they never did understand when it was time to wander graciously home. I go as often as I can to see friends in Scotland. Sometimes it's the time of year when the big stags are rutting and fighting off the young pretenders

– basic machismo sexual stuff. I've that image in my mind of locked antlers. Up there you find the skeletons of massive beasts, antlers entwined, who fought too long, went on with a dispute ages after the combat should have ended, were mortally weakened, could not disengage, starved to death together. It is glorious and pointless. The Iraqi is a Major Karim Aziz who instructs on sniping at the Baghdad Military College. He wouldn't know when to quit. Augustus Peake, in my opinion, has the temperament of a hunter. A gambler never walks away from a final throw of the dice, a hunter never turns his back on a target. More than courage, it is about obsession. Just before I came down to meet you, I spoke with my esteemed American colleagues at Incerlik for an update. There's no word of Peake having crossed the ceasefire line . . . Let's mix the metaphors. The gamblers have probably locked antlers.'

'Did you like Peake?' Willet asked softly.

'Did I say I knew him? I didn't hear myself say that.'

'You knew him because you had met him, and you must have encouraged him.'

A cigarette end was discarded. The packet was retrieved from the pocket, another cigarette was lit. The packet was pitched expertly into a rubbish bin beside the bench. George stood.

'My advice, young man, learn to walk before you try to run.'

'You encouraged him, and you may have helped to kill him.'

'So nice to have met you, Carol. Something for you to remember, Ken. Policy is our god. If little people, silly people, stray off a safe path and into the territory of policy, they will be exploited. Policy is a long game. This game has only recently started – but if we already have a martyr and a myth, it has started promisingly. Good morning.'

When the dawn came, both men – too tired to dream – slept. Between them was the river and the wide stone on which the carcass of the boy lay.

Chapter Nineteen

Abruptly, suddenly, the dreamless sleep was finished.

Gus woke. He jerked up, blinked, and did not understand. He was wrapped in a grey-white shroud.

For a moment, no thought, he flailed at the sheet, beat at it because it seemed to suffocate him, and could not move it. His fists punched the sheet, were absorbed, and it pressed down on him.

He sagged back.

He wiped hard at his eyes. The sheet was pegged just below his feet and just beyond his head, and the memory of where he was, what he had done, filtered back to him.

The rain had stopped. There was a stillness. The cloud nestled over him, but the thunder had rolled on. The sleep had not rested him. Together with the understanding that the cloud over the valley covered him came the tiredness and the slow, aching pains and the hunger.

At that moment, because he had lost hold of the emotion, he could have gathered together his kit and the rifle, and used the cloud as protection to crawl away up the slope towards the hidden ridge. He could put it all behind him and start out on the journey to the frontier, to an airport or to a lorry park.

Gus thought he was blessed.

In the scramble of his thoughts, as the residue of sleep was pushed aside, he realized the value of the cloud that sat tightly on him. Faces and voices slipped across his mind, competing for attention. Each gave him an opportunity, and it was no longer possible for Gus Peake to gather together the kit and the rifle and climb to the top of the slope.

He murmured, 'I am blessed because I am here and because you, sir, have followed me. There is no hate, no slogans of politics, there is no baggage of distrust. I don't know what your shooting range is called, I don't know where you go to pit yourself against opponents and elements. My range is Stickledown. It can be quite a pleasant place in summer – birds, flowers, good light – and it can be a hell of a place in winter, believe me, wind, rain and flat, dead emptiness all the way to the butts and the V-Bulls. Thank you for following me, because it's like I'm on Stickledown and shooting for a silver spoon, and you're on your range and shooting for whatever prize is important to you, and for both of us it is real. You could have walked away from me, I could have walked away from you, and both of us would have been left with dried-out lives. Do you understand me, sir, am I making sense? No-one else will understand me or understand you but, then, I don't think either of us would ask them to. We are blessed, we can only use the blessing. I'd like to have met you, and talked with you, but . . .'

He could not hear the rambled words he murmured. It might have been the tiredness, the pain or the hunger,

485

but he felt, to a slight degree, better and more settled for having talked. He thought those other voices – from the kitchen, the factory, on the Common, at the tent camp, in the office, on the bench – would have understood what he said, and why.

Blessed . . .

He shook himself, cleared the chaff from his mind. The talk was finished. He was blessed because he was given time by the density of the cloud hanging in the valley.

Where he lay there was sparse cover from stubby wind-broken bushes with the first buds of bilberry fruit and a rock that covered his shoulders and flattened lifeless bracken. It was a useful place for a firing position. He felt a keening breath of wind on his face: he must use his time because soon the wind would carry away the cloud cover and he would be able to see what lay before him. He rummaged in the rucksack for rounds of his Green Spot ammunition, took two from the tissue paper in which they were individually wrapped to prevent scrape noise. The magazine was already loaded on the rifle, five bullets, and he did not believe he would have an opportunity to fire more than one. He polished the two rounds so that the Full Metal Jackets shone, would catch the light when the cloud was gone. He had no string, or bandages, so he unwound the towel from the barrel and working parts of the rifle, made slits in it with his penknife at the ends then tore off narrow strips of fraying cotton. He knotted them together. Because of the thinness of the strips, the cotton rope he made would not take a weight and would snap at a violent pull, but it would be of sufficient strength for his purpose. He would have liked it longer, but that was not possible.

He tied one end of the slim rope to a shoulder-strap of the rucksack and tested the knot with a gentle jerk. The rucksack shivered with a slight movement.

He was satisfied. His hand dipped again into the rucksack and retrieved a khaki woollen ski hat, and used the penknife to snip off more stems of the bilberry bushes, weaving them between the stitching.

He placed the rucksack half behind the rock and masked it with bracken fronds. He laid the two rounds of Green Spot ammunition on top, and behind them he put a stone the size of his hand. Over the stone he placed the wool hat.

He crawled away, paying out the length of towel rope, burying its length under further pieces of bracken. He used the sideways crawl – which they had shown him on the common and called the 'slug' crawl – so that the trail was minimal. When he had paid out the towel rope he was some twenty feet away from the rucksack. He was on a flat ledge of broken-down bracken, without stones, rocks or bushes, without serious cover.

Gus could not tell how long he would have the protection of the cloud. He worked at controlled speed, but not in panic, to snatch at the bracken, tear it up and make a blanket of it over his boots, legs, body and head, and over the rifle, the sight and the barrel. Then he draped the hessian net over the brightness of the 'scope's lens.

He settled, waited on the wind, and wondered what his opponent was doing.

Through patience, Major Karim Aziz had learnt to hold the present in perpetuity, at the expense of past and future. The patience was based, as if embedded in concrete, on certainty.

He had slept for three hours. He had woken and immediately felt alert and alive. His resting place, chosen in pitch darkness, was under a flat slab stone that jutted out over a small table of grass that in turn gave way to sheltered ochre bracken fronds. If he had thought of the past or the future, he would have walked down the slope, through the blanket of cloud, and climbed the far side to safety.

Patiently he had watched the wall of lightening grey mist that was around him until, imperceptibly, it began to fragment. He had confidence in himself, and in the man he thought of as a friend, and confidence in his dog.

The cloud had started to break above his eyeline.

First there were lighter points, then blue islands, then a first glimpse of the sun. The cloud served him well, satisfied him. It had blocked out the early-rising sun, which would have peeped over the ridge on the far side of the valley and beamed onto him. He would have been looking into the sun in the early morning and his side of the valley would have been illuminated. It would have been the point of maximum danger when the sun's strength caught the colouring of his face, penetrating under the stone slab, nicking the lens of his 'scope. Later, when the cloud blanket was burned away and the sun was higher, the stone slab would throw down deep shadow over him and his rifle. Much later, towards the end of the day, the sun would be behind him and its power would fall on the far slope. Then it would search for the man, his friend . . . That was the present, and all else was forgotten.

When the sun fell on him, through the cloud gaps, he squirmed as far back as possible into the cavity under the stone slab, and his hand gently, tenderly, ruffled the hair at the dog's throat. His preparations were made and he had no doubt that the man, his friend and adversary, had stayed.

As the cloud thinned, pushed away by the wind, so the vista of the valley opened before him. There were gullies of dark rock with silver ribbons of water from the night's rain; scattered trees, clumps of wild fruit bushes, small patches of gorse, bracken and heather littered the rocky ground. There were dispersed rocks, open stone screes, and pockets of grass. It was good terrain for him and for his friend. He stared out over the carpet of cloud that filled the bottom of the valley, where its dispersal would be slowest, using his binoculars with a cotton net over them. He thought that a lesser man than himself would have peered at the unveiled expanse and harboured doubts.

He would not want to fire the one bullet, ready in the breech mechanism of the Dragunov, until the sun was behind him, playing on the slope opposite, but he had already made the necessary preparations for that moment, still many hours away. His patience would see him through the waiting. He was on his stomach and his head was behind the 'scope, his body twisted so that his legs could splay out under the slab. He would be hundreds of minutes in that position, without food, without water and without sleep. He was as comfortable as he could make himself as he studied the ground on the valley's far side. There was a symmetrical shape to it. He estimated that the twin ridges bounding the valley were 1,300 metres apart. Both then fell sharply before flattening to a more gradual incline that in each case, at its limit, almost made a level plateau. On his side, looking across the cloud floor, he was close to the lip of that plateau. He reckoned that its forward edge on the far side, matched and dotted with trees, occasional protruding rocks, bushes and weather-flattened bracken, was 700 metres from his position. Below the lip, where he looked from and where he looked to, were cliff faces that fell into the cloud, tumbled stones and rare paths where animals or shepherds had made precarious tracks. There were fissures now in the cloud floor below and he could hear more distinctly the roll of a water torrent among rocks. Directly facing him was a rambling track that led up, across the plateau and then towards the far ridge, similar in every way to the one on his side down which his dog had led him before he had veered off and stumbled into the cavity below the slab.

From the side of his mouth, he whispered to the dog, 'You have to be very strong and very patient, but I think my friend is there. In this life, nothing can be guaranteed, but I do not think the man, my friend, would run from me. My concern is the casualty he carried and his desire to find help for the child guide, but he is very tired. He has carried the child, who must have been precious to him, for a great distance – I could not have done that – but I cannot believe he would have had the strength in the time that was available to him to take the casualty up the first difficult climb, then across the easier plateau, then up the second climb. But, more important, I do not think that such a man would pass over the chance to face me. We are solitary people – I laugh when I say it, we are also possessed of a great arrogance – and we wait for the day when we can confront an equal. What else is there, in this life, but to take up a challenge that is offered? I do not think he will have cheated me.'

490

He passed a biscuit to the dog, the last and damp from the bottom of the backpack, and apologized that he had not brought more food for it.

A shaft of sunlight broke the mist cover below him.

He saw the body, laid out on a smoothed wide stone around which the swollen river funnelled.

There was a dark stain high on the shoulder. It had been laid there with dignity and he saw, through the binoculars, that the eyes had been closed and that the arms had been laid at rest at the sides, and he thought the young face was at peace, the pain gone.

The body was where he was guaranteed to see it. The sun blazed down, destroyed the mist. He had not been cheated. He had not doubted the man, his friend.

Very carefully, concerned that he should not make sudden movements, Major Karim Aziz began to scan the steep slopes and the plateau across the valley, over the body.

'Oh, by the way – I should have told you this morning, just didn't get round to it – last night on my voicemail, my leave has come through,' Ms Manning said. 'All the days in lieu that I'm owed, two weeks – thank God.'

'What are you going to do with it?' Willet looked up from the console that he had just switched on.

'I've got to see my mother, she's had a bit of bronchitis, and I thought of a week's sunshine break, Tenerife or—'

'That'll be nice,' he said heavily. He pointed to the screen. 'What do I do with this?'

'Slam it in, and get on with other things. It's finished, as far as I can see – look, it's been good working with you, but there's no-one else to see. We did what we were asked to do.'

Willet said coldly, 'I don't suppose there is anyone left to see.'

'This sort of business always ends with a whimper. I don't like it any more than you, but it's what happens. Maybe we'll meet up again.'

Willet gazed into her face. 'He's a victim. Won't anything be done about the people who used him?'

'Shouldn't think so,' she said. 'They're always forgotten, always hidden, always protected, those people.'

'A *victim*, for Christ's sake . . .'

She fidgeted for a moment, awkward, then said, 'I don't deal the cards. It's been good knowing you. My advice, meant kindly, type it up, hand it in, and start at something else.'

'He deserves more . . .'

She pulled the door closed behind her with the firmness of finality.

His fingers rattled on the keyboard.

AUGUSTUS HENDERSON *PEAKE*

9. (Conclusions after interview with George — (identity unknown), SIS Vauxhall Bridge Cross, conducted by self and Ms Manning, transcript attached.)

VICTIM: AHP in my opinion was manipulated by SIS. A man of limited intelligence and sparse experience, he was encouraged to travel to northern Iraq and involve himself in a hare-

492

brained scheme where other more powerful forces might win, where he would most certainly lose.

BLAME: There was a trail of Open Doors. SIS was at the heart of a programme aimed at deceiving AHP. The trail, and direct responsibility for it, leads to SIS. They and many others should take accountable responsibility for the utter precariousness of AHP's position.

SUMMARY: For a raft of reasons, AHP was allowed to travel to northern Iraq with a 'slim to non-existent' chance of survival, in order to push forward matters of HMG policy. He was an innocent. His inevitable fate is a matter of public scandal.

TO BE COMPLETED

Irritably and impatiently, he flicked into the file for the number. When he had dialled it, and it had been answered, Willet had to wait a full four minutes for the junior-school teacher, Meg, to be brought to the telephone in the headmistress's office.

He blurted breathily, 'It's Willet here, I met you on that disgraceful early morning when we barged into Mr Peake's home. You should know that he is currently in northern Iraq, being hounded by a pursuit force of the Iraqi army. There are many who are culpable for his situation, but you should also know that you are one of the few without blame. I apologize for disturbing you ... It's not your fault but it's in the hands of the gods now.'

There was a shocked, stunned silence, then the phone rang off.

He would deal first with those who were without blame. He dialled the number of a vicarage built in the countryside under old trees, but the phone was not picked up. Then he rang the number for the modern bungalow behind the vicarage, and heard a faint, aged voice.

'Wing Commander Peake? It's Willet, from MoD – I came to see you with Ms Manning of the Security Service. I have to tell you that I have a very poor view of elderly men sending the young to their deaths. Your grandson is somewhere, at this moment, behind Iraqi lines and hunted like a dog – because of you. You indoctrinated him with that rubbish history of your "friendship" with Hoyshar, the Kurd. You fed it like bacteria into his system. You took him back there ten years ago and further infected him. You passed on to him the letter that has probably killed him. You, because of your background at Habbaniyah and in the Kurdish region, had occasional contact with the Secret Intelligence Service, and I believe that you informed them of the letter. You set this process in motion. Where doors should have been locked in the face of your grandson, they were opened and his journey was made possible. What you couldn't achieve yourself, you sent someone else to do. I hope you can live with that, what you've done to your own blood. Good-day, Wing Commander.'

The line of troops had bivouacked in small cluster knots for the night, and endured the storm.

At dawn they'd been caught in the cloud and had had to wait until it dispersed.

The line had formed again, and pressed on. They had reached the ridge and seen the body. The officer, on the radio, reported back to Fifth Army in Kirkūk that, beyond boot marks in the mud at the summit of the ridge, there was no sign of the foreign sniper, or of Major Karim Aziz, and that the valley below him seemed at a cursory glance to be empty . . . except for the body. The officer said that the body confused him: it was not abandoned, not dumped, but laid out as if it were a sign or a symbol that he did not understand.

The troops around the officer squatted down and began to eat their rations.

He lay across the line they took.

They had red-brown bodies and were twice the size of what Gus knew from home.

Each of them, each of the thousands, found him blocking their track, crawled onto his body, then diverted in search of his flesh, and bit him. Every last one of the little bastards bit him fiercely. They had fangs and venom, and they bit his ankles and the skin at his waist, and were up under the gillie suit. They found the skin at his throat and his face, and they bit his hands.

The bites, the injections of the venom, were all over his body, itching and hurting. Anywhere else he would have paused from lining up his aim on the target and would have swept the little bastards to oblivion. He could not move. He could not swat them and could not scratch the wounds they left him with. When he eased his glance to the right he could see them coming for him in a long, limitless line.

It might have been for half an hour that the ants

crossed him and crawled on the rifle, and after them it was the turn of the flies.

The sun was high and had settled a haze over the valley when the flies came in the wake of the ants. There would have been his sweat to attract them and the raw pimple wounds with the blood, and the urine that he had leaked into his trousers. They flew against his hands and face, hovered in front of his blinking eyes, insinuated under his face net, up his nostrils and into his ears. The flies inflicted more wounds and drew more blood. After them were mite-sized creatures from the bilberry bushes, then spiders from the bracken circled him and feasted.

He remembered the bubble. Inside it, where it never rained and was never too hot, where the wind never blew, there were no ant columns, no flies, no mites and no bloody spiders. He imagined himself to be inside the bubble's comfort.

The sun at its height, with its haze, seemed to burn steam off the floor of the valley. His eyes were tiring from the long hours of searching through the 'scope. He whose eyes lasted best would win. It was hard to see the detail on the valley floor through the steam mist and sometimes the body of the boy was reduced to a blurred outline. Hard, too, to gaze across the valley and identify individual rocks, particular bushes and isolated clumps of vegetation that made cover.

He yawned hard, and that broke the walls of the bubble. He yawned again, then swore to himself. The Iraqi would be on the plateau across the valley at his level, not on the steeper slopes above because there the range would be too great, and not among the rocks below, because there the cover would be harder to use.

He searched and could not find, and he knew he should rest his eyes but he did not dare. He looked for light on metal or for a clean line where there should be only a broken one.

When the sun dipped, sank, then the haze over the valley would be gone. The light would be into his tired eyes, and the gentle slope of his plateau would be clearly lit to the man on the far side. He had to believe that inside the bubble his eyes would not tire, or he would lose.

He heard the crows calling, above him, high over the valley floor as they circled the smoothed stone on which he had laid the body.

Did they have doubts, the men he had read of and whom he believed he walked with?

Aziz knew the names of some with whom he believed he walked, but some were anonymous to him except for the reputation of what they had achieved. It was unsettling that he had doubts that gnawed at his patience . . . There was an American marine who had confirmed a kill at 1,290 metres across the river at Hue; and another marine with a known-distance range map who had hit at 1,150 metres, witnessed and written up by his officer, in the Vietnam Central Highlands; and there was Carlos Hathcock who had taken seventy-two hours to move just one kilometre and then had killed a general of the North Vietnamese army at 650 metres. He knew their stories, but did not know whether they had harboured doubts at the moment when they squeezed the trigger.

Had the rifle held the zero? He lay under the jut of the slab and the worry fretted at him. The Dragunov, with the PSO-1 telescope sight, had held the zero the last evening when he had fired on the man and hit the boy, but the doubts lingered because he remembered each stumble in the night and every jolt on the rifle. He had tried to protect it, because the rifle was his life, but he could not be certain he had succeeded. The 'scope seemed solid on the stock, but if it had shifted half a millimetre, he would miss and he would lose, and he would not walk with the great men.

His mind flitted on, sifting the doubts. He had sunk in the bog; the mud had cloyed round him, he had cleaned the outside of the rifle and the inner parts of the breech. What if a speck of mud was in the rifling of the barrel? The round would go high or low or wide, and he would lose.

In front of the muzzle of the barrel, he had cleared a small area of bracken fronds so that he had a clear shot ahead. To the sides he had thinned the bracken. What if, when he identified the position of his friend, a single frond blocked a clear shot? Billy Sing, the Australian – and Aziz knew of him from his reading in the library at the Baghdad Military College – had killed 150 Turks at Gallipoli. He would have squirmed in anxiety lest his bullet nicked a single frond or blade of grass or twig. A bracken frond close to the muzzle, unseen through the focus of the 'scope, would deflect a bullet travelling at 830 metres a second and he would fail.

He thought of the great men of the Civil War in America – Virginius Hutchen, Truman Head and Old Thousand Yards, who was the buffalo hunter – and he believed they would all, in inner secrecy, in their lying-up positions, have entertained nagging doubts about their equipment. He would not know the answer to any

498

of his doubts, or whether he would ever walk with the great men, until he fired.

He heard the crows, and that pleased him. He watched them circling, and he thanked them because they turned his mind from the doubts, and he started again, through the heat haze, to search the far wall of the valley, and the plateau.

Once a month, Lev Rybinsky drove his Mercedes up the winding stone track and brought Isaac Cohen a twelve-bottle crate of whisky and gossip, and was paid for both commodities in crisp new dollar bills.

That midday, mopping his head with a handkerchief and pocketing the money, he told the Israeli of new gun positions on the *peshmerga* side of the ceasefire line, and of what was said in the bazaar in Arbīl about the hanging of the woman in Kirkūk, and of the pillow talk of the *agha* Bekir's treasurer that he had learned from a whore in the UN club at Sulaymānīyah, and of . . . but the Jew hardly seemed to listen.

'Do you remember, Rybinsky, the sniper with her?'

'I met him. I talked to him. He said that a big sniper had been sent from Baghdad for him. I told him of the duels between snipers in my city, Stalingrad.'

'You are so full of shit, Rybinsky.'

'How people in the city watched the duels, wars within wars, primitive, and took grandstand seats and would bet . . . Did he run away, too, and leave her? I have not heard of him since she was taken.'

'I have it from the radio intercepts – you should get yourself there.' Cohen went to the wall map, used his pointer and gave the six-figure reference. 'That is where they are, to duel.'

'He was not experienced.'

'Then you should bet on the Iraqi.'

'I told him about Zaitsev and Konings, at Stalingrad, how they watched for each other, stalked each other. Zaitsev had the experience, as does the Iraqi.'

'I give you fifty dollars, Rybinsky at two to one against, that the Iraqi sleeps tonight with God.'

They shook hands, Rybinsky wrote down the grid reference and hurried to his car.

Commander Yusuf was brought a transcript of the radio signal from the ceasefire line.

'Where is this place?'

He was shown it on the map, a finger prodding into an area of wilderness. He pondered, gazed at the harsh whorls of the contours and the shaded empty spaces without marked roads. He was a man of streets, buildings, restaurants, wide parade grounds, prison yards and cells, and he had no familiarity with such a place.

'How can it be reached?'

Lev Rybinsky found Sarah at the clinic she held each week in the schoolhouse at Taqtaq, and pushed his way past the queue of waiting pregnant women. He shooed out the patient on the couch and ignored her protest.

He told Sarah why he had come.

Her face widened in astonishment.

'Not only do I give you morphine and penicillin, I give you sport.'

'You are sick, Rybinsky, fucking sick and warped.'

But she wrote down the map reference, closed the clinic for the day, and ran out into the sunlight to her pick-up.

*　　*　　*

'Is that Davies and Sons, the haulage company? I'd like
to speak with Mr Ray Davies – it's Willet, Ministry of
Defence.' He waited, listened to the tinny music over the
telephone, then heard the voice. Willet said brusquely,
'I'd like to congratulate you, Mr Davies, because you
damn nearly fooled me. I thought you were merely
stupid. I now know better. I assume that, with lorries
running all over Europe, you quite often do little courier
jobs for the intelligence people. I assume that you had a
call before Gus Peake said he wanted to travel to Turkey
and gave that preposterous story about needing
to understand better the drivers' problems. You made
available a lorry with a secret compartment where
the rifle could be hidden from foreign Customs. To
a degree you are responsible for Mr Peake's present
situation – he is lost in northern Iraq with half of their
regular army chasing him. Well done. My suggestion,
you put a notice in the trade magazines for a new transport manager because you'll be needing one.' Willet
paused, listened to the question from the other end.
'Why are you responsible? Instead of opening the door
you could have slammed it on him, and saved his life.
You ingratiated yourself in the hope of a future favour
– probably a blind eye turned to another of your dodgy
consignments. Good-day.'

He slammed the telephone down hard, and his hand
shook. Then, again, he pecked into the file for a number.

'Mr Robins, please. It's Willet of MoD. No, it's not
urgent, it's not a matter of life and death – it's past that
time . . .' He was told that Mr Robins was unavailable
because he was on business in America. He left no
message and limply set down the telephone. If the

501

connection had been made, he would have said, 'Mr Robins, good to speak to you. I thought you would like to know that in the report I am writing on the journey by Mr Peake to northern Iraq, and what we believe will be his subsequent death there, I hold you partially responsible. I have reason to assume that you were told by SIS to give what help you could to Peake. Of course, you didn't demur – you were advised by a faceless bastard that an opportunity now presented itself to gain Green Role battlefield experience for your .338 calibre Lapua Magnum rifle at a time when it is still under trial. What a heaven-sent chance to find out how the bloody thing stands up to combat conditions. You could have told them at Fort Bragg or Leavenworth or Benning or Quantico, and at Warminster and Lympstone, all of the damned rifle's tested qualities – good for the old export business, yes? Right now, his situation behind the lines is quite desperate. Sale or return, wasn't it? I don't think it will be returned – such a bloody shame.' He would have liked to say that.

'What's it to me?'

'It would be like standing with him, for God's sake.'

Joe Denton knelt in the minefield with his back to her. She had shouted from the road to him what the Russian had told her. The line of V69s where he worked was particularly difficult because they were dispersed into a gully, and over the years sediment had covered them. It was a place too complicated for local men, even those he'd trained. He looked after himself, and thought he did not need emotional baggage.

'If you used your eyes, Sarah, you'd see that I've got a job of work here.'

'Please, Joe, it's important to me – and I think it's important to him.'

He swore under his breath, pushed himself up, gathered together his probes and the shovel and the roll of white tape, and walked back up the cleared path. She showed him the map and gave him the grid-reference figures. He climbed into the passenger seat and planned a route.

The dog's panting was worse. Aziz, himself, even in the heat when the sun was high, could fight thirst and endure a dried-out throat and the aching in the stomach.

He had no water for the dog. Even if he had had water in his bottle, if he had remembered to fill it from puddles or the rushing streams during the night, he would not have been able to retrieve it from his backpack because that would have created too great a disturbance. With gentle movements of his trigger hand, he tried reaching behind him, to soothe the dog's heaving motion, but his eye never left the 'scope as he tracked it across the far wall of the valley.

The crows were lower in their wheeling flight. He found now that they came into view, and sometimes he allowed them to lead him in effortless slow arcs. When he followed them, raking the ground against which they flew, he was more relaxed, his eyes less tired. But the crows, wary and wild, were dangerous to him. The crows, with their suspicion and their needle-sharp eyesight, were on level flight with the stone slab at the plateau's rim. If they saw him move, they would twist away. If they spotted his head moving or his body turning, they would scream their warning. They were his enemy and his ally.

'My friend, how goes it with you? How is the hunger, and the stiffness? Are you well, my friend, or are you suffering? If you move the crows see you, if they see you I see you . . . but it is the same for the two of us. It is my dog that suffers worse than me and I cannot tell him that his suffering is not for a great time longer.'

In front of Aziz, where he had cleared the bracken, there was a small patch of shadow thrown from the stone slab. The shadow reached, now, to the muzzle brake that reduced the flash signature on firing. When the sun had lowered behind him, when the light of it shone with force onto the far valley wall, when it covered the cleared space in front of the brake, then he could loose the dog to tumble down the path and drink in the stream on the valley floor. Then it could go to its work. If he was to win, and earn the right to walk with the great men, then the dog was the key.

Aziz soothed the dog, and watched the crows floating lower.

It pecked at a worm, sodden, lifeless, drowned in the dirt.

The bird strutted in front of Gus, holding the worm in its beak, and gobbling it down.

He had watched the drifting tilt of the sun and in his 'scope there were now small shadows in front of the rocks on the far side of the valley, and in front of the bushes. The advantage was ebbing towards the man across the valley as the haze of the heat cleared.

Gus knew why the crows flew lower, but he could shut that from his mind and the mass of flies that swirled round him. The ants had reversed their march and came back over him, eagerly searching for flesh to bite. Some had crawled into his socks, down the ankle support of his boot, had found the open blister, had used their teeth on it and their venom. He could dismiss that pain and that raw irritation, the stiff ache of his body and the growl of his stomach, the stink of urine in his trousers – but it was the small bird that frightened him.

The instructors who had been with him on the Common then sat with him in the pub bar had said that all wildlife should be avoided, but birds above all. There had been a sniper in the First World War, an Australian – and even eighty-odd years later the instructors had seemed to know the story by heart, searching for his Turkish opponent in a field of ripe barley. It had been extraordinary to Gus that their stories were old, as if past history carried relevance to today's present . . . The sniper, crawling so slowly and so carefully through the barley, had seen a lark. There was no panic about the small bird as it flew for food and came back to one point in the field. On the death stalk, the Australian had been drawn towards the bird and gone close enough to see its nest and the fledglings it fed. Near to the nest, so still as not to disturb the bird and send it chattering away, was the profile of the enemy's face. The Australian had killed the Turk, one shot, and felt no remorse, only 'hot pride'. The lark had made the kill possible, had drawn the sniper's eye to the target.

The bird had finished its feast on the worm.

It pirouetted on its spindly legs then twisted back to preen its wing feathers with its beak, then hopped up.

The bird was the size of the sparrows, robins, chaffinches and tits for which his mother put out seeds, nuts, lard. It had bright colours and a piping call. The bird's new perch was on the foresight of the rifle. He was frightened because he did not know whether a man peering into a ten-times magnification telescopic sight, hundreds of yards away, would be drawn to follow those bright colours, as the Australian had been.

His survival, and he knew it, was about small things. With a newer, harsher intensity he began, again, the search of the imagined squares his mind made across the width of the valley.

The crows were lower, the sun was fiercer in his face, and the end of the towelling rope was close to his hand.

It would be soon.

Chapter Twenty

It was a landscape without pity, a place too barren for the civilization known by the watchers who dribbled towards their positions on the high ground above the valley. Too remote for settlements, too unyielding for cultivation, too boggy or stony or steep for the grass necessary for grazing animals. But each of them, coming to their viewpoints, recognized a savage, cold magnificence.

As they slowly descended, the crows were still wary of the feast presented to them, but were gathering courage as their shadows swept the stone slab, and the body lying on it.

On one side of the valley, facing the watchers, the shadows were lengthening and were darker. On the opposite side, where other watchers searched for a target to hold their attention, the sinking sunlight stripped the ground of cover.

None of the watchers believed that they had long to wait.

The dissembling heat was long gone as Aziz, relentlessly and remorselessly, searched the far slope with his closest focus on the plateau.

It surprised him that he had not yet seen the man. He knew that his own stamina would not survive another night and into another day, that he must force the issue in that late afternoon while the light gave him advantage. The skill of the dog would not last without food through another night, and nor would he. He reflected that the time was close when he must push his luck and his fortune. And he reflected, too, on the core conditions of the counter-sniper. The words he used in the lecture room at the Baghdad Military College, and on the range outside the city, played in his mind. *Pro-action* or *re-action*. The counter-sniper could either locate his target and fire the first shot in the combat, or he could lure the enemy into shooting at a false target, identify the firing position, then strike back. It was the great dilemma, but the choice was not his, because he had failed to locate the target, and the issue must be forced.

He ruffled the dog's collar. The panting was not so fierce, it was now cooler in the cavity under the stone. His tiredness and his hunger worried him. If he did not shoot soon he was anxious that his hands, in fatigue, would shake and his eyes would be misted, and that – from the hunger – his concentration would waver. He talked softly to himself, and to the dog, as if that would calm the shake, clear the mist and hold the concentration. He imagined that he stood at the lectern in the lecture theatre at the Baghdad Military College, with students arrayed in front of him.

'It is a lonely world, and a world where only the strongest win. It is a world of physical strain and psychological stress. It is a world of vendettas, inhabited by eccentrics and solitary men who have, above all, the

508

hunter's spirit, who chase the challenge from which they cannot escape.

'It is a world where time has stood still, where the past is the present and the future is not recognized. More than eighty years ago, a tank first saw combat and in that time the tank has changed beyond belief, in armour protection, mobility, firepower. The artillery has developed since those days and now relies on laser sights, night-vision equipment that highlights targets believing themselves invisible, and the accuracy given by the computer's chip. But, in my world, the sniper's world, little has changed.

'I glory in the age of my art. I am soft-skinned, without armour. My 'scope, the barrelling of my rifle and the quality of my ammunition have changed little in those eighty years. I do not hide behind the advances of technology.

'I live because I employ the old arts of fieldcraft and concealment, because of the patience I can muster, because of my skill.

'I belong to myself.'

There were always blank and baffled faces staring at him from the raised seats in the lecture theatre.

He would do it in a few minutes, send the dog, because the lowering sun would make it the optimum time for success.

Aziz could see, when he raised the elevation on his 'scope sight, broke the search at the level of the plateau, a small knot of people – men and a woman in a pink blouse – sitting on the distant ridge, beyond the range of the Dragunov.

*   *   *

He tried, and tried without success, to control the clutter of his thoughts.

The view through the 'scope's lens, over the rocks, grass, slopes, shadows, bracken, bushes and a jutting slab of stone, threw up the faces. A shepherd gazed at the peace around him . . . A lieutenant paused in the sunshine as he emerged from the darkness of a bunker . . . The officer was going into the command post . . . But the faces were of the dead.

He was responsible. Was he evil? Psychopathic? Could he shelter behind the comfort of the excuse that he served a cause? He had not known them. He had killed men whose names he did not know. Was it wrong? There was no-one to tell him, no-one to give him an answer. Not his grandfather, or the people who had helped him. No message from good old George, smoking himself to bloody death. No-one could say to Gus Peake whether he had done wrong and he didn't know himself.

He saw the pale features of Omar and then they were blocked from him by the fluttered wingspan of the boldest crows. Then he saw the beak rise and fall on the face, and others came and fought around the boy's head.

He tilted the sight savagely and the view ravaged over the valley wall and the plateau, up to the ridge beyond. There were soldiers in combat uniform there, and a small slightly built man in olive fatigues who stood apart.

He knew again that he had much for which to be grateful to the boy. The faces were gone, and the guilt at their deaths had been put aside.

'Come on, sir. I think you are hurt worse than I am . . . And you have travelled with a reputation, while I have only silver spoons. I think the reputation must make it harder for you. Be quick, because soon the sun is in my lens. Hurry it . . .'

Rybinsky had the sandwiches and passed them round, but Sarah watched the crows at the body and refused. Joe ate and shared his water bottle with the Russian.

Rybinsky, between mouthfuls, said, 'They are here, I know that because the body is here. The body is the glove of the challenge. I have two to one against the foreigner from the Mossad on the hill, I am prepared to take other bets. Sarah, I give you evens on the Iraqi, I think that is fair. What do you want, Joe, Augustus or the Iraqi? The odds I offer are good. The Mossad wagered fifty American dollars.'

'You are a pervert, Rybinsky,' Sarah said.

'I am merely a man who enjoys an entertainment. Joe?'

Joe thought for a moment, as if he weighed the form. 'Twenty on the Iraqi.'

Sarah grimaced. 'I feel ashamed of myself and disgusted by you but twenty-five on our man at two to one against, yes?'

Their hands met; the bets were sealed.

Rybinsky frowned. 'What confuses me, why is he here? Why is the foreigner here – for what? I am here to make money, Sarah is here because she has compassion, and she can smoke grass, Joe is here because his inflated wage is tax-free and he lessens a little the chance of children being maimed. The Mossad on the hill is here because Iraq is the enemy of his country. We all have the best of reasons for being here, except him. Why is he here? I do not understand.'

Joe took a sandwich and offered his water. He said grimly as he gulped, 'If either of you sees him, makes a gesture, points, identifies or distracts him, I'll kill you – with my own hands.'

It had been a long journey for the commander. He had travelled by car on the metalled road, then by jeep up rough tracks, then on foot. That he had embarked on the journey was a record of his nervous anxiety. He recognized the vulnerability of his own situation. The man had been in his hand, had slipped through his fingers. If the man escaped him, it might be whispered by the many who hated him that the escape had been facilitated. The many who had cause to loathe him could whisper that the loyalty to the regime of Commander Yusuf should be questioned. If his loyalty were to be investigated, his life was threatened. Suspicion was sufficient for the taking of a life, and those of a family. He thought, in his extreme anxiety, of the men searching a room, stripping the possessions of two sweet small children.

'Who will win?'

Perhaps the officer hated him. Perhaps – and he would not know it – he had interrogated the father, brother, cousin or friend of the officer and was loathed.

'It is not in our hands,' the officer said quietly. 'It is in God's hands.'

He had known where he would find him, and was not disappointed.

Willet saw the solitary figure on the bench and the wreath of smoke blowing from his face. He strode forward, along the embankment, through the crowds who

512

pressed around him and scuttled for their trains and buses home.

He thought that what he had done that day was what was owed to Augustus Henderson Peake. He had phoned those individuals who had helped Peake, and told them where he was and why they were, in all likelihood, responsible for his death.

A cigarette was thrown away; another was lit.

'Ah, the telephone freak – the man with the conscience. I've been hearing what you've been up to.'

'I came because I wanted you to know that I hold you in contempt.'

'That's trite.'

'Listen to me – he was decent and honourable. He may have been immature and ill-equipped, but he didn't deserve the open doors that will kill him for nothing.'

'Trite and romantic.'

'He was sent to his death, and you knew that was the way it would end,' Willet barked.

'I think, from within your little army shell, that you have learned surprisingly little of human nature.'

'I know about exploitation and manipulation.'

There was a small smile, that of an older man forced to explain the obvious to a juvenile. 'Hear me out. We deal in the commodity of grown men who make their own choices. Around the world, in the darker corners, at any day of the week, there are a hundred men like Peake. They work for aid agencies, they are businessmen, tourists, journalists, academics, whatever. They paddle around, and if they come back they are debriefed. They are *volunteers*. We're not nannies and he's not a victim. He is an adult, and he is grateful to me

513

– not that he knows it – because I gave him a chance of personal fulfilment.'

A tired grin, and the cigarette was tossed towards the clutch of pigeons.

'I think you've shortchanged him, Captain Willet, and have not recognized the dream in us all, and the utter thrilling excitement, which so few of us are ever fortunate enough to feel. I believe that Augustus Peake would find you rather dull company . . . Ah, my last one.'

The empty packet was thrown skilfully into the rubbish bin, and the cigarette was lit.

'You know so little. Did his grandfather tell you about blood spilled a half-century ago? Were you told that men died in a mountain village so that his grandfather would live? No? There was a debt handed down, grandfather to grandson, and an obligation that it be, someday and somehow, repaid. If you think it was exploitation and manipulation you are merely naïve. Before he left, he sat where you sit and thanked me for the chance given him – you wouldn't understand.'

George wandered away, as though further explanations were no longer necessary, leaving Ken Willet behind him, bruised.

At that moment, Aziz thought of the future. The future – if he waited for the darkness and climbed back the way he had come – was his family being made to pay for the bullet or the rope, and was his body in the hands of the torturers, and was his life. The future was also – if under the darkness he went down to the river then up the far side and out of Iraqi territory – the existence without dignity or pride of the rootless exile. In the future, he would never walk with great men. This would be the last opportunity.

He pulled the dog from behind him, grasping tightly at the nape of its neck and dragging it into his body. It was only an animal, a trained beast that was eager to please, but it had the power to destroy the future and maintain the present. He held it against his chest and murmured the commands in its ear. It was the moment for which, over many hours, he had trained the dog.

He trusted the dog, as he trusted his rifle. He trusted that the dog and the rifle would hold the zero. He had no other chance but to lay his life with the animal. He saw the bright light in the eyes of the dog and felt the whip of its tail.

With a sudden movement, as he whispered to the dog, he threw it out from the cover of the cavity under the stone slab and towards the track he had come down in the night. It landed, stumbled, then pounded away from him. He could not know whether the dog would respond to what he had whispered in its ear. A great void settled around him, with its warmth and its breathing gone.

He could not see it. Lying under the slab, its descent on the track was hidden from him.

The void was filled. Aziz had never known such pumped-up, electric excitement.

As Gus tracked over the lengthening shadows, there was a fleeting movement at the extreme edge of the lens' view. He breathed hard, then edged the 'scope back. His breathing came faster. He found the spaniel.

The end had started and, if he missed the trick of it, he was the loser, and dead.

Its head was low on the path as it came down, as if there was still a scent to be found after the rain, and still bootmarks to be recognized. It came fast, without hesitation. He thought it a fine animal, but pushed the distraction from his mind. His view was off the slope and the plateau across the valley, where the man waited with his rifle. Gus must follow the dog's run. Everything that had seemed of importance to him now rested with the dog.

It came to the stream and the crows scattered from the body, rose above the bloodied carcass. It leaped into the fast-water pool beside the smooth stone and he saw that it cooled itself, bathed, and drank. The crows shouted at the interruption and flew circles round the dog.

As the dog came onto his bank of the stream, there was a sudden rainbow cloud over it as it shook the water beads, diamonds, from its coat. He thought that the dog was the man's last throw. The dog was there to be shot, to be sacrificed, had been loosed for Gus to fire at, and show himself. When it had shaken itself it squatted and defecated, then began to circle and to search. The dog was a decoy, as important as a plastic pigeon in corn stubble, as valuable as a papier-mâché head poking up over a parapet. He wondered how long the dog had been with the man, how much love had been given it, how much care, and how much misery the man now felt having loosed it, or if the life of the dog did not matter to him.

The crows were back again on the body, their feast resumed.

The dog found the scent in rocks and mud and grass. It came up the path that shepherds had made over generations with their goats and on towards the plateau. Gus was torn: he must follow the dog, watch its progress. He had not seen the point from which the dog was sent, but he had taken note of the strata of the plateau where he had first seen it. Which trail must he follow? The one that would lead him to the man, or the one that would save himself? Near to where he had first seen the dog was bracken, a bush and a bilberry patch; close by was a stone slab with a dark curtain of shadow beneath it.

The dog came up the path and followed his boots' tread from the night.

His attention, concentration, was divided and he knew that that was the man's intention. The sun teetered on the far ridge. If he should lift his gaze, he would be blinded by it.

Gus held the rifle so that the 'scope sight covered the ground where he had first seen the dog, but he twisted his head fractionally so that he could watch its approach. He thought he was losing and was out-thought.

. . . The memory came back – he should have shut it out and could not – of the officer who had come to the school in his last year. Gus, the sixth-former – Gus in the current-affairs session – Gus listening to the paratroop officer, a Falklands veteran of the previous year – the officer talking about combat, but dressing the reality up in the jargon of duty, stoicism, patriotism because that's what he would have thought was right for the kids to hear – Gus realizing that the officer was using fantasy bullshit, not telling them the truth of clinging to life, game time over, survival – Gus, afterwards, alone beside the cricket pitch, wondering if the ultimate truth, never spoken of by the officer, was total and exhilarated, heart-pounding ecstasy . . .

Across the valley, did he feel the mind-bending, addictive, narcotic excitement – or was he sad that the dog might die?

The dog paused at the point on the path where Gus had come off it, where he had started to crawl away from it, and searched, and Gus's finger tightened on the towel rope.

Sarah said faintly, 'It'll find him, the dog will find him.'

Joe said, 'Don't interfere, just watch. It's like nature, it takes its course. You are not a part of it.'

Rybinsky said, 'If you interfered you would break the bet. And, more important, if you interfere you destroy the supreme moment in the lives of them both.'

The dog – Gus was forty yards from it and saw it clearly – scampered in a small loop round that place on the path. Its nostrils were up, flared.

He had been told that a dog could find ground scent and air scent; there wouldn't be much from the ground for it to work off after the night rain, but the air scent would be heavy with his sweat and urine where he lay, and from the rucksack, which lay ten yards away.

It turned off the path, came slowly towards the rucksack and towards Gus, following the trail on which he had made the slug crawl. The care he had used to avoid breaking the twig stems of the bushes was sufficient to have hidden his movements from later discovery by a 'scope at long distance but was wasted effort against a dog coming close. It knew the source of the smell was near. He recognized the quality of the dog's training because it did not blunder forward or bound right up to the source of the smell. From a long way back, out with old Billings – and from a short way back, in the pub with the sergeants – he had been told of the difficulty of teaching a dog not to run over the smell source. It hesitated and strained against its instinct, then it went rigid, with the right paw cocked and the eyes wide, its neck stretched out, and it pointed. The body of the dog pointed towards the rucksack. He could see every hair on its head, the claws on the paw, the saliva at its neat little mouth.

The aim of the rifle would be on the dog and on the ground ahead of it.

He thought the man would now be breathing hard, squinting into the 'scope, locking the butt against his shoulder, feeling for the trigger, and searching the shallow area of ground the dog marked for him.

The end of the towel rope was between his fingers. He gripped it, took up the slack until it was taut, then jerked it.

It was a slight movement. The cap filled with stones and embedded with bracken fronds would have juddered. The polished Full Metal Jacket bullets would have rolled. The rucksack would have swayed. Only the keenest eye, at 750 yards, aided by a sight, would have seen the motions of the hat over the rucksack and the gleam as the low sun caught the twisting bullets.

He hoped, had to, that he had trapped the attention of the man.

The dog's chest heaved, and it maintained the point.

He pulled sharply. The hat would slide away. The bullets would shimmer and fall. The rucksack would surge sideways as if a hunted target tried better to hide himself from the dog.

Gus did not know whether he had done enough to kill a man.

He was surprised.

He had thought better of his friend.

The dog pointed for him. Ahead of the point was an upstanding rock surrounded by a meld of downed bracken and sprouting bilberry. Aziz's track through the 'scope sight had gone a minimum of a dozen times past the rock and not lingered on it because it had seemed to him too obvious a place for a sniper of quality to choose for concealment.

But there had been movement at the rock, he had seen it, and there had been two moments of bright reflected light that had caught the lowering sun. He had blinked, then slipped a finger from the trigger guard and wiped hard at his eyes, which were old for the work and starting imperceptibly to fail him, and he saw the olive-green shape.

On the shape, indistinct, bracken and bilberry were set as camouflage.

He thought the clear, angled line of the shape was the shoulder of the man, his friend.

His eyes smarted and he wiped them again. The dog he loved – seldom admitting it – in whom he trusted, had not backed off from the movement, and still pointed at the target.

The wind had not risen and not fallen; no adjustment was necessary to that turret or to the distance turret.

It was said amongst the best of the snipers, those with whom he wished to walk, that they should cultivate the sixth sense, the intuition of danger, but Major Karim Aziz was too tired, too wearied, to recall what he had read or what he knew.

His last thought, before he fired into the chest of the body, where the clear lines did not match the lie of the ground, was that the man had disappointed him by choosing a place to hide as obvious as the upstanding rock.

The crash of the shot burst in his ears, and the butt hammered against the bone of his shoulder.

The crack.

The gabble of syllables in his throat.

The thump.

Gus screamed.

The scream came from deep in his gut, from far down in his throat. The scream was pain, shock. He tilted his head up so that the scream would echo over the space of the valley, and he gave the final ravaging pull to the towel rope.

When the scream died, when the rucksack toppled and was still, there was a small silence. Then the crows rose from the body, chorused the scream and gave it strength.

It was how Major Herbert Hesketh-Prichard would have done it, and Crum and Corbett, and Forbes, and the glassmen who were Lord Lovat's gamekeepers. It was what Kulikov had done when he lay beside Zaitsev, and Konings had fired.

After the scream, the quiet fell, and the birds circled and dived again.

His 'scope roved close to where he had first seen the dog on the far side of the valley.

He saw the face. It was, because nothing had altered with time, as the old men would have predicted. It was grey against the shadow under the stone slab. Nothing was different since Konings had fired, and Kulikov had screamed, and Zaitsev had seen the face, the target.

Gus took the deep breath to still the beat of his heart, then let the air slowly slip from his lungs, held it – began the slow and steady squeeze of the trigger.

Sarah's head ducked to her knees and the first tears gleamed on her cheeks.

Joe swigged on the water bottle, and threw it – half full – away from him.

Rybinsky reached in his hip pocket for the roll of American dollars, peeled off a twenty, and passed it to Joe, but it was not taken and fluttered loose, drifting in the wind towards the ridge of the valley.

Further down the slope, the dog still pointed.

At the bottom of the slope, the crows again pecked at their feast, undisturbed by the moment.

Across the valley, the commander swore, turned away, and thought of the children who were precious to him and the enemies who would gather.

The sun teetered on the ridge, blood-crimson red, and its flame seemed dulled.

It was the last moment in which Major Karim Aziz, skilled instructor and failed traitor, husband and father, could touch the present. When the moment of triumph passed – and it was clear in his mind – he must confront the past and the future.

To touch the present, the triumph, he squirmed

forward from the cavity, and he felt the aching stiffness, the coming cramp pains.

He could not see, from the back of the cavity, the triumph. He must witness it, indulge himself. Then he would rightfully walk with the great men of history. He could not yet see the body and the now useless rifle of the man he had thought of as his friend. At that great range, Aziz did not realize that the angle of the dog's head had shifted fractionally, that the line of the dog's eyes and nose was towards open ground twenty paces beyond the upstanding rock.

Without witnessing it, the triumph was diminished.

He lifted his head higher.

He did not hear the shot, did not see the vortex of the bullet's swirl, he did not feel the strike of the bullet. He was thrown back into the depth of the cavity.

Gus stood, stretched, then bent down to pick up the ejected cartridge case, and pocketed it.

He trembled.

The bracken he had spread over his body, his head and the rifle barrel cascaded down to his boots.

He left behind him the smoothed hollow where he had lain through a part of a night and the whole of a day, and the length of towel rope that was the mark of a killer's deceit. He walked, awkward and swaying, to the rucksack and could not still the shiver in his hand as he untied the towel's knot to it. Then he dropped the hat and the two polished bullets into it. It was only when he lifted the rucksack to throw it on his shoulder that he saw the clean pencil-sized hole in its fabric.

He walked on, where before he had crawled, with a

drunken stride. There would be guns on the far ridge, at the extreme of their range, but he did not care.

It was over.

Where there had been excitement there was now only a desperate emptiness that numbed him.

He came to the dog and heard the low, throttled growl. If he had died it would have been because of the dog. It did not back away from him and had no fear of him, and the hackles rose on its neck. He had watched the path of the bullet towards the man who had trained the dog, and in two long seconds the excitement had drained, as he saw the man pitched back into darkness, and he did not know whether the man was wounded, in pain, bled, or was dead.

Gus reached down, grasped the scruff of the dog's neck and lifted it – as old Billings lifted dogs – and he slid its small shape up under the weight of his smock, and he thought that was the least he could do for the man who had hunted him and who had been beaten only by the scream. He was crushed by the emptiness in his soul, and he did not know of the wild, thrilled excitement that he had given to the man he had shot.

He did not know that he would shoot again, in two weeks, on the range at Stickledown and that Bellamy, Rogers and Smyth would crawl off their mats to watch the accumulation of the yellow markers on the V-Bull, and that Cox would pack away his Garand rifle, hover behind him and shake his head in awe, that Jenkins would rummage in his kit for an old, tarnished silver spoon and present it to him, that the report of the vintage Lee Enfield No. 4, Mark 1 (T) would blast out over the familiar heathland.

And he did not know that a young officer, from the

Ministry of Defence, would come and grip his hand, mutter apologies to his sun-gaunt and hurt-ravaged face, when he would not understand what offence demanded apology.

And he did not know that for a month the city of Kirkūk would be under military dusk-to-dawn curfew because her name was scrawled on walls and beside her name was painted the crude outline of a rifle shape topped by the bulk of a telescopic sight and that a torturer would be recalled to Baghdad for investigation.

And he did not know that his grandfather would weep an old man's tears when told where he had been and what he had done.

And he did not know that he would light a candle each evening and set it on the window sill of his home, and sit with a dog on his lap and remember the fire over the oilfield at Baba Gurgur, and a faraway place and faraway people.

And he did not know where the road he had walked would finish.

Gus felt the heartbeat of the dog against him and began to climb the path to the ridge.

His shadow danced in front of him.

Behind him the sun fell and its flame guttered.

THE END

A LINE IN THE SAND
by Gerald Seymour

In a village on the Suffolk coast, Frank Perry waits for his past to arrive. A decade before he spied for the Government on the Iranian chemical and biological weapon installations. His information damaged their killing capacity for years.

Now, Iran will have its revenge and has despatched their most deadly assassin to fulfil the task. Codenamed the Anvil, he will move with stealth towards his chosen objective unless Perry's protectors can reach him first.

As he draws nearer, the ring of steel protecting Perry grows tighter. But against a faceless adversary, and with the job fatally compromised by the stifling political bureaucracy surrounding it, there seems little chance that the past will not have its day once more . . .

'Brilliantly written and deserving of the Booker Prize, if only it wasn't so populist'
Mail on Sunday

'Gripping momentum . . . Depth of characterization, wealth of colour and detail, and precision of prose . . . New vintage stuff'
The Times

'Brilliantly crafted'
Sunday Times

0 552 14682 X

THE WAITING TIME
by Gerald Seymour

On a winter's night at the height of the Cold War, in a small town on East Germany's coastline, a young man is dragged from the sea and killed by the regime's secret police. The witnesses are terrorized into silence. But a British woman is present and hears the shot which ended her lover's life.

A decade later, times have changed, the Wall dividing two great ideologies has crumbled, and old enemies have become new friends. An ex-Captain in the Stasi's Counter Espionage section, Dieter Krause is an honoured guest at the headquarters of British Military Intelligence. He is confident that the skeletons in his past are hidden until . . .

Corporal Tracy Barnes, a clerk, attacks him in the officers' mess. She was there at the scene of the young man's murder ten years before. She knows Krause is responsible. But she can't prove it – she needs the witnesses to talk. To make them do so, she must follow Krause to Germany. For her, the waiting time is finally over . . .

'One of the best plotters in the business'
Time Out

'One of Britain's foremost pacy thriller writers'
Sunday Express

0 552 14605 6

A SELECTED LIST OF FINE WRITING AVAILABLE FROM CORGI BOOKS

THE PRICES SHOWN BELOW WERE CORRECT AT THE TIME OF GOING TO PRESS. HOWEVER TRANSWORLD PUBLISHERS RESERVE THE RIGHT TO SHOW NEW RETAIL PRICES ON COVERS WHICH MAY DIFFER FROM THOSE PREVIOUSLY ADVERTISED IN THE TEXT OR ELSEWHERE.

14497 5	BLACKOUT	*Campbell Armstrong*	£5.99
14646 3	PLAGUE OF ANGELS	*Alan Blackwood*	£5.99
14586 6	SHADOW DANCER	*Tom Bradby*	£5.99
14604 8	CRIME ZERO	*Michael Cordy*	£5.99
14495 9	THE LOOP	*Nicholas Evans*	£5.99
13991 2	ICON	*Frederick Forsyth*	£5.99
14597 1	CAUGHT IN THE LIGHT	*Robert Goddard*	£5.99
13697 2	AIRPORT	*Arthur Hailey*	£5.99
14717 6	GO	*Simon Lewis*	£5.99
14591 2	REMOTE CONTROL	*Andy McNab*	£5.99
54535 X	KILLING GROUND	*Gerald Seymour*	£5.99
14605 6	THE WAITING TIME	*Gerald Seymour*	£5.99
14682 X	A LINE IN THE SAND	*Gerald Seymour*	£5.99
14723 0	FIELD OF BLOOD	*Gerald Seymour*	£5.99
14722 2	HARRY'S GAME	*Gerald Seymour*	£5.99
14724 9	THE JOURNEYMAN TAILOR	*Gerald Seymour*	£5.99
14729 X	ARCHANGEL	*Gerald Seymour*	£5.99
14733 8	HOME RUN	*Gerald Seymour*	£5.99
14731 1	A SONG IN THE MORNING	*Gerald Seymour*	£5.99
14732 X	AT CLOSE QUARTERS	*Gerald Seymour*	£5.99
14730 3	IN HONOUR BOUND	*Gerald Seymour*	£5.99
14726 5	KINGFISHER	*Gerald Seymour*	£5.99
14725 7	THE GLORY BOYS	*Gerald Seymour*	£5.99
14727 3	RED FOX	*Gerald Seymour*	£5.99
14728 1	THE CONTRACT	*Gerald Seymour*	£5.99
14735 4	THE FIGHTING MAN	*Gerald Seymour*	£5.99
14736 2	THE HEART OF DANGER	*Gerald Seymour*	£5.99
14734 6	CONDITION BLACK	*Gerald Seymour*	£5.99
14391 X	A SIMPLE PLAN	*Scott Smith*	£5.99
10565 1	TRINITY	*Leon Uris*	£6.99
14047 3	UNHOLY ALLIANCE	*David Yallop*	£5.99

All Transworld titles are available by post from:

Bookpost, PO Box 29, Douglas, Isle of Man, IM99 1BQ

Credit cards accepted. Please telephone 01624 836000, fax 01624 837033, Internet http://www.bookpost.co.uk or e-mail: bookshop@enterprise.net for details

Free postage and packing in the UK. Overseas customers: allow £1 per book (paperbacks) and £3 per book (hardbacks)